MW01152340

The Thief's Daughter

by

MARY ELLEN BOYD

DEDICATION

My editor,
who always manages
to take my dreams,
and give them
polish.

PROLOGUE

1810

The party was in full swing when Reginald slipped through the front door, open to the night air. He could hear the small orchestra, but it sounded far enough away. He had on his finest clothes, clothes his wife had kept in good condition. The clothes she had treated with such care, sponged and pressed so tenderly would certainly pass muster in this crowd.

But the butler was there, waiting for latecomers so that he could prune out those that did not belong.

"Name, please?" The man's voice was so haughty that he could have passed for any of the guests there.

It would serve his father-in-law right to use his name, so Reginald did. "Sir Aldo deRoss." He hesitated, then added, "Baronet." Hopefully no one here knew the man. He did not care to leave his precious Gloucestershire and those sheep, whose manure he carried on his boots everywhere he went.

"Very well Sir," the butler said as he stepped aside.

The ploy had worked so many times, but he was always relieved once he was inside. A few years in the army had given Reginald the straight shoulders and the brisk stride to fool the most discerning of butlers. Most guests, also. The only problem would be if anyone here actually knew his father-in-law. The man had gout, not to mention the family carriage was too old to make it, so the chances were small that anyone here had even seen the man.

The son was another possible complication, the youngest, come along well after all the older daughters. Since deRoss had cut Reginald and his wife off at their marriage, he knew little of what the child had become. The chances of deRoss's son touring London were small. Undoubtedly the boy had been raised to be a tradesman, raising sheep and selling wool.

His hands clenched at the thought of what he could have had were his father-in-law not such a snob. A baronet? And a smelly one? All those sheep, filling the fields and clinging to the very air.

Still, he and Elizabeth had received just enough over the years to help his meagre Packet Service wages stretch. DeRoss would hardly be so generous, so they determined long ago that the money came from the mother. Although where *she* had come up with it with that miser of a husband, they did not know. And Elizabeth, his lovely Elizabeth, knew how to make their pitiful money cover everything.

Neither of them had so much as hinted to young Tessa about her grandfather. No point in getting her hopes up, because the baronet would never accept her anyway. His own granddaughter!

Elizabeth was dead now, and he and his daughter needed money to live on. The war was over, and he had not been paid for a long time.

A man had to do what a man had to do, and this new career paid very well.

He was out of sight of the butler. Reginald searched for the nearest staircase going up to the family's dwelling.

Voices came from behind a door, too close, and he glanced around for an escape. The next doorway showed no light from beneath, and he scurried down the hallway and ducked the through it, holding his breath when he slipped inside.

No sounds followed, no heavy breathing, no excited titters. No couples who had chosen it for a liaison. As his eyes adjusted, he saw himself in a feminine room, from the delicate lines of the desk and the chair. All the chairs, for that matter. Worse, that desk was little more than a small table, with nothing to hide behind should he need to find concealment.

He went over to the pale curtains that hid the tall, narrow windows, the color indistinguishable in the dark, pulled them apart just enough for the moonlight and the faint city reflection to shine in, and turned back to the room. A fainting couch sat in one corner, close enough to the door that it was easy to overlook when one first entered. That would be passable for concealment, but he would try to get out before he risked discovery.

What might a wife keep in her desk? He slipped over to it, taking care with every step. With the party going strong, servants would be everywhere, picking up glasses set aside and then forgotten, or following instructions on cleaning some mess or another.

The desk had one long center drawer, and two more on either side. Nothing else. He tugged on the center one, relieved when it was not locked.

Trusting woman. More fool she. But it held nothing more than a few sharpened quills, several piles of different colored papers, some wax, and a stamp. Probably her initials.

That would not do. It was likely traceable. He needed things that could never be identified.

He moved to the drawers on the right side, smaller but a little deeper. More paper, a few hairpins, and some shiny ribbons. The drawer was not wide enough for much else.

The bottom drawer didn't give, and he knelt down to see why. Aha. That one had a lock. The woman was not as trusting as he first thought. He reached in his pocket for his tools. He had become quite adept during the war at picking locks in houses they searched. If he had been caught the penalty was death, but he was lucky. And quick.

His skill served him well now. The lock gave with a small *snick*, and he pulled it open.

Letters, bound with a soft ribbon. He had heard no gossip in the gaming hells about this family, but letters were always worth a read. Many a juicy tidbit, something worth paying for, was hidden in plain sight to a skilled thief. He slipped the ribbon off and flipped through the correspondence.

Nothing of interest here. Every letter was addressed to the same man, and every return was addressed to the woman. And both were now husband and wife. Reginald pulled the ribbon back over the bunch and slipped them into the drawer.

No, in this house jewels were better.

The last drawer held what he wanted. A heavily jeweled hair comb that must have fallen out of the hair, and been tucked in here for safekeeping. Reginald gave a quiet chuckle. It was underneath some handkerchiefs, so he doubted it would be missed for a while.

And it would bring a pretty penny. Pearls, and what looked like diamonds, even—could it be at that size?—a ruby in the center. If it was not a ruby, a mere garnet that big would bring enough money to keep himself and Tessa fed and housed for a good while.

It was tempting to search further, but a wise thief got out in time. Tucking the comb into his hidden pocket inside the coat, Reginald crept over to the windows.

They opened quietly, without a creak. With a bit of squeezing, he let himself out, just a jump to the ground, and out past the stables.

CHAPTER 1

London, 1814

Her father's hand brushed her arm, and Tessa started. She must have dozed off. How could she, with him so close to the end? What did that say about her?

No one knew anything of what she had endured because of him, and who would ask in this neighborhood? He had been gone more than he had been home most of her life. For a long time she had been far too little to know about money, except for the worry that never seemed to leave her mother's face.

But now was not the time to go into that, she scolded herself, and rubbed the pain that had taken up permanent residence between her eyes.

Her father's hand moved again, and Tessa forced her heavy lids back open. The candlelight in the darkening room made her blink.

"I have set . . ." Reginald's eyes fluttered shut, and he fought for breath, the air rattling in his chest.

"Don't try to talk, Father," she said, and was surprised by the tear that trickled down her cheek.

"You up." Another breath rattled, the sound like the knell of doom.

You up? Tessa blinked away yet another tear, and swiped at that wet cheek. He must be rambling, the end was so very close.

Then the pieces fit, the first part of the sentence coming together with the rest. *I have set. You up. I have set you up.* What did he mean?

Now she truly *did* need him to talk. "What are you saying? Set me up how?" With his sad lack of judgment, it might mean anything, most likely something bad.

"Monies. Jewels. Even letters." The words rushed out on one breath, and then another inhale. "Use them."

Monies? *Jewels?* Her own breath caught. "Jewels? From where?"

"Found . . ." his voice trailed off again. She only heard the rasps of his labored breathing. "In my coat."

"Father? Father, what jewels?" Tessa leaned over him, wishing she could wake him enough to get the answers. "What letters? Please!"

"My coat." Reginald tried to cough, but it was weak, and when he fought to breathe in for another attempt, his eyes widened for the first time all day. With a soft exhalation, he sank in on himself, and his body went limp.

"Father? No, Father, please, no!" Tessa grabbed his hands, the ones that had just been trying to catch her attention, and pressed them together. "Father, please, please talk to me."

But there was no response. No more breaths, no movement of his fingers, no flicker of his eyelids.

His hands were so limp, and heavy. Tessa felt her breath shudder this time as she set his hands down, folding them one on top of the other on his chest.

Tears leaked out, not wrenching, not sobs, just wistful tears of what she wished it had been instead of what it was. She wished she could weep with abandon, pour out all the ache and loneliness, but all she managed were those few tears that slid down her face.

When they had dried, Tessa let herself sit for a moment beside the bed where her father lay. The day had been a long one, and her legs were so very tired. All too soon, she got up and began the work that had to be done.

Plus she had a funeral to pay for.

Monies. Jewels. Letters.

Those last mumbles from him nagged like a burr in her brain. They made no sense, but if Reginald had come up with something worthwhile to sell, it would be a wonderful thing.

What were the tales of the sailors? She wracked her muddled brain. Weren't they allowed to take booty from the captured ships? She remembered him saying something to her younger self about what plunder meant. But the packet ships only carried letters and passengers, and they seldom won battles, they were so lightly armed. Everyone complained that the mails went over the side when they were attacked. Had he saved some those letters? Was she supposed to deliver them?

She would look later. Right now, if someone was going to remove her father from her room, she had to send word to the church with the news and get the process started.

Perhaps one of the men in the neighborhood would agree to take over the washing of Reginald's body, and getting him dressed. There were the bearers to pay, not to mention the coffin rental, and the minister's compensation.

Tessa picked up the water bucket she left next to the door, then glanced back at her father's still body on the bed. There was nothing much to steal, but would a thief be stopped by the sight of a corpse?

The closet door stood open. It had been nearly bare inside before Reginald joined her several months ago. Strange, how full it was now. She could see his coats from the outside door

Monies. Jewels. Letters. In my coat.

She went back, skirting the foot of the bed, and shut the closet against any prying eyes. Even his clothes could tempt someone in her neighborhood.

Then she let herself out, taking care to lock her door behind her with the key she always kept on a chain around her neck. Bad enough her father had cost her extra during these last weeks, but if the landlord found out he had died in the bed, she might be looking for another place herself. Mattresses were dear, and the room had come furnished.

Tessa gave a half-laugh, choked with the heaviness in her chest. Furnished! One chest of drawers barely waist high, one small table next to the bed, the chair on which she sat while her father died. And a small round coal burner for heat in the winter, that piped most of the smoke through a pipe out the roof. She had contributed the teapot for her winter tea, a china plate she rescued from her mother's possessions after she died, and the matching china cup that once had been beautiful but now had a chip on the rim.

Did a coal burner count as furnishing?

On the way down the outside stairs that ran upward along the slender rooming house where she and several other family groups lived, Tessa had learned after several nasty slips to take special care. Those stairs shook under every step and became slippery in the rain and occasional snow, even the fog or mist that sometimes drifted in from the seaport, but it was her only way in and out, and she felt slightly safer knowing someone had to climb them to reach her.

She would need that faint sense of security in the days and years ahead.

Bucket banging against her leg, Tessa rubbed a hand under her eye and caught a fresh tear. One tendril of her long brown hair fell over that leaking eye and gave her a moment of privacy.

The narrow alley bustled with activity, none of it good. The families who lived in the buildings lining this secret alcove had all gone inside to eat what food they had and sleep, and now the pickpockets and footpads who shared the nearby dwellings ruled the neighborhood.

"Eve'nin', Tessa." "Nice ta see ya, Tessa." "'Ow's work comin', Tessa? Stitched any pretty dresses lately?" "Eve'nin', Tessa. I still got that French lace, iffen you want some."

"Walt, Bertie, Alfie, Herb. Evening to all of you. Be careful, you hear? I would not like to learn any of you wound up in Newgate."

"Not even me?" Herb leaned down to look in Tessa's eyes. With his blond hair—presumably it was light under all the grime—and blue eyes, he hardly looked like the threat that he was, until you saw the coldness in the eyes and the hard set to his jaw. "Surely that means there's still a bit a 'ope for me in there sumwhere's in that cold 'eart of yers?"

"If my heart was that cold, Herb, you would not want it." Tessa began to back away. She had no illusions the kind of neighborhood she lived in. For the most part, she felt safe, but when Herb decided she would make the perfect footpad's wife, life had become a tricky dance. Only her father's sudden presence had given her respite. Now she feared that peace was over.

"Sumpin' wrong?" Young Alfie was her favorite of all the local crooks. Tall, wiry, dark-haired, and those striking blue eyes in a face so far untouched by his rough and dangerous life, she often wished she had the means to rescue him before it was too late.

The day's events came crashing down again. Tessa felt her eyes fill, and blinked to keep them back. She did not know how successful she had been, but it was getting dark.

Tessa looked at Alfie, and then at the others. The perfect solution stared her in the face. "Yes, Alfie." Her voice cracked. How odd, after all the grief her father caused her when alive. Surely she had shed enough tears over him already. "My father has died. I just wondered how I would manage to get him buried."

"Ah, that's too b—" Alfie's words were cut off.

"We kin do it tonight, Tessa." Herb rubbed his hands on his pants, as if already dusting off the dirt.

Trust Herb to offer. Unfortunately she was not in a position to turn down help, whatever form it came in.

"We'll jest bundle 'im up and tuck 'im all nice an' snug in the cemetery tonight an' no one'll be the wiser." Herb leered at her. Maybe it was supposed to be a smile, but whenever he got that expression, Tessa knew to beware.

She understood exactly what he was talking about. It was tempting.

Hire them to go dig a hole in the soft dirt on top of a new grave, slide her father in, lay the topsoil back, and slip away. Burial costs being what they were, it was done all the time.

However, grave robbers out for fresh bodies to hand over to the medical schools for study would find her father in no time. Not that she ever expected to go visit his grave, but Tessa did want to know where he was. She had spent enough of her life wondering if she would ever see him again.

"Thank you, Herb. I will think about it, I promise you." Now that she had their attention, Tessa decided to make an offer she could live with. "If I decide to try for a real funeral, can I pay you four to carry the coffin?"

"Will we need new clothes?" Bertie ran his grubby hands through his curly dark hair. Tessa wondered when he last bathed and which would be dirtier when he was done, the hair or the hands.

"I can't afford the expense, Bertie, but you appear to be the same size as my father. Maybe he has something that will fit." Reginald's words came back, a whisper in her mind. *Money, jewels.* She snapped her mouth shut. When would she learn to think before she spoke?

Alfie's eyes lit up. "Fer real? Ye'll really let me 'ave one of yer pa's coats?"

If she hurried, she might be able to go through a couple shirts and pantaloons or breeches of her father's for those letters before the men came up. "You have to agree to carry the coffin first."

"To look like a dandy? I'll do it!" Alfie nudged his friend. "Whatcha say, Bertie? Wanna have some new duds, too?"

The two exchanged a glance, and then turned back to Tessa. "Promise first."

She sighed. Without help, she did not know how to get her father to the churchyard. "I promise. What do I need with my father's clothes?"

Bertie narrowed his dark eyes. He was learning to be a real tough. Walt and Herb, as the older men of the group, had taken the two younger along on their thieving since the boys were small, and now what chance did they have?

"Kin I see 'is duds first?" Bertie exchanged a glance with Alfie. "Don't want no rags."

That brought up something Tessa had worried about, but getting straight answers out of Reginald was impossible. Where *had* he bought such nice clothes? He claimed it was his discharge payment from being in the army. Tessa found that hard to believe. She knew of no sailors who dressed as well as he did.

"Bertie, remember my occupation? I know fabrics. They are nice, I assure you."

He stuck out a grimy hand. "You got yerself a bargain. Tell me when to be there, and I'll carry yer pa wherever you want."

Tessa made herself take his hand, ignoring the powdery leftovers of something nasty under her palm. "I need to talk to the clergyman and see if he is willing to do the funeral."

Bertie dropped his hand and backed up a step. "I ain't gonna have nothing to do with no clergyfolk."

Alfie gave a bark of laughter. "Ye 'fraid ye'll 'ave to confess?"

"All you have to do is carry my father's coffin." She hoped that was true. She could not afford much more than the most basic of burials. Surely that would not bring them into too much contact with the parson.

"An' where we to find this coffin, I ask ye?" Bertie's hands were propped on his hips now, his jaw was stuck out in a challenge.

"I will rent it. You just have to go to the church and pick it up. I promise you won't even have to talk to the parson if you don't want to."

Bertie stood there, hands still on his hips, jaw working as if literally chewing over the decision. Mercenary concerns won out. "Awright. I'll do it."

Tessa turned to the other two men. "Walt, Herb, Alfie, will you make up the rest of the carriers?"

Walt looked at Herb, they both looked at Alfie, and they all turned in unison to Tessa. "'ow much money do ye think ye can pay? Do ye even guess 'ow much we make in one night?"

Backing up and turning away, Tessa said over her shoulder, "I would never force any of you. Thank you for listening so kindly to my request." Then she walked off.

* * *

Monies, jewels, and letters in my coat. Before she handed his clothing over to the men, she had to find them. If they existed. If it wasn't the ramblings of a dying man. Tessa slid her hand into the first outer pocket. Nothing there. She moved over to the other side and did the same. It, too, was empty.

As she pulled her hand back out, it brushed something hard, and she stared at the coat. Cocking her head, she slid it back in, and checked the lining. There it was, the small slit. She didn't sew men's clothes, that was a job for tailors, but she did know what seams in lining should feel like, and it wasn't this.

"You sly devil," she said to the still body on the bed. "What have you got in there?"

Thank goodness she always brought her sewing basket home from work! Thread and needles would be necessary to get this done. With her smallest scissor, she found a stitch in that slit, and snipped it, then another, opening a hidden pocket big enough to reach inside and feel through the layers. There it was, a slender string of finest cording, like the fastening of a pouch. She hooked her finger through it, then caught the edge of the sack in a firm grip, and worked her hand back out. The pouch got heavier with every tug, until it popped free through her hole.

And jingled.

She worked the string off her finger, and opened the pouch. Her mouth dropped at the sight.

The sparkle of gold. Coin. If she had problems breathing before, it was nothing to what clenched her lungs tight now.

Gold coins, several of them.

One hand on the outside, and one on the inside, she felt with care every inch of the lining, in the coat back, along the sleeves, and there it was, the faint roundness of more coins. Tessa reached for the scissors and began snipping more threads.

When she was done, she had another pouch, only this one held silver coins. She spun around from where she sat on the bed and stared at the coats that hung on the hooks inside the tiny closet.

Did each of them hold the same thing?

The night was growing darker. Those clothes were going to go to the men in the morning. If she left so much as a single coin in a single pocket—despite their surface affection, Herb and Walt were mercenary to the core, and Bertie and Alfie followed their lead.

She began tugging her father's clothes off the hooks, and tried not to think of the night's sleep she would lose.

* * *

As she sat waiting for the men to come the next morning, the picture of patience—she hoped—her mind reeled from what she had found. Set her up, indeed! Her father's coats were a veritable treasure trove of money and jewelry, even loose gems.

Most of the jewelry was just empty settings that had been pried open and were now bare. But there were some, hairpins and earrings, rings and a couple of necklaces, still intact.

There were only a few letters, seals already broken. Either someone had received and read them before her father found them, in which case, why had Reginald taken them, or he had been the one to pry them open.

The coins terrified her, gold guineas and silver shillings tucked in hidden pouches roughly stitched in the linings. Chills ran down her arms as she realized how easily she could have given them away, never knowing what lay snugged inside.

The money might be explainable, late wages he had saved for her. When she found the jewelry, however, she had started shaking. It had not stopped all night. Some of the rings were engraved, and each had a different name. Before she noticed that, she had known where they came from.

Her father was—had been—a thief.

CHAPTER 2

The grave yawned in front of Tessa as she stood in the summer morning sunshine, her bonnet doing little to ease the glare. Her stomach hurt. Even though the Neighborhood Four had kept their word and carried her father's body to the cemetery, she felt alone. The two youngest, Bertie and Alfie, wore Reginald's clothes as partial payment for their efforts, but Herb and Walt stood like menacing presences opposite each other at the head of the rented coffin.

What they would do if they ever learned about her inheritance made her shudder.

Her father's last words echoed in her mind, nearly drowning out the curate.

"I have . . . set you up." The words were faint, his voice scratchy, the sentence broken by gasps for air.

"We now commit Reginald Abbott—" A strong voice pounded against her ears.

The echo of her plea startled her, one of the last things she had said to him. "Don't try to talk, Father." If only she had asked for details, information, explanations!

"To the ground—" The strong voice broke through, and the shuffling of feet. When she lifted her head away from that hole, Herb was leering at her. Tessa looked back down at the hole. "Earth to earth, ashes to ashes, dust to dust—"

"Monies. Jewels. Even letters." That wavering, dying voice interrupted again, a faint murmur.

"In the sure and certain hope of —" The curate's voice cut in, thankfully cutting off the voice's whisper in her mind. She looked up.

Alfie's eyes were sad as he gazed across the wrapped body at her. For an awful moment, she thought he was her father, the clothes were right but the person wearing them was all wrong.

"The resurrection to eternal life." The curate sounded final, wrapping up the funeral. He must have given some signal to the men, because Father's white-wrapped body slid into the open hole. The rental coffin the small church kept for those who could not afford the expense of buying sat off to one side, ready to be carried back for the next funeral.

I should have bought Father a coffin, she thought, but was the money even hers to spend? She did not possess much, but she had self-respect, and would not damage it now.

She hoped she had found everything there was to find in the heavily padded coats and suits with the odd pockets where he had tucked his loot. If any of the Four discovered something she had missed in her father's clothes, they would be back to search for the rest. Herb would, for sure, as he was the leader of the group—and the most dangerous.

The avaricious look in Herb's cold unblinking gaze when he had seen those coats and pantaloons, the shirts and vests, laid out this morning chilled her every time she thought of it.

Reginald had been away often, but those Four never knew when he would be back. The threat of him following through on his promise to put a bullet through them if they touched her had been enough to keep them in check.

Father was gone, now. Truly gone, leaving her alone. And vulnerable.

The dirt was shoveled onto Reginald's body with soft thumps, each one landing on her heart. The curate held out his hand. Tessa pressed a coin—her own hard-earned money—into it and whispered, "Thank you." She could not see his face. Tears blurred everything in front of her eyes.

An arm appeared, blurry, like looking through a window in the rain. She did not check who it belonged to, just gripped it and turned from the grave.

Madame Genevieve, at whose shop she worked as a seamstress, had given her the morning off for the funeral, and that time must be almost over. Any tears she shed had to be done between here and the shop, because once she got there, she needed to be presentable.

* * *

Tessa whipped the needle through the fabric in a loose baste stitch, just enough to hold it in place, and the delicate necklace around the lady's throat caught her eye. Again. All afternoon, she had tried not to notice the jewels hanging from ears and around necks, sparkling on fingers. Nothing ostentatious, not for going shopping where thieves prowled the streets, but could no one leave their home without some sign of their wealth?

Had her father robbed any of them? Some of the jewels tucked away in her room might well be the property of the women she fitted for balls and operas, for soirees and parties, and all of the other fancy gatherings the wealthy indulged in.

She took another stitch, and refused to let herself notice again the sparkle reflected by the sconce in the fitting room. She had a job to do, and she had already taken too much time with this morning's burial. This handiwork didn't have to last longer than to get the gown off and into the back room where she could do the final sewing. It was a good thing, because her thoughts refused to settle. All day she had been pushing away memories. Her father lying cold on the bed, the curate with his measured voice, Herb's cold gaze.

She looked at the rich gown in front of her. What was it like to be able to mourn, to cry if she wanted to? Not to be required to smile when inside she felt nothing but grief? Her vision blurred, and she blinked to clear it. A warm drop slid down her cheek, and she mopped it up with her sleeve.

She took another stitch and tried not to think of the mess Father had left for her. Jewelry broken apart, stones wrenched out with no regard for their settings. The work of a thief, ripping out everything that could not be traced and selling it.

The needle went in and out of the fine fabric, taking loose stitches to mark the hem, and another tear blurred her view. This sadness was not like when Mother died. It had been four years, but the bond between them had been strong, and the ache still crept up on her when she let her guard down. Father had been gone often, however, working on the Packet ships, sailing the mails through the deadly maze of French warships.

Or so she thought. Where did he find these things? No one sent such items across the ocean, did they? How could a sailor steal them when they were getting ready to dump the mails if the French attacked? There would have been a group of them carrying it all up to pitch over the side, how would he have found the time?

Someone in the shop just beyond the thin door to the fitting room cleared their throat, and Tessa's mind snapped back to her work.

She took another stitch in the hem of the silver Irish lace gown, being careful to ensure the silk lining remained in place. She just had to mark the last bit of the hem, and the gown was ready for its final sewing. She would have to stay late, but then, she always did this time of year.

"There!" The last tacking was in, and she snipped the thread with care, conscious of the delicate lace threads just an inch away. Tessa measured the gown's evenness with her gaze. The lace was aligned perfectly, the hem skimmed the floor, the train would drape just long enough to toss over the arm or catch up with the little loops she had already stitched in place. Now if she could just carry it to the workroom without having the stitches break! "I will have sew this, but I will do it as quickly as possible. Let me help you take the gown off."

"Thank you." Lady Warrenby turned her back, and, taking the hint as an order, Tessa immediately began unhooking the fastenings. Just like a maid, she thought, as her fingers worked down the hooks.

A maid with over £100 of gold guineas and an unknown amount of jewelry and gemstones hidden in her room. But of course, what remained of the necklaces had to be turned to the owners, bent and broken as they were. She could not keep them. Her father might have been a thief, but she was not! While she had little, Mother had taught her self-respect and honesty, and they were not things she could bear to lose.

At the end of the day, you have to live with yourself. Can you look your own self in the eye, and respect what you see? Those were her mother's words, her mother's values, and she treasured both.

Everyone knew that certain symbols were specific to families. To her untrained eye, it appeared crests were worked into the settings. She would not recognize them, but someone else should.

How did one find an owners of damaged and stripped jewelry without winding up in Newgate?

She sighed as she began working the gown with its fragile connections off, taking care not to stress the loose threads.

"Are you unwell?" Lady Warrenby asked the question through the layers.

Servants never complained. Tessa learned that long ago. They never had bad days, never were tired. And certainly never got ill. "I am fine, my lady."

The dress came off with not a single baste stitch popping. Tessa set it down and picked up the gown her customer had worn into the shop.

"Will that be done by tomorrow evening?" Lady Warrenby turned her back to Tessa so she could be buttoned up.

"Of course, my lady." Tessa's fingers were as quick as any lady's maid doing the fastenings. Of course. Having a whole day to finish a dress was luxury. It was not just Lady Warrenby's gown to finish during the Season, but every other woman who made the same request. *I need that gown by tomorrow night.*

After helping the lady into her day gown, Tessa picked up the new one, left Madame's customer to put on her gloves and hat, and whisked out the fitting room door, heading toward the back room where she kept her sewing basket during the day—and the other unfinished work for the other waiting customers. She dodged a last few lingering women at the long tables who still had not made up their minds which fabric they wished, careful not to catch the lace on anything.

Huge bolts of fabrics of all color and texture were stacked in teetering piles on the tables in front of every woman. They would pull out a bit of material from one and look it over before tugging at another and repeating the process. And of course when the women left, it was up to Rosie, Madame, and herself to put everything back as quickly as possible.

They needed more staff, but it was not Tessa's place to tell Madame so.

A hand caught her arm, and she whipped around at the touch, to look into the warm hazel eyes of her employer.

"*Je suis désolé*," Madame said in a soft voice. In one hand she held another card of pins, so no doubt she had left her own customer to resupply her tools. "I cannot spare you more, but it is . . . *difficile*."

Difficult. Yes, it was difficult, but kind of Madame to recognize it. "Thank you."

"You stay and help Rosie *et moi ce soir*?"

"Yes." She did not relish going home later than usual, but neither did she look forward to the empty room.

Madame patted her shoulder, and opened her mouth to say something else in her French/English blend of words, but a voice, thick with impatience, distracted her. "Madame, Madame, I'm waiting," came from behind one of the fitting room doors. The woman turned away, but the brief gesture of compassion warmed Tessa as she shifted the gown and continued past the corner where Madame kept an elegant carved chair next to her cast iron stove where there was always hot tea for the customers—or her girls if no one else happened to be around—and on toward the back room where the bulk of the work was done, and where she could shed her tears in private.

Before she reached the sanctuary of the workroom, the street door swished open, bringing in a gush of London's summer fragrance, warm river air tinged with the stronger scents of manure and smoke. She turned to greet the guest. Madame was already out of sight in the other fitting room, probably doing the same adjustments she herself had just done, and Rosie's job was mainly sweeping and hauling fabric to and fro. Besides, Madame said she liked the way Tessa spoke.

It was not another woman, trying to slip in before the doors were closed for the day. Tall, dark-haired, icy green eyed, and as handsome and appealing as sin, Lady Warrenby's son stood there. His hair nearly brushed the top of the doorway, and waves fell free as he finished tucking his top hat under his arm.

She wasn't supposed to stare, but it was hard not to. The brown jacket and buff trousers fitted him as though painted on, and she wondered if he had to pay extra for the fabric it had to take to make a coat that size. It must have taken a room of assistants to tailor such an outfit. A cravat billowed out over his vest, tied in a fancy knot. His chest hardly needed the attention.

Broad across the shoulders, with big arms that bulged against the seams of his coat. His legs were long, and once when she had glimpsed him riding up, it seemed even his massive horse was too short for his size.

With her seamstress's eye, Tessa recognized the crimson vest visible between the buttoned coat and that flowing cravat as silk with gold and silver threads. Real gold and silver, like the guineas and shillings in her room. Just like that, her mind was back at her rented chamber and the treasure she hoped was still there. Tessa forced it back to the situation at hand. There was nothing she could do right now. If she lost her father's hoard, would she really be worse off than she had been before it had shown up?

"Miss?" Lord Warrenby glanced around the room, fixed his strange light-colored gaze on her. Those eyes and that commanding gaze always made her feel like a butterfly pinned to paper. "Could you please inform my mother that I am here?"

"Of course." She bobbed a quick curtsey. "She should be out in just a moment." With a wistful glance at the workroom door, so close, Tessa turned back to retrace her steps.

He gave a short nod, and tapped a gloved hand on his leg but made no move to leave. Instead, he leaned against the doorpost and let his gaze wander over the room, nodding at the women he seemed to recognize. Other men had poked their heads in to see when their women would be ready, and they all had a baffled look as they stared at the overly feminine display of delicate chairs with curving legs and brocade upholstery, bolts of velvets, silks, and muslins in every color of the rainbow, only to slip back out to the safety of a man's world outside, where carriages and horsemen rode by and the air smelled faintly of the river, just a few blocks away.

A man of his confidence would hardly be frightened off by floral muslins and Irish lace. Tessa knew his Christian name, she had heard his mother mention it often enough whenever she visited with friends, but refused to let herself even think it.

She tapped on the door of the fitting room she had just left. "My lady?"

Lady Warrenby's voice wafted out. "I heard him. I just have to re-pin my hat, and I shall be out. It will do him good to wait." A smile lightened her words.

"Yes, my lady." Tessa once more made her way around the tables and the customers toward the man who set her heart aflutter, and repeated only the first words of the message. Those strange icy eyes of his held her in place like a rabbit in a snare. His nod released her, and she scurried back to the door that meant a few moments of safety and quiet. Thank goodness she did not have to wait out there with him! She did not think she could sew a straight line if he watched her.

Not that a man of his stature would watch a servant.

Even hiding in the back room it was hard to concentrate. Tessa found herself straining to hear either mother or son's voice.

* * *

Warrenby was relieved when his mother came out of one of the little side doors in the shoproom. He knew better than to watch a servant, which he supposed a seamstress was even though she did not work for any grand house. Yet he found any number of excuses to accompany his mother and his sister to their modiste shop.

He would never consider defiling someone beneath him, but the young woman who just disappeared with the newest gown behind the door held far too much fascination for him.

Her hair was thick, and dark brown, and long. He knew because it was often sliding out from underneath her caps. She would push it back impatiently and always with a quick exhalation of frustration. He often had to hide a grin as he watched her struggle with it. Her eyes were large and brown and her features so refined she could have come from any of the famous families known for beauty. High cheekbones, delicate nose, a Cupid's bow of a mouth, and even a cultured voice. Precise speech told of a good education in her past.

He sobered, and the smile he had been fighting disappeared. So many people were brought low by heirs who squandered money without a thought until there was nothing left, and once powerful families were left destitute.

What a pity that women, the most vulnerable, so often had to fend for themselves.

What was this woman's story? The descendent of a family that had lost everything? Or was she some by-blow of a wealthy cad? There were certainly enough of them littering London's streets, starving and ragged. Women who were reduced to selling themselves to survive, children who begged for coins and fought for scraps stolen from the fruit stands when the owners were distracted.

He knew none of those abandoned children were his. He was much more careful with his dalliances.

A swipe of guilt reminded him of a time when he was younger, when he was not so cautious, but he shoved the thought aside as his mother came closer.

She stopped in mid-step halfway through the room to re-pin her bonnet back in place, giving him a moment to clear any lingering memory from his face. Her maid rose from a chair near one of the tables, being inconspicuous while she waited. "Are you ready to go home, Mother?"

Rebecca, Lady Warrenby tugged her gloves into place as she stopped in front of him. "Yes, I think I have everything I need."

He ushered her out the door, and held it open as the maid followed her mistress out, as well. She was new, as his mother's old maid had retired recently with a bad heart. He wracked his brain for the new servant's name. Wilson? Johnson? Roberts? Something common like that.

As the outer door settled behind them, the bell over the doorway giving a faint tinkle from the other side, he stepped even with his mother. There was something he had to clear with her out of the ears of her new servant. The woman might be privy to his mother's secrets already, but he would not add to her knowledge. Instead, he kept the conversation general. "I am sure you will give Emmy a bit of a run when the two of you make your appearance at the ball." He made an exaggerated wince as they neared the carriage, where the footman had the door open and was lowering the steps. "Even though the ball is hardly my idea. I am just glad it will be held at your house."

His mother smoothed his cravat, though he knew it didn't need smoothing. "There is really no reason you cannot move into the family home. While I appreciate the comfort there, you are the lord now. You belong in the house."

"Mother. Emmy needs that house, and really, I can hardly evict my own family."

She stopped at the open door, and waved her maid in first. The young woman clambered inside and vanished in the dimness. She was too discreet to sit close and overhear, a good sign. With a glance inside the carriage, his mother turned back to him, and sighed. "Tell the coachman we are in no hurry."

The footman waited silently by the open carriage door. "I will take care of my mother," Blake said, and waved the man off toward his place next to the driver.

Blake helped his mother into the carriage and climbed in after her. He waited until they were moving before he spoke. "I have something else to discuss. but it can wait until I get you home."

"Good, because what I have to say cannot wait." His mother pinned him in her gaze. "I have kept quiet for months, but I must speak now. It is time for you to find yourself a bride." Her eyes went sad for a moment. "When you marry, you will no longer have an excuse not to take your rightful place, and take back the house."

Lady Warrenby let out a gust of a sigh, and put a smile on her face. "If your father were still alive, you know he would remind you of your responsibilities to the family name, but he is not. I must therefore take up the mantle in his place." She looked down at her hands, and Blake felt the pain in her stifled sigh.

"I believe he was older than I when you two were wed." His mother's gaze came back, and he managed a smile. "I am right, am I not?"

"That is not the point. He had been looking for some time before he met me." Color tinted her cheeks.

"How do you know I am not?"

"You are only recently returned to England. Were you looking among the French?" Her voice was a bit tart.

"No. Of course not. I was doing my part to support our army." Doing things he could not reveal, just in case his services and skills were required once again. "I was not over there playing."

Her eyes softened. "I know you were at great risk, and I am beyond glad that the war is over."

He did not *have* to go to France, as the heir he probably should not have, but his father wanted him to do something to try to overthrow the tyrant. Just the knowledge that Napoleon was now gone made those months worth it.

Besides, his work had never put him in the danger his mother feared. It could have, but he took great care that no one knew who he was. He was as comfortable in a farmer's rough clothes as in the elaborate garments he now wore.

Neither nor his father suspected they would not see each other again.

His mother was still talking, and on the same subject. "But that does not change matters. We are holding Emilia's first ball at your house, and I have taken great care who I invited. The house will be filled with perfectly lovely young ladies. You really should pay attention to them. You know you must ask a few at least to dance."

He bowed his head. "I will do my very best to take Father's place but I will tell you right now, I am not interested in wedding a child. There mere thought makes me shudder." He didn't have to force one for emphasis, the shiver already ran through his body. Every time he thought of looking at a wife his sister's age he felt queasy. "Bring me all the wallflowers from the past few years, or force me to dance with one of your friends, but I am not going to pay court to an infant."

"Emmy is hardly an infant." His mother gave him a measuring look. "I might consider assigning you one or two of the poor girls. But I warn you, I will not have you waste a dance on a woman past the age of giving me grandchildren."

He chuckled. "Very well. I count that an acceptable compromise."

The rest of the ride was filled with what his mother called. 'satisfying gossip.' Lady Fanny's daughter—"You do remember her, don't you?"—came out last year, and had turned down four—"Four!"—offers of marriage. "You must write her in for a dance." Lady Therese was rumored to be engaged even though no announcement had been made yet, so she was off his mother's list. There had been two reports of duels already, and the Season was barely half over. And on it went.

When they pulled up in front of his old family home, his mother said, with a twinkle, "There! I feel that you are as prepared as I can make you."

When they walked into the house, his mother dismissed her maid with her gloves, hat, shawl, and reticule, and turned to him. "Your father's old office?"

Blake shook his head. The title did not fit comfortably yet. Sitting in his father's office, in his father's chair, would have to wait. "No, let's go to your morning room."

His mother's favorite room was much as it had always been, soft yellowy wallpaper on the walls, fresh flowers on her small desk, and delicate chairs of whitewashed light oak and done in matching yellow upholstery. He wondered yet again how such curving legs could hold people without breaking. The chair his father used to sit in was still in its corner. Solid, warm wood and a rich red, it provided a splash of color to the overwhelming femininity of the rest of the decor.

It never looked out of place, though, and he knew his mother intended it that way. His father had spent many an hour in this room, watching her embroider, or read, or helping with her correspondence. She never needed as much assistance as she pretended, but they both enjoyed the time.

He wanted that kind of marriage. And he wanted his sister to have it, too.

"Can you take your father's chair in here?" Rebecca Warrenby waved to the chair, and sat down at her desk with a great arranging of her grey skirts. He didn't often notice the half-mourning, but now it felt heavy on his mind.

He closed the door behind him, and took his father's chair. This was different, for he had climbed in and out of it as a child. While it carried his father's memory, it did not hold the weight of replacing the man he did not think he could ever equal. "Now for my business. Mother, do you remember my old friend John Holland? He requested an appointment with me, and said he chose to talk to me instead of to you, as I was now head of the family. I have my suspicions, but do you know what he is talking about?"

"I have a guess."

She had a *guess*? Or she knew for certain? "Is it Emilia?" His stomach tightened. "Does he want to court her? And how could he meet her already, she is barely out!" His voice raised toward the end in spite of his efforts.

Rebecca Warrenby gave him a long look. "In the first place, she is not *barely* out. It may be her first season, but it is well under way. She has had plenty of opportunities to meet eligible men. Secondly, your sister and I have always been close. She tells me everything in her heart. If you just found out, I am surprised." She paused. "Well, perhaps not that surprised. Once you found your own house, there just have been less chances for a brother-sister chat. Not to mention, you have not even been in England until recently. How was she supposed to communicate? The Packets ships were regularly attacked. The wonder is that any mails got through until the war ended."

Blake looked down at his hands and then back up at his mother. "You remember John and I were friends for a very long time."

"Yes. And?"

"Mother, I have been in France and Europe for quite a while. I don't know what John is like now, but he was the biggest rake of my group of friends. Gambling, womanizing, drinking. He is not the kind of man I would ever give consent to."

Rebecca leaned back. "I seem to remember a son who did the same. Oh, perhaps not so much drinking, and you were always aware of your responsibilities toward our finances, but womanizing? Really, Blake, are you not the case of the pot calling the kettle black?"

He shook his head. His hands clenched on his knees. "No, I do not think so. He was the most randy, the most daring, of all of us. That was fine then, but now? And for my sister? No."

Rebecca shook her head. "Blake." Her voice held a finality that in his youth had always presaged the final word. He was reminded that she had made the decisions for the household after Father died and he was still away. He would have to take the load off her. "Have you seen John since you came back? You have been home for over a month now. Did you even send him a note?"

He straightened in the chair. "No. I have very little in common with the man I used to be."

One of her eyebrows lifted. "You two have your sister in common."

"Not if I have anything to say about it."

Rebecca played with a quill set out on her desk. The action was not nervous, more distracted. The room went quiet while he waited for her response. Finally she sighed. "You owe it to your sister to speak to the man. You are not, after all, the only one to grow up in the intervening years." Then his mother folded her hands and looked out the window.

Blake gave a quick single nod. "Fine. I will trust your judgment for the moment, and see John! But don't expect me to give in on Emmy."

She smiled. "Good for you, Blake. Be kind to him, now."

He hated it when people talked in riddles. He had endured enough of that in his work in Europe. Hiding who he was, what he knew. Pretending to be a simple traveler about the countryside, all the while listening, watching, gathering all the information he could, and trying to send it back without arousing suspicions. But it was obvious she was not going to say anything more.

CHAPTER 3

The sky was dark when Tessa arrived back at her room. The Neighborhood Four were nowhere around, and in spite of the affection she felt for a couple of the men, the only thing she thought was, *If only I could trust them!*

She ran up the stairs and stuck her key in the door, something she was used to doing without the benefit of daylight. No one lay in wait, leaping out to grab her, nothing looked disturbed. She pushed the door shut again, slipped the latch back in place, set her work basket on the floor, and the cold meat pie in paper wrapping she had purchased from a street merchant for supper on the chest of drawers.

When she lit the candle and the room warmed into view, the memories crowded in on her, the last weeks as her father grew weaker and weaker.

There had been no time for sleep last night, but now, with her father's body gone, the bed felt contaminated. Maybe she would sleep on the floor until she could make another mattress.

Or buy a new one. The thought made her catch her breath. Was any of the coin mixed in with the gems truly hers to spend? Or were they all ill-gotten gains?

She wished he had told her about the thieving before! Goodness knows, there had been time. Of course he would not tell her. It had been his last days, and he knew it. He did not want to see the reproach she felt now, the mixture of disapproval and dismay that turned her grief into a jumble of sadness and anger.

First things first, to make sure everything was still where she hid them, the ultimate check of whether anyone had been in. The Four were deviously clever. If there was a way to get in and back out with the door locked, they knew how to do it.

She went from the hollow base of the vase to the book where smaller gems could be hidden to the corset on the closet shelf to the stockings in the drawers on her dresser. One by one, she searched through her secreted horde, and each stash was still safely intact.

Even the small stack of letters. Tessa pulled them out of their hiding place and looked at them. A couple were ten—she checked again—or more years old. She ruffled through them, picking up words and sentences, skimming what she had not had the time to do last night, shoving aside the guilt of reading something that did not belong to her.

Despite her father's words, it was most obvious she had no claim to these. They had the feel of blackmail, ugly secrets such as the plot to sell shares in a false mine that someone thought funny enough to share with a friend as a joke. One gloated about a friend who had cheated at cards and cost some family she did not recognize their inheritance, most likely casting the innocent victims out onto the street while the man who cheated reaped the rewards of his foul deeds. Another was a plea from a young woman who was pregnant, begging the father to come back from somewhere, marry her and claim his child.

Father had held them for so many years! Did a secret become more valuable after time had passed?

"My father, the thief and blackmailer," Tessa said with bitterness.

As she looked at them again, one name jumped out at her. Blake Glover. *Blake*. The only place she had heard that was in connection with Lady Warrenby's son. How many Blakes were there?

She knew no one else to ask. And she didn't know him either, only knew who his mother and sister were. And that he seemed to watch her when she moved about the shop. Every time he was there and she would look up from what she was doing, his eyes were on her. And he did not look away when she noticed.

Unless she was fooling herself. Perhaps he wasn't watching her at all, and her silly imagination made her see what she wished.

Tessa tapped the letters against her palm and stared across the room. The small dwelling, all she had to call her home, was too small to let her thoughts drift far, not like gazing over the ocean, letting her wishes roam free. No, only a small coal heating stove in the corner of the outside wall, unnecessary now and barely sufficient for the winter, the bed with worn mattress, little table with the room's lone candle, the battered chest of drawers with the still-wrapped meat pie on top, a door to the shallow closet in which her few dresses hung on the hooks, all dark, all worn for work, and the hard chair where she sat.

It felt like her thoughts were trapped in a circle, going around and around, always the same thing.

Someone has to be told. Someone who will believe me, and help. I cannot do this on my own. The elegant scripts and the sturdy weight of the paper—people with that stature would toss me into Newgate and have me strung up without a second thought. How can I, a mere seamstress's assistant, possibly put this right?

That name on the top letter seemed to stare back at her. Perhaps she was a fool, but it felt like a sign.

She was going to bring that letter to Lord Warrenby, and hope for the best. Now all she had to do was find out his direction, but she thought she knew how that could be managed.

The letters carefully hidden again, she ate part of the meat pie, rinsed her face and teeth, blew out the candle, and settled herself to sleep on the floor, sure she was in for another restless night.

Voices came from close by.

"I think Tessa's sleepin'. Whot makes ye think she'll let ye in? She don't let nobody in." Alfie's voice, but what he said froze her in place.

Who would he be talking to, if not Herb? He would not really break in. Would he? She eased off the floor, moved quietly toward the drawer in which she hid the last few possessions of Reginald she chose to keep, including the revolver. She hated guns, but she knew enough to know how to load, point, and pull the trigger. And as it turned out, her father had been more concerned with her safety than she thought and the gun was already loaded. Not cocked, but definitely primed and ready.

"'er pa's the one who kept us away, and 'e ain't 'ere any more. 'Sides, did she or did she not take me arm on th' way outa the cemetery? She were turnin' ta me." Herb, full of himself.

Would she be evicted for putting a hole through the door?

She pulled the levers back, and the sound snapped. Before she could cringe, an audible start seemed to cut the night, the gasp of men recognizing the faint noise from her side of the door.

"It be 'is ghost!" "I ain't takin' on no ghost!"

Steps pounded back down the stairs, and someone slipped on the last few, several bumps in a series, and they landed with a yelp.

Maybe her father had given her one gift. He showed them he did own a gun, and convinced them that he would use it.

How long would that last?

* * *

At dawn the next morning, when the sun crept through the crack she always left in the curtains, sparking against her eyelids, Tessa felt surprisingly well rested. She had gone to sleep after all, despite her makeshift bed, and the threat that Herb and his cohorts would stop and think. But then, their superstitions were strong. It would be wonderful if they believed she was protected by her father's ghost. Permanent relief from Herb's threats.

For right now, getting out of here came first. She dressed as fast as she could, and grabbed the second half of the meat pie. It congealed overnight and tasted stale, but she swallowed it down. She needed every minute of the day to get everything done. The letter and a few of her father's shillings for a hackney coach went into her tied handkerchief, which she edged into the hidden opening of her skirt and pinned. She would take a couple stitches to hold the little bundle more securely once she got to Madame's.

The shop was quiet when she arrived, flushed and breathless, although she heard Madame Genevieve's voice coming from the main room. "I want this floor swept *avant* anyone comes. One *ne quitte ma boutique avec* dust clinging to the skirts!"

"Yes, Madame," Rosie answered. Tessa took advantage of knowing where the others were and darted over to the large tin where the papers were kept. There was no time to write anything down. She would have to rely on her memory.

Thank goodness Madame's records were neat and orderly. Tessa flipped through the cards, keeping one ear on the conversation in the other room. Sure enough, as she suspected Madame kept track of her customers by their bills. As for Lady Warrenby, all the bills went to her son, not to her.

Whispering the house directions, street and number, over and over under her breath, Tessa closed up the tin and slipped over to her sewing basket and the chair she claimed as her own. She had just made it there when Madame walked in.

"*Ah, bien, bien.* You are here. We are busy too much, j*e crois, non?* I am looking for another, you agree?"

"Oh, yes!" She might be able to get home before the sun set. How wonderful to think of a whole night of sleep.

Madame wasted no time, but sent out word. Women popped in at the shop's back door, begging an interview for the position of seamstress, leaving Tessa to handle all the customers herself.

By the end of the day though, and through several pots of tea as each woman was carefully interviewed in her French and English jumble, Madame had made her choice, so tomorrow looked better. The new girl, Ellen, was just as young as Rosie, but seemed to know what she was doing.

As Ellen settled herself at the back room's table and accepted a set of sleeves that had to be stitched before they could be sewn into a gown, she smiled at Tessa, and the strain around her young eyes, pale brown to match her hair, faded a bit. "I's so glad t'ave this job. We needs the money bad. I been 'elpin' me mum since I were old enough t'old a needle. I knowed I could do the work. Me da is sick and we ain't got no money but what mum and me can bring in."

From the energy with which Ellen set to work, her brown hair falling about her face, her mouth pursed as she concentrated, Tessa had no doubt she could do what they needed done. Her nimble mind was as quick with the calculations for yardage as Tessa had ever seen, and managed to mark the patterns with a clever eye for saving as much fabric as possible.

Perhaps, with two competent seamstresses and Madame's skilled designs, the shop would become even more popular.

Madame was French, and never spoke of her native land. And now,

Tessa realized, she made certain that those who worked for her were all women who needed it. Herself, virtually parentless until her father came here to die. Ellen, with an ill father and a mother who had been the sole support.

Rosie popped in to empty the dustpan, and Tessa watched her with new eyes. What was her story? Tessa felt ashamed that she had never asked. The girl could not sew, her work was the most menial, but it was employment nonetheless.

Madame Genevieve had set herself up as employer for those who needed it most.

What must it be like having to sift through all the women who came to the door, begging for a job? Sewing was not a rare skill. How did one pick the most needy from so many?

And thinking of needing help, she herself still had an urgent errand to run, and it would be late before she could do it. Finding her way across London in the dark was becoming far less practical. No, she would have to get up earlier tomorrow.

But it seemed Ellen proved her worth, and Madame wanted to leave early herself, an unheard of event. Providence must be smiling down on her efforts to undo her father's crimes.

Twilight lingered when Madame called the day to a close and shut the door behind them. Tessa checked the handkerchief's knot and the stitches before she headed down the street. For the first time in months, maybe years, she left her basket at work. What she had planned would not permit bringing anything that might be thought to carry away stolen goods.

Her long shadow stretched out beside her, taller and thinner than her actual form. When she got around the corner and out of sight of anyone from the shop so no one would wonder at her direction and ask uncomfortable questions tomorrow, she started for the nearest hackney stand, several streets away.

* * *

The hackney pulled away as soon as she climbed out. Nerves fluttered in Tessa's stomach. She was committed to her purpose now.

Carriages and horses filled the street. Tessa took a look at herself in the nearest window, just to be sure she was presentable. Even the lowliest servants in these great houses had standards. As one last check, she took the risk of removing her hat for a brief moment to make sure no threads, loose fibers, or anything else clung to it.

She looked for the rare numbers on the houses, the equally rare street names, comparing their appearance with the house description she had memorized. She had a number, too, but not all the houses bothered to put them on. It would be wonderful, she thought as she passed another beautiful house, if his house actually were numbered on the outside instead of having post-men delivering mail do it from pure memory. Down that street she walked, until she reached the last house before the next intersection. Still no match.

The houses were only getting larger and more ornate. Wide double doors, large paned windows, shutters in dignified black. In a couple of the houses, she saw enormous chandeliers were already lit, as though these people were not concerned with the cost of candles, their light filling the entire room, sending their glow out onto the green lawns.

Squinting across the street, Tessa thought she saw a number closer to what she was looking for. She crossed over, dodging the manure from the horses, and continued her walk. Her steps slowed.

Something told her, before she saw the—*thank goodness, yes!*—number, that she was at the right house. A white stone wall with an openwork iron fence on top and a recessed gate in the center blocked the sidewalk off from the property. Steps led to the gate, and beyond that, a span of grass further separated house from street. More steps led up to the house's dignified black-painted double door. She looked up at that door, and found herself staring at the number she wanted.

The house was perfectly balanced, the door with deeply recessed panels proclaiming its weight and import. A large fanlight added design even to the space above. On either side, large windows with heavy curtains and lace inner sheers matched width, and above it, another floor had the same harmonizing look. Higher above, still another floor, but with smaller windows, two on each side instead of one large one.

Servants never went to the main door, she knew that from going with Madame to deliver gowns. No, they went around to the back, and came in the servants' entrance. So she followed the side of the house around to the back, where even the servants' door was freshly painted and looked crisp and clean.

A path went further out from the house, and the smell of horse told her it led to the carriage house and the stables. Voices hummed on the air from the unseen buildings, company in the quiet.

The brass knocker on that clean servant's door surprised her. Somehow she had expected that they would not bother with anything so helpful, that anyone relegated to this lower level could just as easily bruise their knuckles pounding until someone heard.

A smile crooked her lips. Somehow the thoughtful touch reassured her. This was a man who cared about his servants.

The smile faded when the knocker echoed into the house, or at least into the bottom of the house. She had to remind herself that she was not one of them, and likely not entitled to the same courtesy. Her very errand made her standards questionable.

The door creaked inward, and a woman, round and with a pleasant, smiling face, stood there. "I weren't expectin' no deliveries today. Kin I 'elp ye?" She swung the door wider, and Tessa wondered if she was supposed to walk in.

She stayed outside. "I have something that I believe might belong to Lord Warrenby. If I might be allowed to deliver it?"

The woman's eyes narrowed. "Now, listen 'ere, we don't allow no women o' that kind."

Tessa could not help herself, she laughed, and the laugh surprised herself as much as it did the woman. "Oh, I am so very sorry. I did not mean it to sound that way. No, it's not that kind of thing." She rushed her explanation out. "My father just died. He was in the Packet Service, and I found some items, letters, in his possession. I don't know the story of them, but I'm trying to track down who they might belong to."

The difficulties with the war's mail delivery was well known. She held her breath and hoped her tale would be believed.

"Oooh." The face resumed its smile. "Well, that is different. Come in, come in." She grabbed Tessa's hand and pulled her inside, then shut the door behind her. "Me name is Mrs. Smith. Wot be yer name?"

She walked into a wall of heat, the air was thick with the scents of cooking, meat and vegetables, and something sweet she could not identify. "Tessa Abbott."

"Well, Miss Abbott, ye jest come in and rest yer feet."

The room was so warm because an enormous brick fireplace took up most of one wall. Iron hooks for pots hung at various levels, and on one side, a small door enclosed what Tessa presumed was a bread oven. Below it, a wide hollow held logs for immediate use. On the side wall, more logs had been piled even with the meagre windows that peeked out into the back lawn.

She wished she could ask Mrs. Smith to open the door again so she could breathe.

"Sit, sit," Mrs. Smith urged. She poured out some tea from a pot kept warm on the edge of the fireplace. "'ave a cuppa. Ah'll go see iffen 'is Lordship is busy."

"Thank you." Tessa sat at the table, and watched as the woman slipped out a door on the far side. She got a quick glimpse of stairs beyond before the door closed.

Aha! Some of the complaints of cold food at dinners that she heard floating around the shop made sense. She wondered idly just how far they had to walk with the food once they got to the top of the steps.

And then she jerked her attention back to the matter at hand. Under the protection of the thick tabletop, she snapped the thread holding the handkerchief, and pulled it out of the opening hidden in her skirt folds.

Letter in hand, she waited for Mrs. Smith to return with Warrenby's response.

A few minutes later, a man dressed in crisp black, as black as the doors on the house, came in, Mrs. Smith on his heels.

"What is this I hear about letters?"

This man would not be as gullible as the cook, and might ask uncomfortable questions, the same ones she had no answer for herself. No one was as snooty as a butler, she had heard, and it appeared she was about to find out if the reports were true.

Tessa held out the letter. "This was among my father's possessions when he died. I don't even know if it belongs to His Lordship, but I can't imagine who else it might be. Even if it is not his, I thought perhaps he might know the name."

The butler took it as if it smelled bad. His first move was to flip it over. The broken seal was as glaring as if a lantern shone on it.

"I found it that way. I don't know who broke the seal." Tessa felt color rush up her face, and the room felt even hotter.

The man glared at her, condemning her already. "Come with me, miss." He turned and stalked toward the same door.

Tessa whispered, "Thank you," to Mrs. Smith, who did not look as kind now, and hurried to catch up.

The stairs were stone, reminding Tessa that the kitchen was built inside the foundation. At the top the butler opened another door, and held it for her. It might have been his normal way of treating people, but she had the distinct impression that he was making sure she didn't slip away.

They walked along a hallway paneled in wood on the bottom with a rich green wallpaper on top. Her shoes clicked on the wooden floor that someone kept polished to a high sheen. Past one door, closed tight, and further along the hall until they reached another door, dark wood and six-paneled, near the end.

He gave a polite knock. Some command must have come from inside, because he turned and glared at her. "Wait." Then he disappeared within. The door shut.

"I will," she said, but he wasn't there to hear.

* * *

Warrenby looked up from the financial registers he went over every month. It was late, the candles were burning low, and his eyes burned from the smoke. He hired someone trustworthy to manage his estates, but a smart man knew enough to keep a close eye on the books anyway. "Yes?"

His butler stood with his usual poker-straight posture, a folded paper in his hand. "Mrs. Smith says a young woman brought a letter she claims she found among her father's possessions after he died. It had already been opened. She *says*" —the word was rich with skepticism— "that she found it that way."

Blake set the quill pen down, and held out his hand. "Let me see it."

As soon as Hodgins set it in his hand, he recognized it. A red haze clouded his vision, and his heart began a drumbeat in his ears. If Hodgins said anything, he could not hear it, just stared at the handwriting of the person who knew his deepest, most shameful secret. The words wavered and he suddenly realized his hands were shaking against the restraint he forced over his body. He made himself to take a breath past the tightness in his lungs, a bellow of rage trapped behind his training and control.

With exquisite care, he set the letter down on his desk. *How did this fall into someone else's hand?* He had hidden it with the greatest caution. If this were to get out, he would not be the only person hurt. And one of them was the most innocent of victims.

His daughter. Who did not even know him, who called another 'father.'

He shoved the memories away with an effort that sent chills down his body. Better than the heat that had threatened to explode through his skin.

His lungs finally released, and he took a deep breath. In a voice he did not recognize as his own, Blake asked, "A woman brought this?" He did not wait for Hodgins to reply, just snapped, "Send her in."

This day could hold no further shocks. He had thought that a moment ago. He was wrong. He recognized the young woman who walked in the instant he saw her. Blake gave a nod to Hodgins, who still stood guarding the door, and his butler slipped out as quietly as he did everything, shutting the door behind himself. "You!"

A strange pressure built inside. Disappointment, of course. Perhaps he had imbued her with qualities she did not possess, merely because of her big, innocent eyes, her perfect speech, and her little quirks.

And what did that say about his ability to judge people?

The young woman bobbed a quick curtsey. "Hello," she said in that same cultured speech that always caught his ear.

"Explain yourself." He had not intended his voice to be so harsh, but the thought that she had read and knew his worst secret, his biggest shame, made his stomach clench.

She made no attempt to walk in further, just stayed by the door. Politeness? Lack of presumptuousness? Or getting ready to make a run for it? He could have told her it was useless, Hodgins would stop her, or see to it that someone else did.

He did not invite her to sit. She was not of his class and would not expect it anyway, but the necessary omission, even in these circumstances, caused an itch in the middle of his chest.

Why, out of all the women in the ton, did he have to find this one so appealing?

The woman shifted her feet, he could tell even beneath the black gown in which Madame dressed all her workers.

And why did that plain gown have to *sway* like that when she moved?

"The letter is yours, then?" Her question sounded all innocence, and her eyes, even from across the room, matched it. Those big, brown eyes.

"You knew it was, or you would not have brought it here." He had to get his anger, or perhaps it was his humiliation, under control. Blake took a deep breath, and held it until his heartbeat slowed. A little.

"No." Those brown eyes went from innocent to angry. She took a breath, fluttering the fabric over her lungs. Her hand clenched in her skirt. Anger? Or perhaps nerves, even guilt? Color flushed up her pale, porcelain skin. "I did not *know* it was yours. I just . . . I had heard your mother use your name and thought it was possible. Nothing more."

"Where did you get this?" He could not bring himself to touch the letter in her presence, but he gestured to the white square on his desk. "And don't give me any tale about finding it among all your father's possessions when he died."

"Not even if it's the truth?" The color deepened in her face, painting her cheeks in bright rose.

She was convincing, he had to give her that. "What is your name? I like to know with whom I am speaking."

"My name is Tessa Abbott. My father's name was Reginald Abbott, and he always *told* me he worked for the Packet Service." She gave a deep sigh, Blake almost felt the gust of air from where he sat.

That sigh, and the bitterness in her words made him decide to listen, to extend the benefit of the doubt. He did not know what it was like to face disillusionment from a parent, but he imagined it would sound exactly like that.

"I think you had better tell me the whole story." The difference in his voice was obvious even to himself. And then he broke the rule that had been bothering him since she first walked into his office. "Come in and sit down, Miss Abbott."

"Oh, no!" Her eyes went big, and he had to blink to break the hold that warm dark gaze had over him. Did she know the power of her stare? "No, thank you, but I could not do that."

"But I'm inviting you." A smile tugged at the edges of his mouth. Didn't he know what she was going to say all along?

If only those eyes didn't catch him with their every change in expression. She was such a treat to watch. She was not of his class, he reminded himself, and he was not the kind of man who dallied with the vulnerable.

"Please." Blake urged, and she crept into the room, like a little black mouse checking to see if the path was clear before venturing toward the cheese.

Which would be either himself, or the chair across from him. The symbolic cheese was probably the chair, but he could wish it was otherwise. "Now. Tell me about this father of yours, and how he might have gotten possession of something so private as my correspondence."

She sat on the edge of the seat. Wary little thing, wasn't she? He gestured to her, and she took a breath before she began. "My father was gone most of the time before his last illness. Until she died, my mother said he worked for the Packet Service. As I got older, I just assumed he was still working on the mail boats. Now, I doubt it very much. In fact, I am not certain he ever worked for the Packet Service at all."

"And why is that?"

She looked down at her hands, and sighed again. When her eyes met his, the force of the plea there was so strong it took all his willpower to stay in his chair, and not go to her side.

"That letter is not the only one I found. He had them hidden in his clothes. He told me so just before he died the"—he saw her calculating—"night before last, and I stayed up going through every coat and suit. He had special pockets sewn in. If there was even one empty, I could not find it."

Her eyes shimmered with tears, and he had a moment of pure male panic. But he didn't move away, didn't get up from behind his desk and cross the room, however tempting. Someone who had lost both parents, one the night before last, was entitled to tears, yet that shimmer was all he saw.

The night before last. Her father had been newly dead the last time he took his mother to Madame's shop! He had seen no signs of grief.

But she was talking, and he had missed at least a few of her words. The last few, however, caught his attention. "I'm sorry, can you repeat that?"

"I said, I need your promise that you will not turn me over to the Bow Street Runners." Her hands were squeezed so tight together that every knuckle was white.

He hoped he would not regret this. "I give you my word. That is a promise."

* * *

Tessa looked at Lord Warrenby. Her hands hurt, and she felt the pain all the way past her elbows. Beads of sweat were forming on her forehead, but she was afraid to brush them away. He had listened to her so far.

But jewelry! One could not put a price on letters, ink on paper, but gold and gemstones? People had gone to the gallows for less.

She took a breath past a tight throat. "Beside the few other letters, there is some jewelry, as well. And gemstones."

His eyes widened before they narrowed into glittering ice-blue flashes. "Tell me, why not burn it? If there are more letters, why not burn them all? Why not keep the rest? Surely you could live better by selling them."

"To whom? Fellow thieves? I know some, they live all around my rooming house. They would have no trouble fencing them, but there is no guarantee I would see any return." She stifled a shudder at the thought of Herb finding out what she was hiding, and hurried on. "And to bring them to a reputable shop, how would I explain them? You don't believe me, how could I convince anyone else."

She thought she heard him say something like, "I never said I didn't," but her words kept coming. How did she explain what it had been like that awful night as she found treasure after treasure? "They are all stolen, I know that. I'm not stupid! They would have the Bow Street Runners on me before I could leave the shop. Transportation to Australia is the best I could hope for!"

Her throat tightened, squeezing her voice. She said, softer than before, "More likely I would end up in Newgate, and then hung. I could not betray all my mother's teachings, her high standards, that way. She was a woman of honor, I would never bring such reproach to her reputation."

Tessa hurried on. It was now or never. "I brought the letter because I hoped if it was yours, you might be willing to help me find the owners of the jewelry. You were always so kind to your mother and sister, and that means a lot in my world. I think some of the necklaces and rings may have had family crests worked into them, but I would not recognize them, and I think you probably will."

The room went quiet. She wanted to fill the silence, but could think of nothing else to say.

Finally, when she thought she could take the oppressive quiet no longer, he cleared his throat. "Your father came into possession of jewelry, as well as letters." His voice was flat.

Her own throat felt tight now. In a small voice, all she could get out after that confession, she said, "And gemstones."

In that same expressionless voice, he said, "And you want me to help you find the owners."

If you can. If you will. If you don't plan to turn me over to Newgate. But all she said was, "Yes."

"Very well then." Blake—Warrenby, she reminded herself, any chance of familiarity was gone—leaned back in his chair. His arms flexed inside his coat. If she had to guess, she would think he had just clenched his hands. That was a bad sign, but he had not thrown her out yet. "I will expect you here tomorrow night. Bring everything you have."

Both relief and dismay flooded her. Dismay, she realized, was first, that sinking feeling, the tightness in her chest. "Are you going to have the Bow

Street Runners waiting for me then? Does the promise hold good for more than today?"

His brows came down in a fierce frown. "When I give my word, it is good for all time."

"Thank you," she said, and hoped her relief did not show in her voice. How little the upper classes knew of the life of ordinary workers!

Warrenby leaned back and pulled on a velvet cord behind him that hung down the wall. The door to the room opened, and the butler entered.

"Have the coach brought around to the front."

"Yes, sir." The butler bowed his head, and slipped back out the door,

A coach? She had seen his vehicles. To drive around in her neighborhood this late at night? His driver would be lucky to get out alive. "Oh, no, sir! I mean, my lord. You don't have to have someone bring me home. Really. It isn't safe to have something as elegant as your vehicle in my area."

He looked like he had been about to rise, but settled deeper in the big wooden chair. "How can I know you will be safe, then? You have just told me you have a virtual thief's paradise in your room. I would prefer you make it back here safely, so I can take them off your hands."

Warrenby folded his arms over his chest. "If you want my help, you had best take care of yourself."

A strange tingle ran through her. Of course he didn't mean it that way. *Take care of yourself.* Regardless, those words warmed her deep inside.

All the way out to the carriage with the footman, all through the ride to Madame's with the silent coachman, and all the walk to her own room in the dark.

* * *

Blake looked down at the letter on his desk. He knew exactly what it said. It hadn't reached him until he returned home from a dangerous trip delivering urgent news and the maps he had made to the War Office. But it had been too late. His hurried call on her father before he was to go back to France had been met with icy disdain.

A million times he had asked himself if he had really wanted to marry Alice when he took her virginity, and a million times he had come up with no answer. He had never even told her he was leaving for the war. No wonder she had it delivered to his house. It was the only address she knew.

Probably better that way, he thought again, a familiar thought that had haunted him ever since he first found it in the correspondence. Had she known, had she sent it through the mails, he might never have heard a thing. Mail was notoriously slow, even non-existent, what with France monitoring all the waterways. It amazed him that England had managed to win the war at all, what with so many of their communiques landing on the bottom of the ocean whenever the sea battles were in question.

Even worse, letters were nearly public property when they did reach the army. Everyone was so desperate for news from home that it hardly mattered whose letter it was.

And the more salacious, the better.

He had pulled Alice's letter out several times since he returned home for good. As it did every time, the day he approached her father came back in hurtful clarity. Marquis Wilton had matched his own soldier's posture with an intimidating stiff stance. His blue eyes, so like hers in color, had been cold as ice. "My daughter is wed. You have no business showing up here. She does not need your attentions now."

He had not even been invited in.

The man had continued, "I could, I *should*, call you out, but that would only cause the very speculation we wish to avoid. You are not welcome here, and I certainly will not give you her new address. She wants nothing to do with you. Had you any care for her, you would have tried to reach her first. After despoiling her, the possibility of a child must have occurred to you. You will stay away from her and her family, and you will not attempt to communicate with the child. If I find you have done either, I *will* call you out, scandal or no."

And that had been that.

He looked at the fireplace in the wall. It was not lit, the day had been too warm. Should he light it now? Should the letter be burned, and spare them all further danger?

A strange need, a link to his child, made him press a hidden button in the middle of his desk. A tiny drawer popped out. No one knew the secret cubby existed. In fact, he had ordered it specially made, and even the old craftsman who had done it had since died. The only one now who knew where it was and how to get in was himself.

The letter safely stored, Blake leaned back and stared into space. Was Miss Abbott as innocent as she claimed? And would she bring the rest of the stolen items? His brow furrowed as he thought back over this night's strange event.

He believed she would. Honor was a rare commodity, even among his own class, but he suspected she possessed it.

He would know tomorrow. If she came, well and good. The thought have him a strange sense of comfort.

If she did not come . . . if she did not come, he would simply go find her.

CHAPTER 4

The sun's first glow jerked Tessa awake. She did not even realize she had slept at all, but she must have, since she woke on the floor, with her head pillowed on her arm.

Tessa sat up, every muscle stiff. How nice it would be to be able to sleep in, even for only one day! She pushed herself to her feet, and stretched, feeling the pull of abused muscles from yesterday's excursion. The tightness eased just enough for her to clear her head.

She was supposed to do something today. . . What was it again?

Her gaze fell on the chest of drawers, and the stockings with their secreted stash jumped to mind, bringing with it the rest of her memories. Ah yes, the gems and their settings, and Warrenby. And the pouches she had not figured out last night. There wasn't much time now, she would have to do what she could with what she had.

She did not own a reticule, which would have helped. Somewhat. All she had were the slits in her skirts, where she hid the money for food from the street venders. The handkerchiefs in which she tied those small coins would never hold all the settings, with their larger and uneven sizes.

Which was the lesser of two evils, to leave the settings here and risk another day when they could be stolen, or tie them as best she could and take the chance that someone might hear her clink as she walked?

The gems were easier, and quickly sewn into a single kerchief, which she fastened with tight stitches against the inner seams of the skirt of her gown. At least, with them tied in the handkerchief, and the little bundle as secure as she could make it, she doubted any sound would rise above the noise of London's streets.

Perhaps even above the noise of the shop.

She had given Warrenby her word. She would do her best to keep it.

Besides, she would sleep better knowing that there was nothing worth stealing here once the gold was gone. The coins, of course, but if they were taken, how much worse off would she be? She knew how to live on little money, she had done it ever since she found herself on her own. Truly, even before that, as her Mother had taught her much during their own lean times.

She would hope for the best, and bring the settings with her. Decision made, or perhaps it had formed overnight as she slept, Tessa pulled out her few remaining handkerchiefs, tucked several settings in each, and repeated what she had done with the gems. Tie every kerchief as tight as she could, only this time she took extra stitches in each knot for safety, then sewed each package down the seams of her black work gown.

She had forgotten to sponge it off, but it was too late for that. Londoners were used to smells and she kept herself cleaner than most. No one would notice that over all the perfumes floating about the shop.

She ignored the few letters. There was no time. They would just have to wait another day.

* * *

"Miss? I'd like to see that blue fabric. Bring it here, please." An imperious voice snapped the command.

Tessa nodded. It had been a busy day, and tense, with the handkerchiefs slapping at her legs as she moved about the shop carrying bolts of fabric or hand-sketched gown designs to women who wanted to see them. Worse was when she was on her knees making last-minute adjustments to hems and trains. More than once she had set a knee down on a dangling cloth-wrapped bit of gold, and had to muffle her yelp.

Tessa tugged the long bolt free, and brought it over. "Here you are, my lady."

The woman gave her no acknowledgement, but then, they seldom did.

Would this day never end? The looming trip across London in the late-night sky haunted her, breaking through her concentration at the most inconvenient times. More than one customer had snapped, "Are you even listening?"

The shadows blended together as the sun neared the horizon.

The bell over the door jingled, and Tessa looked up from setting the bolt on the wide table exactly as the woman directed. Another customer came in, bringing perfume and the scent of rain. Tessa glanced behind her, to see the first fat drops hit the cobbled stones outside.

Perfect. Just perfect. Now she would arrive soaking wet. Maybe, she thought with faint hope, the rain would end before she had to set out.

Nothing would change the weather. If it still rained, if it was dry, she had to show up tonight at Warrenby's. And by the time she got there, she would be more than ready to get rid of everything, she thought as one of the packages slapped against her leg when she walked away from the table and the customer.

"Miss? Oh, Miss? I don't like this fabric after all. Take it away."

Tessa muffled her sigh and retraced her steps to lift the heavy bolt she had just set down, then wove through the tables and chairs, the bobbing bonnets and draped skirts, to put it back in its niche.

Someone pulled at her arm, and Tessa looked down at a middle-aged woman whose bonnet brim partially blocked her face. "I have decided.

You can take the other sketches away. I want this gown," a piece of paper was separated from the others, "and that fabric." She swiveled around to point at the very bolt that Tessa had just put away.

So she headed back to collect the bolt yet again, trying to ignore her aching feet and the scent of tea wafting from the corner.

* * *

The door closed for the last time, and Rose went through the room snuffing all the candles. Madame locked the door with the key she kept around her neck, and turned around with a smile. "*Pour ce soir*, we are done. Home!" She clapped her hands, and started back across the room. "Rosie, *finir le* . . . le . . . sweep."

Tessa bit her lip to hide her smile. Madame's struggles with English often left them guessing, but they were learning some French in the process.

When the shop was dark, she stepped out the rear door into the narrow lane. The rain had not stopped, and water came over the roof's edge in a steady stream. She pulled her bonnet further down—as if that would help, she thought with a snort that got a drip up her nose—and hurried down the narrow gap between the buildings. The sooner she got to the main street, the greater possibility that somewhere along the way she might find something heading the direction she needed to go, however dim the chance was. She grimaced, and swiped at the water dripping off her bonnets brim into her eyes.

And stopped short. A small enclosed carriage and horse sat directly across the side street opening, blocking anyone coming or going. The door swung wide, adding a darker square in the murky night. Tessa whirled away, only to hear a familiar voice from the depths. "Get in. It is far wet to walk."

Lord Warrenby.

She turned around, and hurried toward that welcome bit of black. A white gloved hand came through the door. "Hold on."

A small step was flipped out from within. The hand never wavered. "The longer you stand there, the wetter you are getting."

She grabbed hold, gathered her wet skirts, and stepped in, following the guidance of his strong arm.

"There is a seat behind you. Sit down before we start moving."

Tessa managed not to laugh. She had been in carriages before, if hackneys and mail coaches counted, and knew well where the seats were. "Thank you, my lord."

At a thump from something against the roof, the carriage gave a lurch and started down the street. It was so quiet, just the slight scrape of the wheels against the sodden cobbles and the whoosh of the water as it parted.

Flint scraped, and light flared in the small space. In its glow, Warrenby's face was focused as he set the glass over the lamp, and turned away to hang it on a hook. He reached out and pulled the curtain across the window. Settling back, he turned that odd glittering gaze, more piercing now in the enclosed space of the carriage, on her.

"I assume you brought the jewelry." It was not a question.

Heat rushed up her cheeks at what she assumed would come next. "Yes. I did not have time to package the letters. I hope you are not angry." She tried to read his expression, but nothing showed. "I cannot hand any of the gems and settings over now because they are hidden on my person."

One side of his mouth quirked in an almost-smile. "I would not ask you to. We can certainly wait until we get somewhere warm." His gaze flicked to the window, where rivers of rain slid down the glass. "And dry." He turned back to her. "We will have to work quickly if I am to get you home before you have to get up again. I assume you rise early?"

"Yes. I usually am up with the sun, at the latest." Just the thought of another short night of sleep triggered a yawn, although Tessa tried to hide it, but she was certain the tightness in her jaw and throat gave her away.

She saw a smile pull at his mouth, but it faded. "So." The word hung in the air for a moment, and Tessa waited for Warrenby to add something more. "Had I not seen you working in Madame Genevieve's shop, I would have taken you as someone from genteel society." Although he did not ask, she heard the question hiding in his words, *Who are you, where are you from, and how did you come to be in this state?*

He was not done. "After all, you are asking quite a favor of me. I think I should know as much about who I am dealing with as possible."

The question he had not asked was as much in the open as if he had said the exact words. Tessa tried to find any insult in his comment or his tone, but couldn't. And he was right, she was indeed asking a large favor of him. It was quite presumptuous of her. "Very well. What would you like to know?"

"Have you always lived in London? Is Abbott your family name?" For first questions, they were mild, Tessa thought. He could have asked something much more harsh. He settled back in his seat just as she had in hers, widening the distance between them. And, not altogether coincidentally she was sure, moving his face out of reach of the little lantern.

"I suppose so. It is my father's name. As to whether his family belonged to Society," a sad laugh choked her for a moment until she could clear her throat, "I highly doubt it.

"He would not be the first son disinherited for bringing . . . disgrace to the family name." The words came out surprisingly gentle.

"If so," Tessa felt the bitterness rise, but bit it back. "He never said. I know nothing about his family. My mother's either, for that matter."

She felt a quick movement from the other side of the carriage. "Neither?"

"No. Neither."

"No cousins, no grandparents, no aunts or uncles?" He still sounded surprised, as if the thought of being without relatives was foreign to him.

"No." She feared her face showed the heat creeping up her cheeks. He might be out of the lantern's glow, but she was not.

"I . . . see," he said from the dimness, but his tone sounded like he did not understand at all.

"We are nearly to my house, and I just have one more question. Where have you lived? If your father was in the Packet Service, you didn't live in London all your life, did you?"

Humor lifted the tightness in her chest. Tessa felt herself smile, felt the corners of her mouth lift, even felt the twinkle she was certain was in her eyes. "No. We didn't. Back when I was little, I remember we lived in this small but pretty house before we started moving around. My earliest memories are of it."

"Ah. Where was this? Do you remember?" The question was too casual, but perhaps he was getting bored and just making conversation to fill in time.

* * *

She gave a hint of a smile, just a lightening of the unease in her eyes, and a loosening of the tightness around her mouth. "I honestly don't know. I was young. We've lived in Falmouth, and later in Yarmouth. After . . . after my mother died, my father and I came to London."

He could tell the grief she still felt for her mother's death, it was in the little hesitation, and in the flatness of her voice when she spoke of it. He hated to cause anyone pain but he needed to know. "How long has she been dead?"

"Four years."

"And she never said anything about where she was from?"

Her perfectly arched brows came down. "I already answered that. No."

Ah, that was better. He preferred the snap to the sadness. Blake tried not to give away his thoughts. A mother who spoke cultured English, and a very pretty house. There was a story there, he was certain, but Miss Abbott clearly was not privy to it.

Pity.

Falmouth would fit in with the Packet Service, as would Yarmouth. For years the former had been known for corruption, and it might make sense that someone working on a Packet could live more comfortably there.

Wasn't there a tale about the sailors managing to capture some Spanish vessels, and sell their treasure quietly, then live on the proceeds?

Those abuses were ended about six years ago, if his memory served. She was certainly old enough to remember something of those days.

"Fascinating history, I'm sure, but what about the letter you brought me? *My* letter? How would your father have gotten hold of it?"

"I . . . don't know." All the animation left her face, the smile disappearing as if it had never been there. "He was not home much, not until he became quite ill these last few months. You would know more than I how he might have found it."

"It did not go through the overseas mail. I know when and how it was delivered. It never left the safety of my house—or so I thought—until you brought to me yesterday."

She took an inhale, he could feel how much it hurt even from across the carriage. "Why are we dancing around the subject? My father was a thief. Clearly he stole it. How he did it I don't know, but nothing else explains the jewelry hidden in . . . his clothes." She turned her head away from the light.

He had known some unsavory characters among the *ton*, but had never seen the slightest bit of shame in them. Unfaithful husbands and wives, cheating at cards, phony mine sales, blackmail.

The man might have been at it for years. There had to be victims out there, people who had paid—for how long?—to keep their own secrets from being made public.

He felt a tightening in his chest as he looked at the averted face across from him. His hands clenched as if preparing for a fight. And he wished he could pull the man back from death and have a go at him, just for what he had done to his daughter.

Instead, he had to sit here and watch her suffer. Before he could decide what to do, what to say, as if anything could relieve her situation, the carriage stopped. He lifted the shade, and even in the dark could recognize where he was.

The carriage shifted. He recognized the sensation as the driver climbing down, and the door opened. "Here we are, sir."

* * *

Tessa just stared at the front door as it drew closer and closer in front of her. Her heart began to pound, and embarrassment sent heat up her face and tingles down her hands.

Finally she got enough air to speak. "You can't do this! You know I'm supposed to come in the back."

He turned around and gave her a mock glare. The twitch of his lips at the edges took the bite out of it. "Just whose house is this?" He looked down at her, from his greater height because of the slope of the walk. Pale light seeped across the transom, casting its faint glow onto his dark hair. "I have no intention of tracking you across my house, especially when I know what you are carrying."

Then he turned back to the door, which was opening even as he neared it.

Tessa pulled her bonnet further over her face.

The carriage rattled down the side of the house, jerking her attention from the open door, and Warrenby standing there, waiting.

"Miss Abbott?" His voice pulled her attention from the house's corner behind which the carriage had vanished. He still waited patiently. Just inside the house, a weary-looking footman stood with what she suspected was less patience.

Tessa scurried to catch up. Warrenby ushered her in, and stepped in behind her. The footman closed the outer door, and only then, hidden from any curious neighbors, did she feel she could relax, if just a little.

"Come into my office," Warrenby said, and walked down the short hallway to where it crossed with a larger one.

Funny, how things looked different coming at it from a new direction.

"It is late, and I would prefer we do this quickly." He entered a room partway down the long hall. Inside, it was dark, the curtains pulled tight and no candles lit. He walked around the big desk she remembered, now just a darker shade of black in the room. Tessa stayed near the doorway, afraid she would stumble into something.

"One moment," he said, and did something at the desk. The snap of flint, once, twice, and a small glow started. Another moment, and one by one, he lit all the candles in the candelabra on his desk. The room warmed into light.

He sat down and held out his hand. "If I might see what you brought me?"

Tessa felt her cheeks heat, and knew he saw it. "As I said earlier, I have them hidden on my person. I will need privacy to get them out." The heat in her face grew as she realized how indelicate she had been. *Hidden on my person.*

It looked like Warrenby's cheeks colored, too. "I will give you a couple minutes, no more."

She nodded. "That will be fine." Before he could rise, she said in a rush, "Do you have scissors? Or a knife? I need to cut some threads."

With a slight scraping noise, Warrenby pulled open a desk drawer and took out a slender knife he must use to break the seals on letters. "Will this do?"

Tessa nodded. It wasn't ideal, she didn't know how well it would cut through thread, but, "I think it will be fine."

"I shall leave you to your devices, but be quick. As I said, it is late, and we don't have much time." He laid the knife on the desktop, walked past her, and out the door. It closed with a solid *thump*.

Snatching the knife off the desk, Tessa jerked up her skirt and began sawing at the small packages, one after another. If he would give her more than the couple minutes, she did not know, but she suspected not.

The knife was not meant for this use. The ticking of the clock became a chant to hurry. Not *tick, tick, tick*, but *cut, cut, cut*. As the last handkerchief pouch was set on the desk, a firm rap came on the door.

"Come," she said, and smiled. No doubt knocking on a door in his own house was not something he had to do often. It should be the other way around. She should be the one who had to knock, while he granted entry.

Ah well. She would enjoy this single event while she had it.

He walked in when she spread open the first kerchief, and as he neared the desk and Tessa knew he caught a glimpse of what she had brought, his steps slowed. She pulled at the last threads holding the second kerchief tight, and a low whistle cut the quiet air.

* * *

Miss Abbott worked on the fastening of another one of her little pouches. Blake stared at the two mounds of gold on his desk. These were not small bits of jewelry. She had been right, what was left of them would still be identifiable. He knew nothing about fixing jewelry, but maybe, just maybe, a skilled jeweler would be able to repair these. All except for the jewels that had once graced them.

Tessa pulled open the last kerchief, and motioned to this latest mound. He tore his gaze from her to look at the pile spread out. Stones of all colors, reds and blues, greens, oranges. She could not know the value of what lay on this latest handkerchief. He did not even know how much it was. A lot, for certain.

"I found some . . . coins in his pockets, as well." The words came out slow, and laden with guilt, and her gaze slid away before coming back. He saw her take a deep breath before continuing. "I know it is wrong, but I hoped to keep them. I don't know what else to do, how to find who the money belong to."

A smile quirked Blake's mouth. "That is a quandary, to be sure. It is impossible find out who they belong to. Coins have nothing recognizable to mark them. We can hope people—or their jewelers—recognize at least some of their gems in the pile you have there, but anything beyond that will just have to be written off as a loss."

Relief lightened the burden in her eyes. "Oh, thank you! I have been so careful not to spend them—at least, not many of them."

"Let us see what I can find out about the settings and the jewels we have. I'm sure many families will be happy to get that much back."

Miss Tessa cleared her throat. He raised his eyebrows. "Yes? Is there something else?"

"I didn't bring the letters." Color crept up her cheeks, adding a rosy glow to her lovely face, and again the thought ran through his mind, *who was she?* "If it is acceptable to you, I will have to bring them another day."

Oh, yes. The letters. He waved his hand across the wealth on his desk. "I shall be occupied for a few days with these." Not to mention with John and Emmy, and the announcement he expected to come soon. And the parties that would follow. He suspected the letters would be the least of his worries. "Bring them as soon as you can, I'm sure you would like to be rid of them."

"Thank you." The color that had just begun to fade washed back, and he had to force himself to concentrate on her words. "I do not want there to be talk if I come too many times, but I just did not have any way to carry them"

"There won't be talk." She had no reason to believe him. "Anyone familiar with me knows I do not impose my will on my servants. Or anyone who has no recourse. No one will suspect anything untoward."

Except he did pick her up in a carriage on a late and rainy night, and whisk her off to his house. That might raise some questions even among those who knew him. The skeptical look she gave him showed him that carriage ride was on her mind as well.

Carriage rides made him think of Hyde Park on bright sunlit days, where one could drive with a woman and exchange greetings with friends and acquaintances, or walk along the shady paths if one wanted more privacy. This woman would grace anyone's carriage, and he knew she could hold her own in a conversation.

He had not struggled with Society's rules before, but his time in France had opened his eyes to a great many injustices.

Like a man and a woman who found each other attractive, even intriguing . . . Blake shook his head to clear the inappropriate thought. It was time to bring her back to her own room. She had mentioned that she rose early, and it was creeping close to midnight.

CHAPTER 5

Madame was flustered as she checked over the gowns in preparation for the first customer of the day. "*Maintenant, la dame* Honora Saxton will be here for her gowns. This is the first time she has come *à mon salon*, so we must be on our very, very best."

Our very, very best. Tessa had been through Madame's nerves over new customers before. Until everything was final, the sales were set, and she was certain the woman wouldn't change her mind, she knew her employer would be fluttery over the smallest detail.

As she went about her normal work, pressing the delicate bits with the tiny iron, and checking the hems and seams for any mistakes so the new customer could see how perfect they were, Tessa took great care. She kept one eye on the new girl, Ellen, as she did the same on her own work. Madame checked the inventory of fabrics, and marked the supplies they needed in fine lead pencil on a piece of paper to send to G Sutton. Rosie was sent off with the order.

"*J'espère qu'elle* she finds her way," Madame muttered as the girl slipped out the back door. Guessing her employer's meaning was always a challenge, but Tessa assumed she either wanted this Lady Saxton to come, or she was afraid Rosie would get lost.

She glanced up at the clock. It was time to open the shop. Nine am, early for the *ton*, but not too early for someone desperate to have another gown for a ball the same day.

Women flowed in within minutes. Yawning, blinking, but still eager, well-dressed ladies who reeked elegance and perfume. Tessa knew they had not become so ornate without having dragged their maids out of bed much earlier.

Poor girls. If there had been a ball last night, she wondered if those maids had managed even two or three hours of sleep. As she glanced around the room, it was easy to see which had stolen a few minutes' sleep while their mistresses were at the ball, and which had been silly enough to stay awake wrapped up in their own pursuits. Those maids were almost asleep in their chairs.

Tessa wondered if she could stall enough to give the poor tired maids at least a brief nap. A cup of Madame's tea would help, but it would never be offered to a maid.

Several hours flew by, women being put into gowns, or shown the sketches of new ones, which they either approved or verbally ripped apart. The latter were her least favorite kind of customer.

"Oh, Honora, do you see this color?" The girlishly feminine voice carried like a bell across the shop.

"Oh, my! How did I miss that? You are *exquisite*, Amanda! How can I be so fortunate to have you as a friend?" The overly loud voices had to belong to women who did not mind being the center of attention and would relish causing a scene. That promised the difficult kind of customer, and it was always good to be prepared.

Honora. Honora Saxton, Madame's new customer? Tessa wished she could peek out of the dressing room door sand see who both of them were as the first voice didn't sound familiar either. Might Madame have *two* new customers? She didn't dare so much as move, as she was occupied right now with the Dowager Duchess of Oswald, one of their most annoying and particular customers, who had far too much influence on far too many of the others. One unfavorable comment from the dowager could drive away all but the most reliable clients.

So she kept pinning and listened to the two women talk about the *exquisite* fabric and how utterly *lovely* they both were to have the other as friend.

The woman standing in front of her made a sound much like a snarl. Tessa looked up in surprise, to see her staring across the tiny room at the door. In an undertone meant only for herself, the old woman muttered, "Those two are the most annoying women in London." But the Duchess was not speaking to her, so Tessa remained silent and pretended she did not hear.

The pins were finally in, the Dowager Duchess gave her approval, and the gown was promised for later in the day. Tessa took it to the back room and sat down to stitch.

An hour later, the gown's last adjustments finished and the dress wrapped in paper for the servant to come and collect, she went back into the store. The voices of the two women who had drawn the Dowager Duchess's ire were still there, and Tessa had a chance to see them.

Even before she managed to memorize their faces, the gems hanging about one of the women's neck and ears caught her attention. Not the more subdued jewelry the other women wore so as not to attract thieves. No, these two had come out for show.

It didn't take long to determine which was Honora Saxton. She was stunning. There was no other word for it. Her face had strong features, high cheekbones, firm nose, big eyes, but they were all so perfectly balanced that anything less would get lost in the line of her jaw and the length of her face. Her hair was brown like Tessa's but darker, fuller, glossier. When she turned enough for Tessa to see her eyes, they were so deep and black that it was hard to turn away. The lashes matched her hair and framed her eyes so thickly it was as if they had been outlined in kohl.

But Tessa was a servant, and did not dare be caught staring, so she turned away before the woman would notice.

Had Miss Saxton and her friend left *any* jewelry at home? As she set down a sketch of one of the latest fashions in front of a young woman, she heard someone mention, "Warrenby."

Attention caught, Tessa tried to hear the rest while she answered questions and discussed fabric with the girl she was supposed to be helping.

Fortunately, he seemed to be the talk of the day, and even Honora Saxton and her friend couldn't bear to be left out. With their carrying voices, Tessa was able to hear the rest.

It seemed Warrenby and his mother were having a coming-out party for his sister. Tessa had to smile. Not always did she get to find out what happened to the elegant gowns she stitched, but most likely that silver blue lace dress was for that party.

She would never get to see it, but it was nice to know even that little bit.

* * *

Blake stood at the doorway of the ballroom, and ran his gaze over the swirling mass of colors and sexes. Men and women moved back and forth in the dance, exchanging partners for the twirl only to return to their original one for the promenade. For some it was the happiest moments of the night, for others, despite the usual courtesies, the moment they could turn their back on their partner they let their faces sag into disgust or dismay.

Somewhere in there, Emmy danced with his old friend and sometime foe. From what his mother said, the two had snatched every chance to be together. Ice parlors, book stores, promenades in Hyde Park, and musicales, they somehow managed to 'accidentally' run into each other on nearly a daily basis.

And it was now Blake's job to treat the man with courtesy and be open-minded.

He adored Emmy. There were just the two of them, and such a large gap between, but despite that they had always been the very best of friends. How had they managed it? He felt a smile turning up his mouth. No doubt most of the credit belonged to his mother, who always knew how to rescue him when his ten-years-younger sister began to irritate.

They were the only ones in the class of wealthy and titled (that he knew of, at any rate) who spent more time with their parents than with nannies and tutors. Perhaps because he was an only child and they had given up on more. When Emmy came along, they were used to doing their child-rearing alone, and then to have a daughter! Even ten-year-old himself was thrilled at her little-girl delicacy.

He had blocked the doorway long enough. The current set was nearly over, the dancers would break apart and the next set would form, so if he wanted to catch Emmy he needed to find her soon.

Ah, there she was. Her black hair glistened under the chandeliers, and the jeweled hairpin their mother loaned her sparkled like a queen's tiara. When she turned around, he saw her face light with a smile that rivaled that pin.

Which made this all the harder. If he hurried, he could catch her and see if he could reserve the space of time for a dance. His decision would wait until tomorrow, when they could be alone in his office, but for tonight he wanted to enjoy his little sister's company while she was still speaking to him.

The man talking to her had an eyepatch, the leather band that held it on going all the way around the back of the man's glossy pale blond hair. And the gloved hand extended out to Emmy for the turn looked misshapen, the glove loose over what should have been the broadest part of a man's hand, the palm sagging and wrinkled. Before he had a chance to wonder what the white covering hid, Emmy took that hand without a flinch.

Blake stopped mid-step and stared at that hair color. The only man he knew with hair like that, the blond that had never darkened with maturity, was John.

But an eye patch? The John he knew would wear an eyepatch at the club just to startle his friends, only to whip it off and watch everyone's reaction. But the hand? From this distance Blake couldn't tell if the way the hand was positioned made things look worse, or if it hid something horrific.

Blake dodged through the last cluster of skirts, feathers-decorated head designs in everything from hats to tiaras, and full dress tailcoats in all manner of colors, blue predominating. At last he was close enough to reach out and catch the blond man's shoulder. The man turned around, and Blake found himself staring into the lone eye of his old friend. Where his other blue eye had been, on John's left side, a big black eyepatch now rested.

Around the patch, red scars showed. The patch was not large enough to cover all the damage that had been done to his face. So it was not just the hand that marked his time in the war. Even his once-too-handsome face carried the damage.

Blake's mind went blank. No words came out, no words even formed inside. He had been in the war himself, but somehow got assignments that took him away from the worst of the danger.

His mother had known about John's injuries. Of course she would have. This was what she wanted him to see.

But his own objections still held fast. He would never reject a suitor for Emmy just because he had been injured in the war. Far too many strong, brave, worthy men came back with such. But just as many came back the same person inside as when they left. Or even worse. Men who took their memories out on those who got near. The John Blake remembered had far too many weaknesses of character to give Emmy to him out of sympathy, just because his body was damaged.

Emmy stayed close to John's side, her gaze going from one to the other. Every time she looked at the other man, her face softened. The steel in her spine was almost visible.

"John."

His old friend looked wary, whether about the memories they shared that he must have known would come up, or about the change in his face and hand and the expected thoughtless remarks, Blake did not know. "Blake."

His voice was different, rougher, thicker, like something had happened there, too. Blake did not know what might have caused it, but it was not the voice he remembered.

"*Blake*." The word came out in his sister's feminine voice, but it carried all the iron of the heaviest sword. "You know my dear friend, John."

His mind had still not caught up. Thank goodness he could manage his sister's name without thinking. "Emmy."

"Look at this," Emmy said, holding up her fan and the attached pencil. She drew a line through a name already written on a spine. "I just happen to have a dance free."

Blake and John exchanged glances, and that single eye twinkled. John was biting his lip. At last his own mouth and his mind found something to say. "How convenient," he said, turning to look down at his sister. "I was just going to ask if you could find room for your big brother in your crowded schedule."

The first notes started, so Blake held out his hand. Just before Emmy put her much smaller one in his, she gave him a quick pinch on the wrist, right where it would hurt most. He growled, "Little wench."

"Just remember," she said without dropping her smile, "I know all your weaknesses, so if you don't treat John with the utmost respect I can, and I will, make your life a misery."

"I believe you will try. But I am older and I know how to fight dirty."

She actually laughed as the first steps started. With a saucy lift of her chin, she retorted, "I am a woman, and I know how to fight dirtier."

The dance steps swung them away from each other, and Blake's gaze caught John's, where he stood against the wall. The man actually looked worried, Blake thought as his feet followed the steps of the dance from sheer habit.

Emmy and he met again, and she picked up the conversation. "I know you were in the war, Blake, but you—" the circle interrupted her, and then she was back. "—were lucky enough to come home with not even a scratch."

As the dance continued, he learned that John's hand had been shattered at the same time as the eye injury. A man had pulled a derringer he had hidden on himself somewhere. John threw his hand up in an automatic attempt to shield his face, and the bullet had shattered the hand, then spun off, hitting the eye somehow.

"He was so lucky," Emmy breathed, before adding, "He only had one hand and one eye when he managed to save himself in that fight."

One big question remained unanswered. "So how did you meet John?" He had kept his friends as far away from his little sister as possible.

No doubt those same friends had been keeping their own sisters away from him, as well. *Blake the Rake*. The old nickname came whispering back. He looked down at his little sister as she continued with her tale, and hoped his secrets did not show.

The story came again in bits between the dance steps, but Blake had no trouble piecing it together. "I was waiting for the carriage to come after the opera. The road was so full, the line of people waiting was so long, and I got jostled. I was about to fall. He rushed over and caught my arm to keep me upright." Her face went soft, her eyes glowed and a gentle smile played around her lips, startling her next partner before she swung back around and finished her tale. "I didn't even drop my shawl, he came so quickly."

So John had rescued her. Blake had been in the crowd after an opera, he knew how easy it was to be knocked down, or to have one's reticule snatched off one's wrist, or to lose a pocket watch without even knowing it was gone.

"Blake? Be kind to him. I love him. He is going to be your brother soon."

He needed to thank John for protecting Emmy. Oddly enough, he thought he might actually mean it. In fact, the more often the dance took him into John's line of vision as he waited by the wall with the others who had no partner, the more he wanted to walk over there and say hello, to stand and talk as they had once, now seeming so long ago.

Only those who had been in that war could understand. They tended to gather in the clubs, linger on the streets, as if that horrible time, those shared memories drew them together.

At last the dance did end, and he gave Emmy a bow, then pulled her into his arms for a quick hug. He no longer cared who saw them, did not care if it would be tomorrow's *on dit*. She was his little sister, and almost certainly he would be losing her to a husband one day soon. Emmy believed it, and Mother seemed to support her choice. All that waited now was finding out if the feeling was all on his sister's side, or if John, too, believed he could be a husband for her.

And to bargain for as much time as possible, because he was not one of those who was in a hurry to marry girls off their first season after they came out.

If John was leading both his sister and his mother on, one handed and one eyed or not, Blake would make certain he answered for that.

He did not think, however, that was the case.

"Where do I take you now? Who is next on your card?" He looked down at her. She was flushed, her cheeks were pink, and her eyes sparkled with excitement.

He doubted it was from dancing with him. Sure enough, when he turned around, John stood there, holding out his arm. Blake clamped a hand down on Emmy's small one still curved around his elbow and pinned her to his side. "How many dances does this make for the two of you tonight?"

They exchanged a glance. "This will be our second. Two is still perfectly respectable," Emmy said.

Checking on the actual count was too easy. Blake looked from one to the other, but before he lifted his hand, he gave John a firm stare, man to man. "I expect you at my house tomorrow at eleven."

John did not blink. "I will be there."

"Blake?" Emmy sounded like she might cry.

Before he could say anything, John somehow had slid Emmy's arm out of Blake's elbow and onto his own. "Everything will be fine. Don't worry." The words must have been meant for her, only instead of looking at Emmy, John looked at him.

He would not approve without finding out who his friend was now. And if John was as different as his appearance, or if the changes were only skin deep.

"I can still send you off to a nunnery, you know." Blake gave his little sister his best frown, but he suspected it no longer intimidated her like it had when they were younger. He felt a pang around his heart. His baby sister was all grown up.

She laughed. "I would like to see you try."

John bowed, and Blake returned the courtesy.

As his friend straightened, his gaze was straight and honest. Without the slightest hesitation, John said, "Tomorrow at eleven." It was a promise. Then he walked onto the floor with Emilia on his arm.

CHAPTER 6

There had indeed been a party last night. Tessa could hardly miss the gossip, and made no attempt to ignore it. Lord Warrenby's name kept coming up and whispers wafted across the room like perfume. He could never be hers, but now that she had been in his presence, now that she had her own memories of time with him and knew he was a man she could like —very much—what would it hurt to soak up all the information she could? Maybe someday she would find a man to marry, and she could use Warrenby as the standard to judge others by.

So she tried to listen around her own conversations with Madame's clients and the time she lost in one of the dressing rooms, pinning and stitching.

"And he gave her a hug! Right in front of God and the whole room! It was the sweetest thing ever." "I never! How did I miss that? I would have loved to see it." "You had to be in the right place. The room was so crowded!" "I saw it. I was up on the balcony looking right down. I thought I might cry." "Are you certain it was Warrenby? Would he ever unbend enough?"

And on and on, all day long.

Sometimes it was fun to overhear without people realizing one was listening but times like this, Tessa decided, it was frustrating because the speakers all just assumed the other could fill in the blanks, and as such left gaping holes in the story for eavesdroppers.

For example—who had Blake—no, *Warrenby*—hugged? Was there a woman in his life? A public hug was unheard of. For anyone to do that—an announcement of marriage would have to follow, and quickly. The thought left a sharp pain in her chest. He had to marry someone, she knew that, but she wanted just a little more time to dream!

* * *

Blake watched the second hand creep around toward the twelve. It was almost time. Eleven o'clock. John would be here soon, but it would reflect well on him if he was prompt.

A knock sounded on his office door. "Yes?"

Hodgins stood in the doorway, John right behind him. His friend had dressed for the occasion, black tailcoat and gold vest, frilled white shirt and matching white cravat. He was even freshly shaved.

They were off to a good start, Blake thought. He would have preferred to find fault with something right off. Old reputations tended to stick.

Hodgins still blocked the way in. "Your guest, my lord. Mr. John Holland."

"You don't need to introduce him, Hodgins. We are old friends." Which of course his butler knew. What had prompted this sudden bit of judgmental protection, he had no idea. The scars? Perhaps Hodgins had never approved of John, and finally had a chance to show his opinion.

His gaze caught on John's wounded right hand as his old friend stood waiting. From across the room it looked as if it had been nearly torn apart, several fingers healed together into a solid lump of scarred flesh.

And John was right-handed, as he recalled.

Before he could be caught staring, Blake rose. "Come in, John, come in."

John stepped around Hodgins just as the butler was backing away, and they bumped into each other. Red rushed up Hodgins' face. Such a *faux pas* had never occurred in all the time Blake had known him. Before he could begin his regrets, which would be profuse, John interjected. "Excuse me, Hodgins. Sometimes with my eye, things are closer than I expect. I do apologize."

Blake's brows rose, and he had to force them back down. The John he remembered, while never cruel to those beneath him, would never have bothered to extend an apology, and especially not with such ease.

He reached for the whiskey on the shelf beside the desk. He might not like what was coming, but courtesy still required hospitality. "Have a seat, John. Something to drink?"

John was halfway down in the chair. He paused and the single-eyed gaze followed the movement of Blake's hand. "No, thank you. I no longer imbibe." He settled himself, and looked all too calm, in view of the discussion he had to know was coming.

Blake stopped short, his hand still extended toward the decanter. "No?"

"No." The word was firm, and implacable. He smiled. "This is your house, Blake. Don't alter your normal life because of me."

Blake pulled his hand back, leaving the decanter on the shelf untouched. "I don't usually drink this early. I don't need any liquid support to assure you that if I find out you have done anything untoward with my little sister, not even that patch and your broken hand will keep me from taking it out of your hide."

John laughed out loud. "I promise you, old friend, I have been the very model of propriety." A few more chuckles bubbled out. "Did you really think I had forgotten your fists? We went at it often enough that, trust me, you left an impression."

Blake felt the tension leave his shoulders. One side of his mouth quirked. "Good to hear it," He leaned back on the edge of his desk, legs crossed in front of him. "Well. Care to tell me why my sister thinks she is going to marry you?"

The smile never left John's face. "Because I have asked her. She is of age."

Blake folded his arms. "Why was I not approached first?"

The easy smile vanished. John scowled at him. "*You* try courting a woman from behind this face, and with this hand."

He held it up, and Blake caught himself before he blinked. The injury really was startling up close, and looked like it went up into the sleeve, as if the bullet had plowed along the arm before cutting through the hand and hitting the eye. He had not managed to get such a close look last night. Regardless, he meant his firm words.

"I actually heard some women discussing me at a party. Behind my back, naturally, but I suspect they intended me to hear. If I had more money, I'm sure they could have been persuaded, but I am not rich enough, thank goodness, to be considered a prize catch for any fortune hunters. What the girls said was, 'Who wants a scarred creature like him? And that hand!' I don't think I have to expound. None of the sentiments were things I wanted to hear from a wife. So I have become wary around women."

Blake winced. "My own concern is not your face, or your hand. My concern is what you—and I, if I am honest—did when we were younger. Gambling? Wenching? Dueling? Drinking?" He raised a hand, his own flawless hand, and lowered it, hoping it did not seem as though he was flaunting his own good fortune in coming back unscarred. "I am glad you have given up the latter, but do you still gamble? I won't have Emmy marry someone who risks gambling away her future and the future of any children."

"No, Blake, I no longer gamble. That is for the young and foolish, which I have not been for some time."

Blake snorted a laugh. "We are the same age. I hardly consider myself aged." They both chuckled, and then he sobered and went back to his mental list. "What about dueling? I won't have her risk losing her husband to a hot-tempered rake."

Every bit of humor vanished from John's face, and his shoulders sagged under some awful weight. "I have had enough of guns to last me a lifetime. I do not intend to pick up a gun or a pistol for the rest of my life." He straightened, and looked Blake straight in the eye. "That said, if anyone were to insult my wife, I would do whatever is necessary to defend her."

"There are those who invent accusations. It is all too easy to run afoul of them."

"Then, if I miss any of the signs, I shall count on you to help me sniff them out and find a way to expose them for the safety of others."

"Agreed." Blake took a deep breath. His next question was viewed as the norm for the upper classes, but it was one he never liked. He shoved the memory of Alice and the child he did not know from his mind. That was a mistake he would not make again. "And what about women? It is accepted among our class for a man to have a mistress on the side, but I won't have it for Emmy. Do you understand? She will expect you to be faithful in every way. Do you understand me?"

John seemed to be smirking, it was hard to tell because his mouth did not move, but Blake knew his friend all too well. "I can't wait for you to find a woman. Could you give the same answer I can?" He sat straight, his bearing like the soldier he had been, and the man Blake could only hope he truly was. "I have not had a woman since coming back from the war."

Blake gave a start.

If John noticed, he did not let on. "First, I was very ill and it took a while for me to recover."

He leaned back in the chair. "Can you imagine a mistress—or a wife, for that matter—dreading the touch of your mangled hand? Dreading what the patch conceals? No, I decided I was not ready to be that . . . vulnerable. When I showed myself, it had to be to a woman who is as committed to me as I am to her. And that woman is Emmy."

The room was quiet for a moment. Curiosity finally got the better of Blake. "Might I ask what brought about this remarkable transformation? You look like the friend I used to remember, but underneath the skin, I hardly know you at all."

"It's not a pretty story." John glanced over at the decanter, and then away. "We had just captured a town, and the first thing we did was find all the wine, brandy, and sangria the city held. The next day, we were supposed be on the trail of the French, but we were still too drunk to shoot straight. I thought I saw a scout, and I shot." He swallowed, as if taking a drink of the whiskey he would no longer allow himself.

"It was a farmer. A simple young farmer. With a pregnant wife." After a long breath, he continued. "The bullet broke his pelvis. The man lived, but he has not been able to walk properly since that day. I support him and his wife. And their baby, which she thankfully did not miscarry. He cannot farm well enough to provide for them any longer. If not for the blood money I send them, I think they would have starved to death."

Blake said nothing. He had seen that and worse.

"They have not had another child. In Spain, where family is so prized, that is like a knife in their heart. What happens if this child does not survive? So many do not."

He shook his head. "By then I had had a chance to sober up, and looked at the mess I had made of my part in the war. And that, Blake, *that* is both how I lost my eye and why I stopped drinking."

Blake made up his mind. Perhaps it had been decided the night before when John had faced him so boldly and agreed to be here and be raked over the coals by one of his oldest friends.

"Well, then, John, all I can say is, welcome to the family." He straightened from the edge of the desk, and just in time, remembered. He held out his left hand.

John rose, and took it with his own left.

"Shall we toast with the best cup of tea you will ever taste in England? My cook-cum-housekeeper is a treasure, and no, you are *not* allowed to steal her away. If you want any more of her cooking, you will have to come and visit with your wife."

The handshake did not seem to be enough. They looked at each other, and with a burst of relieved laughter, fell into a hug, pummeling the other on the back in welcome.

CHAPTER 7

Tessa clutched her paper-wrapped pickled salmon, which was both supper and breakfast, and her basket, and hid her moan as she neared her house. The moon, lone light for this part of the city, was high, time for the Neighborhood Four to be going out to do their thievery.

And there lounged Herb, waiting for her on the steps halfway up.

From those awful words she had overheard outside her room, she knew she had taken his arm to walk away from the grave. Now the very thing she feared was here. She dared not show fear. "Hello, Herb. You are not out and about tonight?" Her hand clenched on her basket.

He continued to relax on the steps, taking up the whole stairway middle. "'ello to you, Tessa. 'ow 'as yer day been? I was worried about ye. Ye took a blow wen yer pa died. But ye knew I'd be there fer ye." His hands flexed, but she would not look at them. "I been yer protector, did ye know that?"

That was stretching the facts a bit far, she thought. Her *father* was her protector. When he was around.

But Herb wasn't done. She had not expected him to be. "I watched over ye. Many's the time ye could 'ave been robbed on yer way to and fro, but I says, nah, she's a good 'onest gal. But ye're no dif'rent from the rest a' us, are ye? Out fer yerself, ain't ye? At least we're open 'bout wot we do. Not ye, though."

Something in his eyes made her even more uneasy than usual.

Tessa said nothing.

"Ye've been 'oldin' out on me, Tessa me gal." He bared his teeth in what was not meant to be a smile. "Ye paid me a mere twenty shillin's for 'elping ye bury yer pa. Twenty shillin's an' some old clothes. An' after all I done fer ye."

"They were used, but not old. They were very good quality, and you know it!" Her hand tightened on the wicker handle of the sewing basket, feeling it bite into her palm, and her heart began a rapid beat, pounding away like a frightened rabbit. She had missed something in her search through her father's clothes, and Herb found it. She could feel it coming.

Thank goodness she had left everything with Warrenby! No, not everything. There were still plenty of coins, coins that Warrenby had said she was safe in keeping. Unfortunately, he did not know about Herb and his cohorts.

She had to try, though. "I turned everything over to you and the others. What do you think I might still have?"

He began to rise, the movement slow and ominous. "Weel, now, that be the question, don't it?" Even though Herb was not a tall man, standing above her on the stairs, he seemed to tower over her. "Wot might Miss Tessa 'ave kept to 'erself?"

With equal threat, he went down a step. Even losing that much height over her, he still held the same menace. "Ah don't s'pose ye wonder what Ah'm referrin' to?"

Tessa didn't even shake her head, just stood there, trying not to look up at her door. She was very afraid of what she would see if she did.

Herb came down the last two steps in a rush, and Tessa felt his shove before she even saw it coming, impelled by his sudden speed. Her head slammed into the brick of the building so hard she saw a flash of white. Her legs wanted to crumble, but somehow she managed to stay upright.

Herb's hand appeared before her watering eyes. She turned her head to keep the anticipated blow from hitting her face, but instead he opened it, palm up. Gold sparkled there.

"So wot might Miss Tessa be hidin', I asked meself. And I decided to take a check. I popped in fer a little visit wile ye were out, and guess wot I found?"

Tessa blinked the water out of her eyes, and those tears, from pain originally, became despair. *What did you expect when you kept the coins*, she asked herself as she saw her father's guineas glimmering in his dirty hand.

"An' ye thot t'fob us off with shillin's? Lucky fer me, I jest 'appened to notice a bit o' coin in the breeches I were about ta sell. Yer pa were real clever with them little pockets 'e 'ad sewn in 'em, weren't 'e?" He leaned close, and his rotten breath made Tessa gag. "I said ta meself, wot else might Miss Tessa be hidin'? So I popped over ta find out." He shoved the guineas into his own hidden pocket inside his shirt.

"An' jest so 'as ye remember not ta think ye can fool with ol' 'erb again. . ." This time the blow was real, and her cheek felt like it exploded under the impact. Tessa hardly knew when she fell to the ground. His boot connected with her side, and the scream trapped in her throat burned and tore, but she heard nothing, only the mocking laughter as Herb walked away.

Inside her head, though, the screams of pain continued, until finally she managed to get a breath past her tight throat. She struggled to pull her legs close to the searing pain in her chest, but could not bring herself to move yet. No one came out to help her stand, but she didn't expect it.

Ears buzzing, face throbbing, hot agony wrapping around her middle, she laid there in a limp pile, and tried to find the strength to stand.

She got her eyes open, and somehow felt the basket's rough exterior against her leg, a soft scratching through all the searing pain. Herb must not have noticed it when he walked away, or he surely would have stomped it into dust. Or stolen it for cash.

Every movement an agony, in slow stages Tessa managed to get herself to her knees. The basket was sturdy, it did not crack when she leaned on it to keep her up. Her head whirled, the scene, the familiar crumbling brick buildings that surrounded the small alley, the windows with tattered curtains, the narrow lane that offered escape to the world outside, seemed to be moving.

Just a few feet away on the building's ground floor, the window for the room where a small family lived looked out over this scene. No one peeked out, no curtains in windows on any of the other buildings moved either. Perhaps they were honestly asleep, more likely they knew what would happen to them if they tried to interfere.

Not even now, to help her get up.

One arm braced against the wall, she tried to stand but her legs refused to straighten. One attempt, two, three, and finally her legs pushed her upright, although they shook at the strain.

The arm that could not wrap around her middle a minute or twenty ago now clutched that spot where Herb had kicked. Only that arm seemed to hold her chest together.

Did he break her ribs? Tessa slumped against the brick wall, and fought to get breath in, then out. The world stopped spinning.

The salmon package still sat on the dim ground and the basket was by her skirt, where she had been forced to leave it when she got to her feet. The moon's light faded behind a cloud. Was she was about to faint?

No, her ears were fine, no ringing or buzzing, which she understood was a sign of oncoming faint.

Tessa turned her head, whimpering at the burn of stretched skin, to look up the stairs. The only way to find out what survived in her room was to make it up there, so she had to move.

With as deep a breath as she could manage, Tessa bent down with the greatest of care, and picked up that salmon. She could not carry it unless she set it on the basket, but how would she lift that much? If Herb had left her nothing, if not one of her hiding places had gone undiscovered, that meat was all she had to eat until she was paid.

If she could carry it upstairs. One arm around her ribs, the other holding the basket and shaking so hard she feared the salmon would fall off. The staircase was so long!

There was a mirror in her room, or at least there had been. If he had split her skin, she needed to know. With her father's guineas, she could have hired a doctor, but now any healing or repairs had to be done alone.

Alone. The thought made her want to laugh. Or cry.

The pulsing heat around her chest stabbed when she took each stair, but she had to get inside. There might not be a lock left, but four walls were better than remaining in the open.

Herb may have put out word that she was fair game.

Every movement came easier. She told herself that as she went up each tread. The lie kept her going.

By the time she reached her door, Tessa thought she might be able to release the hold she had around her ribs. Just not yet, she realized when she tried.

The door swung open at the lightest touch, and she could see the gouges in the frame. It could have been kicked in, it could have been pried loose with some metal tool. At least when she turned back to close it and fasten the lock, it seemed to still hold.

It would not stand up to another concerted attack. The only thing she could hope was that Herb got enough to satisfy himself. If there was anything left—a stab of pain stopped the thought.

The basket fell from her hands, landing with a creaking thunk.

Now to find out if anything was left. A hackney ride would be a godsend tomorrow, but she needed those coins to do it. When she turned around and looked at the room in the dark, she knew at least one of her places had been discovered. Her corset lay in a heap on the floor. It was too much to expect that any coins would remain tucked inside after that toss.

The vase with the hollow bottom was in pieces on the floor. The drawers on her dresser had all been pulled out and sat in a heap, their meager contents, her stockings, her nightgowns, shawl, and petticoat flung around, one here, another over there. She did not want to check for boot prints, although it was too much to expect that Herb would not have stomped on them. No coins would be left there, either. If they found her stockings, they certainly found the coins hidden in the toes.

Stumbling over to the bed, Tessa sank down on it, moaning again at the pain in her side. The money was gone. She had to accept it. There was no possibility now of a new place to live, no money to cushion the need that haunted her.

And no way to replace the mattress. She was in too much pain to care now.

A tear trickled down her face, followed by another, and another after that. Tessa did not even lift her hand to brush them away.

* * *

The house was quiet, even most of the servants were done cleaning up, and clomped with heavy tread up to their rooms at the top of the house. He could hear their steps on the stairs from where his office was.

He pressed the hidden button in his desk, and the cubby began to slide, only to catch halfway open. It was not made for all the things he had hidden there. Settings and gems took up a lot more room than letters.

A lone setting, bent though it was, had wedged itself in his mind like a burr. If he could make a quick sketch of it, someone might recognize it. He had drawn enough drafts of the lay of the land in France, surely he could copy a necklace.

He held onto one of the small sacks in which the jewelry was stored, and gave a careful pull. The cubby popped out a few more inches, just enough to get a bag all the way out with a couple cautious tugs. Once that bag was out, the drawer snapped the rest of the way open, showing the other fabric pouches.

This might not be the best place to hide things, he thought as he looked at the display. If he couldn't find the owners soon, one of these times the drawer would stick and stay stuck.

It took a moment to find which of the many sacks the piece he had in mind was hidden, but it turned up.

Abbott had done quite a job on these pieces.

He pulled out a quill and some ink, a piece of paper, and set to work.

CHAPTER 8

Pain ripped through her. Tessa forced her eyes open. A faint glow seeped between the curtains, the first rays of the new day, and she knew in a moment she would have to get up and dress.

And walk, somehow, the distance to Madame's shop.

Before she moved, although she wasn't sure she wanted to know, she raised her hand bit by painful bit to her cheek to determine where the damage was the worst. Best to be forewarned before she looked in the mirror. Her face felt swollen on that side, but she could move her jaw, and she did not think the skin had split. Her arms were stiff, probably she had attempted to break her fall when she landed, although she did not remember doing so. When she tried to roll over, the movement sent a lash of heat across her, from one side of her body to the other.

A tear trickled hot wetness down her cheek. "Get out of bed," she whispered to herself, or rather, to her battered body, but it did not want to obey.

How hard had Herb kicked her?

Gathering all her willpower, Tessa eased herself up on an arm that wanted to shake under the mere weight of a single push. Once she was upright, the room whirled for a moment before it settled.

The light through the curtains was brighter. Not a lot, but enough to see the shapes of her few possessions.

It was late. Tessa went over to the wash basin and splashed her face clean. If she could twist, she would try to change gowns and look at the damage his kick left on her ribs, maybe even sponge out the dirt from the things Herb had thrown around her room, but that was not going to happen today.

Her face, though, her poor, tender, swollen face. Tessa braced herself before she dared to look, and raised the small hand mirror, the only thing she had to check her appearance.

"Oh, no," she moaned aloud when she saw what her fingers had felt. Herb's fist had left a cruel bruise, coloring her face with dark rainbows of blue, purple, and green. Where the bruise stopped, her face was a pasty, sick white. The eye closest to his blow had swollen almost to a slit, and was ringed with the same ugly color as the skin around it. The opposite eye had a faint dark circle, and looked sunken.

Too many women showed similar marks as they moved along the

street. It seemed no class was immune. In the shop, wealthy women came in from time to time with veils and too much powder, and not even that hid the damage beneath. She had never wanted to be among them, and yet now she was.

What would Madame think? She could not possibly face customers looking like this! Wealthy women had resources. They could send a servant out to find powder to hide their bruises. Not only did she have no resources after Herb had gone through her room, but she did not know which stores sold the forbidden face paint. Talking to the prostitutes to find out where they got theirs was completely out of the question.

Well, it had been before. Desperation made people consider things they never would have.

Her single-eyed gaze landed on her paper-wrapped meat pie. Flour! The crust outside always had a faint floury dust. If she could get enough of that flour off, she might be able to hide at least some of the bruising. Tessa reached down and grabbed the package, the movement tugging at her aching side.

Her face wasn't perfect when she was done, wasn't even close to perfect, but it was better. Provided as it didn't rain, or there wasn't wind, it would hide the worst damage.

How long did a bruise like that take to heal, she wondered. Madame might have patience for a day, maybe two but if she looked this bad for much more than that, not even her employer's compassion could let her be without Tessa's help.

She hurried out the door, and locked it behind her. It wouldn't keep Herb out, she knew, but she was not going to make it easy for him, either.

Her side throbbed with every step of the stairs. Tessa tucked her arm close, and that helped. A little, but that injured area felt hot, and the swelling was obvious even through her clothes.

"Ouch!" The yelp burst out at the sudden jar to her side as she stepped off the last tread, the weight of the basket in her other hand seeming to pull all the way across her middle. She curled her body over the injury as much as the swelling and pain would allow, trying to ease the pulsing throb. There, she thought as the next breath came without a catch, that was easier.

The sun peeked over the top of the building next to her. She was late. Not badly, but hiding the bruise on her face had taken too much time. Running was out of the question. If she could hardly step off the stairs, the pounding of a dash was impossible.

It was a long, worrisome walk to the shop.

* * *

Madame had her back to the door as Tessa eased in, and rattled off instructions for the day's work as soon as she heard the click of the latch.

"Tessa? *C'est vous*? Sleeves on Lady Sutton's morning gown, the yellow one. They must be done before noon, she comes for fitting." She turned around with a spool of thread in her hand, to stop short. "*C'est quoi votre problème*? What happen?"

Tessa had decided what to say on the long walk. "I was attacked by a footpad on the way home last night."

Madame's eyebrows went up. "*You?* You will not bring *ce danger ici,* to my shop, will you?" She took a step back, and her brows came down.

The woman was no one's fool, Tessa knew. Although Madame was not pressing, she was astute enough to suspect that was not the whole story. "No!" She hoped. Herb was not going to lose her this position! "It was just a footpad." But there was always tonight, and tomorrow, and the day after that. It was time to look for another room, but they were scarce, and her wages barely covered the one she had. Any others would be in worse areas, with new threats.

Was it better to stay with the threat she knew? Tonight was hours away, but she would be alone again.

Madame patted her shoulder. "I cannot have you out *avec mes clients* looking like this. Ellen will have to be in front. You do the stitching here, where no one can see." She propped a hand on her hip and cocked her head as she stared at Tessa's face. "I think we can cover some of that face powder. I will send Rosie out to a shop and have her buy some."

At that, Madame dropped the spool of thread she had been holding in Tessa's hand, and scurried out.

She had not lost her job. A wave of dizziness washed over her, and she fell awkwardly into her chair, jarring the injury. "Oh!" The cry burst out, she could not stop it. Tessa fought for a breath, and could only hope the sounds from outside, the morning traffic, and the calls of the hawkers would keep that yelp from disturbing Madame or her customers.

Breath shuddered in and out for a moment, and Tessa's hand shook as she held the edge of the table beside her, but at least that was quiet.

"'Ello, Tessa, and 'ow are you this—" Ellen popped through the back door in a rush. Her voice stopped as if cut off with a knife. She hurried over and crouched down where she could get a better look. "Wot 'appened?"

"I was attacked by a footpad." The words came out on a rush of air as a sudden stab of pain surprised her.

"Footpads! They otter be rounded up and tossed inter Newgate, th' lot of 'em." Ellen rose, and Tessa caught her breath enough to notice that the girl's mobcap was slightly askew and a few strands stuck out.

Tessa found words came out if she spoke slowly while the pain began to ebb. "Madame says you are to . . ." The pain let go. She managed a good lungful of air. "To fill in for me out there."

"Me? All by meself, without guidance?" Ellen's face lit up. "I been waitin' fer this."

Tessa smiled. "You won't be completely by yourself. Madame has the eyes of a hawk, and she will manage to deal with her own customers and watch you at the same time. I know, because that is how she trained me. And you are better already than I was."

"That's nice o' you ta say." Ellen set her own basket, worn and likely borrowed from someone in the family, down on one of the tables and peeked in the tiny round mirror hanging on the wall from a string. Her brown eyes narrowed into worried slits. "Whoa! I cain't be out like this!" She clucked her tongue. "My hair is all jumbled. I look like I been sweeping."

"I was just about to tell you." Tessa shifted her position on the chair. That spot was setting sore again. "I would not have let you go out until you were polished up."

Ellen finished smoothing her hair, and settled her cap again. "I knowed ye wouldn't." With a nod at the mirror, she scurried back over to give Tessa a quick hug, setting up another lash of pain. "It might be the nicest thing 'bout ye. I 'ope ye feel better soon."

She grinned as she sat down to pick up her own rush gown to finish. Before she bent to work, she added, "Just not too soon." With a frown, she checked over the fancy gown bodice in her hands. "I left me needle in 'ere's somewheres. Where is it hidin'? Oh, there it be. Now I 'member where I was." Ellen pulled the needle out, and it sparkled in the candlelight from the sconces on the wall. "I best be quick. I think the woman'us comin' in early ta try it on, and I ain't got the sleeves in yet, let alone get the two pieces t'gether."

Her head popped up again. "Early! Them don't know wot early is!"

Tessa sat still for a minute while the lingering fire settled down. She had better find out what movements set it off, because she had to get her work done today, too.

* * *

He was tired of looking at the jewelry and coming up empty of possible victims. Tired of making endless sketches of the details on the pieces he had selected. Into late last night, and again all morning. Breakfast had worn off and he could use a cold collation and good company. It was past time that he went out, Blake thought as he dismounted his horse, past time he paid a visit to his club, see if any inspiration came there. He might see a family crest on a ring that would solve even one of the mysteries.

He had been away from England too long, and he was simply going to need help if he was to solve the puzzle Tessa had given him. He had promised her he would return the jewelry for her, and he would do it. A man did not let a woman down once he gave his word.

Blake pushed open the door to White's, and took a moment to breath in the familiar smoky air. There was something so . . . restful here. The fires were left burning in a couple of the fireplaces, just to take the moisture away. Voices murmured, a distant hum from the dining room, he guessed, punctuated by an occasional male laugh, deep and resonant. Cards were slapped down with a sibilant snap.

After a stop at the bar to get something wet, he scanned the groupings of chairs for the men on his list. Perhaps their wives were the best bet to recognize jewelry, but if any of these settings had gone to the mistress, it could have been a disaster. Or at the very least uncomfortable.

Not all wives were as witless as their husbands thought. Still, a wife confronted with proof could make her husband's life miserable.

Haversham and Addersley were in a corner table, in a small grouping of chairs. Haversham beckoned, but Addersley, true to his nature, gave a laconic nod. Anything more enthusiastic was too much effort. Blake raised his hand in return, and ambled over to his friends.

"Glover. Or should I say, Warrenby?" Haversham's mouth quirked. "Are you used to the title yet? I haven't seen you much since you returned." His brown eyes scanned Blake, and came back up to meet his gaze. Short as he was, it was quite a look upwards.

Blake took pity on his friend, and sat in one of the spare chairs, mentally bidding a bite to eat a sad farewell, at least for a while. He would stop in the dining room after he got this business taken care of. "The title is as uncomfortable as always, as you should know. And how does your own fit?"

Haversham had come into his title in Oxford, and took to it easily, as he scarcely knew his own sire. If he had ever shed a tear, no one had seen so much as a wet eye.

"At least the old man left the estate solvent. He might not have cared about his spawn, but I can find no fault in his concern for his money."

Addersley took a sip of whatever was in his glass. "My own brother is caring well for the family pile of stones, too. There are advantages to not carrying the title like a weight around my neck."

Blake and Haversham laughed simultaneously. "As if you would have the energy," his friend mocked.

"Don't tell Gillem," Blake said. "It's a good thing he loves his brother, because he wants that title. Another man might have killed to get it, with that much passion." He looked around the small group. "Where is he, anyway? Aren't either of you keeping an eye on him? What if he gets into deep play?"

"I think he pushed his father a little too hard with his last losses," Addersley said in his methodical way. "I haven't seen him here for a week."

A faint alarm rang in Blake. "What if he's at Watier's? They don't care what you lose there. Just think how much he could cost his family!"

Addersley shook his head. What would it take to make him lose that vaunted calm? "I heard he's been sent to the family estates in Yorkshire. There's not enough out there to get him into trouble."

The surge of tension eased. Looking at his two friends, Blake suddenly realized he had probably the sharpest minds in London in front of him. "I need some help."

"Are you in trouble, now?" Haversham leaned forward. "What is it this time? You don't gamble anymore, you never did drink too much, you came home from the war with hardly a scratch. What trouble could you possibly be in?"

Blake laughed again as he pulled the sketches he had made out of the inside pocket of his tailcoat. "No trouble, but a puzzle. I was given some things found in the possession of an old man who died. I am sworn to secrecy over who he was and how I got them, but it didn't take much to figure out he was rather an accomplished thief. Among the things he had were some that must be family heirlooms, but no way to determine which family. So, how would you like a challenge? Help me find out whose crests these are, or if they are family crests worked into jewelry at all."

Haversham shook his head. "Just bring it to a jeweler. Let him recognize it or not."

"Out of all the jewelers in London? And Bath? Some might even come from the Continent. It's not just one or two. There are a lot of pieces to identify. That's why I thought I could shorten the work with you, at least pull out a few that might be easy."

Addersley's dark green eyes showed a spark of interest. "Let's see what you have."

Unfolding the four he had done, Blake spread the foolscap on the table. Three heads bent over the papers.

Haversham jabbed at one. "I saw that, or something much like it, around Fothering's mistress in Hyde Park once."

Blake looked around the room, checking for the nearest quill and inkwell. Work was generally reserved for home, White's was for companions and conversation, but he saw what he was looking for at the betting book stand, and went over to collect them. He made the note at that page, and set it aside. If Haversham said it belonged to Fothering's mistress, it did.

Addersley poked at another. "It's out of shape, but that looks like the crest for Malcolm. I remember it was around his wife's neck at a ball several years ago. I think there was a rumor that he was looking for it, but he kept it quiet. Word spreads, though." He looked up, and those green eyes fixed on Blake. "So you have it."

Blake nodded. "Apparently so. Thank goodness the man who stole it is dead, because Malcolm might well have strung up whoever touched a thing of his wife's. He is about the only one of our set who never had a whiff of scandal."

"Your own father," the other man said. "Don't forget him. I was stunned to find out you had taken a mistress the first time. I didn't think anyone in your family ever could."

Blake nodded. "My father never did after marrying, but he was a bit of a rake before my mother came along, or so I've heard."

"I notice you haven't picked your favorite up again since coming home."

Blake let that comment go. His old mistress was now another man's, but he had lost the urge for mistresses. He dipped the quill back into the inkwell, made a second note, and set that paper aside with the first.

They were down to two of his sketches.

Addersley turned one around, and tilted his head. "Can I have your quill, and another sheet of paper?"

Blake slid both items over and moved the inkwell close also. After a few strokes of the quill, his idea became obvious to all three.

Blake spoke first. "That is a corruption of Kendal's crest." He raised his head and his gaze slid from one to the other. "The man has a mistress. He certainly has kept it quiet, but what else would explain it? It's too close to be an accident. Some jeweler was given the real thing, to make something so close. Kendall has no daughters. Either of you know anything about this?"

Both men shook their head. Blake looked back down at his friend's sketch. "I wonder whose idea it was to make something so similar. Hers? Or his?"

Haversham pursed his lips, then growled, "That seems like a lady's trick. Is the man so dense that he did not see the similarity himself?"

Addersley scowled. "I am acquainted with the wife. She is a very nice woman. He doesn't deserve her. I hope she doesn't find this out." His mouth quirked into a rare smile. "As for the setting here, Kendal never was the brightest candle in the lamp. If his mistress handed him a design, he would bring it to the jeweler, and not even think to question where she got the idea."

Blake joined in the laughter as he wrote down their latest conclusion on the third paper, but a part of him remained outside. What kind of wife would he get, he wondered. A very nice woman like Kendal's? After the past few months of peaceful calm, he suspected that alone would keep him home and content. There was a lot to be said for peace.

He had long known that he would never be happy with anything less than what his parents had, but realistically, few expected real happiness in marriage. Contentment, a mild friendship, a woman he did not mind bedding, and one who wanted children.

The odds of finding such a woman were slim.

Before he could continue with the depressing thought, a ripple came through the room, swelling like a rising tide. Blake caught a name, and turned to the next group. “What is it? What is going on?”

The man, one he didn’t know well, shook his head. “Daydreaming, Blake? Did you not even hear the man come in?”

Blake looked at his friends, both shaking their heads, and turned back. “No, why?”

“Mundy came in a moment ago, and said he needed to make an announcement.” The man glanced over his shoulder. “I think he’s about to make it now.”

Blake knew Mundy slightly, through the man’s friendship with his father. When the club was called to order, and everyone turned toward their visitor, he made sure he stood where he could see and hear. Such a thing was quite unusual, in his experience.

Mundy was not in a noticing mood, that was obvious. His eyes were swollen and red. Add to that the grey skin that washed out his normally ruddy complexion, and the first stabs of alarm tightened his stomach.

“Please, I need your help. Everyone’s help.” The voice he remembered as strong wavered. “Please. My grandson was kidnapped almost three months ago. My daughter is too distraught to eat. I have put a reward out on him, high enough to tempt anyone. Five hundred pounds. I will raise it if I need to. I will do anything to get my grandson back!”

Blake shuddered as he listened. Even one time was too many, but there was a market for stolen children. Families desperate for a child could pay thieves, or brokers could sell them for cheap labor on ships or as chimney sweeps.

Mundy was still talking. “I have been to Bath and Falmouth, checked Yarmouth, now London. Any place with a port and ship traffic. Thank God the war is over, but even so, if he was put on a ship, how can I ever find him?” The last was a cry from the heart, and the man’s control broke. In front of the whole club, he dropped down into the nearest chair, and clapped his hands over his face. His whole body shook with his sobs, though not a sound came out.

There was a shocked silence in the club. Men looked at each other with blank faces, at a loss in the presence of such grief.

Trust Addersley to keep his head. In his calm voice, he asked, “Did you ever have a portrait done of the child?”

A shudder wracked Mundy, but he cleared his throat. From somewhere on his person, he pulled out a handkerchief, mopped his face, then blew his nose. "Only when he was an infant, and there was nothing much to see of him. It was mostly just a bonnet and a blanket."

Haversham stepped forward. "Have you contacted Bow Street?"

"I did, early on. They have come up with nothing yet." Mundy took another breath, but the sound shivered. "I'm losing hope.I need all the help I can get. The family has kept quiet far too long. I thought I would come here and ask—no, *beg*, for help. For any assistance you can give."

A servant in their house when he was young came to mind, a man with a bright red blood spot on his forehead, a spot that never faded. As a child, that mark had fascinated him. Since then he had seen the same thing more than once. Blake spoke up. "Did he have anything that would identify him?"

"He had freckles, lots of freckles. His hair was peppered with cowlicks, and wanted to go everywhere." A smile tugged at Mundy's mouth, but faded as fast as it had come. "He has a bent finger on his left hand." He mopped up a new batch of tears. "He was very blond, almost white blond, and it shows no signs of changing. He got that from his father."

At the sight of those tears, Blake spoke quickly, to get everyone's attention on what they had to work with. "His age?"

Mundy cleared his throat again, but it didn't help. In a wet voice, he answered, "Five."

"So we have a five year old boy, very blond, stubborn hair, with lots of freckles and a bent finger on his left hand." Blake turned to Addersley. "Let's get some papers printed, and spread them across London. As fast as possible. There are street sellers just waiting for the next thing to sell. Pay them, and send them across the city. If your grandson is here, we will find him."

Addersley ignored him. "It might be good to have a sketch put onto the notices, so people know what to look like. Mundy, can you draw the finger from memory?"

Mundy drew himself up. "Of course I can. Give me some paper."

Foolscap showed up from all sides. A servant, who had obviously been listening, brought over a quill and inkwell.

The man had not exaggerated. Mundy had hidden skills, Blake thought. A finger appeared in short order. He leaned close and watched it take shape.

"That's quite distinctive." He met Mundy's gaze. "If you can do this, can you draw his face?"

Mundy's brows came together. "Faces are harder, but I think I can get it close enough. Give me a minute." He bent back over the paper.

Despite his words that the face would be hard, the man did a fair job. The hair, it seemed, was most distinctive of all the features. A child, in Blake's opinion, was a child. A curved blotter appeared, and Mundy ran it over the sketch with extreme care, making sure nothing blurred.

Everyone leaned close and stared at it. Heads cocked this way and that, eyes squinted, mouths pursed. No doubt many of them felt as he did, that all children looked about the same, but the man had done a good job. Looking around the group, Blake said, "We need to find a printer who can do etchings. Can I take it, sir?"

Mundy picked it off the table and held it for a moment, as if once he let it go he was losing the link to his grandson. Blake took it, caught Haversham's eye, and his friend rose. They made their way around the others, holding the paper high to keep it from being bent, and out the door.

"Let's get this going right away. If I wanted to hide a stolen child, or put him to work, London is where I would send him. How many of us pay the least attention to the little chimney sweeps sent up our flues? If not a chimney sweep, he might have been hired on in a house as a lesser servant already. And five? I don't like it, but I know I have had five-year-olds on my staff. Five is sometimes viewed as old enough to be sent to work."

Addersley nodded. "And the description? Blond hair is so common as to be ordinary."

"I'll take one printer, and get the notice started." Blake turned to his friends. "Haversham, you take another. Addersley, find some sellers, and get them ready to head out across the city." He swung up onto his horse.

Addersley stopped at the head of his own horse, and looked at Blake. "Perhaps your mother and sister can be convinced to discuss it in their soirees and afternoon teas with their friends. If we get the news to spreading through all levels of London, there will be no place where the boy can be hidden."

"Good idea."

Haversham braced himself against his bay, a smaller horse than the other two men had. "You do know that housemaids are more likely to notice things like a child among the servants? How do we reach them?"

Addersley swung onto his horse. "Butlers can be encouraged to make an announcement to the staff. In addition, if we can encourage our equals to discuss it in front of their servants, they will certainly pay attention. Servants always listen to what goes on above-stairs."

For someone who watched more than he spoke, Blake thought, his friend was best qualified to know.

CHAPTER 9

Blake's mother burst into the office in a flurry of lilac skirts and perfume. He had been pacing, brooding about the child and the jewelry, so at least he did not have to rise when she burst in.

"Oh, my darling, have you heard!" Her voice rang in the room. It was a good thing his ears were healthy and would recover. She gave him a tight hug. "Holland came up to snuff and proposed to Emmy!" Another joyful squeeze, which he returned.

John hadn't wasted any time, had he?

His mother pulled back, fairly danced over to the guest's chair across from his desk, and flopped down. The bonnet's decorations fluttered like bird's wings. Her bright smile changed into a mother's firmness. "I am so glad you approved him." She paused. "He did talk to you, did he not?"

Blake seated himself, and nodded. "Yes, Mother, he did come and we did talk, and yes, I gave him permission to ask." Not that Emmy needed or wanted it, apparently. From what John had said, the two of them had made a decision well before he was consulted. "You were right, as always. He has indeed changed."

Rebecca clasped her hands, and tapped her chin with them. "He is the finest of all the men in the Marriage Mart this year, yourself excluded, of course. No title, but he has done a fine job of managing his father's estates so she will never need to worry about money, or him gambling her children's future away. I am certain when his father is gone, he will continue his excellent supervision."

A rueful smile tilted her mouth. "A few years ago I would not have let him within a mile of Emmy, but as you say, he is so changed. He proves the adage that reformed rakes make the best husbands." She gave Blake a stern look. "I shall expect the same out of you."

He shook his head, and chuckled. "I assure you, I am no longer a callow youth, and much of our foolish pranks belong to the young."

"Well. Since you are no longer a youth, you are of the age to find your own wife. I hope you choose well, because I cannot tolerate an empty-headed daughter-in-law. Nor do I want you being wed just for your money." She leaned forward in her chair, as she always did when sharing a particularly juicy tidbit. "You did hear about Bixly? I would not have thought it possible, but his wife managed to send him to the edge of the poor house. She started to gamble, you know."

"I heard something about it." Blake smiled. "I assure you, I will vet any woman carefully."

"Not too carefully, I hope. I don't want you looking for excuses not to wed. If Emmy can get a husband this easily, surely you can get yourself a wife."

A face appeared in Blake's mind, exquisite features paired with a seamstress's gown. He pushed the thought aside. "Speaking of Emmy, did you come here just for that?"

Thankfully, that was enough to take her off tales of gossip, and her efforts to marry him off. "As if I need an excuse! But you are right, I would like your help. We must have a ball to announce the news before it spreads too far. I always hate when the ball is an anticlimax, don't you?"

Blake could only give her a blank look. "Who cares when it is announced?"

She laughed. "You men! It's a good thing we women take over from here. I want it to be a surprise. I'm sure Emmy does, too. The notice in the paper can come after, and the banns don't have to be read until much closer to the wedding. Now, can you rearrange your schedule to play host at the ball a week from now? We will hold it at my house, just because of the ballroom. I will tell Emmy to keep it secret so it can be a surprise."

"Host?" He should have expected this, as the head of the house since his father's death. It was one thing to talk to an old friend to determine his suitability, but this?

"You are now the man of the family, Blake." She removed the bonnet and started taking off her gloves. He could see the trembling of her lips, and knew his father's death was on her mind also. The busy work was a way of bringing herself under control.

Grief, that awful companion, threatened to tighten his own throat, so Blake shoved it aside, and pulled open a drawer. If he knew his mother, she would be asking for a quill and paper and making lists of things he would have to do.

"It is just you two children. Of course you would be the one to host the event. Naturally, if you can find a way to make it a double announcement, I would be delighted." She laughed.

Ah, yes, here it came.

"Your inkwell and a quill, please, Blake, and some paper. I have to make a list so nothing will be forgotten."

He handed them across the desk one at a time.

The quill scratched across the paper. Blake watched the list get longer with increasing dismay.

It was hard to tell from where he sat if those were names to invite, or items to purchase. Either way, he had better brace himself for far more than a small gathering. He had always tried to avoid attending these events when younger. This one was not optional. A bit more experience on how it was done would have been helpful.

At least his mother knew the proper protocol. Galling as it was, he would have to ask for suggestions.

Rebecca looked up. "We must have a new gown for Emmy. One week is not much, but the news will be out soon, and that will spoil the surprise." Another note on the paper. 'New gown,' most likely.

"You might well be competing with other balls. People need time to check their other commitments."

'There will always be other balls," she said, her attention still on the paper, where she was scratching away. "I guarantee you, people will come."

She lifted her head again. "My dear, you will need a new jacket and trousers as well. Go to the tailors today, please, and have something made. Full dress, my dear. You do not want to embarrass your sister."

Blake looked down at his clothes, the buff trousers and the blue coat, even the embroidered waistcoat. His valet would never allow him out of the bedroom with so much as a spot on his boots. "I grant you that my everyday attire is not what I wear to balls, but I am considered to be among the best-dressed men in London. You have seen me, you know I will not be an embarrassment."

Rebecca raised her eyes from the list and speared him with a stern look. "This is for *your sister*."

He knew when to give in, and rose to leave her to the planning. "Very well. New clothes."

As she stared out into space, his mother brushed the feathers of the quill pen under her chin, thinking out loud. "I'll have my staff start setting up the ballroom." Another note. "I might need to hire extra kitchen maids to help Mrs. Smith. I want to order some special cakes from Gunter's. Then Emmy and I will go to Madame Genevieve and have some gowns made up."

"Very well. Finish your list and then we will set out and get our new clothes ordered."

Listening to the list of places that might be contacted with this one event, Blake put the plan for young Parminter into effect. "Mother, at White's this morning, we found out something and I will need your help."

Rebecca poked the quill into the inkwell, and met his gaze. "What is it, dear? You do know that with this ball coming up, I might not be able to give it the attention I normally would." A smile, then, "Not that your sister is the more important of my children, but this is a big event. If you wed, you will get the same care."

"I have no doubt." Blake controlled his shudder. Perhaps he should look into all the whys and wherefores of a special license. But right now a little boy was suffering. "Back to White's. Lord Mundy came in."

"I remember him," she interrupted. "Good friend of your father's.'

"He has a grandson who was kidnapped."

Rebecca gasped, and pressed one hand to her mouth. "No! Poor child!"

"I assume the kidnappers did not know who they had. He was out with his nurse, and I am certain she had nothing on her to give her status away. The nurse was attacked, badly enough, I gathered, that she has still not fully recovered. Mundy has been all over England trying to find him."

"How long ago was this?" Her hands went immediately to her heart, and her delicate brow furrowed. How much like her Emmy looked!

"Three months, as I recall."

"Why did he not come to London first?"

"He went to the ports first. Such danger of little boys being thrown onto ships as cabin boys, or whatever else they use these boys for. At least if he is in a city, there is little chance of him getting away."

"But, my dear, London is the biggest port in England."

"Let the man do what he thinks is best! He's lived in the countryside since his daughter was widowed. I think he wanted to go to the nearest ports as quickly as possible." Blake straightened the blotter on his desk. He had not realized he had moved it. Much as he loved his mother, she had that effect on him. "He is here now, so has asked help to find the boy."

He pulled a notice out of his drawer. "Here. The only distinctive feature on the boy that I can see is his crooked little finger, and the cowlicks all over his head."

Rebecca took the paper, and scanned the description. "Blond hair on a child is far too common. The cowlicks might help, though." She shook her head. "There are ways around that, though. Shave the boy's head, or let the hair grow long enough to cover them. Either would disguise him."

"Shave the head? Would someone do that to a child?"

"Blake." His mother gave him that look, as if he had said something altogether foolish. "Child thieves are merciless. They are capable of anything. Besides, three months ago it would have still been chilly. They could cover it with a cap."

"I have more hope on the bent finger. That is hard to hide."

She nodded, slow and thoughtful. "True. Who notices hands on servants, other than to see if they are clean or dirty? But even a pair of gloves would not be enough to disguise that bend."

"Now, here's what I need you to do. When you are with your friends, tell them the story, and ask them to check their staff." He realized what he had said. "Or ask their housekeepers and butlers to go through the staff. We need everyone to help."

She nodded. "Consider it done." Then she looked down at the list. "I can't think about this right now, not when there is a child lost. I will bring it home, and finish it there."

She folded it, and tucked it into her reticule. "I shall set our plan in motion today. I am taking Emmy to begin her trousseau, so I will spread the news to everyone I see there." She lifted the notice. "May I take this with me?"

"By all means. They might be all over London by now. We had the printer make hundreds."

As she tucked it in her reticule next to the planning list, she said, "Let us hope the boy's kidnappers cannot read, and decide to move him."

Blake nodded. "That is a risk we had to take. How else can we get the news out? Five hundred pounds should shake something loose."

* * *

Madame scurried into the back room. "Girls, girls, we have *un ordre pressé*. Warrenby's two ladies, *mère et fille*, will be having *une fête,* and need gowns *le plus tôt possible*. You"—she pointed at Tessa—"get out and do *la mesure de la fille*. I will *mesurerai la mère*." She grabbed Tessa's barely healed arm and dragged her through the curtain and into the main room.

Tessa tried not to hold back. This would be the first time she had been out among the customers since Herb's attack. Three days to heal, plus Madame's powder, had helped. She looked better, Ellen had said so, but her first test *would* have to be Warrenby's family.

Then again, no one noticed the help.

Even so, walking out into the shop and facing them with fading bruises and powder on her face tested all her composure. She pretended all was well as she curtseyed to Blake's mother and sister. "If you would come with me, Lady Emilia, you can describe what you have in mind, and then we can sort through the fabrics."

"Oh, good. I am so excited!" The daughter gave no indication that she had noticed anything untoward. She never seemed to care about the distinction between her seamstresses and herself. It was rather charming, Tessa thought. "It's going to be such a party!"

Madame Genevieve was very efficient. A rush order meant she could charge extra, and she obviously intended to do just that. She hurried the mother into the other fitting room.

As she made all the required notations, Tessa tried not to think of the long day ahead cutting and stitching, or the walk home in the dark.

Back in the shop deep in the search for fabrics, the younger Lady Warrenby gave a squeal that turned heads around the shop, then held up the loose end a roll of heavy white lace and turned to her mother. "This is it! Mother, see? It would need to be lined, but I'm sure that will not be a problem." She looked at Tessa. "That is no problem, is it?"

Tessa managed to keep her mouth from dropping open. Sewing a gown of lace with a full lining? In just a few days?

Madame glanced over from where she sat with the mother on the other end of the table, examining patterns and fabrics. The surface was so piled with bolts of every fabric under the sun that it was hard see over the top. "*Bien sûr. Mais* it will cost."

Lady Emilia turned her big green eyes to her mother. "Please? I can see myself in it already."

Lady Warrenby looked between her daughter and the lace. "Of course."

The daughter was not done, though. "I could not tolerate it if anything happened my gown that night, and I have seen it happen. I can hardly leave my own party because my dress got spoiled. Can we hire someone from the shop to come and make repairs? Please? I want to look perfect for John."

After a quick exchange of glances, the mother looked over at Madame. "Might we hire one of your girls? I, too, want the party to be perfect."

Tessa knew what was coming. Madame turned to her. "Tessa, would you go *à leur maison* and be ready to handle *les problèmes?*"

Maybe run into Warrenby again?

Madame came to the rescue. "I am worried *pour mes filles et le voyage* and the trip home. It would be very late, *je suis certain*, and I would not feel she were *en sécurité* on the *longue marche à la maison. Je déteste* to be *impertinente*, but if one of *vos serviteurs* could drive her home?"

Lady Warrenby smiled a motherly smile. "Not to worry. We will make sure she gets home safe when the ball is over. I would never expect her to fend for herself. Would that be agreeable?"

Madame pretended to be thinking, but Tessa knew the decision had already been made. "That would be *très acceptable*."

"Then it is done." Lady Warrenby looked as pleased as punch. "I will send a carriage here to pick her up, and she can help Emmy get ready. I'm sure the other guests would be delighted to have a real seamstress to fix up tears and rips, rather than rely on an unskilled maid." She turned to Tessa and smiled as if Tessa had volunteered. "Thank you. It will be six days from now, so if you can make sure everything is set?" It was not a question, despite the kind and pleasant tone.

"Yes, my lady."

It took a full hour to get the orders completed and the fabrics and patterns set aside. Tessa could see Madame was pleased with the order, and the amount she was able to charge. She gushed and smiled until the two left the store, off to buy something else to make the night perfect for the daughter's engagement party.

Then there were the other customers, all clamoring for their own service, all eager to be their best for some newly announced ball. Tessa was certain they were all preparing for Lady Emilia's, and sure enough, finally she heard the name. An odd sense of pleasure filled her, that this lovely young woman would find her ball such a success.

She also decided the young woman deserved every skill she had. If there was anything she could do to make the gown even a little more special, she would do it.

With all the new gown orders, not to mention the ones that were already being made, it would be a busier week than usual. Much busier.

Tessa had never seen Madame be so short with customers as she was today. Between herself and Ellen, they were nearly run off their feet to get measurements and orders added to the stack, with eagle eyes glaring them along.

Finally the shop was empty, at least for the moment.

As soon as the door shut behind the last group, Madame promptly locked it, closed the curtain, and turned around, her eyes wide with alarm. "We cannot have *un autre client* today, nor tomorrow either. We cannot waste *un seul instant. Maintenant*, let us get to work. Ellen! Rosie!"

The next few days would really be frantic, if even Rosie was going to help. To save time, they made the patterns out of fine cloth instead of paper, which they could reuse as a lining. It saved another step.

* * *

Blake had not dared to get dressed yet. For now, he sat in his father's old office with his plate of food and tried to keep out of his mother's way. She had wrested control of her house from the housekeeper before noon with the ease of a general. Thin-sliced beef and pickled pigs' feet, currant sauce, asparagus, a small roast guinea hen, and two kinds of tarts for dessert had been brought up.

If he ate all this, his new clothes might not fit, but he was hungry enough to give it a try. So here he sat, eating, and trying not to listen to the hubbub from out in the hall. Buckets dripped water, he heard the shouts about incompetence, and the mutters of the servants as they passed his door.

The idea of a special license looked better all the time.

John had not contacted him since their talk. Blake wondered if his world was as busy as theirs. Had he been ordered to get new clothes for the night's festivities? What else did a bridegroom have to do?

A soft tap caught his attention. He tried to ignore it, but it came again, and then the door opened. His sister slipped inside, shut it with a quiet click behind her and leaned against it as if to keep intruders away. Her cheeks were flushed, and she was out of breath. He had been told she would be wearing white lace. The pink sprigged gown she had on was no white lace dress. Blake got a sinking feeling in his stomach.

"Is everything all right?" He looked at her again, and green eyes as big as tea cups met his. "Do not tell me you are having second thoughts?"

"Oh, no!" she said on an outrush of air. "No, of course not. I was just wondering—Blake, what if John and I eloped?"

His own eyes went wide. "Eloped? After all this? I am most sorry, little sister, but after what your mother and the staff have gone through arranging for this, the answer is a firm *no*. You are her only daughter, you know she would be destroyed. She has been waiting since your birth for this event, and you are not going to deprive her of it."

Emmy left the door, seeming to trust it to stay shut and keep her hiding place secure, and tiptoed in, to curl up in one of the big leather chairs. She tucked her feet under her skirt, and propped her chin on her knees, looking over them at him. "Blake, can I have just a small wedding?"

He began to sense the problem. "Nerves, my dear sister?"

She nodded so vigorously her curls bobbed loose. Whoever did her hair was not going to be happy having to do it all over again. "I have decided I don't like being stared at. When I think of standing in front of everybody —" she interrupted herself. "Have you ever noticed how big that ballroom is? Blake, it's the entire floor!"

He worked very hard not to grin, but did not know how successful he was. "I have been up there, remember? I grew up here, just as you did."

"Go ahead, laugh," she snapped at him. "Some day it will be your turn. Not just in front of the ballroom for the announcement, but the whole cathedral. Just remember *that*. The bride has to walk past every single person there, but the groom has to stand up before God and everybody and know they are all staring at him to see whether he is going to faint or not."

His hidden smile vanished, as did the urge. "I'm not the daughter for whom Mother has been waiting her whole life to enjoy all the wedding celebrations. If I run off, no one will care."

Her legs slipped off the chair edge, and she snapped upright. "Ha! Don't fool yourself. You are the heir. Not just Mother, but the whole of London will be waiting to see who snags you."

Snags him. What an awful thought, like he was a fish that swam too close to a hook. "We're not talking about me, now. This is your day."

"Coward." She curled back onto the chair in the same protective position as before. "But yes, I do know it is. Today will be bad enough, the wedding, though, is giving me nightmares. I never wanted a 'day.' I think this is more Mother's day." The sigh that came out sounded too big to fit into her body.

Blake leaned back in his chair. Poor child. She was only eighteen years old. While she seemed to love being in the center of her friends, that was very different from being in front of several hundred people. He hated to do it, but it was time to fight dirty. It might be the only thing that gave her the courage to get through the night's festivities. "You don't want John to think you are ashamed of him, do you?"

Her eyes widened, and her head came up again, more slowly this time, as if she had never thought of that before. "No! Of course not!"

"Then, sister, I believe you do have to go through with it. You will be able to flaunt your new gown in front of all your friends." He remembered the bill that had been delivered to his bachelor's house this morning before he came here. "For that price, it should be really something. I doubt even your wedding dress will rival it."

Emmy sat in her little pink cocoon for a few minutes, legs tucked close, toes poking under the ruffled skirt of her gown, and her head back down on her knees, while her arms seemed to be wrapping everything tight. At last the clock in his office chimed four bells, and it seemed to break the spell. "I do have to go upstairs and get dressed. It seems silly to get into the gown with three hours to go."

"Your hair's fallen down," he felt compelled to say. "Although I love it this way, because it reminds me of the little hellion you used to be, I don't think it's the style your mother wants."

She began to open like a flower, legs down on the floor, her head lifting and the tumbled brown tumbling around her shoulders, then standing up to her full height, small though that was. "Thank you, Blake." Her eyes were back to their normal size, not the wide-eyed alarm when she first entered. When she got to the door, she looked back. "I love you."

The words wrapped around his heart. He wondered how often he would hear them after she was wed. Another man would get the first claim on her endearments, which was as it should be, he knew, but it still left a small hurt in his chest. "I love you, too, Emmy. Don't ever doubt it."

With a sweet smile, poignant in its hope and fear, she slipped back out the door, letting it click shut behind her.

* * *

The hooks were hooked, the ribbons were all tied, and Lady Emilia was permitted to turn around and see herself in the mirror. Her mother had been adamant that her daughter not be allowed to look until she was all dressed and her hair fixed.

Her eyes went wide. "Oh, Mum, it's beautiful. I would hug you until you pop if I were not so afraid of damaging anything."

"You have your own dressmaker here on your command if so much as a stitch pops," her mother said, and smiled over at Tessa. Then she turned to Madame. "We both are very grateful for your efforts on our behalf."

"It has been *un plaisir*." She gave a curtsy, and Ellen and Tessa followed suit.

"Yes, well, the pleasure was ours. You did a magnificent job." Lady

Warrenby looked down at her own gown, still in the lilac of half-mourning but sleek and restrained. "If you, Madame, and your other assistant wish to leave, I believe Tessa can handle it from here?" She raised her eyebrows in question.

"Yes, Madam." Tessa presumed another curtsy was required, so she dropped into her best.

Lady Warrenby turned back to her daughter. "Why don't you stay here and read"—she fluttered her hands—"or something."

Lady Emelia laid her hand on her stomach and made a face of extreme suffering. "I am *starving*."

Her mother was not moved. "I'm sure you are not, Emmy. I happen to know you had a huge breakfast at noon."

Lady Warrenby turned to Madame, who was busy checking the large sewing basket of emergency supplies, complete with swatches of both lace and the lining, pins, thread, and several cards of needles. She must have decided it would be enough for the evening, for she gave it a satisfied nod, and followed Ellen out.

The room emptied, and it was only Tessa and Lady Emilia. The young woman sat neat and prim in one of the chairs. Blake's—no, Warrenby's, she reminded herself—Warrenby's sister had always seemed immune to the separation of staff and her own class, but now they were in a room, alone. Lady Emilia in her stunning white lace gown, and herself in the black servant's dress Madame insisted on. The gulf between them seemed so huge and the colors of the gowns only emphasized that. Tessa held her tongue, however tempting it was to make conversation to fill the silence.

Her stomach rumbled loudly, and Lady Emilia gave a start. She must have been deep in her thoughts. "Goodness! Haven't you eaten? I feel like I'm *starving*," She shivered for added drama. Tilting her head, she looked Tessa over. "You look tired. Maybe a good meal will perk you up." Lady Emilia got up and gave the bellpull a solid yank.

She flopped back down on the chair, the double layers of her lace skirts puffing out around her, examined her nails, and then stared at the wall. After a few minutes of quiet, she turned to Tessa. "Talk to me."

A knock came at the door, sparing Tessa from having to dredge up something for conversation.

"Come!"

The door opened without a squeak. A tall maid who looked slightly older than Tessa stood there, black gown, white apron, and large white mobcap covering all of her hair. Only her dark eyebrows gave the hair color away. That, and her rich brown eyes. She recognized Tessa immediately as one of her own class, looked past her, and addressed her question to Lady Emilia. "Yes, miss?"

"Two plates from the kitchen, just pastry, if you please. And make certain there is fresh tea for both of us."

The maid bobbed. "Yes, miss." Then the door closed with that same silent swish.

"Sit down," Lady Emilia ordered in a friendly tone. "There's no reason for you to keep standing at attention like a soldier."

Sit down? Tessa hesitated, but her feet hurt, and her back hurt, and she had a whole night to get through. She looked at her hostess—or whatever role Lady Emilia had right now—and sat down in the nearest chair. The relief was so overwhelming she groaned before she could catch herself.

"Do your feet hurt?" The girl's voice, and her eyes, were sympathetic.

"A little." It would hardly do to tell this sweet young woman what parts of her body ached. She had an entire night to get through yet, and they needed—*she* needed—to be ready for it.

"What is your name?"

"What?" No one had ever wanted to know.

"Your name. I know the names of the entire staff. I would prefer not to call people as 'you.' We are going to be here for a little while. You know my name, I am certain. It is only fair that I know yours."

It felt strange to be so familiar, but she answered. "Tessa Abbott."

"Tessa." She seemed to be testing out the name. "Well, Tessa, what is it like to work?"

Tessa blinked. "Work?" No one had ever asked her that before. How did she answer? How early she got up, how tired she was at day's end, dealing with customers who were never happy. Having to redo gowns she spent an entire week on, just because some little thing was wrong. Or because someone with money thought it fun to make their underlings jump to their tune.

She struggled for words, trying to put her life into a brief answer. "Well, I rise early, and walk to the shop. Sometimes, if it has been a good week and I have a little extra money, I grab a hackney and get to ride part of the way." She didn't add how very rare that was.

"No, not, not that." Lady Emilia waved a hand, and the fabric glowed in the light of the candles in the sconces and the waning sunlight through the window. Tessa dragged her eyes away from the beautiful fabric. She got to sew it, there was no point in dreaming for something she would never have.

The girl was still talking. "—like I never get anything of importance done. Sometimes I think I will go mad with boredom."

Tessa couldn't help it, she burst out laughing. "I don't think I am ever bored. I don't have time." When she saw the look on Emmy's face, part embarrassment, part wistfulness, she sobered. If only she dared say, *Do you know how much people of my class would give for just a moment of boredom?* Instead, she simply said, "I think it is more a matter of finding the things that make your life happy." Without thinking, she went on, "Like this man you are marrying. He makes you happy, doesn't he?"

Oh, dear! She immediately wanted to crawl under the floor. In the shop, they chatted back and forth, sharing all manner of private bits. To do that with someone so high above her was appalling, a rude question, not to mention a terrible breach of etiquette. What if Lady Emilia was being forced into marriage?

But the girl smiled, and her body seemed to soften. She relaxed into the chair, any pretense at good posture gone, and her eyes glowed. "He makes me very happy. He is brave and smart and strong, and, most of all, kind."

Envy prodded Tessa, sharp and painful. How many times had she wondered if what she had now was all there would ever be?

Her face must have shown something of her thought, because Lady Emilia said, "You look sad. Did I say the wrong thing?"

"Oh, no, not at all." Tessa shook her head.

"Oh, good." Lady Emilia said.

Another stomach rumbled in the room, but not Tessa's this time. A little surprising in view of how hungry she was herself.

Lady Emilia laughed and clapped her hand over her middle. "Where *is* that tea?"

The words had hardly left her mouth when the door rattled loudly, as if someone had to kick with her feet, or bang with an elbow.

The girl sat up straight. "Oh, good."

Tessa jumped up, scurried over and pulled the door open. Not one but two maids stood there, one with two plates, each holding a single pastry. The second maid brought cups and a large teapot.

Tessa swallowed. One pastry to bet her through the night, and into tomorrow morning, when she would have to get something solid from one of the street vendors or she would faint dead away at work.

Ah well. She had been hungry before. All she had to worry about now was making certain Lady Emilia did not spill the tea on her gown.

The maid with the plates turned to Tessa's companion, lifting a large, neatly folded napkin off her arm and handing it over. "Lady Emilia, yer mum said ye could 'ave a napkin for the crumbs."

Lady Emilia wrinkled her nose. "Jenny, you are too thoughtful."

Jenny just laughed softly. "I'm just doin' wot I was told."

As Tessa watched the byplay between employer and servant, lady and maid, it became harder to think of Lady Emilia Glover in the formal terms required. This was a very kind young woman, obviously loved and spoiled.

Her brother had many of the same qualities, a man who glared suspicions at her, then apologized for his thought, even came to pick her up in the rain. A man protective of his stature and reputation, yet rode with a servant.

Perhaps it was better if they weren't so kind. At least with those who looked down their noses at her, she knew exactly where she stood, and what the rules were.

She stared at the pastry, and even though her stomach was still knotted with nerves, picked up the fork and began eating.

CHAPTER 10

Blake stood at the head of the ballroom and waited for the orchestra to finish their current dance. The conductor glanced over, gave a quick nod, then led the members into the last refrain.

Looking around the room, it was clear everyone knew something big was in store. The minute he had started toward the front, eyes had begun looking his way and the dancers were losing interest in their movements.

The music swirled to a finish. The applause sounded frenetic. No one walked off the floor, the whole group turned his direction. His mother came in from the side, and joined him there.

"It's time," she said, and scanned the room to find Emmy. Blake chuckled. The only way Rebecca could see across the room was to stand on a stool.

He knew their guests expected the announcement to be about himself. How would they react to his sister's engagement, instead of his own? This was Emmy, and it would hurt both of them—all of them, John and his mother included—if the response would be, not a cheer of excitement, but a moan of dismay. He could only hope any engagement at all would be greeted with delight.

"Ladies and gentlemen." His voice rang out over the crowd, helped by the silence that had begun to fall over the room anyway. "You no doubt guessed that an announcement would be made tonight. Some of you might already know what it is, but for the rest, I must begin by saying that the news delights me."

He extended his hand, and from within the mass of people Emmy started toward the two of them, her right hand clutching John's left as she dragged him along. Nudges rippled through the crowd, and whispers built. Was it the hand-holding? Or the one whose hand she held?

Raising his voice again, he went on, "I have had a dear friend for many years, someone whose company I value. We had been given different assignments in the war, and I did not know what happened to him, whether he lived or died."

Emmy and John were only two rows of people away now, still working their way through the crowd. John's face was pale, the red scar outside his patch showing up more vividly, and his damaged hand curled toward his body, as if he sought to hide it. .

"Imagine my delight when I found out that my sister and my oldest friend had fallen in love and wanted to marry."

Emmy reached his side and pulled John next to her. The silence was heart-crushing. Rebecca gave John a hug. His sister's eyes glistened with tears, and he realized that Emilia loved John so much that his missing eye, his shattered hand, the scars, were not even there for her. She looked at him with love, and to her, he was perfect.

Grateful that John's hand was free and ready for a handshake, Blake reached over and held out his own left, hoping it looked as natural as if he had been shaking left-handed his whole life. John grabbed it, and through their gloves, Blake could feel the trembles.

John had expected this crushing silence, had known it would happen, and yet still agreed to subject himself to it, just to claim Emmy. Was this why his sister had asked for a quiet ceremony?

A spatter of applause broke into the silence, and built, growing louder and louder. Emmy blinked the tears back, although one slipped down her cheek. Before he could reach out and catch it, John's hand, the broken right one, was there and he wiped it away himself.

Blake smiled as the room echoed. He leaned over and shouted above the din, "I think they wanted me to announce my own engagement. To be told it was my sister just startled them for a moment."

John shook his head. "It's nice of you to say so."

Rebecca pulled Emmy into her arms for her own hug, and said over her shoulder at her future son-in-law, "I think it is a little of both. Before I came up, I heard someone next to me saying, 'Blake's found a wife.' So John, Emmy, there might be some surprise at the two of you, but let's give them the benefit of the doubt and say they wanted Blake to announce his."

John looked down at Emmy and over at Blake, and suddenly gave a roar of laughter loud enough to put a dent in the noise of the room. "Imagine that! What a night that would have been! There would be a rush for the doors, as everyone raced out to spread the news." He clapped Blake on the shoulder. "So, Blake, when *are* you going to look for a bride?"

Blake did not feel like laughing at that, the timing was wrong, but he did manage to smile. "Not all of us are as lucky as you two are."

* * *

Tessa straightened herself out of her slump as the thumping of another group of young women rushed up the stairs. In just a moment they would come pouring into Lady Emilia's dressing room. Her engagement must have been announced in the ballroom, because the house had gone remarkably quiet, and then the muffled sound of applause sent shivers through the air.

She set out her needles and arranged the thread in order of the color of gowns she had seen the most often, folded her hands, and waited for the rush.

And for the gossip, if she was perfectly honest with herself.

The door slammed open, and five young women piled through. A tall blonde girl in a blue gown Tessa thought she recognized from Madame's, short sleeves and layers of ruffles at the skirt hem, seemed to be the leader. Ignoring Tessa's presence, she said loud enough for all the others to hear without straining, "The man is missing an eye! Did you see that hand? It looks hideous! And Emmy is so lovely and flawless. What a contrast!"

A tiny woman, not as young as the others, with wildly curly black hair and a determined chin—and apparently a personality to match—said, "Jane. I think he is very dashing. The patch makes him look like a pirate, and I vow, it gives me the shivers." She giggled, then sobered. "The hand is a bit off-putting, I grant you. Still, there must be ways to work around it. I wish he had noticed me first."

The blonde girl wasn't about to be stopped. "But his scars! I shudder to think what his face looks like without it. You might be able to ignore the hand, but no matter what you say, I could never bring myself to touch it. I have not accepted a single dance from him."

A third girl with tawny hair and a pink gown pushed her way through the cluster until she stood in front of the blonde. "Jane, just because no one has asked you yet does not give you the right to abuse every other woman's choice. And if you remember, my brother is missing a leg. I do not take kindly to having anyone tormenting him, so I will not stand idly by and listen to you vent your spleen against John."

Lady Emilia was indeed blessed with her friends, Tessa thought. Two women in a group of five had the courage to speak up, and to make the husband-to-be the prize Warrenby's sister saw in him.

Jane tried to laugh, but it was a poor attempt. "John, is it? Did you want him, too?"

The other just shook her head. "I have known John since we were children. He and my brother were the best of friends. It would feel strange to call him Mr. Holland, although I sometimes do just to see him make a face at me. So, no, Jane, I do not want him, but from all that I can tell, he is a wonderful catch. I would watch your tongue if I were you, because words get around and if Lord Warrenby hears what you said, you can forget about catching him for a husband, either."

With that she came over to Tessa, picked up her skirt, and ran it through her fingers until she found what she was looking for. "Here it is. The lace came off while I was dancing. Can you stitch it back on?"

"Of course, miss," Tessa said, and selected a needle and a spool of thread.

* * *

Tessa was afraid to close her eyes, for fear she would fall asleep where she sat. She had been up now for most of three days, by her calculations. During the previous nights' sewing, they all, herself, Madame Genevieve, and Ellen, had moments when their heads hit the table, and they would realize they had dozed off sitting upright, with their needles in their hands.

Those brief naps and plenty of tea had kept them going. No doubt the other two were long in bed. She did not know what time it was, or if they had forgotten that she was even here.

Music drifted up from below, accompanied by the din of the party. After the last group left, Tessa had pulled the door wider to hear the melody, and dream.

An hour might have passed, she wasn't sure, but finally someone came in. A middle-aged woman, wearing a rich purple turban and a matching gown far too low-cut for her mature years, shoved the door open and glared. Wrinkles exaggerated her aging skin, and the sagging of her breasts. Her heavy necklace, glittering with all manner of jewels, did nothing to enhance the stretch of flesh that showed above the droop. Undoubtedly she wore a corset for support, but either there was no way to lift what she had, or the corset was badly designed and made as well. Her lone saving grace was a lace shawl that she wrapped around her shoulders.

This woman could not possibly be a customer of Madame's. The modiste would never let her clients leave in anything so unflattering.

Her gaze settled on Tessa. "Some bumbling fool stomped on my gown, and it is about to fall apart. I need it repaired immediately." Her voice had an annoying scratchy whine.

No *please*, not even the barest attempt at courtesy. "Good evening, madam," Tessa answered in her best manner. "If you can let me see?"

The woman turned around and pulled away the shawl. She had not been exaggerating. A finger's length of the gathered skirt had indeed been torn out.

"Not to worry." Tessa began sorting through her basket, picking out a needle, her pincushion, thread, and her small embroidery scissors. "If you can remove the gown, I will get to work."

With a sniff of annoyance, the woman let herself be untied and unhooked, and sat in a blanket while her skirt was stitched together. Because the rip had shredded the ends of both skirt and bodice back and Tessa had to sew further into both pieces to ensure that her mend would hold up, she tried to explain that it might appear slightly uneven from behind.

"I don't care," the woman snapped. "I won't be wearing this gown again. I will never go back to the incompetent fool of a woman who made it. All this wonderful fabric," their visitor continued her rant, "and you don't have to tell me she made a hash of it. I would not have even worn it except that it was the only new gown I had. I think I shall take the other fabric I purchased from her and bring it to someone else."

"I work for Madame Genevieve." It might not be proper to solicit customers while at someone else's house, but they did good work, and this woman could certainly benefit from her employer's gift.

"And which gowns did you make, that you think you can go around begging work for her?"

No, that must not have been proper. At least not with this guest. But she answered the question. "Lady Warrenby's, and her daughter's."

"Indeed?" The woman's eyebrows went up. "Well, I might talk to them and see what they have to say."

A dozen more stitches, Tessa estimated, and concentrated on making them as precise and neat as she had ever done.

* * *

No one would notice him if he left for a few minutes. Blake had his hand on the staircase railing to go up and make certain Te—Miss Abbott had everything she needed when Addersley, Haversham, and even Gillem, who must have slipped back into London despite being in his family's poor graces at the moment, stepped in his path.

"Congratulations, Warrenby." Gillem, who smelled slightly of whiskey, was the first to speak.

"Yes. I am surprised at the change in Holland." Haversham lifted a glass of punch in the air, either a salute to John's improvement or to keep Blake from leaping to the man's defense, Blake did not know. "Not the eye, I knew about that already."

He had added that last rather bit fast, but no doubt John was getting used to reactions, both good and bad.

Haversham was not finished yet. "Remember the old John? I never would have put him down as the one to marry an innocent"—he raised his hand to stop any remarks, especially from himself, Blake was sure —"and despite his old reputation, I am positive your sister is still innocent. In fact, I suspect John will make certain she stays that way to the wedding."

"Thank you, my friend."

Addersley waved toward the staircase. "You were heading someplace with dispatch. Did we interrupt?"

Trust Addersley to be the one to notice. "As a matter of fact, I hired a modiste's assistant to make certain there were no disasters. I want everything to be perfect tonight for Emmy."

"Hired a modiste, eh?"

"Modiste's assistant," he corrected.

"Rather a clever idea. Not just your everyday housemaid, then?"

Blake motioned toward the room. "Look at all the ribbons and ruffles and lace here. Even Emmy's gown is a bit out of the ordinary. I made certain of it, and I intend to keep it that way."

"So did you choose the assistant yourself?" A glint of mischief sparked in the man's eye.

He had better nip that in the bud. "Madame Genevieve sent her most skilled seamstress. It seemed a prudent move. Emmy was happy with the idea. I agreed." Never mind the fact that this was the one he would have chosen himself, and not just for her skills.

Addersley was not done. "Old seamstress? Middle-aged? Young?"

That glint refused to go away. Clearly his explanation did not fully satisfy Addersley. Either that or he was just having fun. Blake did not like the implication for Tessa's reputation, or for his own. "Arthur, you know I'm not the type who dallies with servants. I do not like men to prey on those who cannot defend themselves."

"One doesn't have to prey on them. One can merely look."

The other three turned to stare at him. Addersley looked back with brows up in his usual expression of mild surprise. "Tell me you don't like a pretty woman. I see you in Hyde Park. Do not even waste your breath telling me you are always just out for a little fresh air. With your properties to visit? If you want fresh air, take a trip out of London, not a ride through Hyde Park."

Gillem had the grace to wince, since he had probably come from one of his family's own country places. In a bit of forced seclusion for some unnamed indiscretion, if their guesses were right, but still, out of the lairs of London.

Blake decided to be the first to smooth the waters. Nothing Addersley said was far from the truth. "Just remember, Arthur, one of these days your own trip through Hyde Park will be to get a bride." Then he grinned. "I suppose the seamstress can manage without my assistance. You are right. My place is here in the ballroom, not upstairs making certain she has enough needles and pins. However, I can see to it that food is sent up to her."

It was surprisingly hard to let go of the banister, and turn away. It was also the right thing to do, he was sure.

"As long as you three are here, we need to set a time so I can show you the rest of the jewelry. You only saw my drawings of four. There are more. If we're going to work together, you should see everything I was given."

* * *

Her eyes were so heavy she could barely keep them open. Would this ball never end? Some hours ago, a covered plate had been carried up by some footmen all the way from the kitchen. "His Lordship thought you would be getting hungry by now."

Tessa smiled, not even knowing what those covers hid. And not particularly caring, either, she was so grateful to have a real meal. "Tell his lordship thank you for me," she said, and had to force herself not to snatch the plate out of the footman's hand.

Seasoned goose, a bit of ham, fresh-baked bread, and fruit compote, candied carrots, asparagus—a food she had only ever heard of, but never had a chance to try and found quite to her liking—and as a final treat, cherry pie. She settled down to eat, reveling in the distraction the meal provided. If the servants got to eat the same food the cook prepared for upstairs, what a wonderful place this was to work!

Food-wise, at least. A sudden yawn hurt her jaw, it was so wide.

Lady Emma's bed was so inviting! But she dared not. That was a breach of all etiquette, and she would show that she could be trusted to behave.

If she sat here any longer, she would soon be asleep. Tessa dragged herself to her feet and walked over to the window. She could see that the outer curtain was of silk, but she was too tired to enjoy the fabric. When she moved it aside, an under curtain hid behind it. Two curtains, when she was happy to have one.

She gazed down at the moon-gilded grass below. Shrubbery took on a ghostly appearance, like sleeping gnomes who would change their shape in the morning light. Music had drifted up the stairs over the past hours, but somehow it seemed louder here. They must have doors, and perhaps most of the windows, open in order for the sound to come so strongly through the air.

Where she lived, if the noise got too loud, someone could be depended upon to shout, "Keep it down!" No one would dare do that in this part of town. Undoubtedly, anyone who lived nearby was of high enough rank to have been invited, and was no doubt below making much of the noise themselves.

A headache had started some time ago, and it plagued her. Tessa rested her forehead against the window, enjoying the night's coolness. If only she dared pack her sewing basket, and walk home. But walking London's streets this time of night would be a fool's errand. Her black servants' gown might blend into the darkness, but footpads would be about.

"Please, come and tell me I can go home," she whispered into the quiet room.

"I am so sorry you had to stay this late."

CHAPTER 11

The deep voice made her whirl so quickly she almost lost her balance. Warrenby lounged in the doorway, leaning against the jamb as if he had all the time in the world. His hair was tousled, proof he had been dancing to some of the lively tunes that had drifted up in broken bits.

Of course he would have danced. It was his house, and his party.

"Are you ready to leave?" He straightened, and she was reminded once again of how very tall he was. Even from across this room, he exuded presence.

"Yes, oh yes, please." Tessa let the layers of curtains fall over the window. Oddly, the headache was gone. Perhaps it fled in the knowledge that she could sleep soon.

Packing up the basket took almost no time at all. She was an organized seamstress, and everything had its place. With one more look around to make sure she had not overlooked anything, Tessa wrapped herself in the worn shawl, picked up her possessions, and looked over at him. "I'm ready."

"Very well. Follow me." His face had no expression, and he made no further comment, just turned and walked out the door.

After he stepped through, he stopped to look behind and make certain she was still there. She was close enough to see the lines around his eyes, and a faint grey cast to his skin. His eyelids drooped, something she had not noticed from across the room. Despite the exhaustion in his face, his back was straight, and his stride was long.

This house had a *lot* of stairs.

When they reached the main floor, he did not turn her over to a servant, as she expected. Instead, he walked her down another stairway, through the bustling kitchen, where the cook was busy stirring, and off to one side scullery maids were washing with obvious haste. Their own beds must be calling to them, as well.

Then outside, across the gravel toward the stable, where she could see a veritable herd of horses only as large shifting shadows inside. The smell of horse and manure would have given it away, even if she had not seen the wealth in animals hidden there.

"Is my carriage ready?" Warrenby asked a solid, balding, older man in rough work clothes.

"Yessir, me lord, they are bringin' it out now." A frown added to the wrinkles on the man's forehead. "Ah put fresh 'orses on it. Th' coachman'll need ta move fast this time o' night." He paused, clearly waiting for something.

Tessa had been living among the servant class, and knew what he expected. She glanced over at Warrenby. He should be heading back to the house. Perhaps he had the manners to want to see her safely in the carriage.

A clatter made the balding man turn his head. "'Ere we go. The coach." He looked back at Warrenby, that same expectant expression on his face.

The carriage stopped in front of her. She recognized it immediately, the same one as the rainy night he had picked her up from Madame's. Warrenby turned the door handle, and flipped down the stairs without waiting for anyone else. The man in rough clothes frowned harder.

"Ah could do that, me lord," he said. "There ain't no need fer ye ta take that 'pon yerself."

Warrenby interrupted. "I know perfectly well how to drop the steps out. I used to play in this thing when I was a child, remember?"

He took Tessa's basket, and set it inside, then held out his hand.

Tessa stared at it. He had helped her into the carriage the other night, but he had remained inside, no one could have seen him. They had an audience now: the balding man, the coachman, and anyone who happened to be within eyesight.

Warrenby seemed oblivious to the watching eyes. That hand remained steady. It was obvious he intended to stand there until she cooperated. Tessa took it quickly, and bounded into the waiting vehicle with a distinct lack of grace, haste robbing her of any refinement.

Her mother would be appalled, after all the hours of teaching her how to act like a lady.

She had managed to get herself settled when the carriage shifted again, and Warrenby climbed in. Not to be outdone this time, the coachman shut the door behind him.

Tessa struggled with her smile at the puffed out chest and satisfied nod just before the door closed tight.

"Something funny?" Warrenby raised an eyebrow.

"Your coachman. He acted like someone who finally had the last word."

Warrenby's mouth quirked. "I can accomplish things on my own." He gave her a long look that she could not decipher. "Everyone thinks it must be pure luxury to have everything done for you, but it can be wearing. Not to mention boring and unnecessary."

He sounded exactly like his sister.

"Speaking as someone who has never had anything done for them, I promise you, a little bit of luxury is a wonderful thing." Tessa remembered the music, and the gowns that had come through her room. A rush of pure happiness melted her stiff muscles, and she sank back against the carriage seat. "I want to thank your mother and sister for requesting a seamstress for the evening. I will never forget this as long as I live."

A hum of joy vibrated her throat, and came out as a sinking melody on the air. "Such music! I have never heard the like. If I never hear such again, at least I had this night."

* * *

Sadness slid over Warrenby at her words. Someone that looked like her should be able to go to get out on the floor and feel the music vibrate through her from the soles of her shoes, should be able to let it lift her, move to it, sweep and sway.

Did his servants long to join the dancers, as well?

Again, the contrast between her worker's garb, those heavy shoes she wore, the delicate features that would shine with a better style, and her precise speech and normally graceful movements piqued his curiosity. *Who are you*, he wondered. This time he was too tired to be hampered by Society's restrictions. "Who are you? Where did you learn to speak like this? You know you could pass for a member of the upper class."

Her head lolled against the seat back, and her eyes were shut, possibly resting, or perhaps still hearing whatever music had drifted up the stairs. "My mother taught me everything I know. How to read, write, speak properly, walk, sew. Everything. Didn't I tell you?"

"You said your father told you that you were like her, but nothing about how she spoke or conducted herself." He remembered the occasion very well, the other ride in the carriage coming back to him just as it must do with her.

Her eyes opened, and she leaned forward. "I never thought much about it. My mother was just my mother, and it was a part of her." Then she settled back against the seat. "I assumed he thought she and I looked alike. We had no miniatures of her as a young woman, so I had nothing to compare. I don't even remember her hair color, it had gone grey by the time I formed memories. He *might* have meant how I speak. As for where she learned so she could teach me the same, I never even wondered. I just knew neither wanted to talk about their past." Regret tainted her words.

Blake watched her sink back against the seat. Her eyes closed again, her shoulders slowly relaxed. He could not match her ease. Parents who told their daughter nothing about their background. A mother with graceful speech and no name from before the marriage, a daughter with no history beyond those two.

Despite the questions swirling in his head, the mood in the coach was comfortable, the dark lending to the odd intimacy. Blake leaned against the seat just as she was doing across from him. Miss Tessa seemed to feel no need to fill it with chatter, not that she would, given the distance between their two places in the world. But she did not act tense, although she might be too tired to talk much.

It was brighter outside, moonlight and stars and the odd streetlight lending a certain amount of illumination. It was enough to send splashes of brightness across her delicate features. He could light the lamps, but she needed this sleep. If sleep it was.

Sometimes just closing the eyes gave enough relaxation to ease the worst of exhaustion. He knew that personally.

Buildings took shape, stores closed for the night, the windows dark, displays mere shadowy shapes behind the glass. Lamplighters moved along the sidewalk, ladders over their shoulders. Further back, black forms flitted between the buildings, or dashed from doorway to doorway. Footpads hoping for a victim. Their wheels rattled on the cobblestones, making more noise than he noticed in the daytime.

A carriage moved past, heading the other way, back home after a night in the hells, gambling, or a man returning to his wife after spending time with his mistress or in the brothels. The other vehicle's wheels added to the sounds and helped mute their own rattles.

His father never made any nighttime visits. No, he always remained home with his mother.

That is what he wanted, Blake thought, a marriage where neither had any desire to stray. His gaze was drawn back to the woman across from him. Her breathing did not have the regular, deep pattern of sleep. No doubt she was still alert, wary, and the only things getting any rest were her eyes and her fingers.

He could tell her she was in no danger, that he would never abuse his position, but she needed the moments of peace, and showing her that she was safe was far more effective than words.

The carriage slowed. They had reached the destination he had given the man. Blake looked out the window, and noticed they were near Madame's shop. "How much farther?"

She opened her eyes, and peered out the small window at her own seat. "You can stop here. I can walk the rest of the way."

Blake folded his arms. "How much farther?"

"I can walk, I assure you. You should not take a carriage into my neighborhood."

Blake cleared his throat rather than growl another request. "If it is too dangerous to take an old coach, it is too dangerous for a woman to walk alone."

The carriage settled to a complete stop with a gentle rocking.

Tessa slid toward the edge of the seat, and reached for the basket. Guessing her intent, Blake grabbed the handle first, and held it in place. “Miss Abbott. I am not letting you walk home this late. My mother gave Madame her word that we would see to your safety. Would you have me make my mother a liar? Give in. If you get out and walk, we will simply follow you. Imagine what attention *that* will garner.”

* * *

Tessa looked at the dark shape too close to her, as Blake leaned forward and held onto the handle of her sewing basket. They could get into a tugging match, but the wicker would break before he let go.

She did remember Madame’s request, and a parade down the street would attract every footpad around. Certainly word would get to Herb, and she had barely recovered from his last ‘visit.’ Although she had never seen him with a pistol, she was certain he possessed one.

“Very well.” She released her grip on the basket handle, and sat back. He was not a fool, though, and picked it up to put it on his seat. His smile was not friendly. Instead, it was a warning.

“Give me the address, I will tell the coachman.”

She laughed. “Address? I don’t think it has one. I will have to direct him.”

“No. That is not the way this will work. The minute you get outside the carriage, you will run. I am not going to deliver your basket to the shop tomorrow because you thought you could outwit me. Give me the nearest intersection. If we have to go block by block, we will.”

* * *

Tessa sighed. The man was ridiculous. Did he hear nothing she had said? Did he truly believe his rank and his planning—she must not forget his taking the small old carriage—would be enough to protect him? Very well, she knew an intersection nearby that might be safer than the others. It would make a slightly longer walk for her, take her down an area she had not been this late, but it would keep him safe.

So she gave directions, and he popped through the opening in the carriage roof to relay them.

“There,” he said with a smug tone as he seated himself across from her again. “Was that so hard?”

“You do know that I don’t wander the area in a carriage? I walk, and it is much easier to hide a single person than a vehicle.” She took a deep breath, hoping he had come out armed. What a time to think of that! If only she had asked when she realized he intended to be her escort. “I don’t suppose you thought to bring a pistol?”

Warrenby merely pulled back his coat. She thought she saw his lips curve into a smile. In the dark, it was hard to tell. "My coachman is also armed. I am not such a fool as to think any place in London is perfectly safe." His eyes glittered. "Footpads are hardly likely to prowl where no one has anything to steal. Don't you agree, Miss Abbott?"

* * *

There was a pause, no doubt as she weighed his words for any insult. He had not meant one. "Of course."

"Care to tell me what's behind that tone? I did not mean to imply—"

"One of the men on my block is a footpad, if not worse . . . well, he guessed I had more still in my room. He found the coins I had told you about, and took them." Another pause, and Blake held his breath. What was she not telling him? "He was not happy."

A sharp pain lanced across Blake's chest. The coins. He could only guess what that money had meant to her. Tainted though it was, it was still a cushion against the poverty he knew was her lot. "Why not? What business was it of his?"

"I had paid him just a shilling to carry my father's coffin to the church. It was all I had from my own money, as I did not dare use the coins my father hid. At the time I didn't know what I would have to do with it, didn't know I might be able to keep it."

Guilt joined the pain of a moment ago. "I am sorry. Perhaps I should have taken that also. I could have held it for you."

Miss Tessa sighed. "Well, it's too late. His search didn't miss much." Her eyes glittered, and Blake knew she had just opened them. "That is why I was so glad for this job. Madame promised a bonus for the extra hours."

He smiled. Madame was about to get a bigger bonus than she expected. No doubt the woman would keep a good deal of it and well deserved, but he could specify the amount to go to 'the seamstress for her extra hours.' Madame struck him as a woman of compassion, and he was certain Tessa would get every cent of the extra.

What a pity that the bonus had to be kept within the limits of propriety. He did not know how much the footpad had stolen, but no doubt it was a healthy sum.

The carriage rattled to a stop. Blake stood and opened the ceiling panel. "Are we there?"

"Yes, me lord. We be at the address ye gave me." The driver leaned back, and hissed, "Ah'd get yer gun out and ready, if ye take me meanin'."

"Understood." Blake lowered his voice, although he suspected Tessa could hear every word. "Is it safe for the lady to walk to her house?"

In an even quieter voice, one that could not carry into the bottom of the carriage, his driver answered, "Iffen she knows 'er way about, ah'm sure she can make it 'ome safely."

"Thank you. Keep your gun at the ready until she is out of sight, will you?"

"Already got it out, sir." The man sounded entirely too cheerful, Blake thought.

"You stay up there and watch. I will be back as soon as possible."

A half-shriek came from behind him. "What! You aren't getting out, are you? Are you mad?"

She had clearly forgotten who was who in this vehicle. Blake latched the ceiling opening, and turned to face her. "You don't think I am the kind of man who leaves a young woman to walk about London unattended, do you?" He was hunched over in the cramped space of the carriage, wedged between the ceiling overhead and the seat behind, but it left him looming over her. "Are you getting out, or not?"

Tessa folded her arms. "Not."

"Ah. I thought as much." He remained up, or as upright as the ceiling would allow. "Are you going to give me the true directions?"

She gave in with poor grace, and a huff. "Fine! It is back that way." She unfolded her arms and pointed over her shoulder. "Go back to Madame's."

Blake bowed his head. "Thank you." He opened the panel again. "Madame Genevieve's."

"We're makin' quite a trip of it t'nite, me lord. Gonna be almost mornin' afore ye be in bed again."

"Just turn back around." Blake latched the opening and sat down. At least she had not sent them too far out of the way. He was certain if he lit the lamps, she would be scowling. Let her. He felt a bit like scowling himself.

* * *

The carriage eased around on the street, and they started back. Her nerves grew tighter. It seemed she had lived with stress this whole night, in a house she did not know, among people who lived so far above her, and now she longed for rest. Which she would not get, with them driving her straight to the hornet's nest.

What did the man not understand about the area being dangerous? Did he *want* to be shot? "Are you *trying* to get killed tonight?"

"Well, now, that's an interesting question, isn't it? Do you try to get shot when you work this late?"

"First of all, I seldom work this late, and when I do, Madame will let us sleep in the store. *She* has good sense." That was probably not the ideal way to speak to a lord.

"And I do not?" There was a smile in his voice.

"Not if you think you can drive any vehicle around my neighborhood and stay safe!" She heard him take a breath, and guessed what he was about to say. "Do not tell me again how you picked the oldest coach! That might help, but a carriage is a carriage. They are a rare thing where I live, and someone is always on the watch! Not only are you in danger, but you are putting me in danger, too!"

The night she had to cock her father's pistol was all too vivid in her mind. All she could hope was that Herb and his helpers were elsewhere, threatening other Londoners.

Not that she wished ill on anyone else.

Warrenby leaned forward, unaffected by the rocking of the carriage, and took her hands. They were cold, she could tell from the warmth flooding into them from his gentle hold. "I am only going to make sure you get in safely. That can hardly hurt."

"Dressed like that?" She waved at his evening clothes.

He sat back. "Very well. I will send my driver. Will that help? He certainly doesn't look out of place. People will think you took a hackney cab. They were old family carriages before they became cabs, anyway. If anyone asks, you can tell them that Madame paid the driver to make sure you got in safely. Will that be better? I can keep my word to Madame and my mother, and sleep tonight knowing you didn't get attacked by footpads on the way home."

When she turned his new offer over in her mind, she couldn't find any flaws. He was correct about the coachman. He looked exactly what he was; a member of the working class just like everyone else on the block.

Warrenby had been ahead of her *again.*

She sighed. "Very well, yes." Hard as it was to admit.

They drove to Madame's, dark for the night, then turned right, down the narrow side street. Tessa was grateful for the chance to look out the window and give directions, rather than feel his eyes on her, piercing the shadows of the carriage.

Which could not fit in the cramped opening of her little alcove. The driver pulled up, and climbed off. Warrenby must have known he dared not open the door, lest anyone might be watching, so he waited for it to be opened from the outside. He handed the basket over, and she thought she saw him bow his head, one smooth dip.

Tessa stepped out, and caught herself looking back.

"Turn around and start walking," he hissed, barely audible.

So she did. The driver knew his instructions, and fell in beside her. He didn't touch his weapon, but Tessa knew his hand was never far away from the handle, and he could have it out in a second.

They didn't have far to walk, her stairs stopped just out of view. At the foot, she turned around. "Thank you. You should go back, and be sure he is safe now."

"Naw, them weren't my instructions. I was to see you got all the way inside."

The stairs stretched up, dark and looming, but familiar. In the distance, a dog barked warning. The summer air had a gentle bite of cold, reminder of the big ocean so close. Tessa had gone only a few steps when something rustled, and the night went still again. A rat, or a perhaps cat.

And then the sound gave a frightened whimper.

Whoever it was probably would not come out with a big man nearby. She knew enough about how the rings worked, using children for virtual slaves and keeping them under control with intimidation, so pretended she did not hear, just continued up the stairs and prayed the child would be there after the man was gone.

Tessa unlocked the door, waved at the driver, and stepped inside just long enough to set her basket down and shut the door again behind her, but lightly. The work shoes had to come off, they would make too much noise and alarm the runaway. She counted as she bent over and unlaced as quickly as she ever had.

"One, two, three, four, five." That should give the driver time to get back to the carriage. Easing the door open, she peeked outside. Sure enough, he was gone. There was no time to lock the door behind her, but she would only be at the bottom of the steps.

In her stocking feet, Tessa eased down the stairs.

CHAPTER 12

In this area, there were all kinds of reasons that could cause a whimper, most of which she could do nothing about. But this sounded like a child crying for help, terrified and alone. And probably cold. Likely hungry. The street children were always hungry.

For all Tessa knew, it might be one of Herb's latest victims, some young one sold to him for the money he gave the parents. Or a street urchin he had taken a shine to, and decided to groom for a life of crime.

Almost at the foot of the stairs, she stopped. This was about where she first heard the plaintive noise. With slow moves, she eased herself onto the step and waited for the sound to recur. No whimper, no shifting of a foot.

She did not move, just remained in place. A frightened child might do anything to give himelf away, if only to shift a foot, or tilt a head, *something*.

Moonlight, weak down here in the tight spaces between the narrow houses, found the small head hidden under the rickety stairs running along the outside of the building across from her, heading up to the equally cheap rooms overhead. Blond hair—it seemed to be blond—gave a single shimmer, aided by curls that reflected that little gift of light. One shimmer, and then gone, the child had not moved more than a twitch of the head, but it was enough.

She kept her voice soft, just in case the search was on and close. Even more, she knew what this one might have already suffered, how frightened he must be to take this drastic step, but she had to win his confidence first. "Don't be afraid. I won't hurt you, I promise. Please come out. There's no one here but me, and I will do everything I can to help." *Please, oh please, come out*, she prayed.

The shimmer of hair shifted again. A child too young to realize that the faint moon was *her* friend right now, not his. He would need tenderness and kindness, both of which she longed to give him. She wanted to wrap him in her arms and erase the memories. If only she could lure him out . . .

Tessa whispered the words again. "I want to help. You will be safe with me, I promise." No matter how long it took, she was not going to leave him—or her—behind.

Especially not with Herb around. If he was not the villain who had owned this little one, he would be more than happy to step in and take over. She had seen what he did with the children he used, how he turned them one after another into thieves and pickpockets, probably even worse.

Finally a little voice, wet with tears, asked, "How can I know I can twust you?"

That stumped her for a moment. "Well, I just got home, I've been working all day, I have to get up soon and go back and work some more, and instead of being in bed asleep, I'm out here trying to help you."

With a rush, the child popped out of concealment and raced across the opening toward her. Tessa didn't even have time to rise when the boy—it seemed like a boy, he was dressed in rough breeches, although that might not mean anything—nearly knocked her over as he rushed up the stairs.

She folded him in her arms, praying he didn't have lice or anything she might carry to Madame's and spread across the shop, and struggled to her feet. "You have to let go long enough for me to get up, dear," she whispered, and the boy managed to release her, but never let go of her skirt.

Once upright, Tessa wrapped one arm around him, and lifting her skirts to climb the stairs with the other, she got them up to her door, and inside. Safe from eyes and ears, she locked the door and wished again that it was more secure. Blast Herb and his thievery!

Then she leaned against it as she caught her breath and tried to think. She looked down at the dirty blond hair pressed tight against her skirt. Unless it was brown and just covered with ash or dust. Either way, she would have to sponge her dress off before she went to work.

Much as she hated to bring up the ugliness, she asked, "Why were you hiding under the stairs? Don't you have a place to sleep?"

The head shook vigorously, rubbing more of whatever was on it onto her skirts. "I want to find my mothew, and the bad men took me away, and I don't know how to get home, and I'm scawed!" A sob tore out of the child, and was quickly hidden.

Bad men took me away. Tessa stared down in horror. Was this a kidnapped child? England was reportedly full of them, but most turned out to be poor, unfortunate children whose parents had sold them to traders for the coin. No child wanted to believe their mother or father could be guilty of such a foul deed, as she was in a position to know. Much better to blame the men who made their lives a misery. Those same children were doomed to a life of drudgery at best, likely even dragged into crime.

But if she could save even one? Tessa did not know how she could support a child on her income, but . . . she could not let whoever was after this sweet boy get him back.

Her arms held him tight while her heart bled. If only she had some food! She could feel the delicate bones under the ragged clothes, and the rich meal she had just eaten tormented her. If she had just slipped one pastry into her basket! But she had not, and she had nothing but the pitcher of water that held her wash water, the old teapot on the cold coal burner, and her cup.

She would try, anyway. "Are you thirsty?"

"I'm hungwy."

"Oh, sweetheart. I wish I had some food for you. I will get you something in the morning."

"Pwomise?"

She was making progress, Tessa thought, and that brave little request hurt her heart.

An idea formed. Warrenby's mother had young servants in her house, probably the same age as this one. To work in a place where there were good meals and a warm place to sleep—or at least warmer than normal—had to be better than the child was used to.

"I will keep you safe tonight, and tomorrow—today—I promise I'll find someplace for you to live. And you will be even safer than my room."

She still could not tell if they were a boy or a girl, but they had dirty, wildly tousled hair, and features that promised to grow into at least reasonably presentable looks. Perhaps if a boy, he might be able to be a footman, or something even better.

"Right now we both need sleep. I'm going to make a bed for you on the floor with my blanket, and I'll just stay in my clothes." Never having slept in a corset, she expected she was in for a miserable night, but she could hardly undress in front of a little boy. Much as it hurt to admit, she could not risk him spreading lice into her bed. The blankets would have to be washed before they were used again, as well.

Stifling a sigh, Tessa pried the boy from herself, and made him wait while she piled her meager covers into a sort of bed. He clung to the bedstead as he watched. How much he could see with it so dark, she did not know, but even her shadow seemed to comfort him. "Take off your shoes, dear."

He pulled them off with a bit of a struggle, not attempting to unlace them. It appeared what was left of the laces was more knots than string. The shoes looked worn, with broken-down sides, a hole starting in the sole of one of them. Whatever color they had been was long gone. Now a dingy grey-brown, it was impossible to tell what was dirt and what was the remnant of dye. Worse, they were too small, she could tell the moment they came off.

One of his hands must have been broken. The little finger on his left hand was bent. Anger built, bringing with it renewed determination. "Did someone hit your hand?"

He looked down at his hands, and turned them over, then back. "Sometimes they did."

"Did they break your fingers?"

He rubbed his dirty curls against the post, probably trying to shake it *no*. "They mostly kicked me, and thumped my head."

The flash of relief that he hadn't had anything broken vanished at the rest of the tale. No matter what, she would not return him to whoever had him before. She did not care how much this boy's mother had been paid! Tessa took a deep breath. "Then what happened to your finger?"

"My mothew said it bwoke when I was bownded."

Born? A broken finger at birth? Tessa had never heard such a thing, but at least it was not a new injury from abuse. The rage eased a little, enough for her to be able to smile and point at the rough bed on the floor. "In you go."

He scrambled onto the pile of covers, and she flipped the edges over him. This would be the night to light the stove if she had any coal. She did not, so she could only hope he would stay warm.

"Thank you. G'night."

Tessa straightened in surprise. She had never heard a street child with manners. Her eyes narrowed. Come to think of it, his speech had been out of the ordinary, also.

Bad men took me away. I want to find my mothew.

England was a big place. The chances of finding this poor child's parents was slim. If they even wanted him back.

Which brought her back to Warrenby. As she stretched out on her bed, bare now but for a single sheet, and tried to ignore the tightness of her corset, Tessa gave in to a single tingle of excitement. Warrenby had said he would check on her tomorrow. It might be something a man of his lofty position would tell a poor servant girl, but she believed him. He had kept his word before.

When he came, she had a legitimate reason to talk to him now.

* * *

The door opened right on cue as Blake was dropped off in front of his own house. Had his staff stayed up, hoping he would get home in time for them to get a decent night of sleep? He had never wondered such a thing before, but Miss Abbott had put the thought in his mind.

He turned to the coachman before the man could drive away. "Get some rest. You deserve it."

He made it through the door, and gave the footman the same instructions he had given his driver. Tessa was having quite an effect on him, he thought.

His valet was fast asleep sitting upright in the chair at the foot of his bed, his head bent at an appalling angle on his chest. The poor man bolted to his feet at the whisper of the latch home, teetered, and plopped back down, almost missing the seat. Blake grabbed for him, and caught him just as the dazed man began to lose his balance.

He had tied—and untied—enough cravats in his life to know how to do it without any help whatsoever. He tugged at his cravat, and the fancy bow came loose. Then he started in on the buttons of his vest.

A loud yawn interrupted him in the middle of the third button.

"Oh, no, sir! That's my job, my lord." The valet was back on his feet, and this time he seemed to be able to stand on his own. He hurried over and reached for the last buttons. "I'm sorry I wasn't ready fer ya. I din't mean to fall asleep."

Blake brushed his hands away. "You go to bed, now. I'm perfectly capable of getting myself undressed. I didn't expect you to be up."

"It ain't a problem. I caught me a few winks last night after I finished pressin' yer shirts." He pulled himself up to his full height, which nearly matched Blake's own. It came in handy when tying the cravat in some knot Blake had never deciphered, but that impressed all his friends. "More'n a few, if I'm honest."

He went back to his unbuttoning, and eased the vest off from behind. "Got to be careful o' such finery. The stitches might pop, and that's the end of such a 'laborate piece."

Blake grinned at him. "I'd say I could always order another." He sobered, the months in France having taught him a bit about economy. "Like you, I dislike waste. Very well, if my clothes need your skilled care, I am willing to submit."

A thought hit him, the night's threat, and so much time recently spent in the company of Miss Tessa Abbott. "Jasper, who taught you? I approved of your recommendations, but we have never talked, the two of us. I don't even know if you have family still alive."

His valet stopped folding his vest, and turned. "I dint like to get too familiar, or bother you with idle chatter."

"And if I say I'm really interested?" He was, and that surprised him. Tessa Abbott must be having an impact, forcing him to look outside his own group. What the war had started, she seemed to be completing.

Maybe his friends knew their valets better than he had known Jasper, although he suspected Addersley was the type to pry information out of his servants without them ever guessing they had been quizzed.

He allowed himself a little leeway, since he had been off in France for some time. Most of his staff was new, and his work had forced him to keep secrets. Even relaxing his guard this much sent prickles of alarm down his skin.

This was not the war, he repeated in his mind, before turning his attention to his valet.

"Weel, then, my lord, you be—you *are,*" the man corrected himself, "in for a boring tale." Jasper slid his hands under the collar and began the process of removing Blake's evening coat, lifting it up a bit to get it over the shoulders. "Me—my—dad was a tailor. He knew clothes well, and I helped him from the time I were a little boy." The coat went on a hook in his mahogany armoire right away. "I was taught pressing and sponging off stains."

Jasper's voice was soothing, and Blake found himself relaxing after the night. No wonder he never had trouble sleeping, he thought. In addition to the man's skills with dressing, somewhere along the line he had been taught the talent of being a calming force.

CHAPTER 13

The sun's first rays glared through the curtain's gap and washed across her eyelids, jolting her awake. Tessa struggled to her elbows. It couldn't be morning yet! She had just gone to sleep!

Well, the new day was here. She struggled out of bed, her body slow to move. Exhaustion pulled at her, another reason to get up. If she stayed abed, she would surely fall back to sleep.

There was something heavy that needed her attention and greatest care, a weight that had followed her into her sleep, causing dreams of running and hiding, something at her side that she had guarded even in her dreams.

A sound in the room startled her. She whipped around, and was startled to see big blue eyes under that mop of hair staring over the top of her bed at her.

"Oh, good." The words were barely breathed into the air. "I was afwaid I dweamed you, and I was back with the bad man."

The child! That was who she worried about during the night. He was here, and for the moment safe. Tessa managed a smile past the shakiness of relief. "No. I'm real, but unfortunately, my day starts early and I have to hurry to get to work on time."

"Are you taking me with you? You pwomised last night." Those young eyes held both hope and fear.

"You certainly are coming with me, which means we both need to get washed up and dressed. The first thing we have to do with you is clean that hair. Madame—the woman I work for—will not let dirty hair in her shop." Tessa leaned forward, hands on her bed. "I hate to tell you this, my sweet child, but you are very dirty."

"I know." He ducked his head. "My mothew would never let me get this diwty."

Tessa could not think of anything to say to that. If he had been sold deliberately for the money as so many children were, his mother would not be happy to see him again. Whatever cash she had received was certainly spent, and there would be no way to repay the broker.

But parents desperate enough to sell him for coin were not the kind able to keep their children clean.

The quandary would not be solved today. She turned back to the low chest of drawers where she kept her pitcher of water. Thank goodness she had filled it up . . . was it yesterday? It was still quite full.

“Come over here, let’s get you a drink first, and we’ll get started on your hair.”

The little boy came around the bed and stopped close to her. “How can you wash my hair? You don’t have a tub.” He accepted the cup and drank greedily while she absorbed his words.

A tub. He was used to a tub. She dared not read too much into that. It could mean anything, not necessarily that he had parents with enough money to invest in proper tubs, and wanted to keep him clean. A tub could even mean a big bucket on the floor, or a trough that filled during the rains.

But it did not sound like that was what he said.

“You’re right, I don’t. But I do have a bowl, a pitcher with water, and soap. We will just make do with what we have, shall we?” Scoop of soap in her hand, she set the bowl on the floor, and pointed at it. “If you crouch down and bend over that, I will wash the water off your hair into it. We’ll have you clean in no time.”

The floor was nearly as wet as that bowl, but when she was done, she had learned a few things. First of all, his hair was not curly as she had thought, but instead covered with cowlicks that sent it in different directions. Second, His name was Robert. He even knew his last name, but with that impediment, Tessa wasn’t certain she had it right. It sounded like “Pauwmintew.” An odd last name, but then, whose wasn’t?

Third, It was amazing how badly a little boy could smell. He was not pristine yet but he looked at least passable, and smelled a whole lot better once the worst bits were washed off.

Lastly, his poor body was thinner than it had even felt last night, and sported bruises of all ages, from the dark blue of fresh ones to fading yellow of the older ones. Tessa bit her lip to hide the trembling, and forced herself not to gather him tight.

She had no other clothes for him, but dumped his dirty water out the window, swishing the bowl as clean as she could get it for herself. The clothes were shaken out the window next, pounded as clean as she could get them, shake, pound, turn, shake, pound. Hope nobody saw the small garments and made the connection.

Then it was her turn. Now they were really short on time, so Tessa made her cleaning the fastest she had ever done. Just a wet cloth over face and neck, a few other places she could get at without disrobing, once over on any spots on her gown that needed it with the cloth, and she was done.

The hardest part came when she had to make him put on those awful shoes. Poor child. They should be replaced and soon, before his toes grew out the front. Sadly, she had no money to replace them.

Tessa dug for a few of her pence, the only things not worth Herb's attention, and turned to grab Robert's hand. He was going to need real food, not just bread. "I'm going to buy meat pies from a seller on the way to work. I will get two, but only if"—she held up a finger—"You can eat the whole thing."

He nodded so hard she thought his head might fall off if it were not on so tight.

Using a moment they could not spare, she crouched down and took both his little hands. Beneath her fingers, she felt the callouses. Hard as her life had been on occasion, it had never held this kind of distress. "We have to move fast, and be quiet. Can you do that?"

He nodded again, this time slow. His blue eyes were wide, and full of fear.

How she wanted that look to go away!

She took a deep breath. Herb always seemed to pop up when least expected. While she did not know he was the one who had kept Robert, he knew everyone in the business of crime.

Heart in throat, Tessa turned the lock. "We're going out now. You try to keep between me and the door, and I will reach around you. On the way down, stay close to the wall. That way, anyone watching will see me first."

Every movement, the locking of the door, the quick journey down the stairs, was accomplished with a minimum of trouble. Robert had learned somewhere along the line to make himself nearly invisible.

Her work shoes caused the most problem. Moving silently in heavy-soled shoes was impossible. All she could do was keep going.

Turning the corner of her building into the street, the same place where Warrenby had dropped her off last night, her heart thumped in fierce warning. Despite the dimness, despite the shadows, no one waited.

She scurried him across the gap and onto the walkway of the other side. It was better to be on the same side as the shop early than to have to cross where traffic might carry more than the city's shoppers.

He and his gang would hopefully be asleep after their night of crime, but Tessa could not count on that.

They hurried down the narrow street, pausing at the end of the block, looking down the pathways and alleys before dashing across, to hurry down the relative security of those buildings before repeating the frightening crossing at the next intersection. Dirty rags caught in the faint breeze and rolled about, scraps of stained papers used for who knew what crackled underfoot. The street stank worse than usual, but perhaps that was from the heavy summer air. Some days it felt like the fog of London held every odor trapped against the ground, and this was one of those days, even though the sun had begun to pierce the grey layer.

As they neared the shopping district, closing in on Madame's, newsboys were everywhere, waving papers and yelling, "News! Reward! Kidnapped boy!"

The call of "reward" caught her attention. When one of the boys ran up and shoved a paper in her hand, she took it awkwardly, trying to hold it with the same hand that held her basket rather than let go of Robert.

Before she could ask the price, the boy ran off.

No charge? This wasn't unheard of, it did happen on occasion, but most of the time the news cost a pence. Tessa clung to the paper and her basket, and tugged Robert along. They were so close to safety.

The street seller she was looking for was right where she hoped to find him, and she stopped to get one for each. Keeping an eagle eye out, she let him unwrap the paper and take a few bites before she knelt down. To make such a hungry child have to stop eating, even if only for a few minutes, hurt but she thought she saw some shapes skulk between the buildings across the busy street ahead. "We need to get out of sight. We are safer here than we were, but I still want you where no one can see you. You can finish it in a few minutes."

Tessa made a little pouch with the curious notice and tucked her own meat pie in this improvised holder under the handle of her basket where she could them all in one awkward grip. His one hand clutched tight, the other just as tight in hers, one last dash across one last intersection, and they were at Madame's back door. She pulled the key out from the chain where it dangled inside her gown, set her basket down on the ground, and shoved the meat pie and paper package at Robert. "Here. Hold this for me, will you, please?"

The key went in harder than usual, but it had to be her own hurry.

The lock gave and she wrenched the latch, slipping them inside. Silence came from the shop beyond the curtain, so she took advantage of their privacy to sit him down on the floor. "Here, dear, you finish your pie, and I'll eat mine, and then we'll wipe off our hands so we don't stain the fabrics here."

He didn't need a second urging, just thumped down and took another bite. She sat down in her chair and unwrapped her own meat pie. Just as she was about to take a bite, a small voice came from beside her, filled with excitement. "Tessa! Tessa! I think this is me!" He shoved the crumpled, stained paper into her hand. "Look! I think that looks like me."

Tessa took it, and tried to rub it smooth, but before she could even glance at what she held, the door opened again, and Madame scurried in. "*Ah, parfait*! *Vous êtes* here already. We need to go over *les commandes* from yesterday, and see what needs *être fini en premier.* We have someone new *qui arrive ici* at ten, so I would like whatever project you were working on to be"—she broke off as she seemed to see Robert for the first time. "*Qui est-ce?* You know I don't allow *les enfants ici.*"

Madame's gaze pierced Tessa, and went back to Robert. "This *impossible qu'il soit votre enfant*. So what are you doing bringing such a dirty child *ici, dans ma* clean shop? And food? Tessa!"

Robert shrank back against the wall. His hair and face looked so much better, cleaner, than he had when Tessa first found him, but there had been no way to wash his clothes. Even if they had been cleaned, nothing could hide the wear.

"He ran away from whoever had him. I cannot send him back. He has been badly treated." She rose, and stepped closer to Madame, hoping once more that no vermin had crawled from the boy to herself during the night. "Can I talk to you in private?"

Madame gave Robert a narrow look, and with one sharp nod, led the way out of the back room. Before she stepped through that door, Tessa pointed to Robert, who was trying to meld into the wall. "You stay here, Robert. I'll be right back. And please don't touch anything, As long as you are in here, you are safe."

That seemed to make up his mind, because he gave a nod. The tension that had turned him stiff and rigid, far too much for a child his age, eased.

They barely made it into the store proper when Madame turned on her. "He ran away?"

Tessa nodded. "He is so terrified, I know whatever frightened him is real. I found him hiding under the stairs by my room, shaking like a leaf. Whoever he ran away from, they must have hurt him badly. I cannot let him be taken back."

"*Pauvre enfant.*" Madame sighed. "You know he must be bathed, *et avoir de* new clothes, *avant* he can be here. I need your *aide*, so find him some clean clothes and give him a good bathe *avant* you come back." She wrinkled her nose. "You should wash your own clothes, too. *Je pense* he is getting you to smell, too."

Heat rushed up Tessa's face. "Yes, Madame. I will return as soon as possible."

She nodded, then hurried out of the room, afraid of what she might find when she returned to the workroom.

But Robert was still there, in fact, it looked as if he had not moved a single muscle. When he saw her, he dropped his pie, an awful sound burst out of his mouth, and he rushed to her just as he had last night. Tessa wrapped her arms around him, and rocked back and forth as best she could with a child his size plastered tight to her.

She tried to ease him away, wondering where she could bathe both of them without having to retrace their steps to her own room again. "Robert, we have to go wash up." She crouched down. "I think I know of a place where I can get used clothing for you, but my gown will need to be sponged off, and you need a bath."

She could not go back to her room, just could not. In the daylight, even if this early? With prying eyes everywhere, as her neighbors began their own days? She could hear them now, *Did you know Tessa is walking around with a little boy?*

No doubt many of the neighbors were in Herb's pocket.

The back door opened, and Ellen walked in. The observant girl spotted him instantly. "Tessa! Yes?" Then she shook her head. "Not likely, is it? Yer too young. So where did ye find 'im?" Her nose wrinkled. "Iffen ye don't mind me sayin' so, 'e needs a bath."

Tessa's eyes went wide, she felt it and couldn't stop the reaction. Her answer might be staring her right in the face. "How far away do you live? Will your mother object if I take him to your house and bathe him there? I think there is a rag man living around here. I can pay your mother a coin for his bath, and a sponge to clean off my gown."

Ellen smiled. "A coin'd be nice, though me mum would 'ate to make ye pay to bathe a child."

Madame might be willing to give her an advance on her pay, if it meant Robert would be clean. Warrenby had said she would be paid extra for the work, or perhaps that was his mother. Either way, money would be coming.

All she could do, Tessa thought, was ask. "Can you watch him for me? I need to ask Madame for a favor." No doubt Ellen assumed Robert was still a secret from their employer.

"Ye can count on me. I won't breathe a word."

Madame was only too willing to lend the money for Robert's bath and the rag man, once she knew what the request was for. "If he's to stay even *un jour*, he can't smell like he does. Even in better clothes, he has to stay in that back room. He better not be here tomorrow. Find a place for him now, *vous m'entendez?* You hurry back. And send Ellen *dès qu'elle arrive ici*. We have several projects *à terminer* before someone thinks to come collect them *un jour plus tôt*."

They went into the workroom, and Madame dug through the box in her small desk for some coins. Five pence and hastily scrawled directions to Ellen's home clutched in her hand, Tessa reached for Robert and scurried them both out the door. He clutched the meat pie, biting off mouthfuls, eating as they went.

Ellen's mother refused even a single coin for Robert's bath, just like Ellen said. She also saved them a trip to the rag man's house. "I 'ave some outgrown things from me boys. Ye can 'ave some britches and a shirt for 'im."

Robert still clung to that bit of paper. "Will you hold this fow me?"

"Of course I will. In you go, now."

While Ellen's mother, whose name, Tessa learned, was Mary, refused money for the bath, she did accept a few pence for the clothes. They were in surprisingly good shape, although mended in places, and best of all, they didn't stink.

Mary also agreed to burn Robert's old rags. "They ain't good enough even for the rag man."

Robert's eyes went large as they talked about what to do with his clothes, but he didn't start to cry until the ragged bits were taken away. Tessa crouched down beside the tub. "Why? Robert, they are worn out."

"They wewe the ones Mothew put me in that mowrning."

"Oh, honey." Poor child. Whatever the reason for him being sold to whoever owned him, he truly loved his mother. "Robert, the men who are looking for you will watch for those clothes. If you wear something else, they will have a harder time recognizing you."

He rubbed the tears away, and nodded. "My mothew will give me new clothes when I go back." Then he pointed at the piece of paper Tessa held. "Please wead that? It looks like me."

"You finish washing, and I will read it." Tessa waited for him to pick up the squishy soap, and then spread the paper out on the dry floor.

This was the announcement the news boys had been shouting about. A few words jumped out at her right away. "Cowlicks." And "bent little finger on left hand." She stared at the sketch again, picked the paper up and held it close. The face looked like a good number of little boys running about. The hair, though, was exactly like Robert's. She glanced at him, wet hair exactly like this morning, sticking up all over. Just like the picture, and the description. Because of cowlicks.

That little finger, though. He said his mother told him the finger happened when he was born.

She looked at the title in large letters. REWARD. Then looked at Robert. Then read the name of the missing and abducted child. Her struggle deciphering his last name this morning made sense. Not 'Pauwmintew,' but . . . "Robert Parminter? Is that your name?"

He blew out a bubble of soap that had somehow gotten into his mouth. "Yeth," he said, and blew another bubble out. "I alweady told you that."

"Robert, you were right, this *is* you! Your grandfather is looking for you."

Robert's eyes grew as big as a little boy's could, then filled with tears. "I knewed he would find me!"

"We have to bring you to him. Until I can leave, you will have to stay with me, and be very quiet. Can you do that?"

"Why can't we go now?"

Much as she hated to worry him again, Tessa had to keep him safe. The weight of her responsibility sent shivers down her spine, and raised the hairs on her arms. "Robert, I have to finish my work day. I promise we will go as quickly as we can."

Tessa looked at the amount of the reward, and her head began to spin. Five hundred pounds! She did not know exactly how much money Herb had stolen from her, but it might not have been this large. *Deep breaths*, she told herself. *Deep breaths*. Five hundred pounds would go a very long way.

A new place to live, certainly.

For the first time since her father died, maybe the first time since her mother died, Tessa started to feel hope.

CHAPTER 14

Blake helped his mother out of the carriage. He would have done the same for his sister, but she bounded out before he could catch her hand, and turned around to grin at him. "Thank you for escorting us, Blake. I'm so excited to see how my trousseau is coming. I simply have to tell them about the few changes I want." She scurried past him and pulled open the shop's door.

"Yes, I know," he said to her back, and it was hardly a 'few,' they were all she talked about on the trip, but she was already inside.

He exchanged a look with his mother. "I assume you will permit me the honors?"

"She is so excited." His mother chuckled. "I remember when I felt that way. I do believe I was more discreet about it, however."

Blake ushered his mother in, and followed her. The note from his mother had been more than welcome. After all, he had promised to make certain Tes—Miss Abbott was well after the late night.

When the door shut behind him, closing off the rattle of carriage wheels and streets shouts, carriage drivers cursing other carriage drivers or cursing the people crossing the street too close who made them have to pull their carriages up too quickly, he was met by the usual hum of women gossiping and tearing apart the latest fashions. The sound of his name pulled him up short. An elderly woman, one he recognized but whose own name eluded him at the moment, spoke loud and clear. "I talked to the woman Warrenby had hired for repairs. She said that he brings his mother and sister here. I was most impressed with their gowns."

Blake smothered a smile. It was nice to hear even the garments they wore being praised. He wished he dared pause and eavesdrop, but he had a debt to pay.

The woman who had just been speaking must have been told of his presence because she turned, rose, and came over. He gave a quick bow.

"Lord Warrenby, your sister's ball was a pleasure. I only hope this shop does as good a job on the complete gown as that person did on repairs. I am most dissatisfied with my current modiste."

He feared she was the kind to be most dissatisfied with many tradespeople.

One of the fitting room doors opened up, and Tessa walked out. A funny pang zipped through his chest, and he smiled before he caught himself, covering it with a bow.

As she drew near, he saw the dark circles under her eyes, and the pale cast to her skin, accented by the starkness of the black gown she wore. He needed to ask why she was pale, and whether she had managed to get sleep, if she needed a day off so she could rest.

And on that day off, he wanted to take her into Hyde Park, where she could sit and let the fresh breeze wash over her just to replenish herself, instead of breathe the heavy London air that hung over the city today.

Which surprised him as much as the need he had felt to see her when he first walked into the shop.

He had seen her, and if she was wan and tired, at least she was here.

Emmy caught her skirt as she walked past. "I would like to see some other ribbons for the pink gown, Tessa. I am not at all certain I still like the one I selected."

"Yes, Lady Emilia."

Tessa. Somehow his sister had learned her name, and now used it with an easy comfort that gave him a twinge of jealousy. He had already arranged for his man of affairs to send the extra payment to Madame. The bank draft had probably already been delivered.

Tessa walked past him, presumably on her way to get the ribbons his sister had requested, and he distinctly heard a whisper. "Lord Warrenby? Can I meet you behind the shop in a minute?"

What an odd request. But he would do it. No one would think anything of him leaving. Staying all afternoon, however, would cause comment. He whispered back. "Yes." And went to his mother to tell her he would be leaving. "If I take the carriage home and send it back, will you be able to stay occupied until it gets back?"

Lady Warrenby barely glanced up. "Certainly. There was no real need for you to escort Emmy, but it was good of you to do so. I will send it back when we get home ourselves."

He slipped around the back, to find her pacing outside the small door.

"Oh, good." She heaved a sigh that almost reached him. "I am so sorry to impose on you this way, but I need information.How do I get to Herford Street?"

He pulled back, recognizing the street immediately. "What? Why do you want to know?"

In an excited voice, rushed and urgent, she said, "I found the boy everyone is looking for, and according to the notice, he is supposed to go to a house on that street to meet his grandfather. I'm going to take him there after I get done."

Warrenby's heart sank. He had been with Mundy six times already, looking at little boys, and even one girl dressed as a boy, all being passed off as the missing grandson. Several had broken little fingers, one even on the wrong hand, breaks that would never heal properly. Children suffering for want of the reward.

How did he tell her that? He had no wish to shatter her hopes. All he could do was make sure he was there to give her comfort when she got the crushing news. He could even come here and take her and this child she had found there himself. It wouldn't hurt to get a look at whoever she had.

Since he did not know when her day was done, he said, "Hackneys run up and down the nearby streets all the time. I'm certain the driver can give you directions from the stop."

He did not know if that was true, but it wasn't going to matter, because he had every intention on getting here in time.

"Thank you," she said, and slipped back inside.

Blake looked at the closed door, turned and walked back around the buildings, keeping alert. It was broad daylight, and he was only on the other side of that busy street, but London was London and pickpockets lurked everywhere.

Settled in the carriage, he thought over his plan. As long as he kept his eye on the clock, he could catch up with her before she left the shop.

* * *

The horses clipped down the street, his well-sprung coach smoothing out the ride. No doubt his friends were already on the way to his house. For bored young men, and he still considered himself young, the challenge proved particularly intriguing.

His mind slipped back to the gems. He had gone with his father once to watch a necklace be made, an anniversary gift for his mother. His father and the jeweler had looked at a tray of rubies, sliding them from side to side in a small box, picking one up to scrutinize it over a candle, put it back, only to do the same with the next. They had all looked the same to him, and when he said so, his father replied, "Come look for yourself, son."

Kneeling on a chair, he had leaned over the box of gems. The jeweler explained the vague gradations in color, mixed a small collection together, and let him separate them without help. It had not taken long to see the slight differences. When he was done, he had shoved the box back and watched with a hitch in his breath while the man looked over his work. "Well done, young sir." Then nodded to his father. "You have a bright one there, my lord."

The memory made him smile, even past the pang in his heart. How lucky he was, to have the father he had.

He pulled his watch out of his vest pocket, and checked the time. It would be after two when he got home.

When he strode into the house, they were all milling about the foyer, either just arrived or waiting for him. All three.

"Good timing." He grinned at his friends. "Or wouldn't Hodgins lead you in?"

Gillem grinned back, his black eyes dancing. "Hodgins likes me. I'm sure he would have taken us right in had you not appeared just now. I was just about to knock when I saw Haversham trotting down the street."

Blake felt his mouth twitch as he fought the smile. "Haversham trotting? That must have been quite a sight."

Haversham gave a bark of laughter.

Gillem punched Blake in the arm. "Fine! Not Haversham. His horse."

"Precise speech, my man. Precise speech." He looked past them at Hodgins, standing there looking stoic. "Bring us a bite from the kitchen, will you?"

"Right away, sir."

"Anything new on the hunt for Mundy's grandson?" Addersley settled himself in one of the chairs.

"Nothing." He would not bring up Tessa. What was the point?

"Poor man." Addersley shook his head. "It is a faint hope at the best, anyway, but at least we tried."

Eating came first, that and talking about which women newly out on the Marriage Mart held promise.

"There is the Anderson chit. Barely eighteen, but at least she seems to have a brain in her head." Haversham chewed and seemed to think while the merits of the Anderson chit were discussed.

"She's got dark hair and eyes. Must be Welsh there." Addersley stared at his plate in his usual thoughtful way, as if debating what to eat next.

Just like that, Blake found his mind back in the modiste's shop, and Tessa. What *was* her lineage? And why should it matter? Beautiful, graceful, kind, and intelligent.

And not a childish eighteen. Which to his way of thinking was a distinct advantage.

Haversham seemed to be analyzing the last bits of food on his plate, so when he spoke, it was a bit of a surprise. His subject was not a surprise, however. Right down to business, like everything must be with the weight of his title. Blake watched him, and wondered if that would be him soon, once he grew accustomed to the load of his own responsibilities. "So when do we get to see this jewelry lot you so mysteriously came across? And will we ever find out how that happened?"

Blake shoved his plate aside. "Right now, if you wish. And no, you will never learn how I received them. I gave my word."

"Someone in the *ton* has been robbing us blind? Or were they harboring a servant who abused their kindness?"

"I would say more the latter than the former, but don't pry, David. I trust your discretion, but it is better all around if you know nothing."

Haversham shrugged. "If you say the threat is over, I will accept your judgment. So," he shoved his own plate out of the way, "let us see what you have."

Plates set aside and the bell rung for their collection, Blake unlocked the drawer and pulled out the pouch, spreading the contents out across the desk. He straightened them face up, Haversham helping turn them over, and leaned back. "So, does anything look familiar?"

* * *

The rest of the day crept past, Warrenby's visit providing the lone break in the endless endurance today had become. Despite his promise that he would check on her, it was still amazing that he did come.

Thinking about every word he said, each expression on his face, made it hard to concentrate on her work. Ellen had pinched her several times in passing, 'just to keep her from dreaming foolish dreams.'

They were foolish, Tessa knew that, but keeping them out of her head was impossible. She slipped out to get a pastry for Robert and a bite for herself, leaving him under Ellen's watchful eye, and hurried back.

Measuring women, stitching sleeves, marking hems, passing rejected bolts of fabric from one woman to the next, Tessa worked in a daze of building excitement. Five hundred pounds!

She forced herself to measure each woman twice, because she could not trust her own notes. It did not help matters that her hand shook from time to time. Tessa even broke two pencils, and Madame threatened to take their cost out of her wages. The only times she breathed were the moments in the back room when she could keep Robert under her watchful eye.

After the second visit back there, Madame took her to the side. "Lord Warrenby had offered you *un salaire supplémentaire pour le travail* of last night. I will give you your wages at the end of the day, *si c'est acceptable*?"

Tessa nodded, hanging onto the table to keep her balance. She was so tired! When she thought of the night ahead, exhaustion threatened to overwhelm her. She didn't know how late the hackneys ran, but surely Warrenby's extra wages would certainly pay for the hackney rides, two one direction, one to return. If she had to walk, she feared she would fall asleep on her feet.

Four o'clock came and went, then five. The shop closed at last, but that was not the end of work for them. It only meant that no more orders would come in.

Sleeves and bodices and seams and hems, the needle went in and out until it blurred. Not from speed, she realized, but because her eyes could not focus. Tessa stood and stretched, trying to wake up a little, and looked over at Robert, curled up and asleep on the floor, covered with a remnant of fabric Madame had donated. He knew they would be going to meet his grandfather.

Six o'clock came, six-thirty. Nerves kept her awake now. Five hundred pounds were only moments away. Robert woke several minutes ago, but she did not know what to tell him. What if Madame made her work longer, and they could not make it in time? What if she was wrong, what if Robert was not the right grandson?

He had to be. Poor little Robert just had to be. That bent finger, the hair that went every direction, even the age was right.

At six forty-five, she knew the time exactly because she had been watching the small clock on Madame's desk, her employer came in, pulling the curtain shut behind her. "You said you had a place to take him?" For someone who had not wanted the boy there at all, she had been more than kind and tolerant.

"I think so, yes."

"*Tu devrais* go while there is still *de la lumière. Voici ton salaires supplémentaires.*" She handed over a small pouch, tied at the top.

Tessa tucked the little pouch down the side of her basket. She had no idea how much she had been paid. It wasn't as bulging as the ones her father had hidden in his clothes, but then, this was money she had earned, and she felt no guilt in taking it.

Madame looked at the place in the basket where the coins had been tucked, and back to Tessa. "Warrenby *insisté* you get *le paiement aujourd'hui.*" She looked down at Robert, and a smile tilted her mouth. "You have been *un très bon garçon* today."

The little boy flushed, his cheeks pinkening. It was unlikely he understood her words, but the smile was unmistakable.

"Thank you, Madame." Tessa looked down at her young, so precious charge. If they hurried, they could make it to the nearest hackney stand and get to Mundy's without too much trouble. All she could do was hope no villian in this part of Town was out searching for him.

"Now we have to hurry." Tessa tucked the reward paper with its precious address inside her sewing basket where it could not fall out, pressed the cover tight, and picked the basket up, looping it over her arm. "We can't stop until we get to the hackney stand." She held his gaze for a moment, time they did not have to spare, before taking his hand and hurrying through the crowded workroom, dodging around the leftover bolts of fabric.

At the door, Tessa took a deep breath, hoping that little boy would not sense her fear, and grabbed the big handle. She eased the door open and poked her head out, looking one way, then the other. Clear, nothing there that was unusual, nothing that should not be. Taking Robert's hand, her basket looped over her other arm, she stepped into the alley. "Let's go."

His hand shook in hers, but he knew better than she what dangers lurked out here for him. They hurried to the end of the alley. Tessa did another quick check before bustling them out.

"What'cha got there, Tessa?" Artie's familiar voice stopped her in her tracks.

Robert huddled against her side as she turned around, her chest tight, her stomach burning. He was alone, though, no Herb, not even Bertie, but they would not be far.

"Please let us go, Artie. You can't stop us now, you just *can't.*" She thought of the reward, and mentally bid it farewell. Robert was far more important. “There is a reward for him. You can have it all if you will just let us go.”

“’ow much will ye give me?”

“All five hundred pounds.” It hurt to say that, but she would do anything right now to keep Robert safe.

He seemed to think about it, but then he shook his head and moved closer, casting one furtive look behind him. “Naw, ye kin keep it if ye take me with ye.”

“What?” Tessa asked, half afraid she was imagining things.

“’erb be tellin’ ever’one ’ow he give ye what fer ’bout the money. Ah don’t ’member much about me parents, but from wot I do ‘member, me da niver ’it me mum. Ever.”

Tessa looked at Alfie, and hated the lingering suspicion. “Where do you think we are going? I can’t promise you’ll be safe even there.” Nor that anyone would want to take on someone with Alfie’s background, but she did not tell him that.

“Ah don’t care. Ah jest don’t want ta be ’round ’Erb no more.” Alfie’s chin firmed, his face, which had never taken on the hard look of Herb’s, suddenly went harsh with determination. “Ye ain’t th’ only girl ’e done that to.”

“What about Bertie?” Nerves raced through Tessa, making her so jumpy she felt herself bounding on her feet.

“’E laughed at Herb’s tale. ’E wants ta be jest like ’im, wants ta take over wen ’Erb is gone, but it ain’t gonna be ’im, it’s gonna be Walt.”

Tessa made up her mind. “Come with us, then, but Alfie, you had better not give us away.”

He took Robert’s other hand, and fell into step beside her, his pace almost too fast for the boy. “Niver. Ah ain’t goin’ back.”

She knew where the hackney stand was, but Alfie took them on a couple quick turns, “jest ta be safe,” which made the brief journey a little longer. His eyes were alert and piercing, his head almost on a swivel, as he checked everyone on the street.

The street was busy, filled with carriages and shoppers, men in old-fashioned breeches or the newer pantaloons, boots that might have been polished when they left the house, well-dressed women clomping in their wooden pattens, wearing bonnets of all types. Snug to the head, small-brimmed ones, tall-crowned ones with wide brims and fancy hatpins sparkling with jewels, sheer ones that let the hair show through, straw hats in deference to the warm summer weather. Maids in gowns specifically designed not to overshadow their mistresses followed behind, carrying packages by their strings.

As they hurried along, she was grateful for Alfie on the other side and watching for the recessed doorways of the stores. *We must look like any other poor family,* she thought once, glancing between her two charges, *the widow with her two sons.*

At last the hackney stand appeared. She glanced down at Robert. His eyes were still big, but Alfie's presence seemed to give him extra confidence. A few people already waited at the stand. Robert's nerves seemed to be back, as he huddled close to her side, and kept a grip on her skirt.

The hackney came into view down the street. Tessa let go of Robert just long enough to set her basket down, peeled back the basket cover, and slid her hand down for the pouch. Once she got it untied, Tessa pulled out a few shillings, sufficient she hoped for three fares, hers, Alfie's, and Robert's. And of course, she remembered, the tip.

The pouch secured and the basket sealed once more, she took Robert's hand, and watched their ride get closer and closer. Passengers offloaded while she waited with the rest of the group.

At last they were in the dim, cramped confines of the hackney. She doubted Alfie had ever ridden inside one, but he made no offer to ride outside. She would not have let him, anyway, for fear he might be caught. He managed to melt into the background, a slender youth in quality, if grungy, clothes she suddenly recognized as having been her father's, but no doubt he had plenty of practice not being seen.

They rolled on, pulling into old hotels where the coaches also stopped. She could see large trunks being unloaded from the tops and backs of the vehicles. Alfie kept a sharp eye out the faded window. Even though his watchfulness made her nervous, even though she wasn't sure she fully trusted him, Tessa was committed.

Finally, although it might not have been as long as it seemed, he peered through the window at a hackney stop, lurched as upright as possible as the others began disembarking, and said, "We get out here."

Tessa eased her way around the remaining passengers, holding Robert tight with one hand. With Alfie's support, she climbed down into the mucky ground of the old hotel. Odors wafted up, manure and straw and dogs, even the hens that clucked about in the courtyard.

Her basket banged against her legs as she landed, and Robert tugged her other arm when he took his own jump. "Whewe awe we going now?"

"To the place the notice said." Around the hotel, away from the muck of the courtyard, Tessa saw a bucket with water. And, thank goodness, it looked clean. Somehow Alfie had managed to jump over the worst of it, but even his shoes could use a bit of cleaning. Not all of it, she suspected, came from the inn's yard. "We need to wash off our shoes. We can't go in any place smelling like this." Especially not up to the house of Robert's grandfather, servant's door or not.

"I think I splashed some smelly diwt on my pants." Robert's little nose wrinkled.

"We'll all smell better when we get these shoes washed." She sat down on some cobbles that looked cleaner than most, and started untying her laces. Robert followed her example, pulling his borrowed shoes off before she got hers unlaced. Alfie just tugged his boots off, proving what she often thought, that men's garments were much more simple than women's.

Between the dribble of clean water and rubbing the shoes against the rough stones, they got them almost presentable. The smell greatly improved, and that was a good thing.

Then, shod again, struggling with tying the wet laces into sloppy bows, Tessa looked down at their efforts, and decided that would have to do.

Along the side street they continued, the fancy carriages that rolled along the wide road beside them growing ever larger. Crests marked some of the large, elaborate vehicles, pulled by matching teams of four horses. Other vehicles were smaller and bright colored, yellows, reds, blues, holding on one or two people and pulled by an equal number of horses.

She didn't know much about either the carriages or the horses, but she could tell wealth and breeding. She looked down at her black dress, and made herself hold her head higher. Tradespeople must walk along these sidewalks, dressed much like herself.

"Not much farther," Alfie said, glancing back.

She did not know how he knew, suspected it was better that she not ask, but he had gotten them this far without being caught by Herb, and from the storefronts, and the houses she could see down the streets that intersected the one they walked along, she was confident her nemesis was not likely to be prowling the area when the sun, while low, was still high enough to brighten the shadows and show faces.

What Alfie used to orient himself, she did not know. Street signs were difficult to locate, either showing up on sides of buildings or non-existent, and she had no map, only a location.

Suddenly, on the side of a house partway down the street corner on which they stood, Tessa thought she saw the words, "Herford Street" on the side of one of the houses.

"Here we are!" She caught Alfie's shirt, and pointed. "That one."

She hoped the house had a number, because otherwise they might have to knock on a few doors and beg help.

* * *

Blake's carriage pulled past Madame's shop and around onto the side street. He climbed out and walked through the lengthening shadows to the back door. The shop was closed, but he had seen movement inside behind the drawn curtains, so the workers were still there. A knock would bring someone.

It did, but not the person he hoped for. A girl peeked out. "Wot kin I do fer ye? We be closed, ye know. Ye'll 'ave ta come back tomorrow."

"I came to speak to Miss Abbott."

"Ah don't think she knewed you was comin'. 'Cause she already left." The girl leaned in the doorway, and showed no intention of letting him in.

They were being very protective of her."You're sure she is gone?" He had kept a close eye on the clock while he and his friends went over all the jewelry, did their best to reproduce the patterns to carry to the stores, and divided the list between the four of them. There had been still been plenty of time when they finished.

"She done just left." The girl kept blocking the doorway.

"Did you see which direction she was heading?" Perhaps if he hurried, he could catch up with her.

The girl pointed over her shoulder. "Back that way. Ah think she was goin' to the hackney stand with that little boy. Ah'm jest guessin' though."

"Thank you." Then he turned and ran along the row of buildings. "Herford Street!" He barked the word out as he climbed in. Chasing after a hackney was impossible, London was full of them and how did he know which one was hers?

The street was surprisingly busy for this time of day, but then, was London ever quiet? Even when going home from a ball, he had shared the streets with other carriages and wagons, night workers with their noxious loads, and lamplighters keeping the lamps burning. Not to mention footpads prowling for the unwary.

He hated the thought of Tessa sitting in a hackney with complete strangers. Hated the thought that she would have to roam the streets, however neatly groomed and tidy, to find the right house. Hated the thought that she might have to ask total strangers for directions.

Hated the thought that Mundy's staff might be rude or abrupt with her when she appeared at their back door.

Would she go to the back? Or would she think that since she was so certain she had the grandson, she had the right to go to the front?

As he turned on the street, he could see the house. No one stood at the front. The thought that he might have missed her as she walked along set his jaw. If he had to drive back the way he came, he would do that.

He would have to ask the butler, even send for servants and see if anyone remembered her.

As soon as the carriage rocked to a stop at Mundy's front steps, Blake did not wait for the coachman, just jumped out.

CHAPTER 15

Tessa ordered Alfie to stay at her side when she walked around the side of the house to the back door.

"Why awe we going to the back? Gwandfathew always goes in the fwont." Robert tugged at her hand as they started down the side of the house.

"I can't go that way." She did not add that Robert might not be recognized by Mundy's London staff, and she would not put him through being yelled at and ordered here anyway.

"I will tell him that you need to go in the front." He spoke as someone who was used to giving commands.

She smiled at him. "We have to see him first." She remembered her visit to Blake's. "Besides, the cook might give you fancy cakes to eat."

"Oh." That seemed to satisfy him.

They continued on their way down the long side. This time Alfie's steps slowed. "Tess, I gone far enuf. They ain't gonna let me in."

"Yes. They will." She stopped and grabbed his arm. "Alfie, they must have a position for you. If not in the house, maybe they can use you in the stables. Would you like to work with horses?"

"Ah could learn." He set his jaw. "But if they won't, I promise to tell ya I tole ya so."

Robert piped up. "I will tell Gwandfathew you helped us. He will make suwe you get to stay."

Alfie shrugged, but Tessa felt her heart soften to see that the former pickpocket didn't contradict Robert. She had always thought he didn't belong with Herb, and his actions today were perhaps long in coming but inevitable.

When Tessa rapped the small knocker, she thought she heard an echo inside. Alfie reached around her and banged it so hard she thought the little ring would tear loose.

"Alfie! Servants are supposed to show respect!"

"Yeah, but respect ain't gonna bring nobody ta the door."

Robert tugged at her arm. "Tessa! I alweady told you, Gwandfathew will let us in the fwont."

Just then, the door opened. "Yeah, yeah, I heared ya the first time." An older woman opened the door, her mobcap askew, flour on her hands, blending into her white-ish apron, and the same dusty smudge on her cheek. Her pale blue sleeves were pushed up almost to her elbows, and Tessa could see on the sleeve's band where her hands had often touched, as there was the faintest brown tinge to the fabric. Her skirt was a darker blue where it showed around the edges of her apron.

Tessa's black gown felt more servant-like than ever. She had noticed the maids in the shop come in wearing any color they chose, and it had never bothered her, but there they were on her own territory and her black gown made sense. Here it felt stark and harsh.

"Wot do ye want? I'm in the middle o' baking and ain't got time ta waste." Her gaze ran down Tessa's gown, got as far as her waist, and stopped at Robert. She gasped, and clapped her hands over her mouth, leaving more white there. "Is that . . ."

"This is Robert Parminter. I saw the notice—"

Alfie interrupted her. "She rescued him, so she deserves that reward that be offered."

Tessa had to force herself not to roll her eyes at his abrupt and blatant greed. Perhaps he had changed his mind about getting at least a portion of the reward. She had offered it to him.

"I might not have found my way without Alfie here." Tessa decided if she actually did get it, Alfie certainly deserved a share.

"Come in, come in! All of ye." The door swung wider, and the woman gestured with frantic, jerky movements. She whirled around to a table in the middle of what turned out to be a great big room, a massive fireplace against the center wall, pots on holders hanging over a glowing fire. A sink big enough for Robert to have been bathed in sat on heavy legs against the outside wall, just below a pair of dingy windows.

The woman waved to the table. "You two sit 'ere." She grabbed a cloth and wiped off the worst of the flour, then held out her to Robert. "Young Mister Parminter, you just come with me. The lord, he's been looking everywheres for ye."

His eyes went big. "My gwandfathew is hewe?"

"Yes, little mister. That he be. He's right upstairs."

Robert didn't even glance at her. With an odd sense of loss, Tessa watched him leave clutching the cook's hand, whose name he didn't even know. He was not her son, but still, it would have been nice if he had looked back.

* * *

Mundy appeared to have aged since the last time Blake saw him. *Please let Tessa be right*, he thought, because this man could not take much more. He even seemed to have shrunk behind his desk. The dark green curtains had been drawn, as if the sun's brightness was too garish and disrespectful in a place of such sadness.

A room already dark from the wood panelling on the walls between bookshelves of the same should not be allowed to go without daylight, he thought. Without the mirrored backing of the lit sconces on the walls and the glowing multi-branched candelabra, the room would be dark as night.

Blake glanced around, somehow expecting Tessa to be here already, but the office was empty. Just himself and his host. Even Mundy's butler Piggott was gone, the door shut behind himself.

"Warrenby." Mundy rose and came around the desk, his hand out. "Not that I'm not glad to see you, but this is the first time you've come without me sending for you." The older man took a deep breath, and his throat worked. His voice rough, he asked, "I don't suppose you have news for me?"

Blake waved him back to his seat, and waited until Mundy was safely down before sitting himself. "I don't know, but perhaps. I'm just following a thin lead. There is a young seamstress at my mother's modiste shop who thinks she has . . . " *Don't say 'the boy,'* he caught himself. That was too much hope. "Information."

"Well? Where is this seamstress?"

"I had expected she would already be here. She should be here any minute." What did he know about getting across London without a driver, or without knowing where he was going? She *had* to be coming.

A knock at the door interrupted them. "Come," his host called, and the door opened.

"There is someone here to see you," Piggott announced, his usual butler somberness missing, and stepped aside.

A little boy in worn clothing stood there, clutching the hands of a woman whose apron and the flour liberally dusting it proclaimed her to be the cook. She stayed outside the room, waved to the little boy, but neither servant made the slightest effort to close the door.

Blake turned back to Mundy. His skin, which had been sallow, went totally white. He rose on legs visibly shaking, and stared.

Turning to follow his gaze, Blake saw Mundy's reaction mirrored in the face of the child. And it was the boy who moved first. In an aching yowl, months of sadness and fear and loneliness in one word, he shrieked, "Gwandfathew! Gwandfathew!"

Robert's grandfather reached out, his arms wide, his feet in place as if still frozen from the shock, and called, "Robert! Baby!"

They both began moving at the same instant, and rushed together, Robert making it halfway across the room before his grandfather met him, lifted him up and crushed him to his chest, holding him so tight that the sobs were muted, and it was impossible to tell which one wept the hardest.

Was this Tessa's doing? Or had someone else brought the boy, and was she still wandering about London, trying to find this house? If so, he was not sure he could bear to see the look on her face when she found out.

He was about to step outside when Mundy's voice, muffled around the child in his arms, said, "No, Warrenby, stay." Then he backed up, Blake watching in case the man's legs gave way. Safely in his chair, his grandson on his lap, the reason came. "Did you negotiate this return?"

"No. No, sir, I did not, much as I wish I could claim credit."

Mundy looked to the open door, where the cook was busily spreading more flour across her face as she mopped up her tears. "Piggott?"

The butler gestured to the crying woman beside himself. "Mrs. Good brought him up from the kitchen. I merely recognized the boy."

"Mrs. Good? How do you have the answer to this?"

She mopped up the last of her tears, and managed a wavery smile. "There be a young woman who brought him, together with a rough-looking boy. She said the boy helped get her here."

Tessa! It had to be. So she did make it. And she had been right all along. Blake felt a swell of pride, along with a twinge of worry. Who was the boy? He wondered if Herb had set one of his gang to make certain they got the reward. "Was she afraid of this boy?"

"No, me lord. She din't appear ta be."

That was reassuring.

"Well, bring her up here," Mundy barked. "In fact, bring both of them."

"Yes, my lord," two voices came in harmony from the door, and at last it was shut.

Mundy looked down at his grandson. "So, my boy, what can you tell me about this woman?"

"She's nice," Robert replied in his young, piping voice. "She wescued me."

"Indeed! And how did she do that?"

Blake smiled at the tableau in front of him, the boy clutching his grandfather's vest even as he leaned back to gaze in the aged face, the older man staring back as if afraid to so much as look away lest the boy disappear.

"She founded me and took me to her woom."

"And how did she find you?" Mundy's arms still make a loose cage around his grandson, neither ready to let go of the link to the other.

"I was hiding, and she saw me. She can see in the dawk! Then she took me to hew wowk and she bwought me food. And thewe was a papew with my face on it, and she said she would take me but we had to wait. So I waited all day and I thought I would nevew come but she put me in this big black cawage and we wode and wode and wode, and then Alfie said to get out and walk, so we walked and walked, and then we wewe hewe. And the lady in the kitchen said she knewed me and she said you wewe hewe, and she bwought me up, and hewe you wewe!"

"And who is this Alfie? Is he her own boy?"

"I don't think so," Robert said, and wrinkled his nose as he appeared to give it great thought. "I thought she was scawed of him at fiwst, but he said he would bwing us and he did. And he said he didn't want to stay whewe he was, so she letted him wide with us."

Blake spoke up before he was aware the words were even coming out. "He didn't want to stay where? Did he say?"

Robert twisted around just enough that Blake could see his forehead furrow as he thought. His grip on his grandfather's vest never loosened. "I don't think so. He just didn't want to stay whewe he was. He said he wemembewed his mothew and his fathew and that his fathew nevew hit his mothew."

"That's very good to hear," Mundy replied, a smile tugging at his lips. "Fathers should never hit mothers, should they?"

"No!" Robert shook his head with great enthusiasm. "My fathew nevew hit my mothew eithew."

"Of course not. I should thank this woman who rescued you, shouldn't I? And thank the boy, too."

Robert nodded. "She's weally pwetty, too."

Blake said nothing, but he could only agree.

Mundy smiled again, and nodded toward the door. "Piggott, bring up this woman and this boy."

Their audience disappeared from the doorway, closing the door behind them at last.

Robert continued to prattle on, but Blake found it impossible to pay attention. Even though he did not dare turn around, his attention was fixed on the sound of the latch.

At last it came, preceded by a polite knock and a "come." He turned around when she walked in, unable to keep the smile from his face. Another time when he had seen her walk into a room slid back into his mind. She was as hesitant as she had been the first time she entered his own office.

He turned to see Mundy's expression, but the reaction was not at all what he would have expected. Instead of a gracious nod, the man blinked, squinted, blinked again, then his mouth dropped open.

Blake looked from Mundy to Tessa and back, wondering what was going on.

His friend finally let go of his grandson enough to set him on the floor and rise. Grasping Robert's hand, Mundy started across the room toward her.

Still few feet away, he stopped. "Elizabeth? Miss Elizabeth deRoss? Is that you?"

* * *

She wasn't certain what Warrenby was doing here but she was glad to see him. Right now, however her attention belonged to the old man who had to be Robert's grandfather.

Who looked so puzzled that Tessa hated to disappoint him. "No, I'm very sorry sir, but I am Tessa Abbott. My mother's name was Elizabeth, but it was Elizabeth *Abbott*. I never knew her surname." She knew old people forgot things and got strangers confused with friends, but this man did not seem to have the symptoms. Only this confusion between her and this other woman.

Was that Elizabeth an old love, perhaps? To be sure, that woman and her mother shared the same Christian names. But then, Elizabeth was fairly common, even among the lower classes. Everyone knew England's Virgin Queen, and many baby girls got her name as a gift when they were born.

* * *

Blake looked between Tessa Abbott and the earl. Either Mundy was badly mistaken or something big had just happened. DeRoss. The name meant nothing to him. He would have to ask his mother, unless somewhere he could pick up a clue. Right now, however, Tessa seemed as baffled as he was.

Mundy seemed to know exactly what he was doing, and saying. Blake turned to look at Tessa. She had told him she knew virtually nothing about her background. How odd it would be if the answers stood before her.

* * *

Robert's grandfather kept his gaze on her, and now he shook his head. "I can tell you what it was. Your mother's name was indeed Elizabeth deRoss. If you are not her daughter, then the world has just gone topsy-turvy. I knew her about the age you are now, and the two of you could be twins."

"Where did you know her? The earliest place I can remember by name is Falmouth, and there are no deRosses there that I ever heard. I am sorry, but you must be mistaken."

The old man smiled. "And you, my dear, do not know your mother as well as you think. What was your father's occupation? Was he a sailor, by any chance? Because I seem to recall she married one, but I cannot think of the man's name."

An odd chill washed over her. "I was told he worked for the Packet Service. If that is true then yes, he was a sailor."

"Ah." Robert's grandfather drew the word out, more of an *aahhhh*. "I am right." His eyebrow went up in a questioning look. "Was the feud ever resolved? Did you ever know your grandfather? I cannot understand that he would countenance you living in servant's garb."

The chill had become worse. She glanced down at her arms. Tiny fine hairs were standing up as if it were an autumn day and she was out with no shawl, instead of a summer evening with the air still clinging to the day's warmth. "I never knew them, no."

He nodded his head slowly. "You should be in silk and satin."

"I am more familiar with those than anyone." A smile came out of nowhere. "I work with them every day. The finest fabrics you can imagine."

Those expressive brows came down. "It appears to me that you do not wear them, though." He shook his head. "Your grandfather was a fool. Your grandmother helped moderate his stubbornness, but after she died . . ." For a second time, he shook that shaggy grey head.

"Obstinate old man."

"Sir?" Tessa simply could not let him rattle on. When he found out he was wrong, he would be humiliated, and she did not want that to happen to this kind old man. She should be wearing silk and satin indeed! "I am certain you have me confused with someone else. I cannot be this person you think I am. The only similarity between my history and the one you relate is that my father was a sailor, and my mother's name was Elizabeth."

"Was? For both of them? Your parents are both deceased?"

The heaviness that always filled her when she thought of the loss settled in again. "Yes, both. My mother four years ago, my father died just recently."

"My sympathies." He looked her over with an unhurried and piercing gaze. Then a smile crept up his face. "I am certain I am not wrong. You are the daughter of Miss Elizabeth deRoss, and your grandfather is Sir Aldo deRoss, *Baronet* deRoss. You are from Gloucestershire, or at least your family is. Your grandfather owns a good bit of land where he runs sheep, and he also has a woolen mill. He also has great wealth. Your mother was the apple of your grandmother's eye, the prettiest of all the girls." He frowned, and cocked his head. "I think there was a boy, so he may have taken your mother's place now."

A smile quirked the edges of his mouth, and he stared off into the distance. "I know a parent is not supposed to have favorites, but it is a fact that some children are easier to love than others." His gaze came back to her. "Some day you will find that out, my dear."

Tessa tried to smile in return, but the chances of any children brought a deep sadness. Unless she got the reward. That would help so much. Without that, any children she had would be born into at least straitened circumstances.

Before she knew it, not even thinking of the audience, she turned to Blake—Warrenby, she reminded herself. She had been doing so well wiping his given name from her mind, but perhaps the tantalizing hope of a five hundred pound reward brought it back.

Five hundred pounds did not put them on the same level.

What if—just what if—this man was right? Would a baronet in her family do that? She had heard the title, but its weight and meaning meant nothing. Still, it sounded good. A baronet for a grandfather and a five hundred pound dowry!

You are getting ahead of yourself, she scolded. *That five hundred pounds is not yours, not yet, and even if it is, that is no guarantee Warrenby is interested in you in any way.* The grandfather was not hers yet, either. Aloud, she said, "If that is the case, and I must tell you, sir, that I find it difficult to believe, then why did I never even hear of such a man? What is this feud?"

His face sobered. "Sit down, please, my dear, and I will explain."

* * *

Blake watched the emotions flit across Tessa' face, sympathy, uncertainty, fear. He knew how much she needed the reward Mundy had promised, to really all of London.

He would make certain she got it, although he did not think Mundy would go back on his word. Now, though, he wanted his own answers.

Baronet? Just exactly what had happened to lose her such a family? Those titles passed down, it should still lay over her like a protective blanket.

Was the feud ever resolved? Was your father a sailor? Knowing what he already knew about Tessa's father, he had a guess what the feud might have involved, but the only one who could answer that for certain was the grandfather himself. Depending on how severe the problem had been, and obviously still was in view of the ongoing estrangement, the man might not be willing to give an answer.

Obstinate old man. Obstinate enough not to give any answers? Obstinate enough not to take back a granddaughter?

CHAPTER 17

Sit down, the old man had said, and right now she thought perhaps she might need to. Tessa walked over to one of the chairs, dark polished wood with leather upholstery, and sat down, wishing she could hide her work shoes, and that her gown was out of finer cloth. The color could pass for mourning, but the fabric was not even as nice as the curtains hanging from the windows.

Worse, the candlestands around the room were all lit with expensive candles that gave off no odor, the curtains looked like velvet, and the walls were all richly polished dark wood. The whole atmosphere fairly trumpeted wealth.

Even five hundred pounds, assuming she got it, hardly compared with the money that burned in the candles.

Robert seemed to be tired of being overlooked. "I was telling my gwampa all about you finding me."

Tessa had to smile. "Don't forget, you managed to get away from those bad men all by yourself. I had nothing to do with that. It was all you, being brave."

Grief washed over Mundy's face, and she wanted to snatch those words back. He did not need any reminders of what his grandson had endured.

Robert looked up at his grandfather. "Was I bwave?"

Mundy smiled down at the boy. "You certainly were. You still are." He turned back to her. "Very well, Miss—"

"Abbott," she said. He could not remember the name she had given him, but that was fine, as she could not accept the name he wanted to bestow on her. Not yet.

"I know what you are thinking," he went on. "You are convinced I am wrong, that I am a wandering old man seeing what I want to see. But I tell you, I knew your grandfather. I do not have the entire tale, but enough, I hope, to satisfy you." He reached behind to pull the cord hanging on the wall. "I can see this will take some time, we will need some tea."

Sure enough, when the door opened and the man who had led the cook and herself to this room stood there.

"Have some tea brought up, Piggott." He turned back to her. "I think the rest should wait until we have some refreshment in us. You must surely be as dry as I am. And we clearly have some history to go over."

A knock on the door and a well-dressed man of the kind she had seen often enough to recognize as a footman brought in a pot of tea and several cups.

"Thank you." Until then, Tessa did not realize how dry her mouth had become. She swallowed gratefully, letting the warm beverage soothe as it went down.

Following him, another servant came in with a plate of biscuits and a glass of milk, which he set on one of the tables. "Fer the boy."

Robert bounced off the chair, and raced over to the biscuits. He did stop long enough to look up at his grandfather, although he fairly trembled with excitement.

"Of course," Mundy nodded, and Robert had his hands full of the small treats before the words were even out.

Tessa smiled but it was tinged with sadness. She had not been able to feed him much. Warrenby's gaze was on her, she could feel the tingle along her skin, but this time she dared not meet it. He seemed to know too often what she was thinking. This, she did not want him to guess.

"Now." Robert's grandfather set his own cup down. "Let us go back to the beginning. Your mother was one of several girls, the youngest until a boy came along years later, I believe. I think I heard they had given up hope of an heir. Your grandfather was very hard to please, and I did hear each of the girls had to fight to marry the men they chose. Most of them found husbands that were at least acceptable, but your mother wanted to marry a sailor. Your father worked on the River Severn, but I recall he wanted to go onto the ocean."

Tessa relaxed a small bit. The tightness around her chest eased enough for her to take a better breath. That did sound like her father, always wanting something better than what he had.

"I see some of this sounds familiar." Mundy fixed his shrewd attention on her face.

"Not this, in particular. Just the attitude."

He gave her a strange look. Beside her, Warrenby shifted. He had been so still, listening with what felt like fierce concentration, that she had managed to concentrate. "I was already wed, with small children, so I did not hear as much as others did, but apparently there was quite a battle between Elizabeth and deRoss. She wanted your father, and no one else. Tales about the feud between deRoss and his daughter began to spread about the neighborhood."

That hardly sounded like her mother. "Now I am certain you have the wrong woman. My mother was the most soft-spoken of women. I never heard her raise her voice to anyone. A feud that would spread around an entire neighborhood? That is not the mother I knew." Tessa swallowed hard, and a small pain started in the back of her neck.

Her legs did not feel like they would hold her, so she remained in the chair. In a moment or so, she would have to rise and excuse herself, extend her apologies for wasting his time before she left, but not right now.

"I think you need to hear the rest of the story before you make up your mind. Your grandfather threatened to cut your mother off, but not even that stopped her. When your grandmother saw what was happening, though she could not stop her husband from cutting the couple off, she fought to keep your mother where she could watch over her. I heard there was a house your grandmother owned exclusive of her husband, and she let them stay there. They lived there for several years, as I understand, at least as long as deRoss's wife lived."

Warrenby sat up straighter in his chair and looked at her, just as her own gaze found his. "That matches the story you told me. Remember? You said that you lived in a pretty house when you were young."

She could not speak for a minute. This *did* match. The house was a vague, blurry memory, but it was there. Sometimes, when they were living in poor houses barely better than hovels, at night she would pull the covers over her head and close her eyes and pretend she was back in that little house. If asked to draw what it looked like, she doubted she could come up with more than bits and pieces. How old she was when they left she did not know, only that she was young enough to have to hold onto her mother's hand when they walked away.

No one had ever explained why they moved, but it got lost in a series of moves, just one more in the patchwork her life became.

As long as the woman lived. "So what happened when my—when the grandmother died?"

Mundy's mouth quirked upward. "You can call her your grandmother. She is, you know. And yes, when she died, your grandfather refused to let them, your parents, stay there any longer. He insisted the house be given to another of the sisters, I think. That I am not certain of. At any rate, after deRoss's wife died, I moved my own family to take over one of my family's other estates, and I knew nothing else after that."

He leaned back in the chair, looking satisfied at the result of his story. "Anything more you want to know you will have to get from your grandfather. Or perhaps from your aunts and uncles."

Aunts and uncles. She had a whole family.

If. There was still one other very big problem. "If my mother was disowned, what chance is there that any of them will even talk to me? My mother must have brought shame to the whole family. No doubt no one will want to go against their father's wishes, especially if he has not changed his mind after all these years."

"Ah, but that is the thing." If ever a man looked smug, it was Mundy at that moment. "Your grandfather is getting quite far along in age now, and I think he regrets a good many things. I imagine if given a chance to find even Elizabeth's daughter, he would welcome that child with open arms."

Warrenby turned to her. "Miss Abbott, just think. You are a baronet's granddaughter."

She was English, of course she had heard the title before, but . . . the question would make her sound stupid. Tessa asked it anyway. "What exactly is a baronet?"

Mundy chuckled. Blake did not. His friend, whose name she still did not know and did not know how to find out without being too forward, also chuckled, but he looked at Blake, not at herself.

He certainly found something about Blake funny.

"Ah yes, my dear." Mundy stroked his chin. "Baronetcy is one of the unusual things about English titles. To be titled and yet still a commoner, to have the right to be addressed as 'Sir' and yet have no place in the House of Lords, and to be able to pass the title on to one's heirs. There are baronets who have held the title for nearly 200 years, a goodly thing about which to boast."

Blake spoke up. "They are about the same rank as a knight, but whereas a baronetcy is inherited, knighthood is not."

Titles went to men. Except for Queen. Whatever rights her grandf—deRoss held because of his title, they had nothing to do with her. "Did you say my mother had a younger brother?"

Mundy chuckled again. "I believe I did. He is most likely married by now, with children of his own, but as I said, I have not lived in their area for some time so my information might be out of date."

He was enjoying himself, she thought. All this family history was fascinating, she was beginning to believe it, but she had lived her life, knew what struggles her parents had endured, for she had endured those with them. The men here were all badly mistaken if they thought she was ready to turn her back on the life she had constructed, a life she could depend on, for wishful thinking.

"Miss Abbott?" Warrenby interrupted her thoughts. She turned to him. "You know you have to go meet your grandfather. If he is getting old, there might not be much time left. Put his mind at ease."

Her head was already shaking in negation, even before he finished. "I cannot leave my work. Madame Genevieve has been exceedingly kind to me. I don't think I can find another employer with such concern." She leaned toward him. "If I leave her, I will have to start over. Where will I live when I am doing that? How long will it take me to find another position?"

Mundy spoke up. "If she is that compassionate, she will understand."

Tessa shook her head. "I am not trying to beg off, just to explain. I do not want to cause an old man pain, but my way of life is foreign to men of your stature. I have been Madame's primary seamstress for several years now."

Warrenby interrupted. "She has another young woman. I have seen her there. In fact, there are two other women working for her in addition to you."

"Rosie handles only the minor details, the cleanup of the shop, the running of orders, that sort of thing. Other than Madame and myself, only Ellen does any sewing."

"Could Ellen take over while you are away?"

Tessa could only stare at Blake. She moved her gaze between the two men, staring back at her with equal parts persuasion and concern. "I don't know. We hired Ellen because we were too busy. Losing me, even if I can get just few days off, will be a hardship for them."

Mundy gave her a kind smile. "I will be happy to discuss the situation with your employer, if that might help."

She pressed her lips together and tried to think. Madame would let her go for a few days if she heard the story.

"Miss Abbott." Mundy's smile was gone. "What are you really afraid of? Is your life what your mother would have wanted for you? If she was given the opportunity to mend the rift in her family, if she was as kind as you say, would she not grab the chance to give her child—you—a better life?"

Tessa looked down at her hands. Hard as it was to admit, her mother would have tried to make peace to help her child. She would not have been happy to see her daughter living in a tiny room with a broken door, and a villain waiting for the opportunity to come back and do again what he had already done. Or worse. Had Elizabeth known her daughter had been beaten, it would have broken her heart.

She had put all her hopes on the reward, but even if she could find a better place to live, how far away would it actually take her? Herb must know where she worked, or Alfie would never have found her.

Alfie! How could she have forgotten him? Tessa turned around in her chair, but he had not been included in the invitation to sit and still stood by the door, silent as the grave, only now his eyes were big as saucers.

"Fine." Mundy's voice drew her back into the room. He must have seen something in her face because he leaned back in his chair. "It is settled then. I will go with you to speak with this employer. Time is of the essence. Your grandfather must be nearing eighty by now. Your mother was the youngest girl, and he was not young when she was born, as I recall."

As she looked at the implacable faces looking back at her, Tessa thought, *being on a runaway horse must feel exactly like this.*

CHAPTER 18

Despite the breathless pace of the change her life was about to take, Tessa knew she still had one promise yet to fulfill. She turned around again and looked at Alfie. The surprise on his face had been replaced with the bravado she was sure he showed to everyone else. Not to her the narrowed eyes, the tight mouth, the set jaw of Herb's menacing face, though, never to her. Instead of standing straight, respectful, he now slouched against the wall next to the door, his posture relaxed except for the arms folded tight against his chest. One leg was crossed lazily over the other.

He expected nothing now, she knew that, had taken the brave step of breaking with Herb, and now was braced for a desperate life on the run.

Her responsibility to Robert might be over, but the young man had kept his word. "What about Alfie?"

"Oh, yes." Mundy looked beyond her. "Young man, come here."

The sudden tightness of Alfie's body relaxed. As she watched, he went from a budding ruffian to a hesitant boy. She understood the feeling of walking into a room where one knew one did not belong. To expect at any moment to be ordered out, even tossed onto the street.

There was an extra chair tucked tidily against the wall at the end of the long bookshelf in case the group to visit this exclusive inner sanctum was more than two.

"Grab that chair," Mundy said after a brief hesitation. Undoubtedly no one not of the man's class had ever sat in it, it would probably need a good cleaning after Alfie left because even Tessa could see the layers of London sticking to him.

He grabbed the chair, his eyes going wide when he realized how heavy it was. With more care he hauled it over to her side, and set it down, then eased himself onto the seat's edge, looking like a rabbit about to run.

She did not know what she would do if this did not go well. She had no influence here, but she would speak up for him. Her fingers tightened with nerves and worry as she held them linked together in her lap. Even her shoulders had stiffened.

"So I understand that you helped Miss Tessa and my grandson find their way. I am most grateful."

Gratitude, she knew, would not protect him from Herb, who might well be combing London's East End for him right now.

"Weel, ah wanted Tessa ta be safe. Ah dint know 'bout 'er havin' the boy 'til ah seen 'im, but ah knewed the 'unt were on fer 'im. 'E were just another boy sent out ta work 'til the papers were spread all over the town, and then ever'body wanted that reward. It were quite a stir wen word got out 'e were found ta be missin', ah kin tell ya that."

She could not allow them to give Alfie money and send him back out onto the streets. "Alfie broke with his gang when he brought me here. If they find him, well, I don't know what they will do, but he might be killed."

Alfie went still beside her. She could only hope he hadn't planned to join some other gang, because having him come this far, Tessa would not let him go back.

She didn't think he would, but it never hurt to give him a different option.

The room was quiet for a bare moment, and then Mundy spoke up. "What do you know about horses?"

"Ah 'elped one o' the nightmen with 'is team a couple times."

Tessa felt her eyes widen in surprise. Somehow she never thought of him doing anything but joining Herb and his team on their nightly prowls, picking pockets, attacking young dandies wandering too far into their territory, or sliding into houses and taking what they could. And a nightman! Possibly the lowliest job in all of London. It was beginning to look like Alfie had been looking into a way to break free of Herb and his men for a while.

"Would you like a position here in my stables?"

"Wow! Yeah, ah would!"

Warrenby, who had been sitting quite during this, suddenly spoke up. "Your stable is rather thin of staff most of the year, because you have moved your primary residence to the country. Are you planning on moving back?"

Mundy shook his head. "No, I have found I like the country. London is too fast for me now. Besides, it will be easy to have the entire village watching out for . . ." he tilted his head toward Robert. "I would prefer to be there. But I'm certain this young man would be fine here."

Tessa watched as Bla—Warrenby shook his head. "I live in London. I have a full staff here all the time. No one could lie in wait around my stables without being seen. I think he would be much safer with me."

She looked over at Alfie, and fought her smile at the wonder in his face, although no one who did not know him well would see that his eyes were wider than usual, and even though his mouth was not hanging open, his jaw sagged. To go from fearing he would be tossed out again to fend for himself to having two powerful men both want his skills!

Mundy and Warrenby exchanged a long look, and then the older nodded once. "You are right as usual, Blake. I don't keep many here when I am gone. He would be better off with you."

Then he turned to Alfie. "Warrenby will take you with him when he goes. See that we don't regret this, boy."

"Thankee, sirs! You won't, ah promise!"

Warrenby settled back against his chair. "Do you think you can hang on the back of a carriage?"

Alfie started to scoff, but caught himself. "Ah *know* ah kin."

Oh, dear. Tessa decided she was better off not knowing what was behind his confidence.

Just as Alfie's eyes had given himself away, widening with surprise, for no more than the space of a breath, she saw Warrenby's eyes give himself away, a quick narrowing before they again were calm, and his mouth showing the vaguest thinning before that too went back to normal.

But he did not revoke his offer. And just like that, Alfie had a new life. All he had to do now was grab it and hold on.

Mundy grabbed the cord behind his chair again, and tugged. "I'm going to send you down to the kitchen. You will be fed. Just stay there until Warrenby is ready to leave."

When the stiff butler appeared, he took his instructions with only a "Yes, my lord. I will send him out to the carriage when you are ready."

Tessa grabbed Alfie's arm as he rose. "Good luck, Alfie."

"Thankee, Tess." And then, to her complete shock, he bent down and clasped an arm around as much of her shoulders as he could. In a low voice that she hoped no one else could hear, he said, "Ah cain't niver repay ye for this."

Then he hurried out the door behind the butler.

When she turned back, Mundy was smiling at her. "I think that young man has a tendre for you."

She had heard that word floating around the shop before, and knew it's meaning. "Oh no, sir, it's not like that at all. I just found out that he remembers his parents, and it sounds like they tried very hard to raise him right. I believe he saw in me what his own parents tried to teach him. He never quite fit in the gang, there was always something just a little bit different about him."

Mundy turned to Warrenby. "You might not be taking such a big risk after all."

"I was never worried."

Tessa looked down at her hands, and hoped he could not see her smile. She knew that wasn't true, she had seen his reaction.

"Now, Miss Tessa," Mundy pulled her attention back. "We need to get a letter off to your grandfather, tell him his search is over. Then we need to get you properly attired. It would never do to cause him more guilt over your life. He will learn the details soon enough, but I want you to go looking like you should. Do you think your employer has any gowns on hand that can be adjusted for you?"

"Ye—" she started but Mundy wasn't through.

"I would be honored if I could stand in for him. He can repay me for the cost, but he should see you at your best. We will get you a bonnet and gloves and new shoes to match each gown and take you someplace and get your hair trimmed smooth."

"Mundy," Warrenby interrupted. "You have not asked her what she wants yet."

"She wants to meet her grandfather." Mundy looked at her. "Isn't that right, my dear?"

Tessa looked between the two men, and gave in. "I guess so,"

"Good, good." Mundy rubbed his hands together like someone preparing for a challenge. "I will assign one of my maids for you, and you will stay here. It's too late to begin anything today. Tomorrow we will take you to your employer and see if she has any gowns ready made that will fit you. Then we will get you all the rest of what you need. As soon as we have that done, we will head out."

It all seemed so simple, but they seemed to be ignoring one very important problem. "What if my—this man does not in fact want to see me? I can't turn my life upside down only to find out that nothing in fact has changed."

Mundy sighed. "If I am wrong, and I promise you I am not, you will become my ward. My wife will be delighted to bring you out. We will see you well married and established."

Well married? Did that mean happy? She wanted to be happy when she married, wanted to love the man who would become her husband, to feel safe, secure, protected.

Next to her, Warrenby shifted in his chair. She glanced over, looking for . . . something, hoping he would know what to do or say to reassure her.

But he only smiled.

CHAPTER 19

The trip to Lord Mundy's country home felt endless, even though she knew it would take but two or three days. The air was fresh, the scents drifting into the windows carried growing things. Green land and trees rolled away into the distance every time they crested a hill, dotted with the white of sheep and the brown of cows.

It had been so long since she had lived out of London, out of any city at all. Her memories were those of a child, where the green was only vague memories of making buttercup necklaces, and wearing rings of grass.

Both Warrenby and Mundy had the luxury of spending a goodly portion of the journey outside on their horses. She, on the other hand, along with Robert and the maid, Lewis, were trapped in the coach. Even so, the scenery was ample compensation.

Warrenby, riding alongside the carriage as if he never grew weary of the saddle, showed no signs of growing tired. Perhaps he never did. She let herself enjoy Blake's skill with the horse, his erect posture, his gloved hand resting so comfortably on his thigh as he guided the horse with the other. Both man and horse seemed happy with the arrangement.

Tessa knew. She had been watching him much more than was proper. Who was going to tell tales? Not the maid, who knew her duties and her place all too well. Not Mundy either, for when he was not outside, he was either dozing or enraptured by Robert's constant chatter.

If the dozing was for show, she could not tell.

When she tried to relax at having nothing to do for the first time in so long she could not remember, Tessa had even dozed off herself a time or three.

Riding in a carriage, even a well-sprung one, did not lend itself to deep sleep.

Neither did two nights on the road stopping at noisy inns, sleeping in a strange bed each time, two nights with an a new and unfamiliar maid, middle-aged and gentle, to help her in and out of clothes she had been fastening her entire life. Two days of waiting for Warrenby to decide he had done his duty and leave her to the kind care of Mundy. But he still rode at their side.

Two days of Robert's constant prattling. "My mothew says I would always get sick when I twaveled, but I'm biggew now and I nevew get sick any mow." And, "Look, Tessa! Look! I think I wemembew that twee! And look at that house! I know I know that house! We must be getting close!" Each time he decided something looked familiar, he would lean out the carriage window and shout, "Gwandfathew! Gwandfathew! I wemembew that, don't I?"

If his grandfather was taking a turn riding in the carriage, the volume was about the same.

His grandfather always responded, "Of course you do." He would smile even if his face grew sad as he looked away. She knew as well as if the kind-hearted lord had spoken aloud that Robert might actually remember some of these from his horrible trip to London at the hands of his kidnappers. The last time he would have traveled this journey with his family, he was a baby.

Much kinder to let him think they were happy memories.

* * *

She was watching him again. Lucky girl, Blake thought, to have the freedom to stare. If he turned his head to enjoy the same liberty, he would be noticed, and he was not ready to be that exposed. He didn't know how she felt, and dared not do anything to jeopardize this fragile new connection.

Despite the coach windows being left down so often to prevent motion sickness, on the rare occasions he contrived a casual glance, the shadows hid most of her face.

As had the bonnet Mundy insisted she buy with her reward.

That bit of nonsense on her head made him smile, but he moved ahead of the carriage each time so only his back was visible.

At a soft, feminine chuckle from inside the carriage, Blake glanced over, glad for the excuse to look. Robert must have done something charming.

Thank goodness for Robert.

Tessa's soft skin caught the day's glow, and Blake felt his hand clench on the reins, but forced himself to ease back. He wanted to feel the heat of her face against his palm, though, see if it was as sleek as it looked, see what it felt like when the sun had warmed it all day.

Another house came into view, his vantage of height on the horse allowed him to see it first.

As the road curved, the carriage window faced the building, taking a more distinct shape as they rolled ever closer. Robert let out a shriek that made Blake's well-trained horse shy before he brought it back under control.

"Gwandfathew! We'ew *home*! We'ew *home*! I want to see my mothew!" For the first time in the whole trip, the boy burst into sobs.

Blake leaned down, to see tears streaming down Mundy's face. "Yes," the word came out on a hiccup. "Yes." That was the only thing the man managed to get out. Just, *yes*. Yes, they were home, yes, the boy would see his mother in just minutes, yes, the whole ordeal was over.

But it was not really over, Blake knew that. There would be endless nights of bad dreams and screaming terrors, months of clinging, years ahead of the entire family struggling with trust. Who could come into the house, how could Robert be allowed outside, when—if ever—would he be permitted to roam free? New staff would be scrutinized to the smallest detail before anyone was hired.

No, it was not really over, but let Robert think so.

Tessa met his gaze, and he was certain he saw the same thoughts running through her eyes as well.

Her mother had done a wonderful job of preparing the daughter for life among respectable people. Had the woman ever dreamed of returning to her previous life? Dreamed of being welcomed back home?

Dreamed of leaving a husband that must have become an unbearable burden?

Unless the problems did not start while she was alive? Abbott would not be the first man who had lost his mind at the death of his wife. Perhaps the marriage had been happier than Blake thought. Tessa had not guessed. Her father's crimes had come as a complete shock. Her mother might well have been happy with her choice. Whatever the case, the woman had given her daughter the speech and graces that could fit into any society.

A baronet's granddaughter.

The house came closer, and Blake realized for the first time the status of the man he had come to know. Although he had been acquainted with Mundy before, clearly he had not been paying enough attention. To be sure, they were of a different generation. Still, there was influence here, and the import of history.

The carriage clattered along the graveled drive, stones snapping free of the wheels and settling the low shrubs waving. Blake moved ahead to avoid the flying bits, keeping to the shade from the thin trees lining their way. The house was imposing in the lowering sun, the grey stone glinting in the golden rays, three rows of white-shuttered windows reflecting the yellow glow like shining eyes across the building.

As he cleared the last of the trees and moved into the glare, the front door placed right in the middle slammed open, and a well-dressed older woman stepped out, hands clasped, her mobcap askew. Behind her, a younger woman in a gown that looked as if it had been thrown on without concern for appearance held her hands to her mouth. It drooped off her shoulders as if made for someone larger, and the bodice sagged limply.

Staff clustered in the background, nearly shoving them off the step. The two women began to run, the younger outpacing the elder in the first few steps. Her skirts crawled up her legs as she pelted along. Blake pulled his horse up, and guided it to the side as it pranced from the sudden command.

"Whoa!" The driver hauled on the reins rather than risk mowing the woman down, and the door popped open. Mundy, Blake thought. Or more likely Robert. The carriage was still rolling, albeit slowly now, as the boy hurled himself out, falling to his hands before popping back up and rushing to meet the woman. Up close, he could see her better, see the toll this had taken. Her eyes were red and puffy, her skin sallow from months of despair and being unable to eat.

That would explain the gown that was too large.

Her knees gave way as Robert reached her. His impact nearly knocked her off balance, but she held on to it, and to him, keeping upright by force of will, Blake was certain. Horrible sounds filled the air, hardly recognizable as human voices. Joy did not sound like this. No, this was grief, at months lost, at suffering endured and feared. At months of hunger on both sides, at separation.

This is what his own mother must have gone through during the months he was in France. To lose her husband, and not be able to find her son. Yet she had never shed those tears in front of him.

Now he saw them coming from another woman.

The carriage creaked beside him as Blake dismounted, giving an odd counterpoint to the saddle's squeak. Mundy climbed down so slowly it was a wonder he did not fall. Blake grabbed his arm, and held him upright. The older woman reached them. Mundy stepped away and enfolded her in his arms.

Blake turned away, and his gaze locked with Tessa's. She had climbed out during the reunion, and stood beside the open carriage door. Mundy's hired maid sat inside, a dim shadow in the depths.

He strode over to her. "You did a very good thing when you rescued the boy."

Her dark eyes were wet when they met his. "He tried to tell me, but with that little impediment, it was hard to understand everything he said. If not for the notice, who knows what might have become of him?"

Her gaze drifted back to the group reunited at last. The sounds were finally taking on a note of joy, lighter, an odd whuff that might be a laugh, or an attempt at one, and little Robert finally recovered his childhood exuberance as the tones rang with the sound of his voice.

Tessa's gaze slid past him, and Blake turned, then bowed. The Countess of Mundy stood there, a tentative smile on her face. She did not stand there as the earl's wife, but rather as Robert's grandmother, wondering how to thank the woman who had returned their boy. Behind her, the daughter came in hesitant steps, clutching her son's hand as if she would never let him go.

* * *

Tessa watched the women walking toward her, and wished she could slink back into the carriage. This was all so much. She did not do anything extraordinary. How many children had she walked past, unable to help? Children who might have gone on to die of starvation, of sickness, or injury. This one child just happened to be in a time and place where she could, but that was Robert's own doing, not hers.

Months of worry etched Lady Mundy's face, more extreme in the face of her daughter, but beneath the grandmother's lines were fine, delicate features she thought showed their traces in Robert's face. Faint shading that might be long-faded freckles. The most striking thing of all were the blue eyes. This was where they came from. Robert had his grandmother's eyes.

She turned her attention to the daughter, with Robert's hand clutched tightly in her own. Blond hair, curly like her son's but darker. No freckles, she had not inherited her mother's skin. The same pale color, but where Lady Mundy still showed the freckles that must have tormented her as a young woman, her daughter's skin was clear. The younger woman's eyes behind their swollen, reddened lids were an odd blend of blue and green, both parents rolled into one child.

It was easy to see why Robert was such a good-looking child. His mother's features were perfect, as delicate as Tessa had ever seen. Thin nose, high cheekbones, jaw neither too wide nor too narrow. Whatever Robert's father looked like, the boy had kept the refinement of his mother's face.

The daughter, Mrs. Parminter, spoke first. "Thank you for my son." She reached out with her free hand and grabbed Tessa's without waiting for her to extend it. "Thank you so much! I want to know all the details, every last thing, but"—her voice broke. She swallowed, and bowed her head, her helpless struggle for words clear.

"Later, then." Tessa finished the sentence for her.

Mrs. Parminter just nodded, and stepped close enough to pull Tessa into a one-armed hug, her other hand still clutching her son. Her hand caught Tessa's, a quick squeeze, then she hurried off with Robert, leaving her mother behind.

Lady Mundy's eyes were as red as her daughter's had been. "My dear, I too just had to thank you for the care you took of my grandson. I do not know how to express the depth of . . . what I feel. You must be our guest. I won't think of letting you get away. I need you to know . . . I have to say this . . . we are always in your debt. Nothing will ever be enough to repay you."

Tessa flipped her hands and held Lady Mundy's with the same care hers had been. "Robert did most of it. Somehow he found the courage to run away. If he had not, I would never have seen him. If anyone deserves the credit for his rescue, it is he."

Lady Mundy smiled all the way to her eyes. "He is a wonderful boy. So much of his father in him. And his grandfather."

"Yes." She had seen the iron will of the grandfather. Look where she was because of it! Hundreds of miles from London, in a part of England she had never been, about to see a grandfather she did not even know existed until a few days ago. Tessa kept the smile in place with effort as she let go of Lady Mundy's hands.

"Well, I must go in, show the servants which rooms . . ." Lady Mundy gestured behind her, gave a nod that seemed meant for someone beyond her. "My lord."

Tessa turned and nearly bumped into Warrenby, straightening from a bow to Lady Mundy. "We have been invited to stay."

"Of course we have been." He looked down at her, and smiled. "It is customary, even with strangers, to give hospitality, but you are hardly a stranger. You must get used to this now."

Her cheeks felt hot, her hands when they touched the skin were cooler. "My life will never be the same, will it?"

He shook his head. "But it will not be a bad thing. You heard Mundy. He will see you well married. Have you never thought of being wed?"

Tessa felt the head creep back into her cheeks. Yes, she had, but they were wild dreams, unreachable. Just things to make her life less lonely. After the first time the man in front of her walked into the shop, her dreams had a face.

But she could not tell him that. Instead, she merely said, "Of course I thought of it. I just assumed it would happen on its own."

"Perhaps it has," his voice was low, barely audible. "Perhaps it has."

* * *

The dinner was relaxed, surprising Tessa by how comfortable they made her. Despite the years of eating food wrapped in rough paper from whatever seller was closest, all while walking down the street or sitting on her bed, as a girl her mother had drilled proper table manners into her, and they came back.

Well, she thought later. Perhaps not all of them, but enough that she did not embarrass either herself or her hosts.

The meal was thrown together quickly by the chef, a celebration planned and finished all in a day. They had ordered half a sheep, and the kitchen produced a wonderful boiled mutton with a mint sauce, fresh caught grilled fish, and her new favorite, asparagus, plus beans and peas.

Since they knew Robert was coming soon, they had done some berry-picking—the fruit and cream dessert was so fresh she could almost smell the scent of the bushes and hear the buzzing of the bees.

The meal was quiet, as the stress of the last few months drained away and left the family tired.

The servants, however, were beyond happy that their little favorite was back. They fairly glowed. The elegant plates were polished to a mirror shine, the forks and spoons likewise. New dishes were delivered to the table with a flourish, old dishes removed with a smile. Tessa did not know if anyone else was watching the servants as they bustled about silently doing their duty, but these were her class of people, and she saw everything they did.

Then, much to her surprise, Mrs. Parminter looked up at one of the footmen clearing off the dishes from the last course. “Alfred? Tell everyone they have outdone themselves. We are so grateful.”

The footman dipped his head. “Thankee, ma’am. I will.”

That simple exchange held an odd reassurance. If they cared for their servants, perhaps the promises made to herself were good, too.

* * *

As Lewis untied her hooks and released the bow on the back of her gown, and helped her out of her corset and into the bed, Tessa felt the nerves build again. Tomorrow they would complete the journey.

Tomorrow she would see if her grandfather was who Mundy believed he was.

And if he accepted her, or if she would be coming back to this house, and learning what it took to fit into the society into which they planned to thrust her.

Tomorrow Warrenby would have no more reason to ride with them.

CHAPTER 20

The day had risen dark, not a promising sign. The sky spit rain from time to time, but did not seem to be able to make up its mind whether to get serious or not.

Tessa looked out the window, trying to get a vision of the house appearing in the gloom. Appropriate, she thought, that her first view was so dim, so vague. Even so, the roof cut into the grey sky, announcing several floors at least. It filled the window sideways as well, dark and forbidding. Unless that was just the ivy that crept up the walls, making them look as if they moved in the evening breeze.

He owned sheep and a mill, Mundy had said. Owned a *lot* of sheep, and a *large* mill, from the look of that house.

She could not pin down how she should feel. Her mother's life had been hard, and she had died so young. Would it have made a difference —assuming Mundy had the right family—if Mother had access to the privileges of wealth?

Even the wealthy died.

Her mother was the most gentle of women, and most of her life was spent with just the two of them while Father was out at sea.

Assuming he had been at sea. More memories rushed to the surface.

Sitting at a table with her mother at her side, gently guiding as she learned to write her letters. Wiping the slate with the greatest of care to ensure the precious stone would last. Remembered reading aloud to a loving audience of one, remembered the soft tones of her mother's voice as she corrected the pronunciation of words when Tessa stumbled. Never laughing at her young daughter, unless they could laugh together. Walking to the nearest market holding her mother's hand as a child, or holding the basket herself as she got older. Learning to make gowns from scraps of fabric, or taking old ones apart and reforming them to use the bits that hadn't faded.

Her mother's image in one memory after another came fast now, clearer than they had been of late.

Cooking together, learning to bargain for scraps of meat, stretching meals with whatever vegetables could be picked up at the market or their tiny gardens when they had them. Saying prayers together, her mother on the covers with her underneath, the kiss when they were done. Kneading bread under her mother's watchful eye on the same tables where she did her lessons, then watching it rise. The scent of the bread when it was cooking in the small bread cubby put in the side of the fireplaces.

The carriage turned down a drive, and the house slid out of the window's view. She could see it in her mind, though, see it drawing closer as if there was nothing between her and it.

Would her mother want her to forgive? Her leg started to jiggle up and down, the movement so rapid it sent vibrations through the floor of the carriage.

A warm hand came down on hers. Only then did she realize how very cold she had become. She turned to look at Mundy, but everything seemed to move slowly, ever so slowly.

Everything except for that leg, which still bounced in a jerky rhythm.

His eyes were mild, compassionate, but under that she thought she saw the firmness of iron. "Give deRoss a chance, my dear. I am certain it is hard for him to admit that he might have been wrong to treat your mother the way he did."

Words that had been pounding against her lips, strangling in her throat, finally burst out. "He knows nothing about what we endured! Nothing! How can he? What does he know about hunger? About being cold? About having to scrounge for ways to stretch a meal, about having to take gowns apart, or turn them to the inside to make them presentable? I keep seeing my mother, all my memories of our lives. If he lived in a normal house it would not be so hard. But this luxury?"

She waved toward the carriage window, which showed the house sliding back into view as they followed the drive closer, the candles in a few of the windows beginning to outweigh the oppressive day.

"My father was hardly perfect, but my mother was wonderful. She was the most accepting, most honest, most loving person I have ever known. When I think of what she endured during my life and compare it with *that*," Tessa could not even bring herself to look out the window, "it makes me furious! And I am supposed to grant him some kind of *absolution*?"

Mundy's mouth turned down, and his eyes went . . . sad. "There are other ways to suffer than from hunger and poverty. Your grandfather has suffered as well. I want you to promise you will at least *listen*."

Tessa clenched her hands tight, trying to hold in the pain surging through her. She had to look away from the plea, or encouragement, or *disappointment* she had seen there.

She felt it inside, she did not need to see it on someone else's face.

This anger had surged so quickly that she was not prepared for it, and it still roiled in her heart and stomach. A couple days ago she had only her father's mistakes—no, *crimes*—to work through, the turmoil he left for her. He was gone, there was no way to force him to apologize, to clear up what he had done to her. Her mother, though, if there was such a thing as a perfect person, her mother would nearly qualify for the title.

That someone condemned Mother to such a life when they could have helped, someone knowingly had thrown her aside when they suspected what might be in store for her?

The broken jewelry popped back into her mind, those stolen letters. Had Father shown signs of what he would become? Whatever her mother knew about her husband, she had not spoken against Reginald, not that Tessa could remember.

Mundy was watching her, she felt his gaze but could not look at him just yet. That disappointment could have been on Mother's face, *would* have been if her mother was sitting there instead of him.

She did not want to disappoint her mother, nor the man standing in her place. Even more, she felt if she could not find a way through this awful anger, she would be disappointing herself. She wanted to be as good as her mother, wanted to be a person she could like.

Right now she did not like herself very much, but how did one forget? That was part of forgiveness, Mother had taught her.

There was too much to remember. Too much hunger, too much want, too much struggle.

The last lurch told her they had stopped, they were here. It was either the right family, or the wrong one. Until she knew . . . well, her mother had taught her how to be courteous.

The door opened, and the little steps were flipped down.

Tessa hesitated as she looked at the hand held out to her. Two things could happen. This man she was about to meet, Baronet deRoss, might accept her. Equally, he might not. Mundy thought she looked exactly like her mother. When she saw herself in her small mirror, she did not see her mother, however. She only saw herself.

She looked up at the owner of the hand, although she knew the minute she came out of her thoughts whose it was. Warrenby looked down at her. "We will go in first, if you wish, and leave you in the foyer until you are ready. Would you like that?"

She clamped her hand on his, and let him help her own. "That would be nice, thank you."

Her legs felt stronger as she climbed down the small steps out of the carriage.

Warrenby tucked her hand into his arm and began walking to that door. Halfway there, he drew her to a stop. She looked up in surprise. Had he changed his mind about her coming?

His crystal gaze glittered. "Promise me one thing?"

"Anything," she said, and smiled, knowing the word had more meaning than he could guess.

"Stay behind me, if you will. I can only assume you will be able to hear what is said. I will come get you when I am sure."

"I will."

He smiled, gave her hand in his elbow a pat, and continued toward the door.

Lewis walked behind her, quiet as a good maid should be.

There were no layers of stairs leading up to the door, just one lone step, oddly humble. Tessa was glad, because even with the support of Warrenby's arm, she did not think she could have climbed more than that.

The door was open, Mundy waiting just inside as they walked through.

If the outside of the house had been imposing, the inside matched. They walked into the foyer, wide, with dark wood doors, dark wood floors, dark wood moulding, and no window. Candle sconces made of shiny, polished metal hung on the painted deep green side walls. At least, she thought it was paint, it did not look like wallpaper. Mirrored backs on the sconces reflected the flickering light, brightening what otherwise might have been a gloomy welcome.

"Stay here. I will come through those doors," he waved toward the double doors behind him, "when it is time."

* * *

Blake kept his impatience under control as he waited in the green parlor where they had been shown. A large fireplace with an elaborate scalloped grey marble mantle, an anemic flame burning in the base despite the summer warmth, was the focus of one wall. Small mahogany tea tables sat scattered around the room wherever they would be most convenient. A long settee with curving legs and embroidered covering sat in the middle of the room, surrounded by several reading chairs done in the same style, only upholstered in leather. A backless bench with heavily carved legs ran along the length of the window, extra seating for guests or brighter light for fancywork like embroidery. Dark green velvet curtains, if he guessed his fabrics right, hung over the windows, still partially opened for as much of the daylight as they could catch.

Fat flowers in china vases sat on the tables on both sides of the fireplace and announced a woman's presence. According to Mundy, the man's wife—Tessa's grandmother—had died some time ago so either he remarried in the intervening years, or these were from the daughters.

He wondered what Tessa would feel when she saw all this wealth. A sharp pain ran across his chest, comparing what he saw here with the mean street on which she lived. Even the curtains were better fabric than what made up the gowns she wore.

Thank goodness Mundy had managed to convince her to purchase a couple new ones. Blake did not want her subjected to mockery by those who had no idea how hard she worked. No appreciation for the value her skills held.

What did they know about the lives of the poor? The depth of their struggle? Her mere presence in his life made him look at his own servants in a new way.

A large long case clock of inlaid wood gave a sudden chime, interrupting his survey of the room, and reminding him how long they had waited.

A strange clicking sound from down the hallway caught his attention. Shoulders straight, Blake watched the wide parlor door and waited.

The small front wheel came past the edge of the wall first, followed by the long body of the chair. Legs wrapped in a heavy dark blanket despite the warm night. At the same time as the big wheels came through, Blake saw the man sitting in it. A thick shock of white hair, and a lined face with a straight nose and a strong jaw. At first glance, he did not look sick enough to be in that chair. His color was strong, his cheeks were ruddy. Even the fine black coat he wore seemed to fit tight over arms that looked like they could carry the chair instead of the other way around. Heavy dark eyebrows made a scowl over piercing eyes as dark as Tessa's.

What on her was delicate and feminine, on him made an imposing face.

When Blake looked closer, he saw the grey under all that color.

"Ah, Lord Mundy. Been a while, yes, been a while. Got your letter." The man's head bent forward, his eyes gazing between and around them, as if assuming they were hiding Tessa in the room.

"Might I present Lord Warrenby"—but Mundy got no further.

"Yes, yes, pleasure I'm sure. Where is she? I expected you to bring her." DeRoss's voice boomed out with enough volume to rattle the windows. "Not getting any younger, you know. I have traced all manner of false leads over the years. I am not eager to fall for another hoax. Don't have much time left, not much at all."

Mundy stood straighter. "I am most certain you will recognize her." He fairly radiated conviction.

"Most certain." DeRoss whispered the words. The man seemed to sag, the steam seeping out of him like a kettle off the fire. Then his fierce dark eyes filled with tears. "Is she well?" The words tumbled out in a rush. His hands clenched on the blanket over his legs so tight that the knuckles went white. "I was a fool, a stubborn old fool. So many wasted years." That groan came again, ripped from a deep place of regret. "Why did I not—why did I not—"

The man did not finish. His eyes filled with tears, overflowed. The water ran down his cheeks. He dipped his head, and Blake saw the silvery drops fall onto the blanket. The servant who had pushed the chair and stood so silently behind it that it had been easy to overlook his presence reached around and pulled a small cloth from under the covering. He tucked it into deRoss's hand, and the man mopped his face. His breath shuddered, the cloth he held fluttered in his loose grip.

Blake decided to step in. "The husband died recently, but the daughter is waiting in the foyer."

DeRoss's head whipped upright. Despite the red rims, and the matching red around his nose from crying, those dark eyes pierced into Blake's. "My granddaughter is here? Why did you not bring her in? Why is she standing out there?"

Mundy spoke up before Blake could say anything. "Seeing her might be a bit of a shock, and I thought it best to warn you first."

"What do you mean, shock? Why would I be shocked? How else can I weigh the evidence, unless I see her?" Those sharp eyes filled with tears again, but this time they did not fall.

"She is the living image of her mother." Mundy smiled in reminiscence. "The first time I saw her, I thought she was Elizabeth."

"Ohhh." DeRoss drew the word out, more a sigh than speech. He cleared his throat, a rough and wet sound. "Well, go get her! Need to see for myself!"

"I will be happy to." Blake interrupted Mundy before the man could reply. He wanted to see the look on Tessa's face when she found out how very welcome she was. After a lifetime of living on the outside, at last here was a place where she could belong.

Out in Gloucestershire, instead of at Madame's shop. Out here, where it was several days' journey to see her. He should be happy for her. He *was* happy for her. But it was going to make London a lonely place.

As he turned to walk out, Blake was struck with just how empty it would be. For a moment, he forgot what he was doing, where he was supposed to be going. His legs felt shaky, as if he had been hit hard with something.

Now she was the granddaughter of a baronet. It would have, could have, gone nowhere when she was a mere seamstress. As the granddaughter of a baronet, however small the title, now anything was within her reach.

And within his?

CHAPTER 21

The butler stood at the doors, double ones of the same darkness that seemed to permeate the house, leading to some inner room. Tessa looked at those big doors, and her heart thumped so hard she struggled to catch her breath.

So loud she wondered if he could hear it. She pressed her hand against it, trying to slow it down, hold it in. He noticed, of course he noticed, and she dropped that betraying hand away from the racing beat. As she glanced up, she found herself staring into his crystal eyes. He smiled. At the edge of her vision, she noticed one of his hands lift, pause, then drop back to his side.

She wished she could grab that hand and hold on.

"Don't be afraid. He is excited to see you. He regrets what he did very much." His finger came up under her chin for the barest whisper of a touch, but enough to make her gaze flash up to his face. A faint smile pulled at the corner of his mouth. "I promise I will not leave you here if you are the least uncomfortable. You must tell me." He bent his head, staring into her eyes, and the moment stretched, growing longer, taking on something new and tantalizing, his eyes coming ever closer . . .

A sound cut in, the maid clearing her throat.

He straightened with a jerk, and looked at her with an odd expression in those eyes. "Trust Mundy. If he says your grandfather will recognize you, he will. Will you take my arm?"

She nodded, trying to hide her disappointment at that lost moment. She could feel Warrenby's lungs rise and fall against her hand where it rested so close it was pressed to his coat. Odd, she never thought of him breathing so fast. His breath was coming almost as quickly as her own.

Warrenby's other hand came down on hers where it had clenched on his crooked arm. It was warm, unless hers was cold. "Are you all right? I assure you, I will not abandon you here. Mundy has given his word, also. We will make certain you are well-treated before we leave."

Well-treated. Granted, they had both been kind to her when she was just the seamstress who had found Robert. Now, she was possibly related to A Title. Not a big one, but a title nonetheless. That suddenly made her *acceptable*. She should be glad at least that he could now talk to her without having to treat her like a servant.

Something inside her, something hurt and aching, wished it had been different. She wished she had been *acceptable* when she was just Tessa Abbott, seamstress. To know she had been good enough just as she was. The world was the way it was. It was not his fault. *You are one of the lucky ones*, she told herself. And then the reminder. *Maybe.*

Warrenby's hand was still on hers. His voice came through the clutter in her mind. "I will stay beside you the whole time." He turned to stand between her and the door. Humor crept into his voice. "If you feel uncomfortable, give me word. I helped bring you here, it is only fair that I be the one to take you away if it does not work." He smiled. "Shall we go inside now?"

That moment of claiming herself was all she needed. "I'm ready."

"I thought you might be." He turned to the door, which was waiting ajar. The butler no doubt had sensed they wanted another moment, as he and waited discretely just inside, to swing the door wide just as Warrenby put out his hand.

Those knees trembled again, but his arm beneath her hand was strong, and she had that smile, that quick flash of *something* in his eyes, to cling to.

The man stepped out of the way as he pushed one of the two doors open. Facing her, taking over the major part of the opposite wall was a massive fireplace, with a small blaze burning in the center. She stepped in with less courage than she wished. Candles were scattered about this room. A lit chandelier hung from the ceiling, casting a bright glow, and undoubtedly put her into glaring focus.

As her gaze started to move, sitting off to the side, an old man with grey hair sat in a wheeled chair, a grey blanket covering his legs, eyes fixed on the doorway, and on her. Even as she watched, his eyes went wide and he gasped, a sudden, shocking sound.

Tessa took a step forward, then hesitated.

The butler stepped around her and hurried over. A man was already kneeling by the chair, she did not remember seeing him but he must have been in the room to get there so quickly.

She looked up at Warrenby. In a whisper so faint she did not know at first if he even heard her, she asked, "What do I do?"

He gave a quick nod. "I think you should go to him."

It would have been harder to make the first step if not for the awful sounds that still came from behind the old man's hands. DeRoss, they had said his name was. Some short Christian name, it started with the letter 'A,' but the rest eluded her. Calling him 'grandfather' was too presumptuous this early, but 'deRoss," she could do that.

Her skirts on the new blue gown swished as she crossed the room, brushing the floor. The sound had never seemed so noticeable, perhaps because she wanted to be quiet. Wanted to come up to this man on her own terms.

It didn't work, of course it would not. The man—deRoss—was paying attention to her despite the grief overwhelming him. He dropped his hands from a wet, swollen face, swiped them across the blanket, and held them out to her before she was halfway there.

"Elizabeth! My Elizabeth." Someone hissed something at him, and he snapped, "I know that!" Then he angled his head enough to look over his shoulder at the man who stood by the wheeled chair back. "Bring me to her."

Tessa kept walking. Her steps were both going too fast, and too slow, but her questions about who he was seemed to have their answer. This old man looked at her and saw her mother, just as Mundy had. If the resemblance was that striking, it must be true.

The chair creaked as it was pushed toward her, the old man—her grandfather—still holding out his hands. As they neared each other, Tessa felt her heart soften.

Whatever her grandfather did to her parents, what caused him to cut them off, he deeply regretted it, that much was obvious even from a distance.

It was up to her to determine where they went next. She and her grandfather met in the middle of the room. He stared up at her, and she found herself looking into eyes the same dark color as her own. His eyes were bright. Or at least glistening.

Tessa took a big breath, and held out her hands. "Hello," she said, but nothing more would come. Her throat was tight, from his emotion or from her own she did not know.

He clutched her hands so tight her fingers were pinched together. "What is your name, my dear?" His deep voice came out gravely, and she was tempted to clear her own throat, as if that would help his.

Name, yes. Start with that, and think about all the thoughts tumbling about her mind, roiling in her stomach, later. "Tessa Abbott."

At her last name, he winced. "Tessa." He tried to smile. "Do you know how much you look like your mother?" Those dark eyes filled with tears again. "I was a stubborn old man, I missed out on your whole life. Your grandmother had it right, and I was wrong."

If her grandmother had been over to the pretty little house that was such a vague memory, if the woman had kept in touch with her daughter . . . "I don't remember," she said, and felt a pang at the anguish that slipped across his face.

His eyes went tight around the edges before they closed, a visible wince. His jaw tightened, and he drew a shuddering breath before he looked at her again. "Of course you would not. I tried to keep her away."

Those old fingers that had already been tight on her, clenched more. Not enough to hurt, rather that she felt the shudder of regret running all the way through his hands.

It was hardly the thing to do, to tell him she knew nothing about him. Nothing about her grandmother who loved her mother, nothing about any sisters or brothers in the family. So she kept still, just let him cling to her.

If only she felt some connection to this sad old man. Much as she wished she could, everything was too new, too uneasy. Perhaps if her parents had ever mentioned him, she might have wanted to know more. Right now, he was only a stranger.

So she let him hold her hands and tried to hide her unease. He was so excited, so anxious to claim a link to her.

"I will send word to the rest of the children. I am sure they will rush here to meet you. Your aunt who lives nearest can be here tomorrow, it is a short drive, but they will have to make arrangements." He pressed her hands together, framing them with his own. "They will be delighted, I can promise you that."

Speaking for others was a risky thing. She had seen it in the shop, mothers picking out designs for their daughters—'She will love this color, this fabric, this design'—only to have the daughters flatly reject them. And that was just gowns.

Dropping an unknown niece and cousin into the family was a recipe for disaster.

She had come this far. There was no turning back now. Tessa took a deep breath and made herself smile.

He kept on, plans rushing out. "You will stay here, of course. I already have a room being prepared for you, and another for your maid."

Maid—Lewis! How could she have forgotten her? She wanted to turn and make sure the woman had been let inside, but deRoss—her grandfather kept speaking. This was going to take some getting used to, having a family.

"Mundy and Warrenby will stay the night as well, of course. I will not send anyone out when the sun has already set. I cannot have any accidents, any injuries, on my conscience." He looked up above her, no doubt at one of the other men.

"But—" she bit her tongue. Perhaps Mundy had changed his mind about going back this evening. He said nothing, so the arrangements must be acceptable. Warrenby, too, made not a sound, but it was only logical these arrangements suit him. London was a lot farther than Mundy's estate.

The calendar seemed to be rushing away from her. Three days already spent for the journey here, now another day, two, maybe more depending on how long it took the rest of the family to receive word. Then of course their journey here, then her journey back—she felt the nerves build. If she was to keep her position, she could stay one day, that was all.

How could she explain that to him?

Someone cleared their throat behind her, and her grandfather let go of her hands. "Yes, Mrs. Thompson?"

It was a woman, middle-aged and grey-haired, somewhat rounded. The woman wiped her hands on her apron. "The meal is ready to be served, Sir."

"Very well. Thank you." DeRoss gave a nod, apparently a signal to the man who pushed his wheeled chair, and the little group moved toward the door. "Horton?

Without seeming to rush, Horton—the butler, she discovered—got to the door first, and waved them through. DeRoss held out his hand, and she took it. She had held it before, but walking beside the chair, trying to keep her skirt out of the large wheel on the side, deRoss steering the front wheel's bar one-handed, was awkward.

He picked up the questions. "So you are the only child your parents had? No other sisters? No brothers?"

She thought of their small family, much of the time just her mother and herself when her father was out doing … whatever he did. And smiled. "No, it was mostly just my mother and myself."

He seemed to perk up at that. "Your father left?"

Tessa shook her head. "No, but he was . . . on the Packet ships, so he was gone most of the time." She hoped that hesitation was not noticeable, had not expected to stumble over the statement. Whether Father was actually on those ships, she no longer knew, but she was not going to air that in front of this man who already had enough to hold against her father.

Her mother might have been welcome, she certainly was, but her father? Not likely. Not even in memory.

Horton pushed open a single door near the end of the hallway, and held it as the group walked in.

She noticed the color of the room first. Three tall narrow windows on the outside wall were smothered with heavy black curtains, pulled against the coming night. All four walls were done in a dark blue, whether plaster or paper she could not tell from where she stood. A large chandelier of iron tracery hung overhead, and there were signs of dripped wax on the table near the center of the room.

Sconces had been mounted on the walls, but only a couple were lit. Perhaps with such a small group, deRoss felt there was no need for blazing light. Or perhaps he just liked his house dark and masculine.

It would be nice to see it in the sunshine, with the curtains wide and the sun streaming in.

What had her grandmother been like? Had the house been brighter when she was alive? Or did the woman live in all these heavy hues?

The table that took up the center of the room, mahogany perhaps, or walnut, was dark and imposing and long enough to fit a large family but not long enough for a supper party of more than a dozen couples. Matching high-backed chairs lined it, and a sideboard long enough for Warrenby to lie down on its top sat against one wall.

She heard chairs being pulled out, and turned her attention from the room and her memories to what was happening now. The butler and the servant pushing the chair took her grandfather's arms and helped him to his feet. He could stand, but she saw him flinch, and his steps to the table from the chair were so obviously painful that she winced just watching him.

His feet were wrapped in some thick bandages, and he did not have shoes on. It appeared he was barely able to bear weight on his feet.

For the first time since she walked into the house, for the first time since she had even heard about her grandfather, Tessa ached for him. No wonder Mundy had been so insistent that she come and come quickly.

He would not want her sympathy, though, so when one of the two footmen who had appeared seemingly from nowhere pulled out the chair next to her grandfather, Tessa took it without hesitation.

Then the meal came in, surprisingly large for the middle of the day. First a light soup, flavored with tiny flakes of chicken and parsley. After that, fish cooked to perfection, light and crisp, then the meat, rich and tender.

Through all of the courses, her grandfather peppered her with questions. "Where did you live after you moved away? Your father was in the Packet Service? Was my daughter happy? What was it you did in London? You sewed? That is a good womanly occupation."

By 'occupation,' she did not think he meant actual employment. No doubt he thought of needlework, something to keep the hands busy during long quiet hours sitting by a window. In his chair, Warrenby smiled. He knew exactly what she meant when she said she sewed.

"My mother taught me. After she died, I needed some way to support myself until he got back."

"Support yourself?" He sounded surprised.

"Yes," she said, wondering how she could make her life sound softer. She did not want to cause him more pain, but neither could she make her life something it was not. "I have been working in a modiste's shop for several years now. I am a seamstress."

He only sighed.

Tessa tried again. "Sir deRoss . . ."

"Grandfather!" He barked the word so sharply that she gave a start. "None of this 'sir' business. I know who you are, surely proved that I do. You will call me 'grandfather,' are we clear?"

"Yes, sir."

"Excuse me? What did I just say?"

"I'm sorry. I will try . . . Grandfather. As I was saying, you work, and work hard. Your son no doubt works just as hard now to keep the mill going. There is nothing wrong with work. I actually enjoy it." *Most of the time*, she added to herself, but didn't say it.

"Not my *daughters*," the old man grumbled, and Tessa bit her tongue again. Her mother had worked, and worked hard, at whatever she could get for long stretches of her childhood.

Through the whole meal, between his questions, her grandfather barely ate. The reason why that might be worried her.

CHAPTER 22

Tessa looked around the bedroom she had been given last night. Between the rain that had begun in earnest in the afternoon, and the sunset that brought night's dark earlier, the candle was hardly bright enough to see anything other than the bed, only that the room was large. Now that the sun was out, the sky was clear, she could look around before she had to leave again.

She wanted to stay, she really did, but all she could think was that Ellen's crippled father was home alone without his wife to care for him, and Madame needed to hire a permanent replacement for her soon.

When she got back, there would be no position at all waiting for her unless she left today, and even then, it might be too late. Ellen's mother might have found the work suited her, might have found a neighbor to care for her husband, might be better, more skilled, than Tessa herself. So many "maybe's."

It would be another three days' journey back before she knew if anything awaited her. Five hundred pounds would not last forever.

But her grandfather was not well. How long would she have to stay to ease his guilt over the abandonment of her mother? Stay and risk everything she knew, everything she had, or go back and hope against all rational thought that her position remained? Stay or go, go or stay? Her mind bounced between the questions like a cat chasing a mouse around a room.

The room. She dragged her thoughts away from the jumble inside, and looked around. Had this space once been her mother's? It was beautiful, soft blue walls, large windows with white curtains patterned in the identical shade of blue. The coverlet matched. The old feather layer on top of the overstuffed straw mattress was the best bed she had ever been in.

A thick real fur rug was spread by the side of the bed, ensuring that no one would step on a cold floor in the winter. She remembered that cushioning from last night. A fireplace, not just the small enclosed style that burned coal like the one in her small rented place in London but a real fireplace, took up part of one wall.

She thought she heard movement, rustlings, as if someone had changed position in the bed and it had bumped the wall the two rooms had in common. Who had that other room? It could be either Warrenby or Mundy. It would not be her grandfather. He slept downstairs in a room converted for his chair. For a man of his size who must have been vigorous and energetic when younger, having his body betray him so viciously was one of the cruelties of age.

He promised her before they were all dismissed for the night that at least one of her aunts would be here today. The words had sent a chill down her arms. Mundy and Warrenby were leaving, she would have no support—except for her grandfather, their own doting father.

She fought her way through the enveloping feather layer that tried to wrap around her to get out of the bed. What if she had slept through Warrenby's—and Mundy's—departure?

He would not have left without saying goodbye, would he? A tightness formed around her heart, and moved up into her throat. *Please don't let him have left*, her mind pleaded. *Let me have a few minutes to talk to him, at least to say goodbye.*

After making short work of her morning cleansing with the filled pitcher and the bar of soap left for her—real hard soap! What a luxury!—she fought with the fastenings of her gown until she gave up.

Tapping on the door to the small attached dressing room where the maid slept, she waited for a response. At a grunt from inside, she poked her head around the door. A lump on the bed shifted.

"Lewis? Is that you?"

"Yes." The voice was rough, thick with sleep.

A sharp stab of guilt assailed her. After several hard days of travel, yesterday being the most difficult, surely a woman Lewis's age needed her sleep. Now that she had awakened her maid, though, she might as well get what she was there for. "Can you help me fasten my gown?"

Lewis sat up and straightened the cap on her head, which drooped over one eye. "One moment." A deep yawn, and she swung her legs over the bed. When she rose, she wobbled briefly and grabbed at the bedframe before she steadied. "What time is it?"

Tessa stared at her. In her hurry not to miss Warrenby's departure, she had not even thought to check. "I don't know." She took in the room, and found a small hand-wind clock sitting on the far side of the bed.

"Oh. It's five thirty." Even she knew that was much too early for any of the gentry to arise. It was, however, her own normal rising time. "I'm sorry. I didn't realize how early it was."

A few moments later, everything fastened in the soft pink gown she had set in the bottom of a trunk for a special occasion, she crept down the long, dim stairs, and eased open the door at the bottom to peek through before venturing out.

Other than the whispering of the silk from her gown, the brush of her soft pink slippers that hardly counted as shoes, the house was silent. In a way, the quiet was calming, a chance to browse without feeling eyes on her.

The gown with its darling little cap sleeves that barely covered her shoulders was cool in the morning, and she debated going back for a shawl, but that could wait. If Warrenby was about, she did not want to miss a minute, and besides, with the sun shining, the air would warm soon enough.

Besides, the fine cotton fichu around her neck kept at least part of her warm.

Once in the room where she first met her grandfather, she strolled around, looking at the lovely silver and brass candle holders, the rich embroidery of flowers and ferns on the settee covering, the miniatures on the mantle.

Among the small portraits, she saw nothing that could be her mother, and in the count of woman's likenesses, she came up with only four. Four daughters, when there should be five. On one wall, a large portrait had a slight resemblance to her mother, but from the dated style of the gown, the wide collar, the scarf filler for the fitted bodice, and the upsweep of the hair, she knew this must be her grandmother.

From what she could tell, her mother's existence had been wiped from the house.

* * *

Blake slid an arm behind his head as he stared at the ceiling and looked at the border of painted flowers that went around the edge the entirety of the room. And the whitewashed wainscoting, and the soft yellow wall above. He had not thought to draw the curtains last night, the day had been so dark and in the country there was no one to see, but now the sun illuminated the entire room, showing details that last night's candlelight had not reached. This had obviously belonged to a girl at one time, but then, it appeared that deRoss's offspring leaned heavily toward that sex.

That reminded him of deRoss's welcome and easy acceptance of Tessa. Mundy had been so sure the resemblance to her mother would be undeniable, and he had been right.

You will call me 'grandfather,' are we clear?

The memory of that gruff voice made him smile. While Mundy would have kept his promise and taken her into his house, into his care, it suited Blake very well at the moment to have her here where her grandfather would be in no hurry to rush her into wedlock.

Seeing her at the table last night, so elegant, so comfortable, looking like she belonged, just as she had the night before at the dinner Lady Mundy had set up, proved how well Tessa would fit in.

He had always known there was something about her in servants' garb that did not fit, her speech that announced a training and a background much higher than the lowly position she held.

While a baronet's granddaughter was hardly in the same class as a duke's or even a viscount's, it certainly did not belong in the dingy street where she lived.

The look on her face when Mundy had set up the account at a real bank where he deposited her reward still threatened to tighten his throat. If she had been handed the crown jewels, he doubted her awe would have been any greater.

Of course, one could not spend the crown jewels.

Would she miss sewing gowns? Her skill was remarkable, everyone seemed to think so, even he could see the talent in what she made for his mother and sister. Stitching samplers would hardly be a challenge after making fashions that were the envy of the *ton*.

Faint noises came through the wall from the room next door. Only someone used to getting up early—or someone like himself who frequently found war habits rise up and take him with them—would be around at this hour.

Which meant that Tessa was awake and would soon be moving about the house.

He intended to take advantage of that.

The cord for the valet was right within reach. The man came in rubbing his eyes. "Might this be a bit early for you, my lord? What brings you out of bed on this fine morn?"

"The morning, Jasper. It promises to be a sunny day. We don't get them like this in London."

"Naw, sir, that we don't. Not often." Jasper plucked the pants off the chair where they had been laid and handed them over. He used the cloth sitting next to the pitcher, and wiped out the bowl, then poured the water from the pitcher into it. "You ain—aren't the only one up an' about. I saw Miss Abbott slipping into her maid's room. I think she'll be wanting an escort around the yard. If I'm not too bold in saying so."

"That's good to know, Jasper." Trust the servants to know more about their employers than the employers did about themselves. "You are right, she isn't used to an area like this."

"I'll be getting you dressed quick as a wink. Less you want a shave? That'll take an extra few minutes to get the warm water up from the kitchen."

Blake ran a hand over his jaw. "See how fast you can get some, will you, Jasper?"

"Yessir!" The valet was out the door so quickly Blake suspected a romance was blooming between his valet and someone in the kitchen staff here. He did not want to get a new valet. Jasper suited him just fine, and valets handled such personal details that it took special qualities to make a good one.

Blake used the water to wash up. He could have sent for a bath, but that would involve hauling up the tub, as well, and if no one was awake yet, he certainly didn't plan on waking them with all the noise and bustle. Then he opened his satchel, pulled out the razor and the strop, and sharpened the blade.

A tap came on the door, then it opened, and Jasper picked up the teapot he had set on the floor. "Yer hot water, my lord. I assumed you would use the bowl I saw in the room, so didn't bring one."

"Dump out what's there," Blake pointed to his soapy water, "and get me the fresh."

"Yessir." With his usual efficiency, the water went out the window and the bowl got a quick rinse from the pitcher, and fresh, steaming water waited.

A door nearby opened again, and shut. He thought he heard the footsteps going down the hall, and whipped his head toward the door to track their progress, narrowly missing slicing himself on the chin.

"My lord!" Jasper caught the razor, sliding it out of Blake's hand. "Don't know why you don't let me do it like the other gentlemen's gentlemen, but if you're doing it yourself, at least pay 'ttention 'fore you put out an eye!"

Blake grinned. "Go out and keep an eye on Miss Abbott for me, will you?" When Jasper's brow lifted, he added, "She knows nothing about the country. Make sure she doesn't wander outside, will you? I don't think deRoss has bulls, but she might think a pasture is another lovely meadow."

Jasper nodded. "Don't tie your cravat until I get back, please. You do enough of my work that I sometimes wonder why you got me at all." He handed the razor back.

After all the experience he'd had in France caring for himself, Blake made quick work of the serious business of shaving. Before he finished with his shirt cuffs, the door opened again, and Jasper stepped in, closing the door with care behind him. In a low voice, as if he expected to be overheard, he said, "She's just looking 'round in the house." He took the second cufflink and slipped it through the hole, then stepped back. "I'll tell the kitchen to get the breakfast going."

One deep breath before he grabbed for the doorknob, and let himself out into the hall.

* * *

Footsteps came from the stairs that led into the parlor, and her heart skipped a beat. From the sounds of it, one man, and she knew which one she preferred it to be. Warrenby smiled at her as he pushed open the door and found her there, staring at the doorway where he stood.

She could not read that smile. A simple greeting? Or something more?

"I'm glad I got to see you. I wish I could stay longer, but I have to get back to London, and I must leave today." He motioned toward the front door. "Can we go for a walk while we wait for our breakfast?"

She felt her whole face light up. How embarrassing for him! In a more composed voice, she said, "I would love that very much."

He held out an arm, and Tessa slipped her hand into the crook of the elbow. "We will stay within sight of the house. There is no reason to cause anyone concern, and your grandfather should not be allowed to worry."

The butler surprised them by being at the door. She wondered where he had come from that she not noticed him earlier, but he opened the door with the mild comment, "Breakfast is being prepared."

"Thank you, Horton." With a nod, Bla—Warrenby kept moving, outside and across the flagstone walk. The sun was just illuminating the tops of the trees, the shadows were long, the sky still held a bit of the nighttime on the far side. The drive curved, the marks of their coach wheels showed as fresh grooves in the loose rock. She watched her step in the soft new slippers, keeping an eye out for larger, sharper stones.

Her old work shoes, upstairs hiding in her satchel, would be handy right now.

Warrenby seemed in no hurry, he just kept a slow stroll, matching his steps to her smaller stride. The expressions on his face fascinated her.

Each time she glanced up at him out of the corner of her eye, trying to memorize his every feature to keep her warm in the days ahead, it was different. One moment relaxed, his mouth quirking at the edges as if amused, the next moment frowning, his mouth tight, lines creasing around his eyes as if the thought that prompted it disturbed him.

Her favorite was when his face was at peace, the skin smooth, his eyes without lines around the edges, nothing pulling at his forehead, only a faint shadow marking where a beard would be if he allowed one to grow. Even his shoulders were relaxed.

His free hand came up, almost absently as if he did it without thought, and patted hers where it rested on his arm.

The trees that separated the house from the road were not a large stand but the wide trunks proclaimed their age, and the green canopy shielded them from the rising sun's glare as they continued along. Long shadows covered them, giving a momentary break from the brightness, then broke as they moved from one tree's protection to the next. Rustles came from inside, birds or squirrels disturbed by their unexpected presence.

Tessa suddenly realized she had forgotten her bonnet. She had felt no need for one in the house, and he had not thought to remind her before they went outside.

He did not seem to notice.

After a moment, as they neared the larger road, he cleared his throat.

* * *

Tessa looked up at him, and Blake cleared his throat again. Her eyes were so large, so dark, like mysterious pools. If only he knew what she was thinking! Her face had lit up when he asked her to go for a walk, but that might have been as simple as wanting a moment to get some fresh air before the day began.

It did not mean she wanted to be with him.

But he was an earl with wealth and charm, or so he had been told. Surely he could win her over.

Tessa's fingers moved on his arm, and his mind seemed to freeze. He looked down at her just as she looked upward, into those warm chocolate pools gazing, so open, so trusting, up at him, and forgot why he had even taken her out of the house. He had been going to tell her something. What was it?

"Lord Warrenby?"

He stopped walking and looked back at her, his eyes slipping from hers down to her mouth, rosy lips slightly parted now as she began to suspect what was in his mind.

She made no move to step away. His hands came up, dislodging her hand from the arm. One hand on either side of her head, he looked down into those eyes, confused and yearning, and his head lowered, closer, closer, until he felt her breath against his mouth. Before their lips could touch, a bird burst out of the tree, wings flapping, chirping wildly.

He froze, and wished for a wall to beat his head against in frustration. First the maid, and now *birds*? Would no one leave them alone long enough for a simple kiss?

Although the kiss would have been anything but simple, he feared. Once he started, he was not certain he could stop. She had enough to think about without him putting pressure on her.

His head told him that. His heart had a whole different purpose altogether. If he rushed her, Tessa did not have any reason to trust him when he was not comfortable with his new feelings himself.

For him to suddenly tell her that she was important—why should she believe him? If he insisted that he had wanted more when she was a mere seamstress, that he had watched her in the shop, looked for her, escorted his mother and sister when his presence was not necessary just to see her, she had no reason to accept his words.

Somehow he had to find a way to prove it.

He straightened with great reluctance. The chance for a kiss was gone, but he had one more bit of business. He had some wooing to do, and reinforcing his concern for her welfare was a place to start. "I think we are far enough from listening ears for me to speak. What are you thinking now about whether to stay or leave? This is a bigger decision than you expected, I fear. I like the man."

She pulled her gaze away, slowly, coming back for quick glances before finally settling on something in the distance. He could almost see her brain working, almost feel her weighing the benefits of staying versus the comfort of leaving.

"I do as well. I do not want to hurt my grandfather. It is an odd feeling to have so many pieces of one's past come together so quickly. But I have a position hanging in the balance. Five hundred pounds will not last long, and I liked working there. I like Madame, I like Ellen, I even like working in the back room, of all things. When I think about losing that . . ." She sighed, her breath shuddered. "I am so torn! I don't want to start over, but he deserves this chance. I think he is ill, I don't know how long he has to live. Months, maybe a year."

So she had noticed. DeRoss would never forgive him if he convinced Tessa to leave after just finding her. As for himself, he still had her quest to finish, to make certain she could believe she had worth, that none of her father's crimes clung to her. "I think so, too. If Madame no longer has your position, I will see that you . . . find something that suits you."

Yes, he had a position that would suit her very well.

* * *

Before she could protest, Warrenby added, "If things change, if you send a message to Mundy, he will forward it to me. It might take a few days, but I promise to come as soon as I receive the word."

She knew now how valuable his promises were. The night when she challenged him for the worth of his word came back, distant, almost amusing now.

He reached out and took her hands, pressed them together as if she were praying. His hands were so warm, and large. He could cause pain by accident with them, but his touch was so careful, so gentle.

Tessa's throat tightened, a tingle started in her nose as if she might cry. If only he could stay, *they* could stay, the two of them. Not here with her grandfather, but *here*, in the rising sun, with the birds chirping to each other and the smell of growing things.

Somewhere along the line, she had fallen in love with him. She, the daughter of a thief, had dragged this noble man into her scandal. Had risked his reputation. And now she had the audacity to fall in love with him?

He must never know. It would at best embarrass him, at worst put another burden on him. For he would want to let her down gently, because he was that kind of man, one who cared for the feelings of others.

She could only speak in a whisper, her throat was so tight, but she managed to say, "Thank you."

He gave her hands a quick squeeze, then released them. The morning air was cold on them after his warmth was gone.

"Good. I have one more thing." He smiled, a sudden change from the somberness of a moment ago. "Last night your grandfather gave you permission to claim the relationship. I think it is time we, too, got rid of this stiff formality between us. In public we might have to be circumspect, but when we are alone, I am Blake. I would be honored if you would permit me to call you Tessa. Are we agreed?"

She would have to be careful not to let it slip. Now that she realized her love, the struggle would be harder, but O! what a precious gift he had just given her. "I would like that very much."

His smile broadened, moving to his eyes. "Very well, Tessa." Then he waved about him. "I know very little about trees and flowers, but would you like to stroll along the drive?"

If he could smile, a smile in return would not be alarming. She felt her face crinkle, her brows relax, as she let her own smile loose. "Yes, I would. I so seldom get to see grass and trees. Going from my part of town to yours was a revelation."

He leaned back to look down at her face. "But you came in the dark."

"Not completely dark." Her smile slipped into a grin. "When I came with Alfie, it was quite light."

He began to walk, a relaxed kind of stroll that seemed a new side to this driven man. "Speaking of him, I think he will work out well. My head groom told me he is eager to learn. I think at some point I will want to move him to the country."

They found a path, nearly hidden in the windbreak of trees. He raised a brow, and tilted his head toward it. "Shall we explore?"

"Let's." Anything to keep these moments going.

So they took the path. It was nothing fancy, just a wide opening between trees, but it gave a better view of the road, and let them see a carriage that rattled past.

There was no need to talk, other than to point out a squirrel, or listen to a bird's call. A quick bright flash of yellow led to a happy discussion between a tit and goldcrest, a bird Tessa had never heard of before.

Blake laughed when she said that. "Don't expect too much from me, but I had the advantage of listening to my mother and father when they sat in the garden."

They reached a fence, beyond which she saw a great cluster of sheep.

Blake watched the fat white creatures move about before turning around. "I think we're at the end of the path. We should go back. Breakfast must be about to be served, and your grandfather will want to know where you are." He held out his bent arm, and Tessa slipped a hand between his elbow and his body, grateful for the support and the warmth there.

CHAPTER 23

The foyer was quiet when they entered. Tessa had to let go of Blake's arm to negotiate the doors, and missed its warmth. Once again, her hand felt chilled, but it went deeper than that, now she realized what happened when she wasn't watching her place.

The footman who ushered them into the parlor said, "Sir deRoss will be comin' soon. He said ye should wait fer him in the dinin' room." As he started for the door at the other end of the parlor, he suddenly stopped and turned around. "Iffen ye kin follow me?"

Blake held out his arm again. *Do not show too much eagerness*, she told herself as she reached out for that support. A sigh slipped out despite her efforts.

He looked down at her, no doubt he had heard. "Is everything all right?" He leaned down, just a little, and whispered, "Tessa?"

She gave a start at her name, but had to look up, had to meet his gaze. Perhaps it was her awareness of this new feeling inside, but she was unprepared for that steady pale green gaze, the concern there. He stopped walking while he waited for an answer.

It actually hurt to break the connection, but she had to. What had he asked? Oh yes, the sigh. She had to come up with some kind of answer. "I am well."

It must have satisfied him, because they started walking. The footman poked his head out of a door at the end of the hall. "Breakfast is being set out."

She caught the the pungent odor of fish, a whiff of fresh bread, even the sweetness of fruity jam. Blake must have smelled the food as well, because he picked up the pace.

When they entered the dining room, that long sideboard was covered with food. Sausage, and yes, the fish she had noticed, a plate of scrambled eggs, toasted sliced fresh bread. Fresh rolls, something she had seldom eaten and likely the source of the bread she had scented down the hall. More than one kind of jam, which was why she could not identify it.

Tea steamed in fancy pots, and milk in the pitchers that sat between the groupings of food. Gleaming white and floral plates sat in a tallish stack at the far end of the table, along with a pretty wicker basket holding what looked like solid silver knives and spoons, even forks.

Blake lifted her hand off his arm and led her by that same hand over to the sideboard. "We are supposed to serve ourselves. There is no need to hold off until the others arrive. Yes, we were told to wait for deRoss here, but it doesn't mean wait and go hungry." He picked up one of those fancy plates and handed it to her. "Take whatever you wish."

Tessa took the pretty plate, forcing herself not to stare at the beautiful design, the flowers that filled the center and the scalloped edges that ran around the outside, and turned her attention to the food spread out before her.

One sausage, and bit of fish, and a roll, and a piece of toast, and of course the eggs. She saw Blake set his plate down to scoop out some jams, and did the same. Jam on her toast!

There weren't enough hands to carry everything at once, the plate, the silver, and a cup and saucer for tea, so she made a couple trips back to the sideboard before she was ready to sit. A footman appeared out of nowhere—how did he manage to be so inconspicuous until needed?—and pulled out the chair for her.

My goodness!

Before she could seat herself, from outside in the hall came the rattle of the wheeled chair accompanied by murmurs and soft shuffling. Those footmen helping her grandfather, no doubt. It didn't sound urgent, just the calm hum of speech.

Warrenby stepped up beside her. Not too close, just closer. "I will have to give him my regrets. Mundy should be down momentarily, unless he is coming in that group. We will remain long enough to break our fasts, of course, but then we must be on our way."

Leaning down, he said in a low voice, "Send me word if you feel the need to leave. I will come for you. Mundy will gladly have you stay with his wife and daughter until I can collect you."

Before she could respond, Grandfather's chair edged its way through the doorway. In the bright light from the tall windows, her grandfather's face seemed pale. "Ah, I see you have already served yourselves. Excellent." He waved toward the table. "Well, sit, sit, don't let good food go cold."

The same routine as the previous night followed, the servants lifting him from his wheeled chair, helping him to the table, and seating him with care. One of the men went for the food as he called out his instructions. Warrenby sat down on her right, leaving the view between herself and her grandfather open.

"Eat, eat." DeRoss gestured toward her plate. Tessa looked down at her choices, food she had picked out moments ago, and didn't know where to start. The sausage, perhaps, with a bit of eggs. She sighed with delight at the first mouthful. Oh, it was good. Who could do something like this with a simple bit of sausage and eggs? She refreshed her mouth with a swallow of tea, and even that was excellent, smooth and mellow, subtle enough to complement the food without overpowering it. The fish was her next bite, with the same rush of pleasure.

As she leaned back to let everything settle, her grandfather's sparse plate caught her eye. She had seen the same thing last night, and was struck again with how little he ate. Fish, a small helping of eggs, and a single piece of toast along with tea she could tell was clearly weak even from where she sat, and he only picked at them, playing at eating.

Was he dying?

Grandfather set his fork down on his plate. "I sent a note to the one who lives nearby last night, and she should be here today. I know she has already sent word to the others, and they should be here in a matter of days."

Blake stopped the forkful of eggs halfway to his mouth, and lowered it back to his plate. "So they all have received word?"

Grandfather pushed his fork into his own eggs, and looked at Tessa. "I sent messages to my children. Your aunt Abigail should be here today, she lives . . . very close."

That hesitation sent a shiver of *knowing* through her. *She lives very close*. Mundy had told her when the grandmother died and was no longer there to protect who inherited the pretty little house, her grandfather evicted her mother and father and given the place to another daughter.

She had to look away from her grandfather as she tried to determine how she felt. Oddly, that knowledge brought no anger. Years of moving, of small houses in one city after another. How much would have changed if her grandmother had lived? Would her father have been content to stay in that house?

Reginald had insisted he wanted to go to the sea, claimed he longed to hear the slap of the ocean against the ship, feel the roll of the waves. She could not remember a time when those phrases had not come from his mouth. And to be sure, they had often lived in port cities where tall masts poked the sky, visible even from the streets where their small residences were.

Port cities also had roads leading to London. No doubt Reginald could not have tolerated to live under the largess of his wife's mother much longer, anyway.

DeRoss was hurt by what he had done, sending her parents and her own young self away. He had lost the daughter he tried to punish before he could beg forgiveness. Was that not enough pain and loss?

He wanted to make amends. Her mother would accept his apology, would beg him not to look back.

She would not look back either. Her father had no doubt caused enough harm to equal what her grandfather had done, and to far more people, so what was the point of blaming deRoss? Right now, she would eat her breakfast and remember her morning walk. With her small universe back in order, her appetite picked up, and the scents of the food in front of her penetrated.

Tessa spread some jam on her barely-warm toast and took a bite. It was very good jam, and the bread was thick and yeasty. "What kind of jam is this? It's delicious."

"Blackberry," Warrenby said, and she heard the smile in his voice.

"Oh. Thank you." She smiled back. And took another piece of toast so she could have more of the jam.

The door swung in, and Mundy entered. "I apologize for the delay. I slept better last night than I have in days. Weeks." He bent his head to her grandfather. "My compliments, Sir deRoss, on the quality of your beds."

DeRoss returned the small bow from his seat. "I am pleased you found my humble home restful."

Perhaps there was a crumb that got caught, perhaps she had tried to swallow too quickly, but Tessa suddenly started coughing. Warrenby slapped her back two solid whacks, almost sending her into the table, but it did the trick and whatever had been caught in her throat cleared.

"Thank you, my lord." She turned to him, one hand on her neck to soothe the rawness there, and smiled, knowing Blake would hear the familiarity she could not say in public.

Her grandfather seemed to notice the unspoken byplay and approve, because as her gaze continued down the table, she saw him smiling down at his plate. For the first time since they sat down to eat last night, he took a big bite of his food, and exchanged a look with Mundy.

Who had the exact same smug look on his face.

If she could talk him into staying a couple hours longer, delay his leaving just long enough for her to meet this aunt, she could go back to London today with a clear conscience.

After all, they could hardly expect her to wait while they decided whether they even wanted to meet her. She would then have met her grandfather, and an aunt. Surely that was enough.

Madame Genevieve would likely continue holding her position for the three extra days of her return, after having men of Mundy's and Blake's status make the request. She did not care about losing her room. She was never going back there, anyway, and that five hundred pounds would get her a safe place to live.

She would still see Blake when he came into the shop with his mother, and his sister.

When Tessa glanced down the table, wondering how to tell her grandfather that her stay would be this short, wondering how to explain how important it was to hold her position and have an income she could depend on, she realized he had not taken a single bite since her own last piece of toast. If she did not eat, Grandfather would not eat either. It seemed only happiness kept him eating now.

So she picked up her fork and took a bite of something off her plate. What it was she did not know, the food that had been so delicious a moment ago now felt like sand, but she made herself swallow, and take another small mouthful, and another.

The conversation continued, a stray word cut through her thoughts, and Tessa realized she had to pay attention. They were talking about her family, aunts and an uncle, *all who were coming to meet her*, she heard with dismay, and saying it in such concrete terms that it made her mouth go dry.

Thank goodness for the cup of tea she had poured! It was cool enough now to gulp, even though that was not how tea should be drunk.

Her grandfather kept talking to Mundy. "How much do you remember of my other daughters?"

"I remember you had several."

"There were four other daughters besides the one who lives nearby, and of course my son. Abigail, Caroline, Hannah, and Lavinia, then Elizabeth. My son came much later."

Mundy nodded, but did not speak around the mouthful he was chewing.

"Tessa?" Her grandfather turned to her now.

"Yes?"

"You have a great many cousins. Many are grown, I do not know which will come, but be prepared. Abigail had six and now three grandchildren. As I have said, she is the one who lives closest." He took a breath. "Her husband is a vicar, and the area is in need of his services, so I thought it was best they not have to worry about where they would live. Next is Caroline, and she had four children, all girls, and four grandchildren, also all girls."

Goodness! By her reckoning, that made ten cousins to meet, not counting her two aunts or any grandchildren.

He was not done. The names kept coming. "Hannah had three and merely a single grandchild so far, and Lavinia also had six. Two grandchildren so far, and I expect many more. Her husband died and she shows no signs of wishing to wed again. It warms my heart that she loved him so much she never wished to replace him." A smile quirked the edge of her grandfather's mouth. "I hope you don't mind noise. "

Her position with Madame was slipping away. How could she leave now?

CHAPTER 24

Conversation felt stilted as they waited for the carriage to be brought around.

She had been the one to say 'no,' simply because she did not want to hurt her grandfather. If she had said 'yes, please take me home,' she would be getting into the carriage with Mundy, and riding back with Blake. Go or stay, it seemed each decision was wrong.

Brooding was not going to help anything. Tessa looked at Blake and Mundy, standing on the other side of her grandfather's chair in the late morning sun. The lull in the conversation begged to be filled. No one else was talking, so she said the first thing that came to mind. "Lord Mundy, thank you for telling me about my family."

Mundy smiled. "It was my very great pleasure. I look forward to hearing about the reunion. I'm sure they will all be delighted to finally meet you."

"Of course they will!" Grandfather boomed from between them, cutting off whatever else Mundy meant to say. "I am as anxious as you to have them arrive. It might be as much as a week before they can get here, but I won't mind the wait at all."

Tessa's heart gave a lurch at the number. A week! Just to have the rest of the family get here? Every time someone mentioned a time, it got longer.

Blake's crystal eyes seemed to pierce her, to see something she thought she had hidden, because his brows went up in a question.

But she had no answer. In her hand, which she hoped was hiding in the gathers of her skirt, she held the letter to Madame Genevieve asking for more time off that she had written after breakfast, hoping to entrust its delivery to Blake. But now?

When she tore her gaze away from Blake's astute stare, it collided with her grandfather's smug look. In a voice softer than she had ever heard him speak, he said, "He's a good man. I could not have picked a better for you."

Beyond him, Mundy was smiling, too.

"Oh, Grandfather! It's not that at all." She shoved that look, the almost-kiss in the trees, their new informality, to the recesses of her mind.

He had already turned to Blake. “I enjoyed your company as well, my lord. You must promise to come again.”

Blake glanced over at Tessa. “That is a promise I can make, sir. You have my word.”

A carriage rattle and the brisk clomp of horses’ hooves interrupted them, but it seemed distant, coming from the road. They all turned, trying to stare through the thin trees. A large vehicle was rattling along, but instead of going on past, it turned into the drive.

* * *

“Oh, good.” DeRoss rubbed his hands. “This will be Abigail. I wonder if any of her children are with her.” The man smiled up at Tessa, standing at his side.

Was it Blake’s imagination, or had Tessa suddenly gone stiff? His horse nudged him from behind. He looked around, but there was no one to take the reins from him.

The coach, large but worn, a typical black color that long years of use had worn to a dark grey, pulled up in front of them. The coachman jumped down and hurried over to open the door and flip down the folding steps. DeRoss had said one daughter lived close. She made good time. For this first meeting with a relative other than her grandfather, if Tessa was going to be in any way made uncomfortable, he wanted to be right beside to give her support. He and Mundy could wait to leave for a few more minutes.

Grey hair poked out first, on a tall, lanky man in a nondescript black suit. He turned to help out someone inside, likely his wife. This would be the oldest sister, and Blake’s attention sharpened.

His horse gave him a second, sharper nudge, but he ignored it. The animal knew the saddle meant he was supposed to run, and he wanted to get on with it, but he would have to wait.

The woman was rotund, with large hips, an equally large bosom and a sour face, and Blake’s heart lurched. He doubted Tessa would receive a warm welcome from her. However, deRoss had said something about his eldest daughter having had a large family, and that might be a strain on anyone. He would not know, being from a family so small, just himself and Emmy, and she was as sweet as any sister could be.

If she and John had many children, would she still keep her gentle disposition? He hoped so, but he also believed their sons and daughters would not be relegated to the nursery. That might be a strain, but even with his sister married, he could still help.

The new guest hurried over to her father with a great flurry of skirts. Her bonnet was large, covered with handmade flowers and ribbons and netting, but she was solid enough to wear it without seeming overwhelmed.

She did not so much as flick a glance toward the very point of her visit. He looked over at Tessa. Even in her seamstress garb, to him she had stood out. Now, in one of her new gowns, she glowed like a beacon. Her dark hair shimmered in the sun, and her skin glowed like the finest ivory.

DeRoss took matters into his own hands. "Abigail, we have guests. May I present Lord Mundy. My eldest daughter, Mrs. Fredericks. You might remember him from before. He lived nearby when you were younger."

She curtseyed. "My lord. Yes, I do remember you."

"A pleasure, madam." He nodded in return, and gestured past her grandfather. "Might I present my good friend, the Earl of Warrenby?"

Abigail turned, looked right past her niece, and curtseyed again. "My lord. It is indeed an honor to make your acquaintance."

Blake returned her acknowledgement with a bob of his own head, and waited, but did not move away. "Madam."

At last, she looked at Tessa, although she did not move away from her father. Her lip actually curled, just a bit but then he was watching very closely. "So you are Elizabeth's daughter." She looked her niece up and down in silence.

Blake thought he could see steam coming off deRoss, unless it was his own anger coloring the view with red. "Abigail." This time the warning was clear. "You will be kind."

"My dear." The man with her spoke in a firm voice. "This is the daughter, not the mother, nor her husband."

Good. The husband had the will to take on his wife, too.

Abigail smiled, and Blake relaxed a bit more. The smile seemed genuine. Perhaps the woman was uneasy about her own welcome.

"You look exactly like her. I would have known you anywhere. Well, I probably would have taken you for your mother, I knew she had a daughter, but had never seen you so had no idea that you turned out so like her."

She came over and took Tessa's hands. "You are Elizabeth's height as well. Even your eyes are the same. Did you get anything from your father?"

"No, I don't think so." Tessa's voice was even. Blake watched, but she did not draw away. Her cheeks were flushed, but he already knew she did not like being the center of attention. Two pairs of eyes—discounting her grandfather—looking at her with such scrutiny would be enough to make anyone embarrassed.

Carriage wheels rattled on the gravel, and the group turned, to see it coming around that side of the house.

"Oh, my," he heard, in awestruck tones. The wife? Or her husband? Blake looked between the coach Mundy owned, no more than a couple years old and freshly polished from the dust of the trip by an obviously enthusiastic stable staff, and the worn coach the Fredericks arrived in, and thought he better understood their envy.

Lewis came scurrying out of the house, one of the footmen at her side carrying her satchel. "Put that in the coach for me," she said in her brusque tones.

Tessa stepped forward, hesitated, then extended her hand. "Thank you for all your help. I appreciated it."

Lewis looked down at the hand with the same hesitation, then took Tessa's fingers and shook them once. "It was just my job, but gave me a nice trip out o'London." The woman turned and climbed into the carriage.

Tessa thought she had seen the beginnings of a smile on her former maid's mouth. Out of the heavy day, that little hint of pleasure lifted her mood.

Until she remembered the letter she held. Bits of conversations slipped through her mind. *So you are Elizabeth's daughter. This is the daughter, not the mother, nor her husband. Send me word if you feel the need to leave. I will come for you.*

The decision came. She turned to Warrenby. "My lord?" He turned, one eyebrow lifted in question. "Might I speak to you one moment? Just one moment?" Tessa took a couple steps away from the group, and he followed her.

When she was sure they could not easily be overheard, she hissed, "If I gave you a letter, could you see that one of your servants delivers it for me?"

His face went still until he saw Madame Genevieve's name written clearly on it. He smiled as he looked back at her. "Better yet, I will deliver it myself. Goodness knows, my sister is there often enough now with her trousseau to complete."

The letter disappeared into an inside pocket of his coat. "Is that all?"

No, she thought. *Don't go. Stay here.* "Yes."

No sound came from the group by the coaches. Did he feel the gazes on him, too? Did he wish them all . . . well, not to Perdition, but at least to someplace far away, just for a few minutes?

* * *

Blake looked down at Tessa. Her eyes held the faintest alarm, and small worry lines were forming between her brows. He did not like the way her aunt spoke to her. Something was amiss in this family, but no one had given any clear indications what it might be.

Unless it traced back to some prejudice against her father? Mrs. Fredericks, and her odd statement about Tessa not receiving any part of her father, was causing him unease.

She had made up her mind to stay, and he would respect her wishes, but how he wished he could bring her back!

He could not toss her in the carriage and drive away with her, would not demand she subdue her wishes to his. She had made up her mind, despite her obvious trepidation, a courage he admired more than he could say.

Even so, he would watch the mails. Perhaps, just perhaps, she would write and request a rescue. He would wait. And hope.

Right now, as he took his leave, he had to leave her with something to remember him by. Perhaps something for himself as well.

Blake looked down at her hand, still half-extended almost as if she forgot to withdraw it after handing him the letter. Or perhaps—if dreams could come true—she was longing for one last connection herself.

He reached out and took that hand. Eyes were still watching, he did not have to turn his head to see them, but he raised it, such a small thing in his large one, and pressed his lips to the back of it. Briefly, as he had done a thousand times and could do without thinking. But this time he tried to absorb the flavor of her, the scent of her, the warmth of her. It would have to last until he saw her again.

CHAPTER 25

Tessa swallowed hard before she turned back to her new aunt and uncle. Blake—and Mundy—were gone. He had been so straight and tall on the horse, but he had turned back once and caught her gaze before they disappeared behind the small grove of trees. The grove through which they had walked—was it only this morning? She had decided to stay, she now had to stand on her own.

Her grandfather might not have noticed the glint in Abigail's dark eyes or the tightness around her mouth, but Tessa had clear vision and a wary disposition. Perhaps all that time working in the shop would serve her well. Insults and snide comments came with sufficient frequency that she recognized someone skilled in dishing them out. And Abigail, vicar's wife or not, knew how to hand out cutting words.

Did you get anything from your father?

The servant turned around the chair. Grandfather was not even in the house, but at least out of earshot, when Abigail began. "Lofty company. Where did you meet the young one? What was his name again?"

She knew full well his name. She could hardly have forgotten in in such a short time. Meeting Abigail's gaze, Tessa refused to let herself flinch. "That is Lord Warrenby. I met him through the modiste's shop where I am an assistant to Madame Genevieve. I have done a lot of sewing for his mother and his sister."

"A lord, he said? How convenient. You move in lofty circles, I see."

"My dear." Abigail's husband stepped in. "This is the daughter, not Elizabeth. Enough."

This time, her father safely out of the way, Abigail turned on her husband. "She has no idea what Elizabeth and that worthless man did to this family. Mother aged years in those months before they ran away. Family heirlooms disappeared."

This aunt and she were not destined to become friends. If the others shared her attitude, Blake might receive a message sooner than he expected. The animosity against her father she could understand, even though it galled, but she didn't know what her mother could possibly have done.

From the door, her grandfather called, "Are you coming inside, or not?"

Abigail's husband held out his arm to his wife, and seemed to drag her toward the building. Tessa followed behind, but slowly.

Grandfather waited for them in the parlor. "Abigail, Herbert, how long do you think you can stay? You know you are always welcome."

"As for myself," her new uncle said with what felt like honest reluctance, "I have to leave right away. I have a funeral and a wedding yet to perform today, so can stay only long enough to meet my new niece, and then I must leave." He walked over and extended his hand. "In case I forgot, welcome to the family." With a quick bow, he turned back to his father-in-law. "Thank you for the invitation, Sir. The life of a clergyman is a busy one, as you certainly know by now."

DeRoss nodded, and turned to his daughter. "Do you have to go as well? I know what a helpmeet you are for him."

Breath caught in Tessa's throat. *Say yes*, she thought. *Please tell us you have to go, too.*

"Not this time. One of our girls is filling in for me. I wanted to meet Elizabeth's daughter." But Abigail did not turn to look at her, and her voice had an edge.

Tessa hoped her face gave nothing away.

"You have trained them so well." DeRoss fairly burst with grandfatherly pride. "Even the boys. Have any of them changed their mind and decided to go into the church?"

The father smiled. "No, but I have reconciled myself to their choices. They are going into other worthy professions. I did tell you the one hopes to become a solicitor. He has not changed his mind. As for the other, he has surprised us all by insisting he wants to be a surgeon. He is already in Cambridge, but hopes from there to go to one of the teaching universities. Blood does not frighten him, so he wants to work with the patients. If the awful war were to begin again, I think he would follow the army right onto the battlefield and try to save the wounded. He has his eye set on Leiden for the practical learning, but I say Edinburgh will do just as well."

If they had been able to afford a better physician, would her mother have survived? That seemed to be a question that would never have an answer. If the son did go into medicine, Tessa prayed he did not have his mother's disposition.

Grandfather nodded his head. "Fine sons. Fine professions. If there is anything I can do to help, you must not be too proud to ask."

"Father!" Abigail's brows came down. "Herbert is a man of God. He is not proud!"

DeRoss merely laughed. "Pride takes many forms, daughter. After your husband leaves, I think it would be good if you could take Tessa around, show her the gardens, and the path to the lake. You lived in this house until you were wed, there is nothing you don't know about it. I want her to feel at home here."

She did not dare look at her aunt. Abigail had shown enough distaste, Tessa did not feel like facing more at the moment. Her hands clenched in her skirts. She might have won her grandfather over, but it looked like she had an uphill battle ahead of her.

Rather than stand there and let her life run away with her, Tessa turned to her grandfather. "Perhaps he would like something to eat before he leaves?" She might be overstepping her bounds, but she needed a few moments to collect her wits, and there was no reason to follow them into the dining room and watch them eat.

DeRoss's eyebrows went up. "How right you are." Turning back to his daughter, he asked, "Would you like a late breakfast?"

"That would be very nice. We barely took the time to break our fast before we came. A little something is more than welcome." Uncle Herbert actually rubbed his hands together.

Within a minute, her new relatives were out of the room. The tension seeped out of her muscles. When she turned around, her grandfather was watching her with a strange look on his face.

Tessa could not keep the words inside. They had been pounding at her ever since she learned about her mother's estrangement from her family. A more unlikely villain she could not imagine. "What did my mother *do*? Why does Abigail hate me?"

Her grandfather sighed, and the lines on his face deepened. "What a pity she behaved so badly. A woman of her age should know better. I never wanted to tell you. It has taken me a long time to come to terms with it myself." He closed his eyes. "Your father stole one of the family heirlooms, a necklace that had belonged to my mother, and her mother before her. Rubies that had never been faceted, only polished. I confronted him, but your mother took his side. She was already in love, had determined to marry the man, and nothing I or her mother said would sway her."

Tessa felt her legs give way, and sank into the nearest chair. Her father's thievery had begun that early? Had he kept that necklace? Was it one of the ones she had given to Blake, that he was now taking around to the jewelers? Or had he stripped it of the gems and it was only a broken setting now? If it was one that still had its gems, what if one of the jewelers recognized its true value and offered to purchase it?

She had to get a letter to him!

Grandfather's hand plucked at the blanket across his legs. "I am so sorry to tell you this. A child should be able to think more of her father."

The tears in his eyes rolled down his face, and he brushed them away. "I am sorry, my dear. Sorry that I made you and your mother both suffer for your father's misdeeds. Sorry you had to find out at all."

She took a deep breath. He had to know she had already known some of this. "Grandfather, I had only recently discovered my father was a thief. I never knew all the years I was growing up." She rose and went over, to kneel at his side. "Can you draw the necklace? Do you remember it well enough?"

He nodded. "I am no artist, but I saw it often. I might be able to come up with something close." He didn't say anything more, just looked down at her. Tessa could see him thinking, watch the anguish of his thoughts in his eyes. His hands tightened on the blanket, then loosened, then would tighten again.

He turned his head, and spoke to the man behind him. "Ring for some paper and a pencil, will you?"

It took a few minutes to track down the elusive pencil, and even a bit of India gum, as deRoss insisted he would need it to fix his mistakes. He was not exaggerating. If it were not so serious, Tessa might have smiled watching his struggles. Sadly, it was too important to interrupt as he brushed off the bits of the gum as they crumbled under his diligent rubbing. At last, he declared himself satisfied. Abigail came in just as he handed it over to Tessa. "What do you have there, Papa?"

"Tessa asked for a sketch of Mother's necklace, the one that disappeared."

She snorted, a rough and most inelegant sound. "You mean the one her father stole."

"*Enough!*" This time deRoss's voice thundered. "If you cannot be civil, Abigail, you might as well leave with your husband. If you wish to remain until your sisters come, you will control yourself and bite your tongue. Are we understood?"

"But—"

"I mean it! Courtesy, daughter, or leave." He sat straighter than he had since Tessa arrived.

"Fine!" Abigail turned up her nose, but in a quieter tone added, "I shall be perfectly polite."

"See that you are."

Tessa stared down at the drawing again, and wished the memory was clearer. "I saw a collection of jewelry recently where I did not expect to see it. I can't remember what they all looked like, exactly, but I know how to look at them again." She looked up at her grandfather. "May I make another request? A quill and some ink? I need to write a letter."

"Certainly." He beckoned to a footman. "Take Miss Tessa to my office, and make sure she has what she needs. When she is done, take the letter to Masters and have it posted. She will tell you where."

No question to whom it was addressed, no request even for a hint of its contents. Tessa felt her eyes fill, and her throat tighten. He had no reason for such trust, which made its gift doubly precious.

She followed the footman out into the hallway. He opened one of the doors, and Tessa entered a room that had a strong resemblance to Blake's. Big desk, big chair behind it, both of some dark wood. The chair was covered in cracked leather, proclaiming hard use in the past. Equally dark curtains over the two sets of double windows, only in a rich blue instead of the black of the dining room, chairs for guests out of a lighter blue fabric with a thin padding for the seats but with unadorned wooden arms, even some shelves behind against the wall to one side of that desk. The only color surprise was the light blue walls, lending a bit of brightness.

No rug anywhere in the room that she could see, just polished wood out of the same dark stain that marked the rest of the house, as if an entire forest had gone into the making of the place. A man's room, she thought, and wondered who had designed it. Her grandmother, perhaps, with her husband's preferences in mind?

Tessa found herself oddly comfortable here, but could not bring herself to sit in that leather chair. Instead, she pulled the quill, the small knife for sharpening it, and ink the footman had carefully set out for her over to the front of the desk, the guest's section.

This required careful thought and even more careful wording. "Blake," although he had given permission to call him that, sounded too familiar for a letter that others might see. "Lord Warrenby" was too formal, as if wiping out that breathless moment on the drive. "My Lord Warrenby?" He was certainly used to being called "my lord."

Heart in throat, she dipped the quill into the ink and set it to the paper. Before she could brood any more, the words "My Lord Warrenby" stared up at her.

Once again she looked at her grandfather's drawing at the top of the page. Blake had told her his friends were already working on the stolen jewelry, so undoubtedly, they would see this sketch. She therefore had to leave out more than she could put in.

And she had one chance to get it right.

My Lord Warrenby, I discovered there was a theft here as well as the thefts in London. You will see above what the missing necklace looked like. Can you check through what you have in trust, and see if it might chance to be among them? With sincerest thanks, Tessa Abbott

It was done. With careful folds, she got the letter ready to seal and addressed it. The wax sat in its stick on top of the desk, one edge melted. The seal happily was right next to it. At least she didn't have to dig through her grandfather's desk to find them.

You have learned to be suspicious, she told herself. All the sealed letter needed was Grandfather's address so Blake would know immediately where it was from, and it could be sent off.

Then would come the waiting.

CHAPTER 26

Thank goodness for business, Blake thought as he walked toward White's, where his friends were supposed to be waiting. It kept him from brooding and wondering how things were going in Gloucestershire.

Blake reached for the handle of the big door, when a woman a short distance down the street caught his eye. A woman and child, a young girl, were strolling along, heading right for him. He stepped away from the door and waited, wondering if his eyes were playing tricks on him, wondering if the resemblance he thought he saw was really there.

The woman did not notice him, did not change her stroll or her direction.

He moved toward them, then paused, afraid to startle the mother into changing her course. The girl was the right age as his daughter. She would be about five . . . no, six now. He knew almost nothing about children, but everything about the scene just felt right.

Years had passed, but when the woman turned just enough, he saw his guess was right. He knew those movements, knew that petite size, even knew those hands inside the lacy white gloves because he had held them all too often. The hair, though, it was that wildly curly blonde hair beneath her straw bonnet that made the identification all too certain.

His gaze traveled back down to the girl at her side. The child also had a bonnet, but beneath it, Blake thought he saw dark ringlets along the collar of her little gown.

His throat tightened, and he had to blink to keep his eyes clear.

The mother looked up, and gasped. Alice's soft blue eyes, the color of a perfect summer sky, opened wide, quick panic, and then she came to a decision. He saw it happen in her face, the way it smoothed out, the way her gaze relaxed, the muscles around her mouth eased.

She smiled! A hesitant, nervous smile, but a smile nonetheless. "Hello, Blake."

"Hello, Alice. I suppose I should say Mrs. Howard? It has been a very long time."

Her mouth trembled, as if she fought back tears. "Yes."

"You have no need to fear me. I intend no harm to you or yours. I just want"—his voice cracked, shocking him. He had not realized his emotions were so close to the surface.

"I know what you are guessing," she interjected, "and yes. The answer is yes." Her eyes seemed moist now.

"Mommy? Who is that?" Blake saw a little finger point, kept low and half hidden in the girl's skirt. And directed right at him.

"It's not polite to point, Becky. This is an old friend of mine. We knew each other when we were children, but he went away to the war, and I have not seen him since then." If there was an edge of old betrayal and broken promises in her voice, he did not hear it.

"Like Daddy?"

Blake and Alice gave a soft gasp at the same moment, but the girl did not seem to notice.

Alice hesitated, or might have been unable to speak for a breath or two, and then her answer was hesitant. "Yes, Becky. Exactly like . . . Daddy."

For another moment Blake feared his legs would not bend, feared that their stiffness was all that kept him upright and that he would continue to tower over his daughter, but they finally folded and let him lower himself into a crouch. He held out his hand, and hoped it was not shaking as much as it seemed. "Hello, Miss Becky. My name is Warrenby."

He could never claim this little girl, and did not want to cause trouble in the family Alice had constructed from the rubble he had left her. He merely wanted one moment to say hello, to exchange a word or two. It would be all he might ever have, and he would have to be content with it.

But he would not be deprived of this lone meeting.

Becky reached out, and took his hand. Hers was so small, just like her mother's had been, and cool. In a few years, she should wear gloves, but today her mother must have decided they were not necessary. How glad he was for that! He was holding his daughter's hand with nothing between them. When he managed to look back up, away from their tenuous link, he found himself staring into his own pale green eyes. Emmy called them "ice eyes," and Becky had them.

Some day someone might see them, and guess. He did not know Howard well, could not begin to guess what color his eyes were, probably would have never thought to notice before now.

He was not ready to end this moment yet. "How old are you?" It was not a question one ever asked of a woman, but she was a child and he thought children always liked to brag about their age.

He was right. "I'm six. I will be seven in half a year." She smiled, and he had to squeeze his other hand tight enough to dig his nails into his palms to keep his emotions in check. Becky wanted him to smile with her, and he hoped his own lips were curving to match.

His face felt frozen, but Becky didn't draw away, so maybe he was smiling. It was time to stand, to let go of her hand. Blake allowed himself one last privilege, and lifted her hand to his lips. Just a whisper of a kiss, no doubt like ones she had seen bestowed on her own mother.

Then he let go, made his legs lift him back up, made himself tower over this little girl again.

Their time together was done. He had been permitted this moment, had promised he was no threat, and he would keep his word. On a neck that felt as rigid as his face, he turned to look at Alice again. "So, do you have any other children?"

"Yes." A mother's pride showed in her watery eyes. She patted her cheeks with her gloved hands. Had she been crying, too? "I have two boys, one four and one just turned three." Her hand went toward her midsection, then fell back to her side.

She was pregnant again. That gesture gave it away, while the styles in women's gowns hid how far along she might be. He let the little movement pass unremarked.

"They are not here." It was foolish to remark on the obvious, but conversation was still difficult.

"No," Alice agreed. "I left them with their nurse. They were sleeping, and I did not feel like waking them."

"They are always in a bad mood when they wake up from their naps." Becky was not ready to be left out of the grownup conversation. "If they don't get a nap, they whinge, and if they do get a nap, they whinge."

He laughed. Actually laughed, and the simple act surprised him. He had not thought he could yet, but his daughter sounded so put-upon, so adult in her own complaint about her brothers.

Alice gave a thin laugh herself. "She is right. They can be a trial in the middle of the day. But we managed to plan things just right so we could have some mother-daughter time alone."

"It probably will never happen again." Becky gave a huge sigh, too big for her little body.

Blake had to laugh once more. He could see Alice saying that as she hurried her daughter into walking clothes and out the door for a well-deserved break. When he looked down at Becky, he realized he was grinning at her.

Grinning!

Later there would be time to absorb, to say his final goodbyes in his head and heart, but right now his daughter was being adorable, and he was here and this moment was his to keep and to cherish.

"Where were you headed when I interrupted your stroll?" The air around them felt lighter, his breath was easier, his face no longer felt frozen. Even the tension in his shoulders and his hands was gone. He had not realized how tight he had been until it was released with his laughter.

He had Alice to thank for that. What a generous spirit she had! Once he might have thought of his foolish mistake in wasting his opportunity, but even that was gone. Wiped away with the power of Alice's gift, and Becky's innocence.

"I thought I would take her out to Gunter's, and we just began strolling. I should really take her back. My father's carriage will be there soon, and I didn't realize how far we have come." Alice glanced up at the windows around them, and blinked. "Oh! White's! We really have walked a bit."

"Not so very far. If I had come in my carriage, I would have offered a ride, with Becky as chaperone we should have avoided most gossip, but unfortunately I came on my horse." Blake lifted his hat, and bowed. "I should bid you farewell, I have a meeting inside, but I thank you for staying and talking with me. For . . . well, everything." He trailed off, not knowing how to put what this meant into words that could be spoken in front of a child.

To his surprise, Alice reached out and touched his arm. "It was my pleasure, really. It was long overdue."

Urgency pushed the words from his mouth. "I must tell you one thing before you leave. I did not . . ."—*Get your letter. Know about my daughter* —". . .hear anything for months, I was working as an agent in France and only a select and secret few could reach me. I did not even receive word of my father's death for weeks."

"Oh!" Alice pressed her fingers to her mouth. "I hoped it was something . . . but it was a difficult time."

"I am so sorry."

"Thank goodness the war is over!" The words fairly exploded from

Alice, and he was reminded that her husband was in the army, an officer, and not likely to give up his commission except for a position in the government somewhere.

"So am I. Let us hope it stays that way." He smiled. "I am glad it worked out for you. Three children! That is a nice family." *Are you happy? Is your husband good to you?* But those were questions he could not ask, but he had the evidence of his eyes. A woman who dared to stop and talk to an old love seemed to be a woman confident in her new life and her husband.

Her next words confirmed it. She looked down at her daughter, and that little movement toward her middle and her secret came again before she met his eyes. "It *is* a nice family. A very nice family. I am most content with my lot."

"That is the best of news. I cannot tell you how grateful I am for this meeting. You have set my mind at rest."

"Mine as well."

From the height of his waist, a young voice piped up. "It was nice for me to meet you, too."

They all laughed, and Blake dared one more touch, reaching out to capture her hand and bestow one more quick press of the lips. "It was an honor to meet you, Miss Becky."

A last dip of the head, and he let them go. His heart clenched, but it released more quickly this time, and a smile quirked his lips. His daughter was well-raised, loved, and precocious. He could ask for no more.

With light steps, he headed back toward Whites, up the stairs and entered his sanctum.

* * *

"So, Warrenby, while you were strolling about the wilds of England, we have been busy. Turns out jewelers keep surprisingly good records. At least the ones I talked to." Haversham set some papers out on the table, folded, and shoved them over. "We don't know which were for their wives, and which for their mistresses, but all of mine have been accounted for. Their names are on each sheet."

Addersley slid over his stack of drawings next. "I mostly had crests easily identifiable. The jewelers I checked do not have records of making most items, but they could reconstruct the crests. One belongs to a family where the last heir died, and the title seems to have gone defunct. What you wish to do with it, I will leave to your discretion."

Gillem added most of his to the pile of folded papers growing in front of Blake, but held back a few. "I had the least success, and I promise I worked at it diligently." He didn't smile, but enthusiasm lit his eyes. "I haven't had anything challenge me as much as this in a long time. I never even felt like visiting the gambling hells. Not once."

Now he smiled at Blake. "Warrenby, I have to thank you for this project. I have decided to go into this for a hobby, hang out my shingle, if you will. I even stopped in at the Bow Street Runners to ask about what it takes to be an agent. I have no title, my family is sick of my escapades, but out of them, I have contacts in places no one in our class would ever go."

Blake glanced around at the others, and they all showed the same relief as he felt.

Gillem leaned forward, the papers that still sat in front of him forgotten. "Just think! A Bow Street Runner of their very class, someone they knew they could confide in who understands the rules of the *ton*." He shook his head. "The only reason I've been in such trouble with my family, the only reason I gamble, is that I'm bored."

Arms on the table, intensity flowed off him like an invisible wave. "I want this." His gaze went from one man to the next around the circle. "I really want this." A new maturity straightened his shoulders. His chin lifted as if he expected an argument. "I'm going to do it. I'm going to begin as a Bow Street Runner, gain some experience, and see where it takes me. I have no title at stake, nothing much else to do. Now I will have a purpose, something to challenge me every day."

Blake started to smile, and it grew, matching the enthusiasm inside. "Gillem, I think it's a fabulous idea! I like it. I think you should go ahead, do it!"

Haversham, with the weight of his family title already comfortable on his shoulders, sat, head cocked, his vision unfocused as his thoughts churned. Or at least they looked like they were churning. He snapped back to reality, and like Blake, began to smile. "Warrenby is right. I think you will be perfect for it. I know if I ever need anything investigated, I would rather go to someone I know than a total stranger who might blunder around like a bull in a china shop."

Addersley smiled, and shook his head, not in disagreement, but as if in amazement. "Who would have thought? A simple . . . well, maybe not so simple, challenge, and one of us has a new career."

Gillem became all business. "Back to my sketches. I found out that some of the ones I have are old, very old. The jewelers said they could tell simply from the design. I got a couple necklaces that still had the gems in them, and I made some markings to show whether the gems had been faceted. Those markings helped one of the jewelers I spoke to. He said faceting has become more complex in recent times, so the simple cuts indicate older jewelry. Or at least older stones."

He sifted through the papers he still had, and lifted a sketch up, turning it around so the others could see it. "This necklace interested the jeweler most. He said it was at least a few hundred years old. He cannot tell me who it belonged to, and no one could find any records in their shops, it has no crest, but someone is certainly looking for it."

He pointed to a couple of his notes on the picture. They meant nothing to Blake, but clearly they did to Gillem. "This necklace is only missing two stones." His gaze pinned Blake with this new maturity. "You said you had a collection of gems, as well as these. I suspect, since he had not taken this one apart, not much at any rate, he might have kept the stones." With a dismissive movement of his head, he added, "At least I hope so. These would be hard to replace."

Blake made a quick decision. "I'm going to let you keep going. I have more than enough to do right now, returning the jewelry to their owners. Keep me posted on what you find."

He folded the stack in front of him into a neat pile and filled his pockets with them. "I should have brought a case."

Addersley looked over his shoulder and raised a hand to catch the waiter's eye. "Bring us some wine, please. Red. And"—he lifted an eyebrow at Gillem, who hesitated, then shook his head—"three glasses. And a cup of tea."

He turned to the group. "I think we have a bit of celebrating to do. One challenge successfully completed, and a new career."

* * *

Blake sat down at his desk, and pulled out the sack of jewelry. Time to begin the matching. Hodgins tapped on the door, and entered with the plate on which rested the mail. "I thought you might like today's post, my lord."

"Thank you, Hodgins. Set it on the edge of my desk. I will get to it in a minute." He started pulling papers out of his pockets. They had survived the ride home better than he expected. A few extra crinkles, but nothing that would interfere with his ability to match them to the originals.

The plate clicked as it was set down. The address on the first letter of Hodgins' stack and the feminine curve of the writing caught his attention, and he left his papers and the pouch to snatch it off the top. Gloucestershire.

The seal was thicker than he would have used, showing Tessa's lack of practice, but he managed to peel it off without too much damage to the paper inside.

A drawing of a necklace, and a letter. Blake took a moment to study her writing, so feminine it was almost art, yet eminently readable.

My Lord Warrenby. Not 'Blake,' although he had given her permission to do so. She might have thought a letter was different than personal, private conversation. He glanced at the drawing above. No doubt she anticipated others seeing it, so was erring on the side of being circumspect.

I discovered there was a theft here as well as the thefts in London. A theft 'here,' meant a theft from her grandfather. So she was saying, in terms only the two of them would understand, that her father had begun his career by stealing from his in-laws. That explained the estrangement. No doubt deRoss had discovered the theft and forbidden the marriage, but Tessa's mother, as women in love did, rushed to her lover's defense.

You will see above what the missing necklace looked like. Can you check through what you have in trust, and see if it might chance to be among them?

Her valediction showed the same caution as her salutation, so he refused to try to read anything into the formality of it. Check through what he had in trust, yes, he would do that right away. Blake studied the drawing on top of the page. That necklace was very familiar. He had gone over so many sketches today, but this one . . . looked like the one he and his friends had seen with Gillem's notes on it. Not the same, at least he didn't think it was the same.

He looked at it again. To be certain, he would need that sketch he had told Gillem to keep. If the necklace was in the pouch—he reached for the pouch he had pulled out even as he stared at the drawing—he would have to contact Gillem and compare necklace to sketch. No point in having his friend run all over London if the mystery had been solved.

Settings slid out, and Blake sifted through them, one after another, looking for a match. Aha! Success!

He pulled the necklace out and laid it next to the drawing Tessa had sent. The drawing was rough, smudged a bit and stained here and there from the ink of her letter, but if he had to guess, he would say he had a match.

Now for something to keep it separate from the rest of the settings.

A grin pulled his mouth up. The perfect reason to head right back.

First things first. He had to get Gillem here with his sketch, and compare the two sketches with the necklace.

Once he was certain, he would pack his bags, load the horse, or perhaps the carriage in case Tessa was ready to come back to London, and head for Gloucestershire.

CHAPTER 27

The days crawled by. Two, then three. That afternoon she had finally had enough of her aunt and decided it was time to send word to Mundy when a footman hurried into the parlor where she sat reading while her grandfather took his daily nap.

Abigail had found some embroidery to do, and looked up every few minutes, a scowl on her face. Once she said with the usual edge to her voice, "Reading? Can you not find something more productive to do?"

Tessa merely turned the page and retorted, "I have spent the past four years stitching twelve to fourteen hours a day, sometimes longer. I might not have another chance to read when I go back."

Abigail had been quiet after that.

Now the footman arrived nearly out of breath. "Three carriages are coming down the drive. Should I wake the master?" He jiggled from foot to foot with impatience.

Tessa felt a flash of hope. Blake! She dropped the book on the table beside her, jumped to her feet, and headed for the door. As she passed, she nodded to the footman. "Thank you, Robert."

Abigail stabbed her needle into the fabric to anchor it, set it aside, and rose. Her voice followed Tessa. "No need to be in such a rush. Let us see who it is first."

If she responded to every small dig from her aunt, she would be defending herself most of the day. Her grandfather was a joy, Abigail was a thorn in her skin. Had Grandfather not begged her to stay and meet the rest of the family, that letter pleading for return would have gone off within the first day.

Without waiting for anyone else, she flung open the outer door, and shielded her eyes against the sudden glare of sunlight.

None of the carriages looked familiar. Two were average, showing a bit of wear and on the small size. One appeared quite elegant, but not up to the standard of Blake's. It came first, and when it rolled to a stop, a woman stepped out. She didn't seem to fit the wealth of the carriage. Her bonnet had seen better days, the ribbons looked like they should have been replaced a year or more ago. Her gown was a plain muslin, not light and filmy but more durable weight, and done in a medium green. The bodice was not low-cut, as befitted a woman of her age, but even so, she wore a fichu of a filmy material, deeply ruffled and of the the same color so no shadows would hint at any cleavage.

A woman of a certain age, knowing what was appropriate and not ashamed of it.

Two men climbed out with her, but when they straightened and turned around, Tessa saw the youth in their faces, and in the lean frame of their bodies. Neither had filled into manhood, but it was not far away. From the greying hair of the woman who had ridden with them, she knew exactly who that woman was. Their mother.

A man climbed out of one of the other carriages, and reached back to someone inside. Was this man her mother's youngest brother? He looked too old for that. Perhaps a husband, and therefore an uncle by marriage she had to meet?

The movement outside the first carriage pulled her attention back to the woman and the two young men. When the woman turned and noticed her standing there, her mouth dropped open, and she raised a hand to press to her lips. Skirting her sons, she hurried over, each step coming faster until she was almost running. Not waiting for introductions, she threw her arms around Tessa and hugged her tight. A sob shook her body, and another, then she stepped back, red eyed and wet cheeked. "You must forgive me, but you are the image of your mother, and I loved my sister. I have missed—" Another sob, then a watery laugh, and she went on, "I am your Aunt Lavinia, and I was next to Elizabeth in age. Of all of us, I was the closest to her, not just in age but in friendship."

Another laugh, more choked this time, and she tugged Tessa in for a second hug. Faint shudders gave away the sobs Aunt Lavinia was trying valiantly to hide. "You and I are going to be the best of friends, too, I can tell."

After the coldness from Abigail these past days, Tessa felt a warmth grow around her heart. She smiled as her aunt let go and stepped back, far enough to see the lingering shimmer of tears the woman was trying not to let fall. "I hope so," she said in her turn. "Oh, how I hope so."

Lavinia tucked a hand into Tessa's arm and dragged her toward the boys. "You have to meet my sons. These are the youngest, on break from Eton. My older sons had already headed off for time with their friends' families, they will be back in a week or two, so I could not drag them away. But these two agreed to come with me."

Before they could reach the boys, Tessa noticed the other two carriages had disgorged their passengers. Two women, one outside each carriage, stared at her as if she had two heads.

Her steps slowed, and she whispered out of the corner of her mouth to Lavinia, "More sisters?"

"Aunts, to you," Lavinia answered, then raised her voice. "Hannah, Caroline. How good of you to come."

Tessa watched them as they came closer, waiting for the same reaction of amazement as she had received from her aunt Lavinia. They had further to come, but first one, then the second, gave a start, and two mouths opened in surprise, then closed.

The closest woman, drawing near enough to see the medium brown hair piled on her head beneath her bonnet and walking next to the man who could now be clearly identified as her husband, spoke up in a firm and carrying voice. "Elizabeth?"

Her husband nudged her, and she corrected herself. "Elizabeth's daughter? Are you Elizabeth's daughter?"

A hand at her back—Aunt Lavinia—gave Tessa a push, and she made herself start walking to meet the rest of these strangers. Her family.

How very odd.

"Yes," she heard herself answer. "Yes, I am."

That same first woman said in that brisk tone, "I thought so. There is no one else you could be. I suppose you know how much like your mother you look."

"I had never given it much thought until now. My father told me I sounded like her, but after all, she taught me to speak." Tessa did not know if she had brought up her father deliberately, but both women's mouths pursed as if they had just eaten something sour.

This one, though, recovered quickly. "I don't see any of his features in you." She gave a start. "Oh, how thoughtless of me. I have not introduced myself, or my husband. I am your Aunt Hannah, and this is my husband, Mr. Jones."

A laugh came from behind Tessa. "Honestly, Hannah! Even I managed to call my husband by his first name." Lavinia stepped up beside Tessa. "Tessa, this is your Uncle Harcourt. You, of course, can call him whatever you wish. Since we are all so new to you, if you wish to call him Mr. Jones you certainly may, but you should at the very least know his name."

She waved toward the other woman, who had nearly reached Aunt Hannah. "And that is your Aunt Caroline. She and I are both widowed, the other sisters still have their husbands."

Tessa jerked around to look at Lavinia. "You are widowed? I am so sorry."

With a faint bob of the head to the two young men still standing by the carriage, Lavinia whispered, "I'm not. But I never say that in front of my children." After checking behind herself again, she added, "At least he had the decency to leave me money."

Aunt Caroline reached them. She was so slender that despite knowing all the aunts had children, her lithe figure surprised Tessa. "I could not bring any of my children with me. They are all wed, and several have children of their own. Leaving is not simple for them."

Lavinia stepped into the pause again. "Abigail and I were the only ones to have several of each, but Hannah had only boys and Caroline had only girls.Which means you have a number of cousins."

This she did know. "Grandfather told me there are nineteen. I suppose with me, that makes twenty grandchildren."

Hannah, despite her brusk appearance, smiled. Perhaps being the mother of nothing but boys taught her to find humor in things. "We hardly expect you to learn all of them at once. Thank goodness Lavinia brought a couple of hers so you can begin with a small group. She and I are the two youngest before your mother, but she is already a grandmother herself. None of my sons are wed yet, so they have not added to the crowd."

"Not yet," Lavinia piped up. "Give them time, and you will likely have as many as Abigail and I."

Through all the byplay, Caroline had remained quiet. Tessa did not know if that was a good thing, or a bad.

Bad. "Just so you know, we had good reason to cut your parents off." Tessa thought she heard a gasp, and knew it did not come from herself.

Caroline went on, ignoring the pinch Hannah gave her and made no secret of hiding. "I believe Abigail is already here. She suffered a good deal because of your father. He ruined her life, and what he did changed her entire future. She is still suffering the effects. It would be asking too much to expect a warm welcome from the whole family."

"Speak for yourself, Caroline," Lavinia snapped. "You did not suffer, you have just been poisoned by Abigail's sour disposition. Tessa does not need to be punished for something that happened so long ago. It certainly had no effect on my offers nor, I think, on yours."

"Nor mine," Hannah said. "I got the man I had hoped would ask for me, and want nothing more. I never longed for jewels."

Caroline turned to her. "This is not about you, is it? It's about Abigail, and you cannot deny her life was ruined."

Hannah propped her hands, clenched into fists as if bracing for a fight, on her hips. "She has a perfectly fine husband. Honorable, respected, faithful."

"A vicar! Not even a rector, who might have had a chance of providing well for her and their brood, but a vicar! And they had six children! How easy do you think her life has been? Providing and caring for them, her husband so involved in the congregation." Caroline stepped back one step, just far enough to avoid any more of Hannah's pinches.

Tessa remembered Abigail's husband having to leave, and wondered now how much of that rush was justified, and how much was an excuse to avoid his wife's complaining company.

"But that is not the worst of it. As the oldest, she was to inherit Mother's ruby necklace. And now it is gone! Not only was she robbed of the husband of her choice, but her inheritance as well."

Tessa caught her breath, struck by a pang of guilt that should not have to belong to her, but did. She noticed a brief hesitation from the other aunts, and then both Hannah and Lavinia spoke at once.

"He would have been a horrible husband! I hear he flaunts his mistresses in front of his current wife."

"Gems cannot make up for a brute of a husband. Ask me, I can tell you."

The latter comment seemed to come from Lavinia, and Tessa turned to stare at her. A brute of a husband? What her own father had brought on the family might have been partially to blame for this kind new aunt's fate. Having a wealthy, respected man offer for a daughter might have made Grandfather feel like his own name, his own respectability had been restored.

"She should not have to listen to this." Lavinia took her arm in a firm grip and moved back toward the house. Hannah walked on her other side, her hand hooked in her husband's arm. He had been silent through all of this, seeming to let the women handle their own mess.

Caroline followed behind, not speaking but grumbling to herself.

Thoughts, fears tumbled through Tessa's head, questions and more questions. What if the owning of the family heirloom was enough for Reginald, and he had never wanted to strip it of its stones? There were several things in the pile still untouched. Would the necklace be in the pile of jewelry he had stripped, or might it belong to the intact pile?

Broken or intact, would the family feel better if she could give it back? Even broken, it might be repairable. Would they suspect she had known about it all along and was as guilty as her father?

She stepped through the doorway into the house, her mind barely registering where she was until Lavinia shook out her skirts, and she heard them brush against the floor. When she came back to the world around her, she had to scold herself for letting her wishes run away with her. As of yet, she did not know that the necklace was there at all.

Foolish to make plans to reconcile with the family until she had proof it still existed.

If only there was a way to find out whether Blake had received her letter! Tessa had never had anyone with whom she corresponded, she honestly did not know how long before she heard back from Blake. Much as she felt it was time to leave, she could not go until he replied.

CHAPTER 28

Blake knocked on the doorjamb of his mother's morning room, though the door stood open. She had not noticed him until then, so absorbed was she in her writing. He could just walk in, but he had never intruded on her that way. Not even as a child. This room had always been her sanctum.

She would lose it soon, when he and his wife moved in. Let her relish it while she had it.

Rebecca turned from the delicate whitewashed desk, her gown a splash of lilac in the yellow room. His father's red chair was still in the corner, far enough to the side not to clash with the gown's color. He would have to duplicate the room as best he could in his house, so when she moved, the memories could come with her. He could live with all the soft yellow for a few weeks. Tessa might even like it.

"Blake! Come in, come in." She set aside the papers, and laid the pen in its ink-stained holder, the only thing in the room not pristine, then swiveled to face him. "Sit down. You look like you have something on your mind."

Blake still didn't trust those delicate guest chairs with their fragile-looking curved legs, but he wanted to be close, needed to watch her expression. He was going to marry Tessa anyway, but they deserved to know, as he fully intended to come back with a wife.

He always thought the mother longed to plan her daughter's wedding, but it was enough to simply get the son married. How it happened did not seem to be the issue.

"I do. I have news, and I hope very much you will be happy for me."

Rebecca reached out and rested her hands on his, giving a gentle squeeze. "I am always happy to support you. I will admit you gave me some bad moments when you were younger, but you have turned out very well." She let go and leaned back with a sigh. "Your father was proud of you, too. I am so sorry he never had a chance to tell you how much."

Blake's throat tightened. "I'm sorry, too." Then, after his mother fumbled for her handkerchief and he cleared his throat, he blew out a breath. "I have found the woman I wish to marry."

"Marry?" Her hands went up to cover her mouth, her eyes went wide. In face, he thought she might have gone pale. She would not faint on him, would she? "You—you have found a wife?"

"Yes."

"Is it anyone I know? Why have you said nothing before? How long has this been going on?" The color raced back into her face as questions came fast, tumbling out. "You have kept it so quiet. Is it because I have been so occupied with your sister's wedding?"

Blake concentrated on the last one. "No, Mother. It all happened very quickly." Although, when he thought back, it had not been quick at all. In fact, he had been watching her for months. "I have to get her agreement first. It will be a bit of a journey, but I wanted you to know before I left."

"How far?" With a sharp inhale, Rebecca asked, "She is not French, is she?"

A smile quirked his lips and he shook his head. "No, she is not French."

She gave a sharp nod. "Good. If she was, I might have some trouble explaining things."

"The war is over, Mother. I would think a French daughter-in-law would be less objectionable now than even a year ago, but as it is, you do not have that worry." The chair bit into his thighs. It was not designed for someone of his height. Or at least, that made a handy excuse. Blake rose, and went around it, to lean on the curving back.

He took a deep breath. He was head of the family now, but she was his mother, and had a stake in things, too. "You remember the seamstress at Madame Genevieve's? The one who came here for Emmy's engagement ball?"

His mother's face went slack. The color that had just come back faded a little. Blake could see her shoulders tighten, her fingers tighten into tight fists. Her mouth opened on a shuddering sigh, and in a shaken voice she asked, "Is it a relative of hers?"

Another deep breath. "No, mother. It is she." Rebecca knew Tessa's name, at least her Christian name, but he wanted to hear it. Wanted to *say* it. "Her name is Tessa Abbott.

He felt like he was standing in a pool of silence, the room was far too quiet, his mother too still. The first trickles of alarm had just run along his skin when she made a soft, sad sound. "Oh, Blake. A French wife would be easier to explain."

Guilt poked him. He should have said this right away, prevented the misery she now felt, but he wanted her to accept Tessa for herself. In the society in which they moved, he realized that was too much to hope for. "Did you know her grandfather is a baronet? Sir Aldo deRoss."

Those eyes widened again. Not *appalled* wide this time, though, more *curious* wide. "Indeed?" Her shoulders relaxed, her hands went soft again, even the color seeped back a shade in her face. "A baronet? What is she doing here in London, working in a shop?"

It was not a big title, he knew, but if it made a difference with his mother, as kind a woman as there ever was, it would definitely smooth Tessa's path. "There was a family quarrel over her mother's choice of husband. The couple ran away to marry, and since her father moved them about, the grandfather lost track of where they were."

Rebecca scowled. "How was this discovered? Did she know all along?"

"No, she didn't. It was a shock to her. Mundy—you remember that his grandson was missing?" She bobbed her head once. "She is the one who found the child. When Mundy saw her, he immediately recognized the family resemblance. Apparently it is quite striking. That is where I have been. Not just going with him to bring the grandson home, but Tessa came along. He knew that deRoss had been searching for her. If you have not seen her in the shop, it is because she is up with her grandfather."

His mother did not look ecstatic, more resigned. "I assume she has been well chaperoned?"

"Mundy provided an experienced maid to accompany her on the trip. Now that she is with her family, there is no need for someone to protect her name."

"And this is the woman you have chosen."

He straightened, and felt his shoulders go back. A smile tugged at his mouth. "Yes, Mother, she is the one I have chosen."

Rebecca gave a single, slow nod. "I did see how pretty she was, and often worried about her. At least she was in a shop peopled mostly with women. I noticed her cultured speech, she was a pleasure to talk to. Such exquisite manners, as well." Pressing her hands together, she tapped them to her chin. Blake said nothing, just let her process his news.

Finally her hands went back into her lap, and she pinned him in her gaze. "DeRoss? I think I might have heard that name before." A frown formed between her eyes, then smoothed away. "But perhaps not. Still, I would have preferred you pick someone who had not been in trade. I wanted someone higher for you, but I suppose a baronet's granddaughter is perfectly acceptable. No one will find it unusual that she was doing something so ladylike. And sewing! A very feminine pursuit. Much better than a maid." A laugh bubbled up. "I have no doubt all my friends will want fashion advice from her before they pick out their new gowns."

Blake chuckled. "That is a benefit I had not considered. Her previous occupation will make her a handy daughter-in-law."

"What does her grandfather say?"

"I have not even asked *her* yet, but I am certain he will be delighted. He and Mundy were exchanging looks during the meals. I'm quite certain the man can add two and two and get the correct answer."

His mother gave him a shrewd look. "Does she even know your intentions? What is *her* wish?"

That moment in the drive under the trees came back, and Blake had to work to control the shudder of longing. "I believe she will say 'yes.'" Then he leaned on the chair back again. "It is only fair you know I plan to wed her before I come back. I have no desire for a large wedding, and I want her to have the protection of my name when she gets back to London."

Her head tilted to one side, or perhaps she was just glancing at the paper beside her on the desk. Then she straightened. "We have some property near Mundy, I seem to recall. How far is her family home from Fernwood? Do you remember going there as a child? We used to summer at it quite often. Why don't we plan a house party, and we can combine the wedding with the party?"

Blake felt his eyes go wide. "I had not thought of that land in some time. Is the house still there?"

"I don't see why it wouldn't be. It's not a large one, only about a dozen bedrooms, no ballroom, but I'm certain we can send some staff up and get it in shape." Rebecca rose, as if this new project had lent her energy.

Her gaze went firm, the old earl's wife with all her consequence was back. "You have to give her some time, a couple months at least. I will not have it said that you were forced to marry. If you must stay away from London, I suppose I can't talk you out of it, but I would prefer you spend at least a few weeks there during the wait. Besides, she will want a proper gown made."

He did not like it, not at all, did not like any of this delay, but he saw the sense in her words, begrudging as it was.

His mother went on with her planning. "I will send for Masters, and see how many of our staff we can spare. Or who is best to hire for the journey. You check and see if a caretaker is still there." She plopped back into her chair. "I must get another list started. We must hope the house is in good shape, get the furniture uncovered, see if anything needs repairs. Someone must climb up and look at the roof."

Blake came around the chair and dropped a kiss on his mother's cheek. "I will take care of managing the house. You can locate servants."

"Goodness!" His mother looked up at him, a sparkle in her eyes. "How exciting! I must get going. There will be much to do, with two weddings. Who would ever have thought!"

Blake backed away before she came up with more for him to do. Just fixing anything that might have fallen down or worn out with the house, plus convincing Tessa to marry him, would be more than enough. "I will leave you to it, then. I'm going to get myself packed for the journey."

* * *

He checked the pouch he had tucked in his inside pocket again. Odd, that the very necklace Tessa wanted was one of the few relatively untouched. Two stones were missing from the back of the neck near the clasp where they might go unnoticed, but other than that, the necklace appeared undisturbed.

Which brought up more questions as to why her father had gone into thievery if he had a piece, gold filled with rubies, the sale of which would keep his wife and child in food and housing for the rest of their lives.

The only answer he could come up with was that Abbott had stolen this necklace to get even with deRoss, and not for the money at all.

His trunk was tied onto the roof, the outriders mounted up, the driver climbed onto his seat, and turned to him. "Was there anything more, me lord?"

"No. I have everything." He hoped. Jasper and Hodgins had gone over everything twice, plus the valet insisted in coming with to make certain he was presentable for meeting her grandfather. For meeting *her*. He thought she would agree, hoped she would agree, but he might have a struggle on his hands. He could think of a few things he had said that he wished he had not. "As long as you know how to get where we are going, I think we can leave."

Much as he wanted to take a horse for speed, he hoped to bring Tessa back sooner than his mother desired, and that required a carriage. A footman stood next to the coach's open door, the step in place. Blake did not need it, but as long as it was there, he used it, climbed in, and the door thunked shut behind him. Jasper grinned at him from across the carriage.

Now all that was required was to return the necklace, convince Tessa to marry him, fix up the estate for guests including any possible repairs, have the banns read, and get married. All in a couple of months. Or less.

The audacity of his plan made his head spin.

CHAPTER 29

Tessa stood outside in the late day gloom, the sun low enough that the shadows had become one with the encroaching darkness. Her ears rang from the constant din inside the house. Even her neighborhood in London had been quieter than this.

Of course, it got quiet once everyone was in bed, but after the endless conversation, and occasional bickering, during the day, she found it hard to sleep.

She felt trapped between two camps, Abigail and Caroline who seemed determined to make her pay for her parent's misdeeds, and Hannah and Lavinia, who took her side in everything, and were a delight.

And then there were her cousins, both at the age where they had just discovered girls, and were tongue-tied around her. She knew nothing about them other than their names and what humorous family secrets their mother spilled, eliciting groans and "Mother, please," from the young men every time.

Lavinia being such an open and lighthearted woman, her comment that first day nibbled away at Tessa. *Gems cannot make up for a brute of a husband. Ask me, I can tell you. I'm not sorry I'm widowed. At least he had the decency to leave me money.* She absolutely could not shake the feeling that Lavinia's miserable marriage had something to do with her father's misdeeds.

Many women wound up in unhappy marriages, or worse. There was nothing unusual in that. But for a family where one daughter already had a suitor take to flight over a scandal, with no need for a wealthy marriage, the only advantage would be marrying into a loftier title or important influence. Such as removing the tarnish a daughter had brought to them?

If Aunt Lavinia had a title, she had never mentioned it.

Birds fluttered and pipped as they settled for the night. Somewhere in the distance an owl hooted. Almost a whisper in the air, she thought she heard dogs barking. The flowers along the house released their fragrance, as if they had been hoarding it during the day's heat, and now exhaled it in the coolness, sending heavy perfume just for her.

Someone would find her soon, but for now, she relished in the peace.

A carriage rattled along, drawing closer and closer. Carriages were not rare, so she paid no attention until it turned in the drive. The crest on the side was not legible in the dimness, but it didn't have to be. She knew that shape, knew those colors.

Her heart leapt, going from a restful rhythm into a flutter as fast as the birds' wings of a moment ago.

Blake. Excitement tingled down her arms, raising the faint hairs there, while all the air in her lungs rushed out, leaving her dizzy with joy. The reason did not matter. He was here. Tessa flew toward the vehicle, remembering to slow down before she frightened the horses.

"Blake!" There was not enough air in her lungs to say more, she just swiveled, ran around the back of the box, and kept pace with the carriage as it plodded along toward the door.

The window came down on her side, and his handsome face appeared. "Hello, Tessa." She heard him fumble with the handle, as the vehicle rolled to a stop, and then he jumped down, leaving the door swinging behind him.

And swept her into his arms, pulling her tight against his body. His heart seemed to be thumping as strongly as her own. Standing on the opposite side of the carriage, knowing no one could see them, Tessa hugged him back.

This was not a moment to let slip by.

His mouth came down on hers, his lips firm but gentle, warm and eager. She fell into the kiss, thrilled at the unfamiliar feel of a man's lips on her own, their warmth, the tingle that ran down her arms, even the thud of his heart where their bodies touched. With a suddenness that left her reeling, he released her and stepped back.

Heat rushed up her face. What prompted that switch? Had she done something wrong? Did her inexperience annoy him?

Tessa heard the footsteps then, hurrying around the vehicle, and took her own step back. *That* was why he stopped. She dared not check her hair or smooth her gown, that would only give them cause to speculate, but when she managed to drag her dazzled gaze up to his face, those crystal green eyes were twinkling. A smile slipped up her chest, and she felt it curve her mouth.

"We have to talk," he whispered, the words coming out with a strange sense of urgency while his eyes seemed, for the first time, hesitant and uncertain. Before she could wonder what that expression meant, or what those words were hiding, he turned toward the footsteps.

Abigail and the boys, with Lavinia behind, rounded the carriage. She knew why Lavinia was so close upon Abigail's heels. Once again, her favorite aunt had come as her protector.

Even though she felt she had done a creditable job on her own in standing up to the constant pricks from the two oldest sisters, both Hannah and Lavinia must have decided she had endured enough.

Blake bowed at the women, who gave quick curtseys in return, and turned to the boys. "I am Lord Warrenby. And you are . . .?"

"Edward," the oldest answered. "This is my brother—"

Mark interrupted. "I'm Mark."

The boys stood awkwardly, and Blake bowed, a quick dip of the head for each, which they returned with eagerness if less grace. "A pleasure meeting you both. Am I correct in assuming you are Miss Abbott's cousins?"

"Yes," both boys answered simultaneously.

He turned his attention to the Abigail. "Mrs. Fredericks. A pleasure to see you again." Then he turned toward Lavinia. "You must be another aunt."

Tessa remembered her manners, and stepped up. "Lord Warrenby, this is my aunt Lavinia Haversham. She is the mother of my cousins."

"It is a pleasure to meet all of you. I hate to be abrupt, but I have some information that I believe will benefit all of you. Most of all, your grandfather. If we might go inside?"

"Oh!" Abigail turned red, and motioned toward the house. "By all means. Come in, come in."

Blake gave Tessa an apologetic look and stepped forward, extending his arm to her. "My privilege, if I may."

Abigail's eyes went wide and she looked at it for a second as if she had never seen an arm before, then slipped her hand into the crook of his elbow. "Why, thank you, sir."

Tessa watched them go, fighting the giggle that threatened. She knew he did not like Abigail any better than she did, but manners were manners. The look of surprise and confusion on her aunt's face was one she would never have missed.

A familiar hand caught her arm, and an ebullient voice said, "And who might this man be? He is quite the thing, isn't he?"

If only she had time to think about the embrace and the kiss, to hold that moment close and relive it, to lick her lips and taste him there. But

Lavinia's eyes were bright with excitement, and she nearly pulled Tessa's arm out dragging her to the door. Her boys gave up any pretense of decorum and dashed around them, trying to stay as close to this elegant man as they could.

Blake had some information that would benefit them all. He had found the necklace! What else could it be? She hurried along with Lavinia, until both were nearly running those last few steps.

Inside the parlor, her grandfather sat by the fireplace, still at its low burn, blanket over his legs. Hannah and Caroline sat on one of the settees, the boys stood near Blake on one side of the fireplace. Abigail took the chair closest to her father, while Lavinia took the next one. Tessa remained standing, she was not sure the excitement bubbling inside would let her stay down.

The man himself, tall and dignified, dressed well enough to be at a ball instead of in a lowly baronet's house, and Tessa's heart leapt again.

We have to talk. The way he said it, the look in his eyes, and the kiss—she could not forget the kiss—did not sound like it was bad news.

"Good. You are all here."

"My son has not come yet." Grandfather shifted under the blankets, as if his legs bothered him, then settled.

Blake looked around the group, all watching with wide eyes. Or narrowed ones, depending on the aunt. "I cannot wait for him." He pulled her letter out of his inside suit pocket. "Miss Abbott wrote me, and included a sketch you"—he turned to Grandfather—"might remember drawing."

He unfolded the letter, and Tessa was glad she had chosen to be formal in it, because he held it up. From where he stood, she doubted anyone would be able to read it. They could, however, see the sketch.

"I don't think it will come as a surprise to this group that her father . . . may have taken something that did not belong to him." He looked at her first, and dipped his head in a quick bow. "I must apologize to Miss Tessa, as she entrusted this information to me in utmost confidence. She did not know the import of her secret, as it came as a shock to her. She knew nothing about it until after his death, when she went through his possessions. Because she was acquainted with my mother and sister, she took a chance that I might be willing to help."

This time when he turned to her, his eyes danced with amusement. Which of the memories brought that on, she did not know. That look, though, just for her, started flutters in her chest, and warmed her cheeks. "I was happy to do so." He turned back to the group. "However, I had no success finding the owner until I received her letter."

Blake returned the letter to his pocket, and from another hiding place in his coat, he pulled out a velvet pouch. Turning to her grandfather, he handed it over. "If you would do the honors, Sir." It was hard to tell if that lone word, 'sir,' was an acknowledgement of Grandfather's own minor title, or a simple sign of respect.

Everyone sat forward on their chairs as he fumbled with the silk cords. The tension in the room could almost be seen. It was certainly felt. Finally, he was able to pull the pouch open, and tilted it over his lap. A tumble of gold with red flashes rained out.

Grandfather gasped. "My grandmother's necklace."

"I must warn you, there are two rubies missing at the back of it, but I believe they can be replaced."

Tears built in her eyes, her throat clogged with sobs that she could not shed. With that move, he had done as much as possible—with all the years that had passed, all the things that still could not be changed, the suitors that were long gone, Lavinia's miserable marriage that might not have happened, the division between the sisters—to wipe out the stain she brought into the family merely by being who she was.

Would the other families her father had robbed feel the same? This necklace was in good shape compared to the number that were mangled and missing stones. No doubt there were many her father had stolen that were long gone, sold or bargained away and long since melted down into new jewelry.

One question remained that would never have an answer. Why he had not ripped this one apart over all the years, other than to take two stones.

The noise about the room penetrated her jumble of thoughts, and Tessa blinked to clear her vision just in time to see the aunts, every single one, jump up and rush over to their father. They all clustered around, touching it with reverence. Abigail dropped her head onto Grandfather's shoulder.

And she sobbed, the sound wrenching and filled with grief. Tessa's eyes filled again, and for the first time she actually felt sympathy for this prickly aunt. Intuition struck. How much had Abigail loved the baron who broke it off? This sounded like she had carried a torch for him all these years, through marriage to a different man, through raising children, through the grandchildren they gave her.

Perhaps she could be forgiven for the slights and digs of the past days. She had looked at Tessa and seen the sister whose own marriage had cost the one she wanted.

* * *

Blake stepped away from the huddle. This was family business, and he did not belong. Jewelry had never mattered to him before now, but he could feel a kinship with them.

In his pocket he carried a piece of his own legacy. His mother had given him a ruby ring she received from her own mother, a chain that had run for several generations. Hopefully it would fit, but if not, he would simply get it resized. In that event, he also brought along a gold chain so she could wear it around her neck until he got her back to London.

Now that she had a grandfather to handle her interests, he had to speak to the man before he went further. Regardless of Sir deRoss's decision, he only wanted Tessa's answer.

Before he left today, he fully intended to put his claim on her.

CHAPTER 30

"Warrenby!" DeRoss called over the heads of his daughters. When their gazes met, the man mouthed, "Thank you."

Then to his daughters, he said, "Put it back in the pouch when you are done passing it around so nothing happens to it." He motioned to one of his grandsons, and gestured to the bellpull. The aunts were in no hurry to finish looking at the necklace and chattering among themselves, so Blake eased over to Tessa. He could tell she felt like an interloper, not yet a part of this family.

The servant he was accustomed to seeing behind deRoss's chair came into the room, and over to the man, bent down and listened. He hoped deRoss was not so tired that he was about to prepare for bed.

He wanted to speak to the man before the day was over.

DeRoss stopped at his side. "I would like to speak with you in private, Warrenby, if I may?"

One glance into those shrewd brown eyes, and Blake knew the man guessed what he was going to ask. "Certainly, Sir."

Tessa smiled at him as he stepped away. "Give me a few minutes. We still have to talk," he said before he followed deRoss out of the room.

Sure enough, they entered an office, the room where men conducted their business. The big desk looked to be the same wood as the rest of the house, as it matched the floor. No rug adorned it. Whether deRoss liked it that way all along or had rugs removed for the chair, he could not tell. A large chair with worn leather sat in the expected place behind the desk. He felt for deRoss, who likely had not been able to stride in and seat himself behind it in some time. The dark blue curtain covered what had to be windows, and from the layer of dust near the top, probably had not been opened for equally long. He waited for the man to wave him into one of the guest's chairs before sitting down.

DeRoss stopped at the side of the desk, and waved the servant away. "Close the door behind you, will you?"

Instead of asking his intentions toward Tessa, the question surprised him. "So. Tell me the true tale of that necklace. I don't believe Tessa had anything to do with it, but just how deep was the scoundrel in his thieving? I'll have you know, he robbed several of my neighbors, and only my good name saved me from being ostracized." Those dark eyes under the heavy brows pierced into Blake.

But he was made of tough stuff himself, and would not break his word. "I'm sorry, sir, but that is her story to tell. I gave my word, and I will keep it." Not being one to pass up an opportunity, he went on. "I have my own question. Will you give me your blessing to ask Tessa to be my wife?"

DeRoss started to smile, and shook his head, not in reply, but in defeat. "Very well, I can respect your secret. I think I know the answer to my question, anyway. Tell me something else before I answer your question. Just how bad was her life? She gives away almost nothing."

Blake weighed that look."She had done well for herself. Her neighborhood was bad enough, but most of them lived a hard-scrabble life, just as herself. There were thieves and footpads, but she managed to keep out of their way." Most of the time, he added to himself. "That part of her life is not well known, not even to myself. She had an excellent employer, who watched over her like a mother hen and was fair in her wages."

"So what makes you think you know her well enough to wed her?" Those eyes bored into him again.

DeRoss was not going to let him coast, and obviously cared nothing about his title when it came to the fate of Tessa. If it wasn't making this so difficult, he would appreciate that quality. "I care not what her situation in life was. I know the woman, know her integrity, her honor, her intelligence. In my experience, those things are rare, at least among the women I see."

"And you think to toss her into that nest of vipers? Why should she accept you?"

Blake didn't know the answer, but . . . "I am not so conceited to think all I have to do is ask, and she will fall into my hand like a ripe plum. I can only ask, and pray that she cares for me enough to trust that I will watch over her, and protect her."

"You could have made her your mistress before you learned of her connections. Why didn't you?"

The man was her grandfather. He had the right to ask."She is not the kind of woman you insult that way. I knew that long before I began thinking of marriage. Furthermore, I do not take advantage of those unable to defend themselves. I have never dallied with a servant."

DeRoss gave a single nod, but he did not stop. "What about love? She is not a piece of china that you can set on a shelf and take down only when you need her. You watch over women, and protect them as well. Tessa is warm and loving, she deserves a man who is the same." He leaned forward. "I can care for her, provide for her, and have every intention of doing that. So tell me, Warrenby, do you love her?"

Blake had never spoken those words aloud, not even when he told his mother. Sweat prickled along his chest, and his palms went clammy. His throat threatened to close, but he would not give deRoss the impression that he was afraid to speak the words aloud, and clear it. He swallowed, hoping the tightness would ease, and said, "Yes, Sir, I do."

At last, Tessa's grandfather smiled. "That is all I needed to know. You have my permission to ask her, and I hope she has the good sense to say yes." He held out his hand, and Blake leaned forward to take it. "It might be too early, although I doubt it, so let me be the first. Welcome to the family, my boy."

Blake smiled back. "Thank you, Sir. I promise I will cherish her."

DeRoss waved toward the door. "Well, go, go, find the girl and ask her."

* * *

Hannah noticed her standing behind the chair and beckoned. "You know what this looks like, I'm sure, but come see it. It is really something, and we are so grateful for its return."

Rather than admit it had been in a pile of stolen jewelry so large that not a single piece had made an impression, she went over and knelt by the settee. Abigail seemed to have first claim on it, as she had held it longer than any of the others. If she reached for it, Tessa had no doubt Abigail would be slow to let go.

"Actually," she said when there was a break in the conversation, "I never saw it until Father died."

That got Abigail's attention. "You never saw it? Your mother never wore it?"

She shook her head. "Never. Not once." Any more denial, she thought, and it might sound overdone.

Maybe it was the simplicity of her answer, maybe having the family heirloom back was enough to soften Abigail's harsh shell, but she tilted the necklace so Tessa could see it.

Not having owned a piece of jewelry in her life, the rich red glow of the rubies against the heavy gold setting was truly striking. She had seen such things, but the mere idea of touching them had been out of the question.

She had the same feeling now, that touching it stepped over a line. Why should she anyway, since she would not be able to afford such things when she got back to London? The reward for Robert had to go to finding a new place to live, away from Herb. Gems, while beautiful, were not necessary.

The door to the hallway opened, and Blake stepped through. His eyes scanned over the room, and settled on her. Taking that as a hint, Tessa rose and took a few steps in his direction, then waited for his next overture.

"Miss Abbott, it is such a pleasant evening. Would you care to take a turn outside?" He gestured toward the foyer door.

Her nod of agreement might have been too eager, but Tessa wanted nothing more than a few extra minutes with him. Maybe she could find the courage to ask about the kiss.

He made it to the door only a step behind her, and reached for the handle, his arm brushing hers. They stepped back together to let it open, then he guided her through with the same gentle touch between her shoulder blades.

Outside, flowers still perfumed the air, but the birds had settled down for the night, as had the far-away dogs. In the stables, the horses whuffed, and one thumped a hoof on the stoned floor. The coolness of moisture and a sudden gust of wind suggested the possibility of rain overnight.

"I recently learned I have some property nearby, but it is growing too dark to leave now. It is about an hour away, it would be quite black by the time I reached it. I shall stay overnight, your grandfather has invited me to stay." He held out his arm, and Tessa took it, thinking how familiar it had become. Not ordinary, nothing to do with Blake would ever be ordinary, just . . . comfortable.

They walked only a short distance before he stopped, and turned her to face him. The movements were so slow, lifting her hand off his arm and kissing the back, pressing her palms together between his much larger ones, even the way he looked down at her, each felt heavy with import.

"We should not get too far from the house." His mouth quirked up on one side in a half-smile. "I want no gossip to come back on you."

He looked down at her, his eyes glittering in the setting sun. "I thought you might like to know the latest on the jewelry situation."

She wondered if her own eyes were at all visible, or if they had blended into the encroaching shadows. He might not have meant his comment as a question, but she replied anyway. "Yes, I would like to know." That sounded too flat, and he had not released her hands. "Thank you for all you did for me, and now what you have done for my family. I don't think there is any way to repay you for that."

He smiled. "We will get to that later. First of all, one of my friends enjoyed the project so much he has decided to become a Bow Street Runner. I thought to give him the settings and the gems and allow him to handle the rest. We know who most of them belong to, and he can contact the individuals and determine what they wish to do, have them returned if for a wife, or sold, if a past mistress's. That should make you happy. Neither of our names will ever be connected to the thefts, and he can build his investigator reputation."

A sigh slid through her body, weeks of guilt seeping away. "What a clever idea."

"I told you it was not a problem." He gave her hands a slight squeeze. Then a chuckle vibrated from him to her through that link. "Not even I thought the solution would be so perfect." He shook his head. "My friend was well on the way to a life of dissipation, but this has given him a whole new purpose. Your burden, as you thought of it, has been the saving of a life."

The smile faded from his mouth, and he cleared his throat. She waited, but he only cleared his throat again, then shook his head. "I have never done this before, so please excuse me if I sound like the most callow of youths." That half-smile peeked out again. She wished there was more light because she could barely see his eyes.

His hands, that had not let go of hers since he first held them, tightened. "Tessa, will you be my wife?"

Her knees buckled. He let go of her hands, and caught her around the waist, holding onto her until she could stand again. *Yes*, her longings seemed to shout the answer. That surge of joy was washed away by the cold practicality of life.

She knew, more than he, the gulf between them. Too many of his mother's and his sister's friends had been in the shop, or worse, had seen her at the party, tucked away where no one would see her until they needed her skill. They knew what she had been, knew she was no more than a servant. The pain of what she had to say crushed her heart, like fire burning from the inside out.

Taking a deep breath for courage was impossible. In a voice thinner than she wished, she managed, "Thank you." Her voice began to shake, but it had to be said. "I am most flattered and honored by your offer, but that is utterly impossible. You know it as well as I do."

"I know no such thing, and it is not impossible. You are the granddaughter of a baronet. No one will dare speak a word." His confidence in another situation would be humorous, but this was much too painful.

"Your mother and your sister, think of what this would do to them."

"I have already taken care of that. My mother knows, and she has no objections." His smile was bright enough that she saw it even in the growing dark.

Say yes, her heart joined the chorus. Her most cherished dream and her worst fear collided, and she cried out, "You would never have asked before. I was just a servant, too far beneath you. Admit it!" *What are you doing*, her mind screamed, but this was too important.

His smile vanished. In a deep, rough voice, Blake growled, "I cannot deny that you were off limits. And then you came to my house with that letter. I could not believe it when I saw you there. I behaved like a cad when I thought you were involved in the theft. I know I insulted you, and have regretted it more times than I can say. The more I got to know you, the more I found to admire. But I could not prey on a woman with no defenses. I have never taken advantage of my position to molest a maid, and until I knew you had protection, that made you off limits."

He bent down enough to hold her gaze. How lovely that his eyes were so light, because now she could see them, see the heat in them, and the determination.

"There was no need for me to accompany my mother and sister to Madame's shop so frequently. My mother does not need my help, and we have plenty of maids and footmen. Groomsmen, and drivers. She could have come without me."

His voice went deeper, softer. "I came because I wanted to see you." She found herself closer to him than a moment ago, but never noticed herself move. "If this had not happened, I would have spent my whole life wondering if you were safe, happy. Trying to find excuses again and again to go to Madame's, just to watch you. Only, my life would have been a torment. I had come to know you, I would know what I was missing. Know the courage and integrity in those brown eyes"—one hand touched the side of her face—"and that perfect skin"—his hand moved down to cradle her cheek—"that cultured voice. I would know what I had lost. All because I was too blind to realize that I was in love." That smile started again. "Your sudden connections were the greatest gift I could imagine. They saved me from myself." His lips came down on hers, softly, almost reverently, a very different kiss from when he arrived. When his mouth lifted, he whispered, each breath another kiss, "I love you. Have loved you for so very long. Please love me back?"

She found herself standing against his legs, her skirt no doubt rumpling from how close they were together. His voice still quiet, the moment seeming to require this kind of deference, he went on. "Will you put me out of my misery? Say yes?"

Her mouth curved, she felt the smile tug on the skin he was still touching. The hurt, the fears, washed away. How like him those reasons were! She had one thing to say first, a secret she had been keeping for so very long. "Do you remember you asked once if I ever dreamed of being wed?" Her hand rose to cup his face just as he had just touched hers. How lovely, so very sweet, just to be free to do that. "After I met you, the face in every dream was yours. Only ever you."

He turned his face just enough to kiss that hand, but his gaze never left hers. "What are you saying?"

"Oh, Blake, what else could my answer be? I love you, too, so much. Yes. Yes, of course I will marry you."

They were back in each other's arms, his mouth came down on hers, deeper than before, more insistent than before, only now there was no restraint, only giving. His arms wrapped her tight, holding her against his warm body that only wanted to protect her. His big hands released her only long enough to frame her face, and his lips came down again, soft, almost reverent, before any restraint broke, and he clutched her close again, his mouth came down again, swallowing her air, giving his own.

He pulled away just far enough to speak, his voice a husky tone. "Say it again. Please?"

Tessa tilted her head back, and started to laugh. "Yes, I love you. Yes, yes, yes, yes, yes!"

His laugh mingled with hers, soaring into the dark sky.

Manufactured by Amazon.ca
Bolton, ON

38025886R00131